THE BEAST WITHIN

CONVERSION BOOK FIVE

S.C. STEPHENS

This is a work of fiction. Names, characters, places, brands, media, and incidents are either the product of the author's imagination or are used fictitiously. The author acknowledges the trademarked status and trademark owners of various products referenced in this work of fiction, which have been used without permission. The publication/use of these trademarks is not authorized, associated with, or sponsored by the trademark owners.

Copyright © 2017 by S.C. Stephens
Cover design by Okay Creations
Editing by Madison Seidler Editing Services
Formatting by JT Formatting

All rights reserved.
Without limiting the rights under copyright reserved above, no part of this publication may be reproduced, stored in or introduced into a retrieval system, or transmitted, in any form, or by any means (electronic, mechanical, photocopying, recording, or otherwise) without the prior written permission of the above copyright owner of this book.

First Edition: 2017
Library of Congress Cataloging-in-Publication Data
The Beast Within (Conversion Series) – 1st ed
ISBN-13: 978-1974359479 | ISBN-10: 1974359476

For the fans. Thank you for your continued support!

CHAPTER ONE

Hunter

I WAS THIRSTY, but that was nothing new. I was always thirsty. My throat was like a wasteland that had been devoid of any hydration for decades. When I swallowed, my muscles tightened and rubbed together like course sandpaper, permanently scarring the tender flesh inside me. There was only one reprieve from my misery, but I wouldn't allow it. I couldn't. Just the thought of what I needed made me light-headed, nauseous.

Blood. What I craved, what I hungered for, was blood.

And I hated myself for it.

Against my wishes, against all my hopes, desires, and dreams, I'd been turned into a vampire. My father had all but done the deed himself. I was a monster. A demon. Condemned. All because of him.

It had happened four months ago, on a cold, dark November night, when I'd found myself in a fight to the death with my girlfriend's family. They were vampires, almost every single one of them. But, in some strange way that I still didn't fully understand, most of them were human too. An impossible blend of both races. I'd dated Nika without even realizing her true nature, and when I had realized, it had been too late. I'd already been in love with her, even though I'd done my best to deny it.

When I'd refused to fight the Adams, my father had set a trap for them—with me as bait. But Dad hadn't anticipated just how many vampires were in their family. If he had, maybe he would have done things differently—done things that would have ensured my safety, instead of my death. But his plan had failed, and I was the casualty. The collateral damage.

But that wasn't the worst part.

I would have been okay with dying in the line of duty. It would have been an honorable way to go. My ashes would have been set inside my urn, marked with the prized fangs of a hunter, and I would have been given a place of honor in my father's home, next to my sister. Yes, *that* fate I would have been okay with. But Dad had done the unspeakable. He'd forced a vampire to change me. I couldn't even fully comprehend what had compelled him to do that. *Why couldn't he let me die? Why did he damn me? Why did he abandon me?*

These were questions that plagued me, and I was positive I'd never receive answers to them. Dad was gone. My brave, sickly sister was gone. I was alone for the first time in my life. But no, that wasn't entirely true.

Thanks to the curse passed on to me with the vile blood pumping through my veins, I was bonded to the monster who'd created me. Halina. Just the thought of her made me cringe, and at the same time, made me long for her. Not in any sort of sexual way, but how a child longs for a parent when they're alone or scared. I wanted to reach out for her, let her hold me, comfort me … and yet, her very existence utterly abhorred me. And I was eternally stuck in this dichotomous relationship. The bond was permanent. It couldn't be broken. I would always want her … and always revile her.

Escape was impossible; I'd tried. I'd only get a few hundred miles before the yearning was too much, before I couldn't go on until she was near me. And she *always* came to me. No matter how far I tried to flee from her, she always followed. She wouldn't leave me. Ever. A part of me was thankful for that; I didn't know what I'd do without her.

I certainly wouldn't drink if it weren't for her. I knew enough about my species to know that not drinking wouldn't kill me, but it would be bad enough to make me wish I were dead. Then again, I *already* wished I were dead, so starvation wasn't much of a threat. Halina would never let me get that hungry though. She forced food on me, either exposing it to the air when my will was gone, or even, sometimes, pouring it down my unwilling throat. I hated every time I ate. And I loved it.

Blood filled every thought, every dream. I smelled it in the air, on Halina's skin, on my clothes. Every animal we passed as we traveled the countryside had its own distinct, rhythmic heartbeat. I'd become so attuned to them, that I could tell what creature was lurking in the night, just by the sound of its pumping organ. I'd imagine that creamy warmth traveling down my parched throat and want to crumple into a ball and scream in pain and longing. I wanted it so much, but it sickened me. I wouldn't become one of those mindless, blood-lusting animals that killed everything in sight. I wouldn't kill a single creature. I would suffer in silence instead. That was my penance, and I gladly accepted it.

I stayed far away from humans. In fact, I hadn't seen a single person since I'd said goodbye to Nika. God, Nika … if I wasn't thinking about blood, I was thinking about her. When the cravings got so bad that I wanted to suck on my *own* blood, Nika was the vision I held onto—the innocence in her countenance, the deep brown, soulful eyes that were too old for someone her age, the small freckle on the corner of her left eye that nearly disappeared when she smiled, the fullness of her lower lip, a lip that tasted as sweet as strawberries … or blood. I held onto her image when the nights were bad, and they often were. I wondered if she thought of me too. I hoped so. I hoped not. She deserved so much better. She deserved the world.

"Hunter?"

My name echoed back to me from the high canyons that surrounded me, but I didn't turn to see who'd spoken. I already knew. Ignoring the undead creature behind me, I continued staring out into the moonlit vista before me. I'd been hiding in the outskirts of Canyonlands National Park, hundreds of miles south of Salt Lake. It was the farthest from Nika I could bear to be. It was very secluded here. Halina was growing restless with the vast nothingness, but I'd come to enjoy it. My sensitive ears welcomed the silence, and the spires and rock towers were a thing of beauty. Even in the darkness, my keen sight could make out the different hues of the striations in the centuries old formations. They must be amazing in the light of day, but I would never know. I was chained to darkness now. Midnight's captive.

"Hunter." The voice was more insistent now, and an undisguised huff punctuated the syllables of my name.

Sighing, I tore my gaze away from the thin archways of rock soaring hundreds of feet over my head. "What?" I asked, looking behind me.

Halina was standing there with her thin arms crossed over her chest. Wearing a short dress that left most of her upper thigh exposed to the elements, and heeled boots that came up over her knee, her outfit was in no way, shape or form suitable for our surroundings. It didn't hinder her any, though, thanks to her many supernatural "gifts."

Much like my eyes, hers were casting a faint glow on everything around her. All vampires had that calming, hypnotic, phosphorescent gaze. Well, all except for Nika and Julian. Their eyes were deceivingly normal. A vampire's stare was one of the things that made hunting them in pure darkness a bad idea. Those eyes could trap you, lull you into a false sense of security. I'd lost a friend that way before, a fact I was reminded of every time I noted the glow of my own eyes.

A slight breeze caught Halina's long, black hair, emphasizing the wildness of her demonic nature. A nature she succumbed to far more than I did. With a droll expression, she asked, "Are you done here? Can we please leave?"

She asked me this so often, my response was immediate. "I want to stay, but you're free to leave at any time." My stomach clenched just saying it. For all my talk, for all my bravado, I didn't want her to leave me. Just the thought of feeling her presence blurring away made my stomach tighten into anxious knots. It pissed me off. I didn't want to be tied to a stranger like this ... tied to a beast. Irritated, I turned from her again.

Halina walked over to me and sat down. Almost as if she could sense my mood, she put her hand on my arm. "I'm not going anywhere without you, and you know that. But ... I've been gone too long. I miss my family, my nest, my daughter. I want to go home."

The ache in her voice was palpable. It pulled at something in me, some buried desire to please her. Pushing it aside, I again said, "I want to stay. I like it here." And in truth, I did like it here. It was quiet, reclusive. I could suffer in peace, if she'd just let me.

Exhaling in a steady stream, she mumbled, "Fine. We'll stay ... but you need to eat. It's been weeks."

As I shook my head, a flash of pain ripped through my stomach and up my arid throat. *God ... what I wouldn't give for a nice, steaming cup of ...* "I'm fine," I grunted, disrupting my aching desire. "I'm not even hungry."

"You're a terrible liar," she retorted, picking up a stone at our feet and chucking it into the sky. It ricocheted off an archway, sending a small splattering of pebbles to the ground. "I can see how weak you are. You're half-dead."

A smirk touched my lips. "No, I'm all dead. You killed me, remember?"

"How can I forget," she mumbled under her breath. "Regardless, you should eat tonight."

By the imperative tone of her voice, I wondered if she'd force-feed me again. I hoped not. She'd only done it a few times, but I absolutely hated it. I was weak, she was right about that, and she could easily overpower me, forcing food into my mouth, and then forcing me to swallow. It was uncomfortable, for both of us. She usually held me after she did it, sad and apologetic. And I usually clung to her, both needing her comfort and detesting her for it. Such was the duality I lived with daily.

Trying to avoid that unpleasantness, I told her, "There's no food anywhere close to us. What would I eat?"

Standing, Halina looked down at me. "I will get you food, have no fear of that." She switched her gaze to the third person in our unmerry band. "Watch him for me, Gabriel?"

I rolled my eyes. I hadn't been left with supervision since I was ten years old. It was humiliating to have a babysitter. I said nothing, though, and managed to contain my groan when a cool, detached voice answered, "Of course, my love."

Leaning down, Halina gave me a swift hug, then kissed my head. "I will be back before you know it, and I'll have something juicy—something you'll really like."

I couldn't stop the horrified, sickened reaction I had to her words. Leaning over, my head between my knees, I clenched my stomach and breathed in and out, trying not to be sick. I couldn't drink blood. It was wrong. Twisted. Evil. I wouldn't. She would have to make me ... I just wouldn't do it.

Oblivious to my distress, or perhaps ignoring it, Halina streaked away from me. The ache in my chest grew with every mile we were separated, and I wanted to yell at her to come back. I also wanted to scream at her to keep going. I was sure these opposing feeling were going to drive me mad one day, if the hunger didn't first.

After a few moments, Halina's forward movement slowed, and the tugging in my heart eased. I breathed through it as best I could. She would be back. That was one certainty I could count on.

Gabriel sat in the spot Halina had vacated. His face impassive, he watched me in silence. I didn't know what to make of Halina's boyfriend. All I knew for sure was he made me uncomfortable. He was a legend among vampire hunters. An ancient vampire who was well-connected and highly protected. There were several hunters who had gone after him and never returned, and here I was, sitting less than a foot away from him. If I'd been feeling anything other than pain and apathy, maybe I would have made a move on him, finish what my father and I had started in Los Angeles when tracking the blood ads had led us to his nest. But I didn't have it in me, so I did and said nothing.

His face was attractive and youthful, with dirty blond hair and softly glowing, emerald green eyes. Looking like he did, he could have gotten a modeling or acting job if he'd wanted while living in L.A. But that wasn't where his interests lied. Science was his passion. And not just any science, vampire science. He'd been studying the blood of his race, our race, for more centuries than I cared to count, and had devoted his undead life to making things better, easier, for his brethren. It made being around him even more unnerving. This was a dangerous man with dangerous knowledge. I should be ramming a stake through his heart, not stargazing with him.

When he finally spoke, his voice was just as aloof as his expression. "You have not acclimated well to the changeover."

Since there was no question in his tone, I didn't answer. Anyone could see I was struggling. And who wouldn't struggle with becoming a blood-thirsty nightmare? In my silence, Gabriel seemed to find the answer he was looking for. "I can help you."

That got my attention. Looking over at him, I muttered, "How can you possibly help me?" Getting an idea, I turned to face him. "Can you stake me?" Opening my jacket, I exposed my chest to him. Besides lying out in the sun, staking was a surefire way to kill a vampire, a surefire way to kill *me*. I'd contemplated it before. I'd even stuck a sharp stick to my chest once, but I'd never had the willpower to pierce the skin. Like I said, I was weak.

Gabriel raised an eyebrow. "No. Halina would not approve if I destroyed you."

My momentary hope fading, I jerked my jacket back around me. "Well, great. Then my earlier question stands. How can you possibly help me?"

"I can break the bond. Then you would be free to live ... or die ... on your own."

Not sure that I'd heard him correctly, I twisted my head to stare at him. "You can ... you can do that? I didn't think it could be done."

Gabriel gave me a simple shrug, like his statement hadn't just rocked my world. *I can be free?* "My partner was able to break the link. I'm sure I can as well, given enough time."

My mind spun faster than I had the energy to keep up with. "How much time? What do you need from me? When can you start? What do I need to do?"

Gabriel smiled, his face softening for the first time. "I can't imagine it will take longer than a few weeks, not if I give it my utmost attention. But ..." his lips compressed into a hard line again, "... you will need to return to the ranch with Halina."

My entire hope-filled bubble burst. He was just messing with me to help her. Shaking my head, I turned away. "Why do I need to go back there?"

His answer was brief and to the point. "My lab is there. I can't help you without it."

Tendrils of longing tangled throughout my body, and I was again reminded of just how dangerous this man was. "Can you really help me?" I asked, turning to face him again. "*Will* you really help me?"

He nodded once, the movement curt. "I give you my word."

Recalling his earlier remark, doubt filled my mind. "Halina won't be pleased if you break the bond, any more than she would be pleased if you disposed of me."

Gabriel pursed his lips, then sighed. "True. Killing you would destroy her, but, I believe if I break the bond, it will also break her connection to you. She won't feel as ... compelled ... to be near you. She will also be freed."

I looked back up to the archway. Breaking the link filled me with such a painful ache that I wasn't sure if I could do it. If we were no longer bound, if I no longer felt her presence in my mind ... how would I go on? But, Gabriel was right. That very thought was *because* of the bond. Break the link, and the feeling would be broken as well. We'd both be free. Then I could leave. Then I could die. There had to be someone out there who would be more than happy to pierce my heart.

Looking back at him, I asked, "Is that why you're doing this? So you don't have to share your girlfriend with me?"

Without the slightest bit of remorse or self-consciousness, he answered, "Yes, that is precisely why."

I didn't know what to say. I didn't know what I wanted, other than relief from my life. As I stared at the hollowed columns dotting the terrain, I felt my salvation, my curse, returning with food for me. My stomach roiled in protest and anticipation. God, what animal had she found around here? Was it already dead, or did she want me to do that part? She was going to be extremely unhappy with me when I neither drank nor killed whatever poor beast was on the menu.

I fidgeted, wrapping my arms around myself. It was freezing outside, but I was comfortable. That was one bonus of being dead. I never got cold. But I never felt warm either. I simply ... was. I missed feeling heat—the warmth of the sun upon my face in the middle of the day, the warmth of Nika's skin against mine when she held my hand. There were a lot of things I missed.

Halina materialized in front of me, a tan animal slung over her shoulders. I blinked in disbelief as she dropped it to my feet. A deer? She brought me ... a deer. I looked up at her, horrified. "You want me to drink Bambi?"

Halina pursed her lips at me. "Blood is blood. The body merely keeps it warm. And drinking this animal is no different than eating its meat. Don't tell me you've never had venison?"

I remained silent as I stared down into the animal's lifeless eyes framed in thick, dark eyelashes. My father was a traditional hunter, as well as a vampiric one. He'd taken my sister and me on several expeditions. We'd hunted for sport, and to improve our skills, but we'd always used the meat from the kills—waste not, want not—and I'd had deer on several occasions. But never the blood. Somehow, drinking from the animal instead of eating it changed *everything* about hunting.

While Gabriel watched with curious eyes, Halina squatted on the other side of the deer. "Eat, Hunter. You need your strength."

Again, her voice pleaded with me, and again, a small part of me wanted to do whatever she asked, whatever would make her happy. I couldn't do this though. My jaw quivered, and every cell in my body screamed at me to drink the animal while the blood was still warm, but instead, I whispered, "I'm not hungry."

Frustrated with me, Halina bared her fangs, then lunged for the creature's throat. A smell more appealing than anything I'd ever known as a human instantly flooded my senses, overwhelming me. Blood. Fresh blood. It was thick in the air as it gushed out of the hole she'd created in the still creature. I was momentarily grateful that the beast was already dead, and wouldn't suffer by bleeding out, but that feeling was fleeting. It was instantly replaced by longing so sharp and severe that it pounded through my skull and reverberated down my body. It coalesced in my chest and released into the night as a resonant rumble.

Lifting her head, Halina smiled at me in encouragement. Blood dripped from her chin. I wanted to catch the drops. I wanted to bend over and lose my stomach. No … yes.

"Have some, it's delicious," she cooed, licking her bottom lip.

An intrinsic part of me knew she was right; every drop of blood I'd ever had was a delight beyond expectation, beyond reason. But just because the evil was glorious and intoxicating, didn't mean I would cave. I couldn't.

But even as I told myself that, I leaned over the beast. The blood was flowing down its fur now, spilling onto the dusty earth below it. Each drop soaked into the hungry ground. I wanted it to soak into me.

God, the smell … it was so …

My breath was heavy as I brought my face to the gaping wound. Just a taste. Could I have just a taste? My tongue dragged over the bloody pool that had formed. My fangs, uncontainable now that I'd had a taste, crashed into place. I groaned as the hot liquid seared my withered tongue. So … good …

When I pulled my tongue back in to savor the scant collection on the tip, reality crashed into me. I was licking a dead animal. I was growling and groaning over how much I wanted ... blood. I had blood on my tongue. I had blood in my body. I was a monster. This was wrong. So very, very wrong.

Not letting myself swallow the rapturous treat, I spat it out; the ground could have it. Needing to get away from the tantalizing smell surrounding me, assaulting me, I shot to my feet.

Halina immediately yanked me back down. Smashing my back into the hard rock, she pinned my shoulders to the ground. "Hunter! Stop this and eat."

Knowing where this was headed, I pleaded with her, "Don't make me—please."

Her eyes reddened as she leaned over me. "What choice have you left me with?"

I tried to scramble away from her, but she was so much stronger. Straddling me, she easily held my arms pinned to my sides with her knees. Holding one forearm across my chest, she dragged the carcass over with the other. Even though she was smaller, it was as if she weighed a thousand pounds. I couldn't remove her, and I couldn't stop this from happening. Panic set in.

"I'm not hungry!" My voice was raspy, my need evident. I couldn't even fool myself with my words. I *did* want this, I just didn't want to want it. "I don't want to be a vampire! I don't want to drink blood!"

Furious, she dropped her fangs and snarled, "And I did not want to kill my husband! But life doesn't always give us what we want, so stop being such a child. Grow up, get over it, and find a new way to live." Her expression softened, and the redness in her eyes thickened. "Please."

I was still shaking my head when she pulled the neck of the creature over me. Her icy hand came up to hold my head and open my jaw. I could do nothing. As the sweetness poured into my mouth, I clawed at the dirt, both wanting to get away and wanting to pull the animal closer. As my mouth filled, I sputtered and choked on the liquid. I was so panicked by what was happening that it didn't occur to me to spit it out or simply let it run out of my mouth by not swallowing. Then again, maybe it was the starved vampire inside of me that just wouldn't hear of that option. For whatever reason, my body instinctively swallowed without my permission.

My eyes widened as the ambrosia coated my aching throat. My stomach rose in protest, and nausea roiled through me in waves. Even so, my mouth was filling again, and I couldn't stop the contraction of my throat any more than I could remove Halina from me. My eyes stung, and the thick moisture of bloody tears ran down my cheeks as I swallowed a third time.

Halina looked just as affected as me as she held the creature to my lips. "I take no joy from this, but you must eat. And you're doing very well," she murmured, her voice shaky.

Mouth full of hot, sweet blood, I could only whimper in response. So much of the creature's life-force had been spilled with Halina's initial bite, that only one small mouthful was left. I swallowed it down and closed my eyes as my vision swam and my stomach threatened to heave. Then I felt the wet fur being dragged across my skin as the wondrous smell was removed from under my nose. I sucked in deep breaths, trying to shake the scent from my mind, but I couldn't. It was all over me, all around me; I was laced with it.

A soft hand brushed over my forehead. "Much of that animal was wasted, but that should hold you over ... for a bit." Halina sighed, sounding as exhausted as I was.

When I felt her weight retreating from my chest, I rolled to my side and curled into a ball. I gagged, dry-heaved, but the blood was too far into my system to remove it now. It was a part of me, making me minutely stronger than I was before, but still not strong enough. Clenching my hands into fists, I smacked the ground muddied by the deer's blood, then I grabbed my T-shirt and scrubbed my mouth. I needed the blood gone. I needed the smell gone. I needed to *be* gone. Still dizzy and nauseous, I crawled to my hands and knees, then pulled myself up to a low crouch. Sprinting, I blurred away as fast as I could.

I hated her for doing this to me again, and yet, when she predictably raced after me, I stopped and waited for her. I couldn't run. Not for long. I needed her too much. I felt dizzy from the brief jog, and wanted to sink to the ground, never to stand again. Halina searched my eyes, then cupped my face. Unable to hold the weight of my head, I leaned into her palm.

Compassion and remorse were clear as she spoke in choppy tones. "I am sorry it has to be this way. I am sorry this is hard on you. But you're so weak. So very weak. Someone could ... You could be ... I won't lose you, Hunter."

Gabriel came to a stop behind her. His expression wasn't pleased. Whether that was because his girlfriend was holding me, or because I, yet again, had made Halina force a meal upon me, I wasn't sure. The air was clearer here, the smell of blood not quite so pungent. It was still a part of me, though, and I needed it removed before it drove me mad.

My voice barely more than a gust of air, I said, "I need to clean up. Can I please be alone?"

I hated that I had to ask for privacy, but I knew she would grant it to me if I did, especially now that I'd eaten some. At least for a little while. She nodded as she searched my eyes. "Of course, my love."

She tossed her arms around me, squeezing me tight. I was so tired, I collapsed like a ragdoll, but she easily held me upright. Over her shoulder, I locked gazes with Gabriel. His cool look spoke volumes. I could be free from this hellish captivity, from her, if I wanted. I just had to trust him. I just had to return to the ranch.

When Halina released me, she smoothed my shirt like a child. "We'll be nearby," she stated. I nodded at her. I'd already known that. Turning, I walked away at a regular human pace. I couldn't make myself go any faster. I might have eaten tonight, but it wasn't nearly enough. If anything, the few mouthfuls I'd had only made the thirst worse. It was easier to go completely without, than to have a small taste of what I was yearning for. And the yearning tightened my throat in disgust.

Hearing a stream to my right, I trudged toward it. Not caring about anything other than washing away the scent, feel, color, and taste of the blood layering me, I walked right into the water, sank to my knees, and submerged myself. My hearing was muffled under the surging brook; only the sound of rushing water entered my consciousness. I scrubbed my clothes with pebbles from the rock bed, and opened and closed my mouth to rinse my palate. When I felt clean, I dug into the earth to keep myself submerged in the water, then I closed my eyes and took a moment to relish the isolation.

Holding my breath brought me no pain or anxiety, and the temperature of the water was just as chilled as my skin, so I was comfortable, and I remained submerged for what felt like hours. When a familiar prickling sensation crawled up my spine, I knew it was time to leave. The stinging sensation meant the sun was drawing near. I knew from experience that the feeling would worsen as the sun reached the horizon. It was my body's version of a sixth sense, warning me about an approaching danger, one of the few dangers vampires had.

I'd entertained the idea of staying topside for one last sunrise before, but I'd always chickened out and run away at the last minute. And besides, I knew Halina would never allow me to die in such a way. She'd fry to a crisp herself before she'd let that happen.

Emerging from the stream, water dripping off every inch of me, I felt for her presence. She was close, but I didn't want to go to her. Well, no, that wasn't true. I *did* want to go to her, but I wouldn't. I needed space today. I needed to think over my options before I succumbed to sleep. Moving close to a rock spire, I began digging my nightly grave. Halina hated sleeping inside the earth, and complained about it nonstop, but it felt right to me. We were monsters; we should be buried.

When there was enough room for me, I crawled inside and buried myself. The dirt clung to my damp clothes, damp skin, coating me with its gritty protection. Wriggling and digging, I crawled deeper into the earth to hide from the sun. The weight of the world compressed against me, shutting out the air, shutting out the light, but it didn't bother me. Much like being under the water, I found it peaceful.

I felt Halina walk over the grave, checking to make sure I was securely buried, then I heard her lovingly whisper, "Goodnight, Hunter," before phasing away to find her own place to hide.

The evening flickered through my mind—the horror, the desire. And Gabriel's words. *I can help you.* Could he? As the rocks far above me warmed under the light of the rising sun I would never again see, I knew what I had to do. I couldn't live this way anymore. When I found the courage, I would tell Halina that I wanted to return to the ranch with her. And then Gabriel could begin his work on breaking the bond. Within a few weeks, thanks to his miraculous science, I would be free from Halina.

Just the thought made me want to weep with joy. And sorrow.

CHAPTER TWO

Nika

MY BROTHER WAS happy. I could feel it. Thanks to the emotional bond that Julian and I shared, I could always feel what he was feeling, and for the last few months he'd been in a never-ending state of bliss. It was annoying. Right now, Julian was upstairs in his room, doing homework with the girl he was dating—my best friend, Arianna. They were talking and laughing, and generally doing very little actual homework. I was going to have to help him with it once she left, I just knew it.

I was in the kitchen with Mom and Dad, helping them make dinner. Tonight, we were having pot roast. While the cooking meat smelled incredible, I wasn't really looking forward to eating it. I just wasn't in the mood. I wasn't in the mood for a lot lately. Like listening to Julian flirt. *That* I definitely could have gone without.

Standing beside the kitchen sink, I started peeling a huge pile of carrots. Even though I could have used my enhanced speed to peel, slice, and dice the vegetable in a matter of seconds, I took my time. Doing things at a normal, human pace had been drilled into me since birth. On occasion, I sometimes forgot that I could move super-sonically. But tonight, the regular pace was soothing. Somewhat.

While long orange strands of carrot flesh piled up in the sink, Arianna's giggling intensified. I wasn't sure what the heck Julian was doing to her, but it was clearly making her happy, and I was already wishing it would stop. Just when I was debating snapping at him to get to work, since they were supposed to be studying, Arianna squealed, "Julian, stop tickling me!"

Ugh. How long were my parents going to let this non-studying continue? Mom was stirring a pot of blood on the stove, while Dad watched her. The smile on Dad's face was calm and peaceful as he leaned against the counter, arms crossed over his crisp blue dress shirt; he didn't seem to be concerned at all that Julian was slacking off on his schoolwork.

Julian and Dad were startlingly similar, with jet-black hair and sky blue eyes. It was a deadly combination; Arianna constantly told me it was her undoing. She'd even jokingly told me once that my family's signature blue eyes made her want to have an Adams baby one day. Thankfully, that "day" was a long way off. Arianna and my brother weren't even technically boyfriend and girlfriend yet, and Arianna had no intention of sleeping with him until they were. While I thought that was pretty smart of her, the delay was a huge blessing for me; I didn't like *thinking* about my brother having sex, and I definitely didn't want to emotionally experience him doing it. I didn't think I'd survive it. Just feeling him make out was bad enough.

Mom paused in her task to smile at Dad. Looks-wise, I took after her with warm brown eyes and wavy brown hair. It seemed a less dramatic combination than Julian and my dad shared, but it certainly worked for Mom; she was gorgeous. And I'd been told I was pretty, even by people outside of my family. A boy once told me I was beautiful, but I didn't like to think about that. Or him.

Dad had a small smile on his face while he gazed at Mom; he usually did when he was looking at her. You'd think the novelty of being around each other would have worn off after the first decade or so, but not for my parents. They still acted like teenagers in love, still hopelessly head over heels for each other. For as long as I could remember, I'd wanted that. I'd wanted a boy to look at me with as much love and adoration as my parents had for each other. I'd longed for it. And, for a split-second, I'd thought I'd had it, or was close to having it, but it had slipped away from me. No, it had been forcibly ripped away from me. And I still couldn't get over it. I didn't think I ever would.

Trying to ignore the laughter upstairs, and Julian's buoyant mood, I returned my concentration to the carrots. While I went about my work, Mom grabbed glasses from a cupboard and poured some steaming blood for her and Dad. The smell of the warm liquid in the air made my mouth water. I didn't need blood like my parents did, but it was still the most incredible thing on Earth. Better than pizza, better than chocolate, better than a kiss from a boy. Well, almost better.

Dad took the blood from Mom, thanking her with a peck on the cheek. Mom clinked glasses with him before taking a sip. When the beautiful red liquid slipped past their lips, their fangs dropped. It was a reaction none of us could control. We normally held our teeth in twenty-four-seven, but the moment a speck of blood touched our tongues, our teeth were impossible to contain. Mom and Dad made satisfied noises as they closed their eyes and enjoyed their plasma.

Seeing and hearing so much contentment around me almost made me want to leave the house, walk down to Jacen and Starla's place or something, but I knew I wouldn't. For one, Jacen and Starla were just as content—the aging, mixed-blood vampire who played my mother was very happy with her seemingly younger, undead, mixed-blood boyfriend. Secondly, Mom and Dad wouldn't let me leave right before dinner. But aside from those facts, the real reason I wouldn't go out for a walk was because I knew I'd be tempted to walk by *his* place. And I tried not to do that. It hurt too much.

I started chopping the peeled carrots while my parents drank their meals and chatted about their mutual workplace—Mom was Dad's assistant, a fact they both found amusing. As Dad teasingly told Mom that he would like his secretary to start making him "Bloody" Marys in the morning, the sound of laughter upstairs faded away, and heavy breathing and lip-smacking took its place.

Frowning, Dad instantly looked up at the ceiling and said, "Julian, I think you and Arianna should come down now."

He spoke at a normal volume, like Julian was in the room with us, but I knew my brother heard him; there was rustling upstairs as he moved away from Arianna. Nerves and embarrassment washing through him, Julian cleared his throat. "Umm ... my parents want us to come downstairs now."

Arianna instantly remembered just what she'd seemingly forgotten in the last few minutes. "Oh my God! Can they hear us kissing?"

Brimming with equal parts unease and joy, Julian hastily told her, "Yeah ... Sorry, I shouldn't have started that. Sometimes I forget that they're around when I'm with you. I forget a lot of things when I'm with you ..." Arianna giggled, and the sound of soft kissing filtered down again.

Knife in hand, I glared up at the ceiling. "Oh my God, Julian, if you're not going to do your homework, which is what you're *supposed* to be doing, then get your ass down here and help with dinner."

Anger rushed through Julian so fast, I had to close my eyes. "I know you're going through a lot, Nick, but you don't have to be pissy all the time."

Until recently, Julian and I had always gotten along. While I called Arianna my best friend, truly that honor went to Julian. But lately, we'd been butting heads. I knew it was in large part because of the bond. He was happy, and I was miserable, and I resented having to be submerged in his never-ending joy. I knew it was wrong of me to be irritated by his happiness ... but knowing that didn't stop the arguing.

"Bite me, Julian," I growled.

Dad finished his glass and set it inside the sink. "Stop it, both of you," he snarled. Dad was cool, but he was starting to lose his temper with us. I didn't blame him, I would be irritated with us too, but I glared at him anyway, because I just couldn't be reasonable and mature right now. I was a sixteen-year-old girl with a shattered heart. I felt like that gave me some leeway to be a little bitchy.

Seconds later, Julian blurred into the room with Arianna in his arms; she was giggling, but she was holding onto Julian for dear life, and that was probably the real reason why Julian had moved into the room so quickly.

Mom finished her glass of blood then set in the sink with Dad's. Over her shoulder, she gave Julian a reproachful glance. "Normal speed, Julian. You know better."

Clearly only half-listening to Mom, Julian set Arianna down near the island in the middle of the kitchen. Still not entirely used to zipping around so fast, Arianna wobbled on her feet a bit. My friend had always been adorable, flirty, and cute, but being with Julian was changing her some. She'd grown out her caramel hair so that it was just past her shoulders. Her hazel eyes were highlighted in a spectacular burst of mascara, and everything in her wardrobe had shrunk a half size. It was as if teasing Julian with the promise of what he could one day have with her had become her goal in life. It was working too. Julian thought about Arianna nonstop. I could tell, just by his emotions.

While Julian stood behind Arianna, wrapping his arms around her trim waist, Dad lifted his hand and pointed upstairs. His voice authoritative, he told Julian, "I think studying should be done at the kitchen table from now on."

Arianna flushed with color, and every vampire in the room looked her way. Blood rushing to the surface of the skin was just something we noticed. None of us would do anything about it, but like admiring a gorgeous cake in a bakery window, we appreciated the beauty of it. Arianna didn't seem to notice the inspection of her skin tone. She was too wrapped up in her embarrassment. "Sorry, Mr. Adams ... won't happen again."

Chuckling, Julian buried his head in her neck and murmured, "You sure?"

Dad cleared his throat, before his disapproving face shifted to a soft smile. Addressing Arianna, he politely told her, "Please, call me Teren, Arianna, even in private. The people here don't know my true connection to the children. You'll be less likely to mess up, if you only refer to me by name."

Arianna's face turned thoughtful as she nodded. Since she knew the truth now, Arianna was part of the deception, and the world believed our father was dead, and our *real* father was only related to us through marriage. In the lie, Dad's last name wasn't even Adams. It was Thompson, which still sounded strange to me.

Understanding the oddness of what he was asking of Arianna, Dad gave her a sympathetic smile as he motioned to the kitchen table. "Dinner is almost ready. Why don't you have a seat?" His eyes flashed to Julian's. "And why don't you help Nika cut the vegetables?"

Clearly not wanting to let Arianna go, Julian sighed in a lovesick way that irritated me. Feeling my mood, he shot me a cool glance. "Sure," he said to Dad as he walked my way.

Grabbing another knife from the block, Julian stepped beside me. I moved over a step, and Julian grunted, then grabbed a fistful of the peeled carrots. While I went back to tenaciously Julienne slicing the carrots, Mom and Dad sat at the table with Arianna and asked her about school. Julian watched his girlfriend bonding with his family with a satisfied smile on his lips. It made me want to poke him with my knife. Just a little.

While the sound of people talking filled the air, Julian leaned over and said, "What's your problem?"

Intent on my carrots, I muttered, "I don't have a problem."

Julian shook his dark head, and I studiously ignored his intense gaze. "You can't lie to me, Nick. I know you. I know you better than anyone."

Hating that he was right, I glared up at him. "If you know me so well, then you don't have to ask, do you?"

The heat in his eyes faded as he stared at me. "Nick ..."

Compassion and sympathy surged through Julian, and my eyes watered as a ball of pain climbed up my throat. I pushed it back as best I could. I couldn't think about it. I couldn't think about *him*. I needed to press the memory of what we'd had, however briefly, from my mind. It was gone. Dead and gone, and we were over. Swallowing, I snapped, "Just cut your freaking carrots, and leave me alone."

Confusion and irritation swirled through my brother, and under his breath, he told me, "I know you miss him, I know you worry about him, but why are you always taking it out on me?" Anger flared inside him again, and he muttered, "I'm not the one who hurt you, so quit being such a bitch."

"Julian!" That admonishment came from both my mother *and* my father who had easily heard Julian's almost imperceptible speech.

Julian glanced at them, and Arianna looked at all of us, confused. Turning to face them, Julian shrugged, "I'm sorry, but you know I've got a point. She's been nothing but prickly and moody ever since Hunter converted." Hearing Hunter's name was a physical blow to the chest. I even inhaled a sharp breath and took a step back. Julian's pale eyes returned to me, painful compassion filling him again. "I'm so sorry it happened, Nick, I really am, but you've turned into this cold, bitter person I don't even know anymore. I want my sister back. I want my best friend back."

The tears in my eyes built to an intolerable level. "I'm sorry if my pain is an inconvenience to you. I'm sorry that I'm having trouble dealing with the death of the only person I've ever loved. God, how selfish of me, to rain on your perfect parade with my own petty problems. Why don't me and my patheticness just go somewhere else, so you don't have to listen to my 'pissy' attitude anymore." With those words, I adjusted the knife in my hands and slammed it into the cutting board. Thanks to my revved-up strength, the blade went right through the board and into the granite countertop beneath it.

I stormed away from Julian. "Nika, wait, that's not what I—" He reached out for me, but I avoided contact with him. Arianna's eyes were huge as she stared at the knife impaled into the countertop like the famed sword in the stone. Saying my name, Dad stood from the table, but I ignored him too. I didn't need a lecture right now. I needed to be alone.

Hating my life, I stomped out the front door. I wanted to go somewhere, anywhere, I just didn't have anywhere to go. And there was nowhere on this Earth where I could escape my family anyway. I could sense every relative who was a vampire. I could feel their exact location; my parents and my brother were in the kitchen, two of my grandmothers were miles away at the ranch. I could close my eyes, spin around three dozen times, and still flawlessly point each one of them out. But what hurt most of all, was the fact that I could feel Hunter too. Hunter had my family's blood inside him now, and his pinpoint inside my head ceaselessly banged like a drum, one I could never escape from. There was no peace for me, because I was constantly "aware" of him.

Currently, Hunter was with Halina. They were several miles south of the city, away from the ranch where the others were staying. Hunter still refused to accept what he was ... what *I* was. There was an obstacle between us that we would never be able to get past. Even though we could both potentially live for several millennia, there was no future for us.

Spring was fast approaching, but it was still frigid outside. I didn't care as I paced the porch. Clenching and unclenching my fists, I willed the tears I wanted to release to remain inside my body. Through the walls, I could hear my family debating who should come out to talk to me. Arianna wanted to go, but she didn't really understand the situation. Julian wanted to talk to me, but he didn't want to make me even madder, and feeling the mood I was in, he knew he would. Mom started approaching the door, but Dad cut her off. "I got this, Em."

I closed my eyes and grit my teeth, wishing, just once, that my parents weren't so involved with our lives. Couldn't I wallow in pain like any normal teenager? Couldn't I get any peace? When Dad opened the front door, I looked back at him and hiccupped a breath. A part of me wanted to fall apart in his arms, and a part of me wanted to stay strong, stay pissed. Anger was such an easier emotion than pain.

His youthful face concerned, Dad quietly shut the door. He sat on a bench nearby while I continued pacing. He didn't say anything, just watched as I made back and forth patterns across the worn wood of the deck. As the boards under my feet creaked, fury swam through my heart. It felt good, and I embraced it. "He's such a jerk," I bit out.

Tilting his head, Dad asked, "Julian? Or Hunter?"

Hearing his name, I stopped and stared at Dad. The hurt in my chest amplified tenfold. I struggled to hold onto the heat, the wrath, but like the crispness in the air, icy devastation leaked around the outsides of my heart, slowly suffocating the flames. "He said he loved me ..." my voice warbled as I whispered my inner torture.

Dad nodded as he leaned over his knees. "I know," he answered.

I swallowed the sob that wanted to escape. "Then he left ... and he won't come back." I'd felt so hopeful for us when Hunter had snuck into my bedroom and shared his feelings for me after his conversion, but that had been months ago, and I hadn't heard a peep from him since. My hope had turned to despair long ago.

Face full of compassion, Dad again said, "I know."

Wanting him to somehow fix this, like he fixed everything, I tossed my hands into the air. "What do I do?"

Dad patted the bench beside him, and I reluctantly sat down. There was a light breeze that sent a shiver up my spine as it stirred the ends of my long locks. Winter was hesitant to release its hold on the earth, but spring would soon be erupting throughout the city. I could already smell the emerging life in the air. New romances would blossom around school as well—it happened every year—and I didn't want to see the new crop of delighted, joyful faces. I'd rather we just skipped past spring and tumbled directly into summer. That used to be my favorite time of year. In the past, I'd longed for those lazy days, when my obligations were fewer and I could spend more time at the ranch with my family. Now, free time was about the last thing I wanted. No, it was better to be at school. At least I was busy there; it helped keep my mind off things.

Voice soft, Dad told me, "There isn't anything you can do about Hunter, Nika. He has to deal with what was done to him. He has to deal with who he is now. There's nothing that you, or me, or even Great-Gran can do to help him. His happiness is up to him, just like your happiness is up to you." Reaching over, Dad grabbed my hand. His was ice cold, chillier than the breeze washing across my exposed cheeks. "Even though it hurts, and believe me, honey, I know exactly how much you're hurting right now, you have to let him go."

I nodded, sniffing back tears. Dad had suffered a huge loss when he was my age, so he really did understand what I was going through, but I still clung tight to the agony, not yet ready to release it. Letting out a long exhale, Dad wrapped his arms around me. The warmth in his freezing embrace was more than I could handle. The wall holding back my reservoir of pain broke, and my cheeks instantly flooded with moisture. Dad calmly rubbed my back while I sobbed in his arms. I hated crying about Hunter; I felt like I'd done it way too much. My family was right—I was becoming someone I didn't know, someone I didn't like. I needed to release Hunter, for my own sake. I had no choice but to let him go. He wasn't coming back anyway.

When my tears were all used up, Dad and I sat side-by-side in silence. His arm was wrapped around me, and I laid my head on his shoulder. He didn't offer any more words of wisdom, just held and supported me. Dad was my rock, and I knew, without a doubt, as I sat next to him that I could do this. I could emerge from my funk and once again be the hopeful girl who looked at life through optimistic eyes. One failed romance shouldn't be the end of my world. I was stronger than that. At least, I wanted to be stronger than that.

Tuning out my pain, I listened to the world around me. Someone was playing loud music a few doors down. I wasn't sure what song it was, but there was a definite Reggae rhythm to it. In the other direction, an elderly woman was snapping at her tiny dog to stop barking. She always got after her dog about its incessant yapping, but she treated the tiny canine as well as any human child, possibly better. I could make out birds chirping in the trees, an undeniable sign that warmer weather was indeed on the way. I could make out traffic nearby, moving and stopping, creating a symphony of sound that was beautiful in its own way. All around me the world was alive—full of opportunity, hope, and potential. A part of me wanted to embrace it, and I clung to that slippery thread. I wanted to be my own source of happiness.

Lifting my head, I looked at Dad. "Thank you."

Smiling, Dad kissed my temple. "No need to thank me. I'm always here for you and your brother ... even if you sometimes don't want me to be." He smirked, and I laughed at his expression. Patting my thigh, he said, "Ready to eat?"

I nodded as sudden hunger overwhelmed me. I hadn't been eating a lot lately—wallowing in grief was a surefire way to lose weight. But I was going to try tonight; I wasn't sure how long this peaceful, hopeful feeling would last. As tightly as I clung to it, I could already feel the edges of it start to slip from my grasp. But instead of giving up and releasing it, I clung even tighter. I was the only one who could make me happy.

When Dad and I walked back into the kitchen, Mom was setting the table. After she set down the roast, she swooped me into a tight hug. "I love you, honey," she whispered into my hair. I sighed as I patted her cold back. I hated worrying my parents; the last several months had been hard on them too.

"Love you, too, Mom."

When I turned to sit at the table, I noticed that Julian and Arianna were sitting as far apart from each other as possible. From Julian's mood, I could tell it was intentional. He was trying to make things easier for me by not being overly affectionate with her. My heart softened as I considered just how much of a bitch I'd been lately. Julian had been put through hell by his first crush. Raquel had led him on, toyed with his emotions, but all her torments had never turned him into a sullen, bitter asshole. Well, not fully. After everything he'd been through with Raquel, I had no right to resent the fact that he was now happy with Arianna. I didn't want to. I wanted to embrace his happiness, wanted to encourage it. He deserved it ... they both did.

Pointing at Arianna, I told them, "You don't have to do that; you guys can sit together."

Julian shook his dark head. "We don't want to rub it in your face."

Inhaling a deep, cleansing breath, I looked at them both. "You're not. I promise."

I turned to stare at Julian, letting him feel my emotions. They were level for once, moderately happy even. Feeling me, understanding me, Julian stood up. "I'm sorry I said you were a bitch," he said as we crossed paths.

The corner of my lips jerked up into a smile. "Don't be, you were right." Remorse filled me as I looked over my family. "But that's not who I want to be, so I'm going to try to be better." I locked eyes with Dad. "I'm going to try to let him go."

Julian gave me a quick hug, then flitted over to Arianna's side of the table. My friend shot to her feet to give me a warm embrace. "Love you, Nick," she whispered in my ear before returning to Julian's side. She'd started using Julian's nickname for me once they'd started dating. As much as I hated to admit it sometimes, they were very cute together. Almost perfect.

Mom and Dad sat down. We didn't talk about anything deep or anything hard. We mainly stuck to school topics, work topics, and family topics. And, for a moment, I felt just like my old self.

When Julian left to take Arianna home, I did my best to ignore his soaring mood, and tried not to let his joy sour me. Instead, I shifted my pain to happiness for him. And happiness for us. Julian was driving Arianna home in our new car; Dad had finally caved and bought us one. It was a very practical four-door station wagon with absolutely no frills, and Julian and I had to share it, which sometimes led to arguments, but the small amount of freedom it provided was exhilarating.

After saying goodnight to my parents, I headed upstairs. What I saw while I was brushing my teeth was nothing short of miraculous. Julian's room was clean. Everything was off his floor, every item in his closet was properly hung, and every book in his bookcase was facing the right direction ... I think they were even alphabetized. Even his bed was made. Rumpled, but made. This was typically how his room looked nowadays. It was such a huge change from the pigsty it had always been before he'd started dating Arianna; I couldn't help but be awed every time I looked in here. Definitely a positive side effect of dating my best friend. One of many.

I closed my side of the bathroom door once I was finished, then changed and got ready for bed. It was early, but I hadn't been sleeping well recently, and I really wanted a decent amount of rest tonight. Maybe I'd feel better in the morning. Maybe I'd be able to hold onto this sliver of hope I'd found tonight. After changing into my pajamas, I stared at my dresser; just looking at it made a searing pain rip through my chest. Sitting atop the dresser were two items that were very morbid to have in a bedroom—urns. One was gray granite mixed with specks of rose quartz, and the other was pitch black; the black stone reminded me of a pool of deep red blood. Both had fangs engraved into the stone, so subtly that you wouldn't realize what they were unless you firmly believed in my kind.

An internal battle stirred my soul as I stared at the inanimate objects. These things were important to me, but they were also holding me down. If I was ever going to be free, I needed to be rid of them. I took a step toward my dresser, then stopped. Just the idea of removing them from my sight was difficult. I could see Hunter's face with picture perfect clarity whenever I looked at his urn—the darkness of his hair, the intensity of his eyes, the course stubble along his jaw. His features were clear as day when my eyes traced the etching of his name upon the blackness. As was his voice.

"*I want you to keep it. Store it next to my sister's. I don't deserve her company.*" And the last thing I'd ever heard him say to me. "*I love you, too.*"

The memory was too much to bear, and I felt the edge of defeat crawl up my spine. Knowing what I had to do, I picked up each urn. They felt like they weighed a thousand pounds as I held them to my chest. Keeping my emotions as level as possible, I walked downstairs and into the garage. Some cardboard boxes were lying on my dad's workbench. Finding one that was the right size, I placed the urns inside it. I packed them carefully so they wouldn't break, then I taped up the box.

Pulling out Dad's ladder, I dragged it over to the access panel for the storage space. Popping open the hole that led to a small attic caused a light layer of plaster to fall around me. Feeling sniffly for a few different reasons, I grabbed the box and gently pushed it up into the hole. Once it was in the attic, I climbed up and stared down at it.

With a loving hand, I traced the line of tape across the top. Tears pricked my eyes as I murmured, "Goodbye, Hunter." Then, before I could lose my courage, I shoved the box to the far end of the space. It smashed up against some long-forgotten boxes that had been here prior to us moving in. That felt appropriate. Maybe one day, I'd forget they were there too.

It was several minutes later before I returned to the main portion of the house. Mom was right there, her brown eyes searching my tear-streaked face. "Are you okay?"

All I felt now was relief. I'd physically let Hunter go, and now I could begin to emotionally let him go. I could get past this ... I could move on. I was sure of it. I smiled at Mom as I answered, feeling better than I had in a really long time. "Yeah, I'm fine."

CHAPTER THREE

Nika

"SO, NIKA, WHO are you going to go to Junior Prom with?"

Sighing, I lifted my gaze from my lunch to stare at Arianna sitting across the table from me. Posters for the big event at the end of the month were everywhere I looked. It was Cinderella-themed, which I was trying to appreciate, since I had, at one point in my life, really enjoyed fairytales. I wasn't going to prom though; I could appreciate the fantasy just fine from my living room couch.

"For the twentieth time, I'm not going." Amused at the bewildered expression on her face, I resumed eating my pita pocket.

Arianna had the same surprised reaction every time I told her I wasn't going. I really thought she'd be used to it by now. "But it's *Junior Prom*, Nika. It only happens once in your life. I don't want you to miss out …"

Trey, sitting beside me, pointed his fork at Arianna. "It doesn't necessarily only happen once. My cousin went to Junior Prom three times." He looked over at me; the red tinge in his eyes implied that he'd imbibed in a little herbal refreshment today. His smell confirmed it. "Course, my cousin's a skank. She only got invited to go every year because everybody knew she put out."

I smirked at him. "Nice."

With a shrug, Trey returned to his watery mac-and-cheese. Julian paused to laugh at his best friend. My brother was sitting as close to Arianna's side as a person could get, so close that he had to eat with his left hand so he didn't bump her with every bite. He ate that way every single day. Julian was quickly becoming ambidextrous.

Crunching on a particularly loud piece of lettuce, I told Arianna, "I don't want to go. And besides, nobody's asked me." I smiled around my food as I chewed. That *had* to end the conversation, since I couldn't go without a date. I should have known better though. Arianna could be persistent when she was on a mission, and apparently getting me to prom was her newest mission.

Smiling bright, she said, "You still have two weeks. That's plenty of time to be asked. We just have to put the word out that you're available."

She looked around the cafeteria, like she was scouting for potential suitors in the crowd. I suddenly felt like a sack of meat about to be auctioned to the highest bidder. *Look guys, she's got shapely hips and a decent face. And, as a bonus, she promises to not make you buy her a corsage or do the Electric Slide.*

Frowning, I reiterated, "I don't want to go. Really, I don't mind missing out on this one."

Ignoring me, Arianna muttered, "Clancy just broke up with Julia. He probably needs a date. Or Luke … he's gay, but I'm sure he'd go with a girl if we asked real nice." Her gaze shifted to the other end of the room. "Or Austin. He's new. I'm sure he's still single. He'd probably take you."

Now my face shifted into disbelief. Openmouthed, I twisted to glare at Julian. "Can you please stop her? The more she talks, the more pathetic I sound."

Julian smiled over at Arianna, then gave her a swift kiss on the cheek. His mood amused, he told her, "Nick doesn't want to go … we shouldn't force her." He glanced at me. "She'd just pout the entire time anyway."

Giving him a dirty look, I chucked an apple slice at him. He easily caught it, shoving the entire thing in his mouth. While he noisily chewed, Arianna said, "But it just won't be the same if we don't all go together." Getting an idea, she turned her attention to Trey. "Who are you going with?"

My eyes widened as Trey shrugged. "I don't know. Hadn't thought about it yet." Tucking his dirty blond hair behind his ears, he scrunched his eyes in confusion. "When the heck is that anyway?"

Arianna's face brightened as my heart sank. Oh no, no, no. I was *not* going with Trey. "Perfect! You two can go together." Clapping her hands, she gave Julian a satisfied smile. "That solves everything."

No. No. No.

Trey gave me a languid smile as he wrapped his arm around my shoulders. I felt lightheaded just by the smell imbedded in his clothing. "Awesome. Me and Little A, dancing the night away." He pressed his body against mine. "Sounds heavenly."

As politely as I could, I shoved him away from me. "No, I don't think so."

Arianna's expression turned sympathetic. "Please, Nika. I hate the idea of you staying home, hurt and sulking. If you're truly going to move on … let go … then you need to get back out there. And we've been planning prom since freshman year. I know deep-down you want to go. I don't want you to leave high school with regrets."

Remembering our past excitement, our many conversations about who we'd take and what we'd wear, made my resolve weaken. Prom had always meant more to Arianna than it had to me, but I'd loved the idea of experiencing it together. And she made a good point: I didn't want to leave school and regret not sharing the night with my best friends … because of a boy. And if I went with Trey, at least my date would know for certain that there wasn't *any* possibility of a romantic hookup. I was already used to Trey's outlandish flirting, and I rejected him on an almost daily basis. He wouldn't be shocked if I told him I'd rather paint my nails than go out with him. And dancing with Trey might be fun. Maybe. "Okay, Arianna … you win."

She squealed in delight, then reached over the table to hug me. "This will be fun, Nick, I promise!" Repressing a weary exhale, I hoped that she was right.

When lunch was over, Arianna gave Julian a goodbye hug that lasted for several eternities. I could almost feel myself aging while I waited for my friend so we could walk to class together. You'd think Julian was going off to war by the way they clung to each other, but instead of interrupting, I let them have their moment.

My eyes unintentionally swung to my prom date. Trey was sitting on the edge of the table, kicking his legs as he stared off into space. He seemed oblivious to the world as he waited for Julian, but I wondered if he really was. Trey had shown a lot of insight when the ordeal with Hunter and his father had blown up in our faces a few months ago. He was a lot smarter than he let on. If only he'd stop baking his mind nearly every day, he'd probably be a lot quicker.

Just as I was wondering if Trey was even using his brain at the moment, he glanced up at me and indicated across the room with his head. "Looks like Julian's got an admirer."

My eyes instantly flashed to where Trey had been staring. Sure enough, someone across the room was openly watching my brother and Arianna. I frowned when I recognized the dark-haired girl. Raquel. She was with a group of kids who were slowly filing out of the room as they meandered to class. Her boyfriend, the obtuse Russell Morrison, was nowhere in sight. That was probably why Raquel was taking the opportunity to blatantly stare at my brother. Russell was the jealous type, especially when it came to Julian. Raquel had actually broken up with Russell a while ago, finally choosing my brother over the brute. But unfortunately, she'd been too late, and Julian had already started dating Arianna. Surprising, and pleasing, the hell out of me, Julian had turned down Raquel when she'd hit on him. But instead of remaining strong and tough on her own, Raquel had gone right back to Russell when it had become clear that Julian wasn't going to leave Arianna for her. Made no sense to me. She would have been happier alone.

Raquel's dark eyes were glued on Julian, so she didn't see me watching her. To get her attention, I stepped between her and my brother. Her cheeks flushed with color, and her eyes refocused on me. She immediately turned away, tucking her hair behind her ears and laughing at a friend ... who wasn't even looking at her. It was a sad attempt to make it seem like she hadn't been ogling Julian. It instantly irritated me. She shouldn't be longingly staring at Julian, not with how long she'd toyed with him. Julian was happy now, dating my best friend, and Raquel needed to accept that.

Feeling my surge of aggravated protectiveness, Julian pulled away from Arianna to look my way. "What's wrong?"

His eyes looked beyond mine to Raquel gathering her things and preparing to leave. A frown formed on his lips, as Arianna asked, "What is it?"

Curling her arms around Julian's bicep, she stared up at him like he held all the answers to life's many mysteries. Smoothing his expression, Julian smiled down at her. "Nothing that matters anymore."

Arianna glanced past me, to see Raquel leaving the room with her friends. Arianna's expression grew guarded, and her brows furrowed as she nibbled on her bottom lip. As happy as Arianna was with Julian, a part of her still worried that he'd dump her any second for Raquel; that was why they weren't officially boyfriend and girlfriend yet.

Stepping in front of Arianna, blocking her view of Raquel's retreating form, Julian said, "I'm yours, same as I was yesterday, same as I'll be tomorrow. You're the one I want to be with, Arianna."

Right in front of my eyes, my friend melted into a puddle of romantic, sappy goo. I was a little surprised her knees didn't buckle. Julian was getting good at this kind of stuff. He must have picked up a thing or two from Dad. Or Halina, although her form of romanticism was usually a little more X-rated. Giggling, Arianna laced her arms around Julian's neck and pulled him in for another kiss.

Groaning, I turned away again. "We should go, Arianna. We need to get to class. You can maul my brother later."

Arianna giggled in a way that made a flash of desire wash through Julian. I shot him a glance, and he grimaced in embarrassment. Damn bond. Studiously ignoring me, he told Arianna, "I'll see you after school." The lovebirds didn't have another class together today, hence the epically long goodbyes.

"See ya," she sighed as I dragged her away.

When we were free of the cafeteria, I rolled my eyes at her. "Jeez, Arianna. You could at least *try* to play hard to get."

She cuddled into my side just like she'd cuddled into Julian's. "Why would I want to do that? Your brother's dreamy." Laying her head on my shoulder, she sighed again.

Looking back, I saw Julian and Trey heading off in the opposite direction. Julian was laughing, his mood light and happy. It was a far cry from his disposition earlier in the school year when he'd been the dour one.

Twisting around to Arianna, I laid my head on hers. "I'm glad you guys are happy."

Arianna broke our contact and looked up at me. "Are *you* happy?" she asked, her lips curling into a frown.

Watching the cracked concrete at my feet, I debated what to tell her. I felt something sort of like happiness at times, but I certainly wasn't Julian's level of giddy. I was mainly ... resigned. This was my life, and I had to deal with it the best I could. Not sure how else to answer her, I simply said, "I'm not miserable. And that's enough for now."

Arianna sighed and stared at the ground. "Have you heard from ... him?"

I knew exactly which *him* she meant and woefully shook my head. "No, not since the night he told me goodbye in my bedroom."

The memory started bubbling to the surface, but I pushed it down. I didn't want to relive the moment when Hunter had left my life for good. I was trying to move past him. I'd even tried to stop cataloging his location, which was still miles from the ranch.

Arianna rubbed my arm, while I forced myself not to wonder why Hunter was so far south. "I'm sure it's for the best, Nick. I mean, what future could you really have with a vampire?"

So only my ears would hear her, she'd barely breathed the word *vampire*. I gave her a smirk in response. "That's an interesting question, considering who *you're* dating."

Scoffing, she shoved my shoulder away from her. "Julian's barely a VP, and you know it. He's pretty much just got the sexy teeth." Biting her lip, she giggled, "And, oh my God, they're so freaking hot."

Cringing, I tried to scrub the image of my brother dropping his fangs and playfully growling at Arianna. Unfortunately, I'd heard him do it on more than one occasion. "Ugh, Arianna, I don't want to hear about how hot my brother is to you. It's disturbing."

Arianna continued laughing for a moment, then she sighed. "I'm serious about you and Hunter though. Maybe it's for the best that the two of you ... aren't together. You're so different now." She pointed up at the sky. "He's up all night, you're up all day. He's got an entirely different ... appetite than you, and kids ... kids are definitely out." I frowned at all the truths she was spouting at me. Face sympathetic, she gently added, "And don't forget that his entire family wants to kill yours."

I was about to tell her that her concerns weren't *all* warranted—the blood one was fine, since that would eventually be my diet too—when a thought struck Arianna, and she stopped walking. "Oh, my God ... will Hunter still try to kill you? Even though he's kind of ... one of you?"

Adjusting my backpack, I stopped with her. "I don't ... think so."

She narrowed her eyes. "But you don't know for sure?"

I lifted my chin, exuding more confidence than I actually felt. "He won't hurt me. He won't hurt my family. That's not who he is anymore."

Arianna smiled in support, but I could see the doubt in her eyes. "That's what you hope, and I hope for everyone's sake that you're right ... but you haven't spoken to him in a long time, Nika. His head might be in an entirely different place than you think it is ..."

A part of me wanted to disagree with her ... but I couldn't. She was right. I didn't know for sure where his head was, and I didn't know how much he was hurting. All I knew was that Hunter was now something he'd never wanted to be, and he was struggling with that fact. And truly, it wasn't completely beyond the realm of possibility that he might take his grief out on my family. I think he would hate himself even more if he did, but I couldn't just blindly pretend that it was an unthinkable scenario. Hunter could still want to kill us.

Resuming our walk to class, I morosely told Arianna, "You're right ... I don't know. But Grandma is watching him closely, and I *do* know that she would never let him hurt us. She'd kill him first."

I stopped talking after that. I had to. My throat had cinched tight, and no amount of swallowing could loosen the knot.

The rest of school went by mundanely enough. Arianna told me all about her master plan for prom; she'd already spotted the perfect dress. She was so excited that we were all going together. I wasn't as excited yet, but I liked the normalcy of the idea. I could use a little normalcy in my life right now.

After school let out, Julian and Arianna rekindled in the parking lot. Even though Arianna lived within walking distance of the school, and getting out of the parking lot took longer than driving to her house, Julian insisted on taking her home each day. It was a nice gesture, but it meant I had to watch them be all sweet and lovey-dovey for even longer.

Arianna lived on the other side of a graveyard behind the school. While Arianna chatted with Julian in the front seat, I watched the tombstones passing by the window. Before I could stop the thought, I wondered if Hunter was sleeping in the earth right as that very moment. Was he covered up like a grave, or had he found a home to wait out the day? I felt like I would never know the answer to that question. And it was only one of many things I'd never know the answer to.

Julian got out of the car and walked Arianna to her front door. It was so sweet it made my jaw ache. I shifted around to the front seat while the lovebirds smooched on her porch. Believing they'd never separate without assistance, I tapped the horn. When Julian looked back at me, I told him, "I only have so much time, Julie."

He heard me loud and clear through the windshield, and reluctantly said goodbye to Arianna. She lifted her hand to me in a wave as Julian jogged back to the driver's side. Sensing his sadness, I told him, "Cheer up. You know you're going to call her the minute you get home, and now, because of me, you have more time to talk to her." He smirked at me, but his mood lifted as we left Arianna's driveway.

From there, Julian drove me to Salt Lake City Public Library. Besides Arianna's house, Trey's house, and our house, the library was the only other place we could drive to without special permission. And besides the ranch, the library was my favorite spot in all the world. It was also the most painful spot in all the world. It was where Hunter and I had first officially met. It was where he had died.

As Julian drove, both hands studiously holding the wheel at ten and two, I contemplated why I kept going back. In the end, I think it was plain pig-headedness that made me return. I'd loved this place before Hunter had entered my life, and I didn't want my ex to taint something I loved. And maybe if I kept coming back, it would hurt a little less each time. That hadn't happened yet, but I was hopeful.

"You okay?" Julian asked.

"Yeah," I murmured.

The feeling always passed ... eventually. Julian knew that, so he didn't question my answer. Instead, he said, "I'm glad you're going to go to prom. I think you'll have fun, even with everything ..." He sighed and stopped talking, guilt filling him.

Forcing a smile, I told him, "It will be fun hanging out with you guys."

He grinned, then bit his lip as nerves cropped up inside him. "So … I'm going to ask Arianna to go out with me at prom. Like, officially go out with me. It's been a few months now, and I think she'll say yes. God, I hope she says yes …"

I wasn't too surprised by his comment; I figured they were heading that way, but I was a little surprised by the fear and anxiety he was feeling; he was genuinely worried that she'd turn him down. And if she did … would they still date? Sending encouraging feelings his way, I told him, "She's crazy about you. I think she'll say yes, too."

He looked over at me with a dopey smile on his face. "You think so?"

I Indicated the road, so he'd look where he was supposed to. "Yeah … I do." I hoped. If they stopped dating, Halina would wipe Arianna's mind. She wouldn't remember what we were, and I'd have to lie to her again. And I really liked being open and honest with her, even if it was painful sometimes.

Julian's mood shifted once again, from hope to discomfort. Twisting in the seat to face him, I studied my suddenly uncomfortable brother. "What?" I asked, not sure if I wanted to know the answer.

Reluctance oozed from him in waves that made my skin pebble. He let out a weary sigh, then embarrassment flooded him. I furrowed my brow in confusion. Sometimes it would be a lot easier if our emotions had maps we could follow.

"Ah," he began, "It's just … if Arianna says yes, and we start getting serious … you and I … well, we should talk about …"

His emotions twisted from embarrassment to mortification, like he wanted to crawl inside a very deep hole. But there was an edge of determination about him too. Whatever it was he wanted to say, he really wanted to say it. His courage slowly built up, but it was laced with dread, and he was nervous when he pulled the car over in front of the library.

Concerned for my brother, I told him, "Just tell me whatever it is you're dying to tell me … because your anxiety is giving me heartburn."

A small, nervous laugh escaped him. "Sorry, this is just … weird to talk about … especially with you."

I started to say, "What is?" when I suddenly understood what he might be so nervous about. "You're thinking about having sex with her."

Julian sank his head to the steering wheel, and I knew without a doubt I was right. His emotions tumbled from horror to embarrassment to excitement to fear. He wanted this, but he was nervous about it. And now I was too. Julian couldn't experience sex without *me* experiencing sex, emotionally at least. That wasn't something I wanted to feel. Ever.

"Julian, you can't. You guys are ... too young."

Julian peeked up at me, and a flash of amusement washed through him. "Really? That's the objection you're going with?"

My gut churned, and now I was the one letting out a nervous laugh. "No, not really, it's just ... I don't want to feel that. Feeling you make out with her is bad enough."

Julian sighed and twisted to face me. "I know, and I don't want you to feel it either." He cringed, and the look on his face matched the feeling in my stomach. "I'm not saying it's happening now, but maybe in a couple of months? Or maybe in several months, I don't know. But I think ... I think I'm falling in love with her, Nick, and I want to ... one day ..." With a sigh, he looked down. "It's just something we need to talk about, that's all."

Panic filled me—this might be happening much sooner than I'd expected. "Are you sure you'll be ready in a few months? Why don't you wait a year or two? Or ten?"

Julian smiled at me, his embarrassment easing now that the topic had been broached. "Not ten, Nick. Maybe one, but *definitely* not ten."

Closing my eyes, I nodded. Asking Julian and Arianna to wait a decade wasn't reasonable, I knew that, but I wasn't ready. I didn't think I'd ever be ready. With a sigh, I opened my door and got out of the car. Julian waved goodbye, then sped off toward home so he could talk to his soon-to-be girlfriend. And soon-to-be lover. How were we going to get through this?

Putting aside the question I didn't have an answer for, I turned and trudged toward the library. It truly was a spectacular building, a sight that every person visiting town should make a point of seeing. Fountains and parks ringed the building while a curving path sloped up to a garden on the roof. The library itself was a stunning mix of glass and mortar, allowing for plenty of natural light. Hunter and I had spent countless hours talking and holding hands while we sat at a table near the wall of windows that overlooked the city. It had been idyllic. I loved it, I hated it.

As I did most times I came here, I went to the self-help section and found the book on abandonment that Hunter had first introduced me to. I'd never checked it out again, but I read it whenever it was here. I must have read the book about a dozen times by now. I could probably recite it word for word. In an odd way, it was helpful, therapeutic. Hunter hadn't abandoned me, but the feeling of loss was similar. Or maybe he *had* abandoned me. It was hard to say.

Just as I was reading about how to be comfortable with being alone, something I could never truly experience, since I was never truly alone, I felt my mother and father approaching. With a sigh, I returned the book and left my sanctuary. Voices, rustles, and whispers hit my ear as I emerged from the quiet of the library. Once outside, the sound of splashing water joined the cacophony of noise. Looking past a flowing staircase of water, I saw my dad's Prius. Mom waved at me out the window, and I gave the library one last glance before heading toward them.

So many memories resided here; it always took me a minute or two to disengage from them. I didn't speak much as we left, but my parents were used to that by now. I think this place was hard for them to be at too. They'd almost watched their children get killed here. That had to hurt. Once we were clear of the plaza, Dad picked up Mom's hand and kissed the back of it. She gave him a soft smile, then looked back at me. "Everything okay today?"

Her question was all encompassing, open to any sort of problem I might be struggling with. Not wanting to talk about my past, I instead focused on my future. "Yes, no ... I don't know."

Dad's eyes focused on mine in the rearview mirror. "What do you mean? What happened?"

An edge of worry laced his voice and I made myself smile; I didn't want him to worry about me anymore. I was perfectly fine. Well, perfectly safe anyway. "Arianna talked me into going to the prom with Trey."

Both Mom and Dad relaxed. Dad kissed Mom's hand again, as she told me, "I think that's great. It will be nice for you to go out and have some fun with your friends."

I nodded as I imagined how the night might go. "Yeah, I think so too." Resting my head against the window, I watched the world flash by. At least it would be fun to go dancing with everyone. And not a whole lot in my life had been fun recently.

Once we got home, I headed upstairs to put my bag on my bed. Julian was on the phone with Arianna. He was pacing his room as he talked, his face and mood joyous. They were discussing the dance, but I did my best not to listen. Downstairs, Mom and Dad were starting to make pizza from scratch. I was on my way to join them when Julian suddenly told Arianna, "Hey, can I call you back in a minute? Nika just got home, and I want to talk to her."

I locked eyes with Julian, and, after saying goodbye, he tossed the phone on his pristine bed. Shoving his hands in his pockets, he walked through our shared bathroom and into my bedroom. "Hey," he said, his mood content, but concerned.

Julian's eyes drifted to the floor, to where our parents were jokingly telling each other that they should hide some veggies in the pizza crust so we'd eat more. "About what we talked about earlier ... are you okay?"

Forcing back the embarrassment, I told him, "Yeah ... I'm fine." And I was fine, or I would be at any rate. Julian and Arianna were my best friends, and there was no way I'd selfishly stand in the way of their happiness. If this was what they both wanted ... then when the time came, I'd deal with it.

Julian's smile was soft and hopeful. "Yeah?"

Walking over to him, I smiled. "Yeah. This won't be easy for us ... but we'll figure it out. Together."

"Thank you," he said, searching my face. "I know you're not excited about all this, but I am, so ... thank you."

Letting out a morbid laugh, I told him, "Just keep in mind that when it does happen, you'll owe me big time."

Running his hand down his face, he shook his head. "Oh, I know. Believe me, I know." He peeked up at me. "And I know I'll have to return the favor one day, when you're ready. And we'll get through that too. Together."

I nodded, swallowed, and looked away. Julian had nothing to worry about there. The day when I was ready to have sex with someone wasn't happening for me. Not for a really long time.

CHAPTER FOUR

Julian

I'D DONE IT. I'd started the hard, awkward conversation with my sister—the dreaded sex talk. Usually, that was a parent/child thing, but with the emotional bond Nika and I shared, discussing it beforehand was vital. And embarrassing. But it needed to happen, because soon, I was going to ask Arianna to be mine. Officially. And after that...

I knew Nika wasn't ready for Arianna and me to take the next steps in our relationship, but I sure was. We'd been dating for about four months now. Four wonderful, blissful months. And every day that went by, I felt so much closer to her. We laughed, talked, opened up to each other in ways I'd never done with a girl outside my family. I felt like Arianna got me. I felt whole around her. Complete.

Being with her made every feeling I'd once felt for Raquel seem two-dimensional in comparison. My infatuation with my former crush had never gone as deep as my feelings for Arianna; I'd barely scratched the surface with Raquel. But Arianna … Like I'd told Nika, I was steadfastly falling in love with her, more so every moment I was around her, or thinking about her, or wondering if she was thinking about me. It was an incredible feeling, one I wanted to expand on, when the time was right. And I couldn't wait for it to be right. But for now, I was satisfied with asking her to be my girl. At prom. It was going to be perfect.

As I hopped out of bed, I thought about different ways I might ask Arianna to be mine at the dance. During her favorite song? With flowers? Inside a piece of chocolate? Everything seemed hokey, but I wanted to do something hokey for her. Something she'd love, something she'd always remember. I wanted every moment with her to be special. Maybe I could ask Nika for advice. From the lack of emotions coming from her room, I could tell she was still sleeping; that was really the only time we were unaware of each other. I felt guilty asking Nika about much of anything lately though. And talking about Arianna with her was hard, and not just because of the sex stuff. I just felt ... bad, like I was doing something wrong by being in a good mood. Like I was reminding her of everything she'd lost with Hunter.

I didn't want to feel bad, and I didn't want Nika to feel bad. I just wanted everyone to be happy, but right now, that wasn't possible.

With a sigh, I stepped into the bathroom and turned on the shower. The water was colder than expected, and I immediately turned up the temperature. I hated being cold. That was the one thing from my childhood abduction that I really remembered ... being cold. And alone. In a tight space. I hated all three of those things now. I hadn't had a panic attack since Arianna and I had started dating. She grounded me, gave me strength. And the ordeal we'd gone through with Hunter and his dad had given me strength. I'd definitely been tested during the battle, and I'd come out of it stronger, surer of myself. And with a potential girlfriend who I didn't have to hide anything from, who I ... loved. If Nika were happier, and Hunter's father wasn't still out there somewhere, hating all of us, I'd say life was kind of ... perfect.

After my shower, I dressed and headed downstairs to get some breakfast. Nika was awake now, and melancholy blanketed her as she ambled around her room. As I walked, I contemplated if my sister would ever be like she'd been at the beginning of the year. Sure, she was a lot better now than she'd been immediately after Hunter had ... said goodbye to her ... but she still wasn't the Nika I knew her to be. She was darker, not as hopeful. It saddened me that she was different now, but I understood her pain, her sorrow. I was trying to be supportive and help her through it, but sometimes that was difficult, sometimes I lost my patience. I regretted it whenever I did; Nika needed me.

Mom and Dad were in the kitchen when I got there. Dad was dressed for work in a blue button-up and khaki slacks, and was pouring blood from a steaming carafe into two mugs. "Good morning, Julian. Want some?" He lifted an eyebrow to top off his question.

I eagerly nodded. There was nothing quite like a little plasma jolt to start the day off right. Dad poured me a small glass while Mom came up to my side. Wrapping a cool arm around me, she asked, "Are you excited about the dance next weekend?"

Trying to play it cool, I shrugged. "Yeah, it should be fun." Possibly life changing. I hoped Arianna said yes. It was entirely possible that she might not believe I was over Raquel, that she might turn me down. God, I didn't even want to think about that outcome.

Dad handed me my glass of blood and glanced up at Mom. Some secret conversation passed between them as I took a sip. My fangs automatically released as the tangy refreshment hit my tongue. So good. Dad handed Mom her mug, then turned back to me. "About the dance ... I think you should know ... your mom and I are going to chaperone."

Setting down my glass, I gaped at them. "You can't go to the dance. You're not technically our parents."

Dad nodded. "We know. That's why we had Starla clear it with the PTA. They were short volunteers, so we're helping out."

Confused, I could only stare at them. "Why would you want to chaperone a high school dance?"

Mom gave me a care-free smile. "What? It will be fun. We'll get to watch you and Nika clowning around with your friends, listen to some music." She peeked up at Dad. "Maybe dance a little ourselves."

I knew that wasn't it. Not entirely. Something else was going on here. "Dad?" I asked, looking his way. "Is something going on?"

Dad bit his lip, then sighed. He exchanged a glance with Mom before answering me. "Okay, the truth is, while things have been quiet around here for a while now, Hunter's father is still out there. He knows what we are, and he knows where we live. We need to be cautious ... Your mom and I just feel like it would be safer for all of us if we accompanied you to the dance."

It made sense, but still ... it was weird. My parents were going to watch me bumping and grinding with my girlfriend. Or at least, I hoped she'd be my girlfriend by the end of the night.

Feeling weird about the whole thing, I sat down at the table to finish my liquid breakfast.

Done with his drink, Dad rinsed out his cup and put it in the dishwasher. Turning to Mom, he asked, "Ready?"

Sighing as she rinsed out her glass, Mom mumbled, "Do we really have to sit through a seminar on sexual harassment today?"

A playful smile crossed Dad's face. "It will be fun, and informative. And I think you could use the reminder."

Mom scowled at Dad. "Me?"

Dad nodded, his expression serious. "I'm your boss. You shouldn't hit on me nearly as often as you do. It's unprofessional."

Mom gave him a blank expression, then reached out and smacked his bottom. "Is that unprofessional? Jackass."

Laughing, Dad grabbed her waist and pulled her into his body. His fangs dropped down as he growled, "Careful. That may get you fired ... or promoted."

He made a move like he was going to bite her neck, but Mom artfully disengaged herself. Dropping her own fangs, she hissed at Dad, then murmured, "You'll need to be quicker than that, Mr. Adams."

Delight filled Dad's eyes, and I tore my gaze away from them. I swear they forgot Nika and I were here sometimes. Nika reminded them when she entered the room. "Ugh, guys, seriously? It's too early in the morning for all of this."

As she sat across from me, I tossed out, "Yeah, aren't you guys going to be late?"

Dad smirked at Mom as he apologized to us. Mom sighed and handed Nika her bloody breakfast. "Guess we better get this over with. Have a good day, kids." She gave each of us a cool kiss on the head.

Dad did the same, then told me. "Remember, you're only allowed to go to shopping after school, then right home." I nodded as Nika sighed. She didn't really feel like going shopping, but Arianna had her heart set on it, and she didn't want to let her friend down. And she did need something to wear, so she'd grudgingly agreed to come along. I hoped she felt better by this afternoon. I hoped she let herself have a little fun. She needed it.

THE BEAST WITHIN

She stared out the window as I drove us to school. It was still frigid outside, but flowers were starting to bloom in gardens, the trees lining the sidewalks were turning pink, and every morning birds chirped their greetings. This one tiny bird that insisted on loitering around my bedroom window was particularly annoying. I'd debated snatching and eating the damn thing on several occasions.

As we drove past the street that led to Hunter's old house, Nika swiveled around to stare at it. I didn't think she was consciously aware of it, but she always looked. Hunter wasn't there though. He and our grandmother, Halina, were miles south of Salt Lake ... doing who knows what.

Trying to get her mind off things, I tossed out, "So, did you hear ... Mom and Dad are chaperoning the dance. They got Starla to get permission for them."

Nika smiled over at me, but it didn't reach her eyes. "Yeah, I heard." Instantly, her grin evaporated. "I heard why too ..."

I instantly wanted to kick myself for bringing it up. It would have been kinder of me if I'd asked her if she'd rather go to the dance with Hunter than Trey. God, I could be thick sometimes.

Feeling my guilt, Nika forced the smile back to her face. "Don't beat yourself up, Julian. It's fine." Clearing her throat, like she was clearing away her pain, she sat up straighter in the seat. "Are you still going to ask Arianna out? With our parents there?"

My throat tightened as I considered that. My entire family was going to witness me throwing my heart out there. But they'd been there when I'd realized I had feelings for her, and they'd been there when I'd asked her to date me, so maybe it wasn't so odd to have them there. Maybe it was good luck. "Yeah ... yeah, I am." And if the fates were with me, she'd say yes.

The closer we got to school, the lighter my stomach felt. It was almost like Arianna and I had the same type of bond that my parents did; just approaching her made me feel buoyant.

Like she was fortifying herself for a battle, Nika inhaled a deep breath while I parked the car. She was preparing herself to get through another day; I felt her determination, as well as her pain. Even though I was eager to see Arianna, I waited in the car with Nika. Twisting her head to me, she forced a smile to her lips. "You can go. I'm fine."

Even without the bond, I knew that was a lie. She was far from fine. She'd pulled back from the bitterness and anger, but now she was hollow.

Even though she didn't want to admit it, she longed for Hunter. The bright, enthusiastic girl I'd known my entire life was a shadow of her former self, buried under a mountain of grief. I desperately wanted her to feel the joy I felt ... I just had no idea how to get her there. "Nick ..."

Reading my mood, she shook her head. "Don't feel sorry for me. I'll get through this. I promise." She smiled even brighter, but it still didn't touch her eyes. "You know, I think I liked it better when I was the one constantly worrying about you."

Cracking open my door, I smirked at her. "Yeah, it sucks, doesn't it?"

Trey rolled by on his skateboard just as I said that. "What sucks?"

Shaking my head at my friend, I told him, "Nothing." Nika wouldn't want to talk about her ex with Trey; plus, he didn't remember anything about what had happened that fateful night.

As the three of us walked toward the main building, I thought about the arrangement I'd made with Halina regarding Arianna. Generally, we didn't let people know about us. In fact, when we left Salt Lake after graduation, no one here would remember us, not even Trey. But I'd convinced Halina to let Arianna keep her memories. I couldn't bear the thought of her not knowing what I was, of having to hide anything from her. Thankfully, Halina had agreed to let her keep her mind, but only so long as we were dating. If Arianna and I ever broke up, for *any* reason, Halina was going to wipe her. Arianna wouldn't even remember me.

I didn't want to think about the possibility of that ever happening.

Shaking away the thought that was as chilly as the wind seeping through the seams of my jacket, I stepped into the heated hallway and breathed a sigh of relief. Arianna was right in front of me, talking to a couple of her girlfriends. Even from our distance, she smelled amazing. She was growing her golden hair out, and had it in a cute ponytail today. Her long neck was completely taking up my vision. Even though I'd never tasted human blood before, a desire was growing in me to taste hers. I didn't want to kill her or anything—definitely not—but I *did* want to taste her. I wanted to know if that sweetness was anything like the smell of her. It had to be. I just knew it. We'd never talked about me biting her, though, and I was a little scared to bring it up. I wanted Arianna to see me as human as possible.

Arianna turned when she felt me approaching, and my stomach flip-flopped. How could she still do that to me after all these months? I wasn't sure, but I loved it. Nika sighed as she followed behind me. I was trying to control my moods, keep them as even as I could, but it was impossible. I was so damn happy it was ridiculous.

"Hi," I said, snuggling up to Arianna's side.

Wrapping her hands around my arm, she leaned up and kissed my cheek. "Hi, you." Her lips were so soft I had to turn my head so I could feel them against mine.

Between pecks, I again told her, "Hi ..."

She tasted incredible, and I instantly lost myself in kissing her. There were vague whistles and giggles nearby, but I tuned it all out as I cupped her cheek and intensified our connection. Not able to help myself, I pressed her body against the wall. Her hands ran up my chest as she melted into me. I instantly wished we were somewhere more private, like the storage closet. Wondering if she'd consider it, I brushed my tongue against hers. She made a quiet, erotic noise that surged straight through my body. That was when we were forcibly yanked apart. Breathing heavier, I looked over at my sister holding us away from each other.

"Keep that stuff behind closed doors, 'kay?" She glanced up the hall at the group of friends Arianna had been talking to before I'd started mauling her. Several of them were looking back at us and laughing as they walked away. "You scared everybody off," Nika commented.

From behind me, Trey spoke up. "Not everybody. I'm still here." He smiled at me, then mouthed, *That was hot.*

Arianna tittered, embarrassed. I felt the same way as I twisted back around to my girl. It was so easy to get caught up in her. "Oops," I muttered.

Reaching out for Arianna, Nika grabbed her shoulders and stole her from me. "This is for your own good," she said, before forcing Arianna to leave with her.

I lifted my palms into the air as I watched them go. "Hey?"

Arianna giggled as she twisted around to leave with Nika. Over her shoulder, she waved and said, "Bye, babe."

Knowing I'd see her again soon, I waved back. Trey was silent a moment, then said, "By the looks of it, you guys are already sleeping together, so ... man to man, be honest with me ..." he laid his hand on my shoulder, "how amazing is it?"

His expression was completely serious. Knocking his hand off me, I started walking to first period. "We haven't yet, I already told you that."

Trey snorted as he fell into step beside me. "I know. I just don't buy it. You guys are too ..." He twisted his face while he searched for words. "Touchy-feely ... so, no, I don't believe that you haven't touched and felt everything."

I felt my skin warming as I thought about what we *might* be doing in the next few months, if everything worked out like I hoped. "Sorry, but we haven't gone there, yet."

Trey held onto my shoulder to stop me. "Where have you gone? Spell it out. Slowly. I need to know."

Frowning, I shook my head. "No, you don't."

He groaned. "Come on, I'm never gonna get any action, so I need to live vicariously through you. What have you done? Second base for sure, right?"

Shaking my head, I walked away from him. That only seemed to encourage him. "Okay, I'll take that as a yes. Third base?"

Our English class was on the first floor, and we were standing in the doorframe when he said, "Please God, tell me she's gone down on you."

Speechless, I could only gape at him while my cheeks flamed. I couldn't even form the word no. From off to my left, I heard someone softly clearing their throat. When I glanced over, Raquel was standing just within ear shot. She pointed at where Trey and I were blocking the door. Not meeting my eye, she whispered, "Excuse me."

A weird, uncomfortable feeling washed through me. I knew I didn't owe Raquel anything, and she'd done quite a number on me earlier in the year, but, well, she had some sort of feelings for me, and I didn't want to be callous about that. Satisfied that he knew what was going on, Trey clapped my shoulder and walked inside. Stepping out of the way, I let Raquel move into the classroom before me. When she passed by with her head down, her dark hair hiding her face, I muttered, "Sorry you had to hear that."

I wasn't sure she'd heard my apology until she peeked up at me. "Don't worry about it. I get it. You're a couple ... couples do things."

Feeling embarrassed again, I shook my head. "Arianna and I haven't ..." I didn't finish my sentence. I couldn't. It was too mortifying, and none of her business.

Understanding, Raquel stopped on the other side of the door. This was the one and only class we had together this semester, a fact that had barely even registered with me until now. A shy smile on her face, she asked, "Are you and Arianna going to the dance?"

There was something in her dark eyes that bordered on hope. Not wanting her to unfoundedly feel the two of us had a chance, I adjusted the backpack on my shoulder and told her, "Yes. We're looking forward to it."

A flash of pain struck her features before her soft smile returned. "That's ... good. Russell and I are going too." She frowned. "He doesn't really want to, though, since we went last year."

I walked through the doorway while she worried her lip. "You could do better, you know?"

She studied my mouth before moving up to my eyes. "I thought so once, but it was too late. You were already with Arianna."

There was a time when those words would have meant the world to me, but now I just found them frustrating. She started to turn away, and I grabbed her arm. "I didn't mean *me* ... I just meant in general, you could do better than Russell. Even being alone would be better than being with him." Firmly believing it, I put every ounce of conviction that I had into my statement. I didn't have feelings for her anymore, but I still wanted to help her see the truth.

Raquel's eyes darted to where I was touching her before returning to my face. Smiling softly, she nodded. I hoped she hadn't read too much into that, but even still, I'd felt compelled to say it. That was all I would do though. Raquel had to leave him on her own. She had to learn to put her life first.

Trey beamed at me as I sat down. He held his fist out, wanting me to bump it. "Congrats on the third base."

Rolling my eyes, I ignored him.

I met up with Arianna a couple of classes later. She looked upset, and she didn't cheer up when I kissed her on the cheek. "What is it?" I asked, caution in my voice. Arianna was usually very happy when I kissed her.

She glanced at me, then redirected her gaze to over my shoulder. My sharp vision caught a question in the depths of her shimmering hazel eyes. Shaking her head, she started turning away from me. I gently grabbed her arm to stop her. "Hey, what's going on? Talk to me ..."

Arianna's lips quivered as she stared at me. Just when I was positive I'd go crazy if she didn't say anything, she spoke, "Did you tell Raquel that she would be better off with you than with Russell?"

I blinked, hardly believing the words that had left her mouth. "Did I ... what?"

The shimmer in her eyes condensed into thick tears waiting to fall. "Raquel? Did you tell her that she'd be better off with you?"

She was minutely pulling away from me, so I released her arm to grab her hand. "No, of course not. Where ... where did you hear that?"

"A group of girls were talking about it last period. They said you were all over her this morning. Did you talk to her?" As the question left her lips, so did the tears. My heart cracked as I watched her pain. Damn high school gossip.

Wondering how to answer her without hurting her even more, I mumbled, "I ... yes, we spoke ... but I never said—" Arianna turned her head away from me, and I saw the splash of more tears falling. Wanting to fix this fast, I told her, "She asked if you and I were going to the dance, I said yes. She said she was going with Russell, I told her she could do better. That's it. That was the whole conversation."

Arianna turned back to face me, wet trails down her cheeks. "Why would you tell her that? You had to know it would sound like you ... like you meant ... you?"

Cringing, I shook my head. "I couldn't keep it in. Russell treats her like crap. Everyone knows it, but no one says anything." I glanced at some of the people walking by us for emphasis.

Arianna sniffled as she wiped her cheeks dry. "Except you. You had to say something?"

Sighing, I tenderly grabbed her other hand and pulled her closer. "Yes, I had to say something. I'm completely over her, Arianna, but what I'm not over is watching someone get stomped on and not doing anything about it. That's not who I am. That's not the guy you're in love with." I completely froze as what I'd just said registered in my head. I'd opened a door in our relationship *and* thrust her into the spotlight, and she might not appreciate that.

Her eyes widened as she watched my shocked expression, but then her expression softened into a smile. "Yeah ... I know."

She looked down like she was embarrassed, but joy flooded through me so hard, I knew I was being swept away. *She loves me.*

Biting her lip, Arianna looked up at my face again; her heart was in her eyes. "You know I have ... issues with you and her. I'm sorry, I just keep waiting for you to ..." With a sigh, she looked back down.

Abhorring the insecurity I saw on her face, I pulled her into my arms and kissed the top of her head. "You don't have to worry about her. I'm with you, and I'm not going anywhere. You're the only one who gets me ... who knows me." Pulling back, I stared deep into her eyes. "And ... I ... I love you." Saying it lifted a weight off my chest. I wanted to shout it from the rooftops, let everyone know how amazing I felt. Instead, I stroked her cheek, drying where a new tear had fallen. A happy tear this time. "I love you, Arianna," I repeated, putting my entire soul into the words.

Arianna gave me a glorious smile. "I love you, too," she murmured.

Hearing her say it was a million times better than merely having it implied. Giddy grin on my face, I lowered my lips to hers. When we separated, Arianna was a picture of joy. Demurely biting her lip, she stared at me a second, then said, "Yes."

Confusion mingled with my happiness. "Yes ... what?" I asked, feeling like I was floating.

Arianna giggled, then smiled. "Yes ... I'll be your girlfriend. Officially."

I froze in shock, but then euphoria took over. I'd been so nervous about asking her, and here she was, offering me an answer without hearing the question. I laughed as I pulled her into me, then I frowned. Pushing her back, I said, "I was going to ask you at prom ... make it special."

Smiling, Arianna stroked my cheek. "Maybe we can make prom special ... another way."

My earlier shock was nothing compared to what I felt now. Was she suggesting ... ? "Do you mean ... ? Do you want to ... ?" I looked up and down the hallway. "Are you saying we can ... ? You're ready to ... ?"

While I felt stupider with every half-formed question leaving my mouth, Arianna giggled. Holding my cheeks, she made me focus on her face. "Yes, I'm ready. In truth, I've been ready for a while, but I didn't want to rush you."

I lifted an eyebrow at that. *Rush me?* Arianna laughed, then gave me a soft kiss. "I guess I also wanted to make sure you were over ... her. And I finally feel like you are. So, yes, I want to be your girlfriend, and I want to … share myself with you. Because I love you … and it feels so good to finally say that out loud."

I nodded my agreement. "Yeah it does …" Leaning down, I gave her a sweet kiss. "Okay, if you're sure you're ready. Because I *know* I'm ready, then let's do this … on prom night." Laughing, I squeezed her tight. I couldn't believe this was not only happening, but might be happening soon. Really, really soon. Damn. Nika and I were going to have to figure something out fast. Prom wasn't that far away. Double damn. My parents were going to prom with us.

"Oh … shoot." I pulled away, and Arianna's eyes were curious. Glancing up and down the hall, I whispered, "My parents are chaperoning the dance. We won't really be alone prom night." I sighed after saying it. That was true in more ways than one. Arianna didn't know about my emotional bond with Nika.

Her face fell as she realized what that meant for our impromptu plans. "Oh … that complicates things. I guess we won't be able to …" Her cheeks flushed with color as she looked away. "Well, maybe we can still get together later. I could sneak out and come over? Their room is soundproof, right?"

"Uh, yeah, it is." That could actually work. If it was late enough at night, Nika would be asleep, my parents would be asleep. So long as no one woke up, we might actually be able to spend the night together. Holy shit. I might be losing my virginity on prom night. I genuinely hadn't seen that coming.

Arianna squeezed my arm tight. "Okay, then. We'll just have a date after our date." She giggled like the idea was cute. So much blood was traveling down my body that I thought I might pass out. I was making a plan with my girlfriend to have sex next weekend. Holy crap … I had a girlfriend.

I spent the remainder of the day running through different scenarios in my head—really good ones, and really bad ones. On the good side was an amazing night of intimately connecting with Arianna. On the bad side was Nika, or my parents, walking in on us. I had no idea how my parents would react if they caught us, but I was pretty sure they'd be upset. But they'd have to wake up *and* open their door to hear us, and that rarely happened. Nika was the larger concern. If she woke up, even just a little bit, she'd feel what I was feeling ... and that would mortify us both. I'd have to talk to her soon, let her know this was really happening. Oh my God ... this was really happening.

After school, I thought about mentioning it to Nika ... but with Arianna and Trey joining us for our shopping trip, there really wasn't a good way to tell her. All I could share with her was the fact that Arianna had said yes. She was my girlfriend—fully and completely. Nika's smile was small, supportive, and not surprised when I told her, and I figured Arianna had already filled her in on the news.

"Congratulations, Julian," she said, wrapping me in a quick hug. I could feel she meant it, but I could also feel the lingering pain that was always buried inside her, like a layer of sludge weighing her down. After separating from me, Nika pulled Arianna in for a hug. "Congratulations to both of you."

As Arianna squealed and my sister laughed, Trey bumped my shoulder. "Dude? I thought you guys have been going out for months? What is she talking about?"

Tossing him a smile, I nodded toward my car. "Come on, I'll explain on the way."

As we headed to the department store where Arianna had already found a dress, I couldn't stop thinking about prom night. I was almost numb with joy over everything that had happened today. Arianna had told me she loved me. I'd told her I loved her. She'd agreed to be my girlfriend. She'd offered to share herself with me after the dance. If I could pick a day to repeat forever, it would be *this* day. No ... the night of the dance just might trump today. I'd pick both days, one right after the other for eternity.

Trey and I left the girls to it while we went looking for suits. There was a tux shop a couple of doors down, and it took us about twenty minutes to get everything we needed. Sometimes being a guy was easy. When we were done, we sat outside the dress shop and waited for the girls to finish up. I swear to God we waited three hours. I debated talking to Trey about my upcoming plans with Arianna, but I knew he wouldn't stay silent about it. He'd say something inappropriate at the wrong time, and Nika would find out before I was ready for her to know. I needed to tell her in private first.

Standing and stretching when the girls finally emerged, I asked Arianna if I could see the dress. She held the bag tight to her body. "No way, not until prom." Her eyes sparkled with playfulness, and, for multiple reasons, I couldn't wait until next weekend. Turning away from the playful look on my girlfriend's face, I turned to Nika. "So, what color did you end up getting?"

Nika raised her lip in amusement. "Blood red."

My face matched hers. "I should have guessed that."

She shrugged. "The dress spoke to me. But Grandma will need to alter it. It's a little too long."

As Trey yawned, Arianna flung her arms around Nika. "We are going to be so hot! This will be the best night ever." Her eyes locked onto mine, and there was an intensity in the greenish-brown depths that stole my breath. Yes, prom night was *definitely* going to be a night to remember.

CHAPTER FIVE

Nika

MY BROTHER AND I needed to talk to Gabriel *soon*. Arianna had surprised Julian by shaking up his plans and agreeing to be his girlfriend before prom ... so now, the timer had been set. They'd be ramping up their relationship, and eventually they'd start sleeping together. I did *not* want to still be emotionally tied to Julian when they finally had sex. Hopefully, I still had awhile, like Julian had ensured me. Hopefully that was enough time to create some sort of ... cure. Hopefully Gabriel was around this weekend so we could ask him about it. He hadn't been around much though. He didn't like to leave Halina alone with Hunter for long, and Halina didn't like to leave Hunter on his own, so I hadn't seen either vampire in a while. Gently folding my prom dress, I shoved it into my backpack. I really hoped Gabriel was there today.

Once I was ready, I headed downstairs to join my family. Julian was both sad and elated as he picked at a frayed seam on his bag. I had to assume the happiness was because Arianna was now officially his girlfriend, and the sadness was because he wouldn't see her again until Monday. If my own love life was going better, I would have found Julian's devotion sweet. Now, it just reminded me of what I didn't have anymore.

We were having dinner at the ranch—it was Grandpa Jack's birthday—and as soon as Dad was finished with his nightly project, scouring the online classifieds, we were heading out. Leaning against the counter, Dad stared at the website on his laptop with a determination that most people didn't have when they looked through the personals. But he wasn't looking for a job, and he wasn't looking for a date. He was looking for "Blood Wanted" ads.

Dad was right about Hunter's father still being out there, still being a threat, and so long as he was, our family was a target. Everyone in our nest was keeping an ear out, waiting for any sign that Conner had recovered enough from the emotional blow of Hunter's conversion to resume killing our kind. Hopefully, he was still too distraught to be hunting. My shoulder still ached sometimes from where Connor had shot me with an arrow. I didn't want to be in danger like that again. I didn't want to be on the run again. I just wanted a normal life. Well, as normal as my life was ever going to be.

Smiling, Dad stopped on an ad. "Hey, Em, grab my phone. I think I found one."

Mom picked up Dad's cell phone and handed it to him, then leaned over his shoulder as she read the ad. I tried to read it, too, but couldn't see anything from my angle. Dad dialed the number, then stood up. He'd changed into his ranch attire after work—dark blue jeans and an untucked button-up shirt. With the slight stubble across his jaw, he reminded me of one of the ranch hands that helped during the busy times. Mom often referred to Dad's ranch look as "incredibly attractive." She giggled whenever he put on a cowboy hat. It was embarrassing.

One hand casually shoved into his pocket, Dad waited for the person on the other end to pick up. When they did, he said, "Hi, I saw your ad online for donations ... for the food drive? Is that still going on?" The other person cheerily told Dad that it was, and she could take down his information if he wanted to stop by with "food for the hungry."

Tilting his head, Dad said, "I was actually wondering about the recipients. I'm on a special ... all-liquid diet, and I would love to donate food to people with my same condition. Do you accept liquid meals?"

The person on the other end hesitated, then said, "We do have special-needs clients who would greatly appreciate your offer."

Dad exhaled in relief. "Good, I think we're on the same page. I just wanted to warn you about a group who is opposed to 'all-liquid' diets. They're going around answering ads like these. You had any problems lately?"

There was a small gasp on the other end. "No, no we haven't had any ... issues. But we'll be extra cautious. Thank you for the heads-up."

Dad said goodbye and hung up with a smile on his face. "No problems at that one either. I don't think Connor's active yet."

Julian's mood darkened. "At least around here. He could be active somewhere else."

Dad nodded, his expression also darkening. "I know, and trust me, if he *is* killing, no one feels worse about it than me, since I let him go, but, our family is my top concern right now." His pale eyes swung around the room, soaking in all of us. When his eyes finally settled on Mom, they were carefree again. "Now, let's go wish my dad a happy birthday."

The drive to the ranch was peaceful, with Julian staring out the window, lost in thought, and my parents having a quiet conversation about how much longer Grandpa Jack could do as much around the ranch as he did. Not that any one of us could stop him from having a hand in just about everything out there. Alanna would have to tie him up to keep him down. But Grandpa Jack was pretty sprightly for being in his sixties. I was sure he'd be running the place for years to come.

A sense of familiarity washed through me as we approached the wrought iron gate. The family name proudly forged into the black metal gleamed in the spotlights as the gate creaked open to let us inside. Cobblestones thudded under the tires as we drove toward the massive home. The ranch house was an impressive sight, one that could be featured in a "unique and amazing home" magazine. Arched peaks and tall chimneys soared into the air, up to four stories in some places, while rooms beneath the earth extended down just as far—a structural diamond protecting the mythical creatures inside. The lights were on, and I could feel two of my grandmothers, Imogen and Alanna, shuffling about the kitchen as they prepared for tonight's festivities. Halina was still down south. With Hunter.

Driving past the main doors of the house, Dad headed for a dome-like building with a car-size hole in it. He drove the car straight through the space to get to the garage on the other side of the building. After Dad turned and parked the car, we all grabbed our bags and climbed out. Marveling at how clean the air was, I inhaled a deep breath and stared up at the red brick home. More spotlights bathed the bushes and gardens along the bottom in a warm glow, while the bright moonlight above cast its blue-gray light upon the tall spires and towers. I preferred the muted light of the moon to the softly humming man-made lighting. It was natural, peaceful. The way the moon blanketed the sleepy pastures surrounding the ranch was almost sensual. In my opinion, no lights should be turned on outside when the moon was at its fullest. When nature was putting on a show, why try and compete with it?

Mom and Dad were all smiles as they walked around to the back of the house. They loved coming here; we all did. It was a sanctuary, a place where we were free to be ourselves. Grandpa Jack was sitting on the living room couch with Grandma Linda when we entered; they both looked tired, but they stood up when they noticed us. Dad was shaking his head as he walked over to Grandpa. "You don't have to stand, Dad. I'm sure you've had a long day."

Grandpa swished his hand. "It's all right. I've been sitting here for far too long anyway."

Dad lifted his eyebrow at him. "I highly doubt that."

As Grandpa chuckled at his son, I stepped into his side and wrapped my arms around him. "Happy Birthday, Grandpa."

Grandpa patted my back, then gave my head a light kiss. "Well, it sure is now."

As I gave Grandma Linda a hug, and Grandpa embraced Julian, I felt Imogen and Alanna zipping into the room. I glanced over at the pair as I helped Grandma Linda sit back down; even though she tried to hide it, her leg was bothering her more and more recently. The seemingly youthful vampires who had just blurred into the room were physically near identical—jet-black hair, ice blue eyes—but their different styles defined them. Alanna was a rancher's wife, right down to the crisp denims and tucked in flannel. Imogen was a prim and proper lady with a tight bun, high-collared blouse, and long flowing skirt.

Both Grandmas hugged me simultaneously, then moved on to Julian. "Welcome, children," they cooed, kissing his cheeks.

Julian grimaced under their affections, but it was an act. He loved it. "Ugh, guys, I'm sixteen. The kissing needs to stop." He smiled at them as the pair laughed.

Just as I was about to tell Julian that he shouldn't complain about kissing, I felt something that just about made my legs give way; it was like my entire world had just crashed to a stop. The blip on my internal radar that was Halina had just started to move, fast, toward us ... and Hunter was a half-second behind her. My head jerked around to where I could feel them streaming closer, and my body surged with adrenaline. Were Halina and Hunter coming *here*? I hadn't seen Hunter in months. I wasn't sure if I even could see him right now. I'd said my goodbyes, made my peace with the fact that I'd probably never see him again. I wasn't ready to fall back into the pain I'd tried to bury for months. But God, I wanted to see him so badly my chest ached.

As Grandpa Jack asked the suddenly tense room what was wrong, Julian blurred to my side. Tossing his arm around my shoulder, Julian comforted me in silence while Dad answered Grandpa. "Great-Gran is on her way here ... and Hunter is with her." In my periphery, I saw Dad turn to Alanna. "She's coming to the party? I thought ... I thought she was busy and couldn't make it?" He seemed disappointed that she'd changed her mind, but I knew it wasn't Halina he had a problem with.

I couldn't see Alanna's reaction—I couldn't pull my gaze from the spot on the wall that was directly between Hunter and me—but I heard the surprise in her voice. "That's what she said last time I talked to her. She wasn't going to be able to make it because she didn't want to leave ... She must have convinced him to come with her."

Forcefully turning my body away from the wall that had me enraptured, Alanna brightly proclaimed, "Dinner is ready. Shall we eat?"

Food was about the last thing I wanted right now. I wanted to pace. I wanted to count the seconds as Hunter streaked toward me. I wanted to run to him. I wanted to know why he'd agreed to come here tonight. I wanted to know why he hadn't come back before this. I wanted to know if he still loved me ... I had so many questions, and none of them were going to get answered by me sitting down to a plate of steak and potatoes.

Wriggling out of Alanna's grasp, I murmured, "I'll be right back." I knew none of them would let me go, but I had to try. I couldn't just sit here and wait. I'd go crazy.

Just as I was about to blur away, Dad zipped in front of me and grabbed my forearms. Eyes wide, he stared me down. "No, Nika. Stay here and have dinner. Great-Gran and Hunter will be here soon enough."

My eyes watered as I started shaking. "Dad, please, I need to go. I need to see him, talk to him. I just ... I need to. Please?"

Sighing, Dad shook his head. "I'm not going to let you run deep into the countryside on your own. It won't take them long. We'll wait here, together."

I felt like I was beginning to hyperventilate as I stared at him. *Wait?* The word sounded impossible ... and long. Not knowing how to ask for what I wanted in a way that wouldn't sound like childish whining, I instead told him, "Fine," and strode to the table.

There was an unnatural silence in the room as all of us focused on the feeling of Halina and Hunter rushing toward us. Alanna brought out the meal while the rest of us sat and waited. Noting the empty spot where Gabriel typically sat, I asked, "Is Gabriel with Grandma?"

Alanna paused as she set down a platter of T-bones—way too many for the scant amount of people eating food tonight. "Yes. He's been bouncing between Grandma, the ranch, and California, but he was with Grandma last night." Turning her head away from me she added, "He doesn't like to leave her alone for long."

I knew why he didn't like to leave her alone, and a sharp ache cracked my body. Hunter. Gabriel didn't trust Hunter, and Halina wouldn't leave him. Here I was trying to forget about Hunter, and it suddenly felt like he was the focal point of everything in my life. No one was even talking, because all anyone wanted to talk about was Hunter. Julian was the one who finally broke the silence.

As Alanna unloaded a couple of large baked potatoes onto his plate, Julian said, "Has Gabriel had any luck studying Uncle Ben's blood?"

My eyes snapped to Julian's, then Alanna's. While Gabriel's original nest lived in Los Angeles, that wasn't the reason Gabriel had been visiting California. He was studying Ben. Ben had just a trace amount of vampire DNA in him. Just enough to make him impervious to compulsion. It was something that had us all mystified.

Alanna shrugged as she loaded up her husband's plate with a giant helping of green beans. "You know Gabriel ... when he discovers something fascinating, he has a hard time letting go of it. Poor Ben has been poked and prodded quite a bit, but ... I'm not sure what, if anything, has come from it."

Dad's eyes turned speculative as he watched his mother. He didn't like Ben being turned into a guinea pig. Not much he could do about it from up here though, and Dad wasn't comfortable heading down south right now. Not with Connor and Hunter on the loose.

Once Alanna had filled the plates of everyone who was eating, she started pouring glasses of blood. Aside from Grandma Linda and Grandpa Jack, we all got some. I could tell from the smell that it was fresh, but even though my mouth watered, I didn't drink it. I couldn't. My appetite was gone. Everyone else around me dug in while I sat in silence and waited. Dad encouraged me to eat, Julian nudged my elbow, but the desire wasn't in me. All I cared about was the fact that I was about to see Hunter. It filled my every thought, superseded every need.

When Alanna brought out the birthday cake, my plate was still untouched. I sang the song, because I didn't want to be rude, but my heart wasn't in it. As Grandpa blew out the sea of brightly shining candles, I tensed in anticipation. Halina was almost here. She was almost to the door, and Hunter wasn't far behind her.

Once everyone was done cheering for Grandpa, they all looked at me. Sympathy oozed out of my brother, and all I saw in my parents' eyes was concern. Not able to stand it one second longer, I blurred to the front door. Opening it, I waited, and counted. Long seconds breezed by as Halina and Hunter streaked even closer to me. My heart hammered in my chest when they were almost upon me. Oh God, was I ready for this? Trembling, I closed my eyes.

"Someone holding the door open for me. Now that's what I call service."

I gasped when I felt Halina's presence right in front of me. My vision blurry with tears, I made myself open my eyes and focus my gaze solely on her. "Hi, Grandma." I forced a smile to my face, but it felt just that—forced.

Halina's long black hair was loose and wild around her body. She smirked at me, then tossed her arms around me. "Good evening, Nika." She sighed a little as she held me tight. "It's been too long."

Pulling back from her chilly embrace, I risked a glance outside. Gabriel was right behind Halina, but no one else. He was staying back, in a clump of trees, out of sight. He'd come all this way, and he wasn't going to come in, wasn't going to say hello. He was hiding. Still. My heart fell to the floor.

Fighting back the pain, I nodded in response to Halina's statement. "Yes, it has been." I scanned the palely lit landscape where I felt Hunter, looking in vain for some trace of movement in the trees. But all was still … cold and empty. It made me rethink my earlier assessment of the moon. Maybe it was better to drown out the desolate moonlight with garish incandescence.

Halina and Gabriel stepped into the house while I waited at the wide-open door, reluctant to close it on Hunter. Mom and Dad appeared at the entryway to give their greetings to the long-gone pair, along with Alanna and Imogen. Halina squealed when she hugged her daughter; all of us had missed her, but Halina and Imogen were usually inseparable, and the distance had been particularly trying on them.

The comparatively slower humans—Grandma Linda and Grandpa Jack— walked into the foyer with Julian, and even more merriment went around the room. My heart sank as I realized Hunter really wasn't going to come inside. He hadn't rushed here to see me. He hadn't missed me. Feeling my despair, Julian paused in hugging Halina, and mouthed, *I'm sorry.*

Either Halina heard Julian or understood his look, because she glanced back at me still holding the door open. Studying my desolate face, she asked, "Waiting for Hunter?" The way she said his name was oddly affectionate, like the way she said her daughter's name. I shook my head, then wiped a betraying tear from my cheek. Halina tilted her head at my conflicting reaction, then pointed to the clump of trees where we all felt him. "He didn't want to come inside just yet. He said he needed a minute."

I looked toward the woods again, but I still saw nothing to give away a lurking vampire. I strained my enhanced ears, but I didn't hear him either. Hunter was being exceedingly quiet. I wanted to call out to him, beg him to come inside and see me, but the fact that he was hiding hurt too much. I couldn't speak. I merely shrugged and walked back into the entryway, like it was of no consequence to me.

Halina saw right through my bravado. Glancing at the walls separating Hunter from us, she stated, "Don't worry, he *will* come inside when he's ready. He won't be rude by hiding all evening long." The irritation in her voice was unmistakable.

A tired, sullen voice answered her. "I'm not hiding. I just wanted some air." Hearing Hunter's voice again sent an electric shock through me. It was so familiar, yet so foreign at the same time. I wanted to run over and comfort him, but I didn't want to forgive him so easily for disappearing. And a part of me wanted him to come to me first. I needed to see that he'd missed me ... like I'd missed him.

Halina smirked at Hunter's remark. "A three-hundred-mile jog through the countryside wasn't enough air for you?"

His face impassive, Gabriel stated in a detached voice, "You said you would try, Hunter."

As quick as taking a breath, Hunter blurred into the room. "I *am* trying."

Halina beamed at her "child's" appearance, and Gabriel let out a small sigh as he glanced at her. Dad tensed, like he thought Hunter was immediately going to start attacking us, and Julian's concern for me skyrocketed. The crack inside my chest split wider as I stared at the man in front of me. Hunter Evans. He was really here. Finally, after all this time, I was looking at him again. And he looked ... awful. He was thinner than I remembered. Gaunt almost. He had deep circles under his eyes, like he hadn't slept in ages, and he was pale. I'd been expecting that, since he hadn't seen the sun in a long time, but this was an unhealthy pale. Sickly. His dark hair was dull, lifeless, his sexy stubble unkempt. He was dirty, his clothes stained in reddish-brown dirt. Everything about him was off, and if I didn't know any better, I'd assume I was staring at a man with only a few months left to live. He used to be so confident, so sure of himself. He was a shadow now, a shell of a person, and seeing him this way scared the crap out of me.

Rushing up to him, I almost touched his cheeks before stopping myself. He might run away if I was too aggressive. "Are you okay? You look ..." Dad hissed my name, warning me to keep my distance.

Hunter glanced at Dad, then blinked at me with slow, languid, empty eyes. "I'm fine."

I searched his body, then his face, looking for some clue as to what might be the cause for his unsettling appearance. Only one thing came to mind. "No, you're not ... you're starving."

Hunter shrugged, like it was no big deal. I couldn't help but wonder how long ago he'd eaten. If he'd run here, he'd been keeping his strength up somewhat, but who knew how long ago his last meal had been. Angry, my eyes flashed to Halina. "I thought you were making sure he fed."

Her eyes narrowed into dangerous pinpoints. "I am doing my best, but he's extraordinarily stubborn." She locked eyes with Hunter, and her expression softened. "I have had to do several unpleasant things to get him to eat."

Hunter sniffed and wobbled on his feet like he might fall over. "Don't remind me," he whispered. If I'd thought he'd looked pale before, it was nothing compared to how he looked now, and I couldn't help but wonder just what Halina had done to get him to drink. Fixing his haunted expression, Hunter stared toward the kitchen. "It smells like blood in here ... and ... cake." He made a disgusted face, and I wasn't sure which food source repelled him more.

"It's Grandpa's birthday," I explained. Knowing his answer, but thinking I had to try anyway, I told him, "There's a lot left over. Do you want something to eat?" Dad took a step toward me, like he thought Hunter might take my words as an invitation to nibble on me.

Hunter's eyes flashed to mine. For a second, they blazed with interest. They even settled on the vein in my neck, and he tilted his head like he was listening to my surging heartbeat. I wished I could calm my blood down ... for his sake. But seeing him again was making the disobedient organ throb in my chest. "No, I'm not hungry." He smirked, but then the defeated expression of exhaustion seeped back into his eyes.

Dad stepped next to me, his face and body full of caution. "When was the last time you ate, Hunter? Starving yourself is dangerous ..." his eyes shifted to me, "... for everyone."

Still looking utterly despondent, Hunter reiterated, "I said I'm not hungry. I don't want to eat."

My concern for Hunter rivaling my brother's concern for me, I shook my head. "Not wanting to eat and not being hungry are two very different things, and I can tell that you're hungry." Hoping he still cared for me, and trusted me, I held out my hand. "Just try, please ... for me?"

Hunter seemed torn as he stared at my palm. Surprising me, he looked over at Halina and Gabriel for guidance. Gabriel gave Hunter a small nod. Halina looked eager, like she wanted Hunter to eat more than she'd ever wanted anything in her life. Maybe I was imagining it, but I could have sworn Gabriel frowned as he glanced between them. Ignoring everyone else, Hunter slowly started reaching out for my peace offering. Dad stepped in front of me, stopping our potential connection.

Hunter blinked then looked up at Dad's eyes. Tension filled the room as two of the most important men in my life stared each other down. I tried to move around Dad, but he grabbed my hand, holding me in place; his grip was as solid as the cold metal gate guarding the house. Immovable. "Dad," I whispered. "It's fine. Let me go."

His eyes not leaving Hunter's, Dad spoke to me over his shoulder. "If he's underfed, I don't want him near you." His attention refocused on Hunter. "If you want to touch her, you eat first." With his free hand, he pointed down the hallway that led to the kitchen.

Looking like he was too tired to argue with my father, Hunter dropped his hand and took a weary step toward the front door. Sensing that he was leaving, I broke free from Dad and grabbed Hunter's elbow. He looked back at me with disheartened eyes, like I had betrayed him for asking him to feed. "Okay. Don't eat. Just come and sit with us while we have cake. Be a part of our family and help us celebrate a birthday."

"Family?" he murmured, his voice cracking.

I nodded as I stroked his arm. "Yes, we're your family now, remember? It's fine if you don't want to drink, just don't ... leave."

Halina surged forward and grabbed his other elbow. Eyes imploring, she begged, "Please, Hunter. I don't want to go yet, and you know I can't leave you. I made you a deal. I promised you I wouldn't force blood upon you again if you agreed to return with me, and I meant it. No one here will make you eat ... if you really don't want to." Her eyes seemed to age right in front of me as she admitted that. She desperately wanted him to eat.

Dad objected immediately as he pulled me back into his arms. "There are humans here, Great-Gran. Linda. My father. The children. He could attack them. You can't let him stay here when he's starved."

Halina's head snapped to Dad. "This is *my* home, and if I say he can stay, then he can." Sighing, she added, "And you don't need to worry. He won't harm anyone." Twisting back to Hunter, she placed a palm on his cheek. "He won't even bite Bambi."

Hunter smirked, and a twinge of jealousy zinged up my spine. They'd had moments together, bonding moments. They even had inside jokes, although, from the look on Hunter's face, they were morbid jokes. I hated that they had those intimacies, but I understood why they did, so I tried to ignore my feelings.

With gentle urging, Halina finally coaxed Hunter away from the door and into the hallway that led to the kitchen. When they were gone, I yanked away from Dad. Proving that I was indeed my mother's daughter, I smacked his arm with all my supernatural strength. "He wasn't going to hurt me."

Irritated, Dad leaned into my face. "You don't know that ... not for sure. He is dangerous. You have to be smart about this, Nika."

Bristling, I raised my chin. I *was* being smart. I wasn't in danger when it came to Hunter. At least, not when it came to him drinking from me. He still might stake me, he still might shatter my heart into a million pieces, but his thirst wasn't an issue. I wasn't in danger from *that*. "I know what I'm doing."

Seeing an epic battle of wills going down, Mom came over and wrapped her arm around me. "Let's just ... finish Grandpa's birthday party." She pulled me away from Dad; he followed right behind us.

When I walked into the dining room, Hunter was standing in front of the table, staring at the remains of our meal, and the cake that Alanna had prepared for everyone who was eating. The scent of blood was strong in the room, my full, untouched glass was cooling in front of my full, untouched plate. Hunter's eyes were locked on my blood-red glass. He was breathing heavier, his fangs were down, and his entire posture was rigid with tension. He was even leaning forward, ready to pounce, but he didn't make a move toward the sparkling crystal glass ... he just continued to stare at it.

Halina stood beside him, watching him carefully, waiting to see what he would do. Thinking of removing the glass, removing the temptation, I slowly moved toward my table setting. Hunter's eyes shifted to track my movement, then they flashed back to the glass, and a low growl cut through the room. He definitely wanted the liquid on the table; he nearly panted as he stared at it.

Just as my fingers curled around the glass, Halina spoke. "No, leave it there."

Reluctantly, Hunter pulled his eyes away to look at Halina. "You said you wouldn't force me."

Halina put a hand on his arm. "And I won't. But I won't shelter you either. I won't sit idly by and watch you be in pain without trying to help you. You need this. I had to carry you most of the way here because you were too weak to run on your own. Eventually you will become so weak you won't even be able to move. You will atrophy. You will rot. I can't bear that thought, so I will keep trying to make you okay with what you are. Because you're my child, and I love you."

An irrational irritation swept through me at hearing Halina address him so tenderly. *She loved him?* Keeping my eyes focused on Hunter, I again pushed away the jealousy blossoming in my chest. They had a bond that he and I would never have, but I didn't need to be upset about it. Shifting my course, I sat down at the table and waited for Alanna to pass out cake. I didn't want it, but I would gladly eat it if it gave Hunter an excuse to be close to me. I patted the seat beside me, but Hunter was glued in place and didn't move an inch. Dad sat next to me instead. I rolled my eyes at him but didn't press the matter. If I pushed Dad any harder, Julian and I would be in the car, heading back home before the night was through, and there was nowhere else I wanted to be other than right here by Hunter's side.

Alanna passed out the plates while everyone sat at the table and tried to act like Hunter grunting and huffing at the far end was perfectly natural. Everyone with cake slices started digging into their food, and tense conversations bubbled up. Halina wanted to know what everyone had been up to recently. Her eyes rarely left Hunter though. Mine either. He was just standing and staring, but the turmoil was clear on his features—he wanted to sit and drink ... he wanted to run away. A whimpering sound escaped him. It broke my heart. It was so painful to watch him in such distress. I ached for him. I wanted to fix him. I wanted to help him.

My words barely audible, I whispered, "Stop hurting yourself, Hunter. Just drink it."

He blinked and inhaled, like he was waking from a trance. He took a step toward the table and all conversations stopped, all eyes turned toward him. Halina partially rose from her chair, eagerness and trepidation on her face. Dad tensed like he was preparing for battle.

Looking at all of us, Hunter cleared his throat; his body shook with restraint. "I appreciate the ... invitation, but ... I'm really tired. I'd like to rest now." His eyes locked on Halina. "Please."

Halina sagged back into her chair as she nodded. Her expression was just as exhausted as Hunter's, like she had no idea what to do about his refusal to eat anymore. Standing, Gabriel stepped forward and extended his arm toward the hallway. "I'll show you to your room."

Fearing I might never see him again, I scooted free from the table and blurred to Hunter's side. Dad growled at me, but didn't drag me back. "You won't leave, right?" I asked, my vision hazy. "Just tell me that you're not going to run away again."

A trace of a smile lightened Hunter's fatigued expression. "Nika," he murmured, "I've missed you." The smile dropped from his lips as he turned away. "I'm not going anywhere. There's nowhere else for me to go." His sentence should have lifted my heart, but the grief on his face and the despair in his voice broke me. Tears were streaming down my cheeks as he walked away.

I'd believed that his coming to the ranch was a hopeful sign, a sign that he was beginning to accept who and what he was. But I couldn't have been more wrong. His relenting and coming here, being *carried* here, was in truth a sign of defeat. Hunter was giving up. He was slowly and surely losing the will to go on. Like Halina, I had no idea what to do for him. And it scared me to death.

Everyone started talking about Hunter after he left the room with Gabriel. Grandma Linda was concerned about Hunter losing control and going on a rampage, Dad debated with Mom if it was safe for us to stay here, and Imogen and Halina discussed ways to turn around Hunter's passive mood. Alanna and Grandpa Jack were the only ones still focused on Grandpa's birthday, since it was his special day, for a little while longer. I purposefully said nothing. Hunter was hearing enough right now; I didn't want to add to his confusion.

Excusing myself, I went upstairs to get ready for bed. It was torturous. It was so difficult to know that, after all this time, Hunter was finally in the same building as me, but I still couldn't be with him. I wanted to go to him, but I knew he didn't want to see me. Not yet. He was still adjusting—to being here, to being what he was. I needed to give him space. And that was so hard to do.

After changing and brushing my teeth, I laid in my bed and listened to the swirling words blending together in a dull buzz that occasionally crackled with the pop of Hunter's name. It drove me crazy; I just wanted everyone to go to sleep and stop talking about him.

"It will be okay, Nick," Julian said, entering his bedroom.

Sighing, I adjusted my position for the millionth time. My mood had been shifting all over the place. The barrage of feelings was hard on Julian, almost as hard as it was on me. Feeling so much turmoil at this proximity sometimes made us feel physically ill—nauseous. It was draining, and giving him a headache, but all I felt coming from him was support.

"Thank you," I muttered, tears pricking my eyes. I wished I could talk to Hunter, or about him. But that conversation wouldn't be private, so I didn't say anything. Anything other than, "Can I sleep with you tonight, Julie?"

His response was instant. "Of course."

Hopping out of my bed, I plodded over to Julian's room. Wishing I could block the image of Hunter's wan face from my mind, I crawled under the covers with Julian. Reaching out for me, he clasped my hand, just like he used to when we were children; the warmth and familiarity was soothing. Squeezing my palm, he murmured, "Night, Nick."

I smiled as best I could. "Good night, Julie."

CHAPTER SIX

Hunter

I'D WAITED WEEKS to tell Halina I was ready to return to the ranch. As eager as I was to be free of her, I dreaded it too. I probably would have gone several more weeks without telling her, except she'd attempted to force-feed me again, and in a moment of sheer panic, I'd blurted out that we could go home so long as she promised to never pour blood down my throat again. I just couldn't take it. Halina wanted to go home just as much as she wanted me to eat, so she'd agreed to my compromise. While I knew she hoped I would succumb to the monster inside and feed, I'd seen the joy in her eyes as she'd started making plans with Gabriel to surprise the family with an unannounced visit.

But, if I were honest, one of the reasons I'd been reluctant to return, a large reason actually, was Nika. I hadn't been ready to face her. All the feelings I'd been trying to repress since converting had rushed to the surface the moment I saw her. She was gorgeous. With dark amber eyes and long silky hair that my fingers itched to touch, she was just as beautiful on the outside as she was on the inside. Seeing her again had pierced my silent heart as surely as if someone had staked me. And the way she'd looked at me, with such compassion in her eyes. She might not be in love with me anymore, but she still cared about me. And I still cared about her. Just seeing her again made me want to do anything she asked of me. Even drink. I'd considered it, briefly, but in the end, as always, I couldn't go there.

The smell had been thick in the air, Nika's heartbeat had raged in my ears, and all I'd wanted to do was drink that glass down. And another. And another. But my stomach had instantly knotted and my guard had instantly gone up. Dressing up blood in fancy crystal didn't alter the reality of what it was, and what *I* was if I drank it. I probably should have just sat at the table with the family, acted as human as possible, but I'd felt my willpower fading, and I'd known that if I *had* sat at the table, the glass would have ended up in my hands, the blood would have ended up in my mouth, and another tiny part of my soul would have shriveled and died. I did *not* want what I desperately *did* want. So, in the end, I chickened out, asked to leave, and further removed myself from the only people who were attempting to help me. And from Nika, who said I was a part of her family, who begged me to stop hurting myself, and then begged me not to leave. She still cared … but she shouldn't.

Pushing aside my dramatic reunion with a family of monsters, I focused instead on the ancient one walking beside me. Gabriel's eyes watched the stone steps as we walked, so I was free to study his expression, not that doing so helped me any. His face was a blank slate, an empty mask. He hadn't said a word since leading me through the hidden entrance in the living room that led to the lower, sun-proof layers of the home. Everyone else in the house had mentioned me after we'd left, most were worried about what I would or wouldn't do. I had no plans to do anything, so none of them needed to worry. I'd listened for Nika to speak her fears, but she hadn't. Her silence unnerved me more than Gabriel's.

After traveling down several hallways and three flights of stairs, we reached a set of heavy gilded doors. Gabriel pushed them closed after we walked through, and all sound shut off from above me. The isolating silence was deafening. It put me on high alert, and I spun around, searching for an enemy. All I found was Gabriel watching me with a slight lift to his lip. "The lowest level is soundproof. Don't worry, you get used to it."

I hadn't experienced pure silence since being turned. The closest I'd come was being submerged under water or under the earth, but that was nothing compared to this. After the disorientation passed, I found that the solemnity was comforting. Knowing no one above could hear our conversation, I asked him, "Will you begin working on me now?"

The short stone hallway in front of us came to a T, with lights on the walls extending both left and right. Gabriel turned right, so I followed him. "Yes. Your room is directly across from my main lab, so no one will question your location. We'll have plenty of time for testing." He looked over at me. "No one can know what we're doing down here."

I nodded. No, if anyone found out, they would tell Halina, and she would never allow the bond to be broken. She'd probably stake Gabriel if she realized what he was doing. She might afterward if her feelings weren't severed like Gabriel thought they would be. But that was his problem, not mine. Sighing, I wondered if any of this was going to hurt. That didn't matter though. I needed these shackles removed, as much as that thought pained me.

My chest constricted, and I automatically searched for Halina's presence above me. And Nika's. I knew I shouldn't care about either woman, but they both had a place in my heart, and they would both be affected by my quest for freedom. I wouldn't be deterred by that fact though. Returning my eyes to Gabriel, I calmly stated, "Let's get started."

Gabriel led me into his laboratory. I suddenly felt like I was in a horror movie, entering the mad scientist's lair. Glass containers bubbled and percolated with red and pink liquids, all of them releasing the scent of blood into the air. I struggled against the conflicting urges running through my body—desire and disgust—but the blood was laced with so many other, unappealing smells, that I quickly pushed aside the longing.

The smell of sulfur burned my nose as I watched Gabriel stride from one experiment to another. A full smile was finally on his lips. This place was clearly where he preferred to be. Turning down the heat on something simmering on a burner, Gabriel poured a small sample into a cup, then, using an eyedropper, squeezed a few red drops onto a slide. His smile grew as he examined the slide under a microscope. "Perfect," he murmured.

He lifted his eyes to mine. "I have several experiments running, plus the never-ending job of creating the drug that keeps mixed vampires from converting until they are ready." I remained silent. Gabriel had already told me about the lifecycle of mixed vampires. Nika, while as alive as any human now, would die and convert like any other vampire before her 26th birthday, unless she took the drug Gabriel supplied. It made my leeriness of him fade some, to know that he might extend Nika's living life. She could find love, have children, grow old ... even die and stay dead. She could live a completely human life.

I pondered for a moment how I would survive if Nika chose that life. But then I remembered that my plan wasn't to survive at all, so Nika's death wasn't something I would ever need to worry about. Selfish, yet comforting.

Gabriel continued while I silently berated myself. "I asked Imogen to look over things while I was gone, but she doesn't know this room like I do. It's good to be back." His smile was radiant as his emotions finally showed themselves.

Feeling lost in this confusing, stark room, I asked, "What do you need from me?"

Gabriel raised an eyebrow, like he thought the answer was obvious. "Your blood, of course." He pointed across the room, to a wall-sized refrigerator with a clear door. Inside, I could see rows and rows of vials full of blood. "I already have a sample from Halina, but I'll need yours so I can compare the bond."

I snapped my eyes back to his. "The bond is in the blood?"

Gabriel's expression grew even more amused. "Everything is in the blood."

Well, of course it was. What in my life didn't revolve around blood now? Gabriel extended his hand to a chair nearby, and I collapsed into it. With barely an examination of my arm, he found a vein and plunged in a needle. I flinched, but was soon mesmerized by the sight of the vial filling with deep red liquid. "I may wake you periodically throughout the daylight hours to perform other tests on you. The middle of the day is the only real time we'll be alone."

He filled up another vial while I nodded. "That's fine. Whatever you need from me."

"Eating would help," he replied.

I raised my eyes to his; it was a struggle to keep them open. I was so tired. "Is that necessary for the testing?"

Filling another vial, Gabriel shook his head. "No. But it would keep Halina off your back and happy, and it would increase your stamina so I could take more of your blood if needed." He capped off the vial and indicated the four he'd filled. "I'll have to make due with these for now. If I take anymore, you may pass out."

I looked over at his collection. Some sick, twisted part of me wanted to drink the blood, even though I knew it was mine. I shook my head. "Blood loss won't kill a vampire; if you need more, take it." It took a lot of effort, but I refocused on him. "If I don't have to eat, I won't."

Gabriel glanced down at my arm, then removed the needle. "There's no need to completely wear you out ... I have enough for now." The tiny prick in my arm healed the second the intrusion was gone. "And if you choose to live in pain, then I guess that's your choice." He started to turn away from me, then stopped himself. "How you live is up to you, Hunter, but I care a great deal about the living vampires in my care. If you hurt Nika or Julian, or any of the humans in my nest, not only will I end your life, but I'll do it in the most painful way possible."

Even though his words sent a chill through me, I smiled at him. "And here I thought you wouldn't stake me?"

He frowned. "Not without good reason." He lifted a pale eyebrow. "And I think I made it quite clear that I would *not* be staking you." As if he hadn't just been talking about my gory demise, he smiled and indicated upstairs. "While you are here at the ranch, you should check out the living room during daylight hours. I've protected the windows to a level that allows purebloods up to thirty minutes in sunshine. I think you would enjoy it."

An explosion of painful need burst through my soul. Sun. I'd gone so long without it. I never thought I'd see it again, feel it again. If I could have it, even for just a few minutes a day ... maybe it would keep the insanity at bay, give me a reason to go on, to keep trying, to keep living through this hell, at least until I could be free of it. "Thank you," I whispered, too blown away to say anything more.

I stumbled to my room, anxious for the sun to rise, for night to end. I wished I was tired enough to fall asleep, to speed up the process, but I wanted it too badly and sleep was impossible. My plush room had every amenity—four-poster bed covered in a solid black comforter, a dresser full of clothes, all in my size, a chaise lounge beside a bookcase overflowing with novels that piqued my interest, a leather couch opposite a flat screen TV, and even a private bathroom.

Since I was covered in grime from living outdoors and sleeping in the ground, I decided to take a shower. Filth swirled down the drain as the hot water removed all traces of my former life. Savoring the stinging sensation of scalding water, I turned it up even hotter. Even though my shower was longer than most baths, the hot water never ran out. The plumbing here was designed for those who liked being warm.

When I was clean, dry, and dressed, I laid down on my bed and waited; I was too tired to do anything else, and too eager. Straight across from my king-sized bed, where a normal room would have had a window, was a painting. The intricate brushstrokes depicted a glorious sunrise. It made my eyes brim. The sun. I was going to see the sun.

Halina came downstairs before the night was through. When I felt her approaching my room, I feigned sleep. She cracked open my door, whispered my name, then sighed as she walked into the room. I had to consciously fight the innate need to turn and acknowledge her. But if I did, she would want to talk, and I didn't want to do that right now. I just wanted to be left alone. "Are you asleep?" she asked. I laid perfectly still, stopped my breathing. The undead didn't breathe while we slept, while our bodies were shut down. I heard her move to the end of the bed, felt a blanket covering me. The kindness in the gesture almost caved my will, but I still ignored her. I needed to maintain distance if I was going to separate from her. God, could I do that?

Leaning down, she kissed my forehead and spoke soft words in a language I didn't recognize. The tenderness in her voice was unmistakable though. I clenched my concealed hand into a fist to stop myself from turning to her and seeking comfort. What comfort could she really give me anyway? She was a monster. I was a monster.

When she left the room, I opened my eyes. Grief crushed me—despair over what I was, horror over what I was about to do. There was no way to win this battle warring within me. Whichever way I turned, I'd already lost.

I felt like I waited forever, but eventually, even miles below the earth, I could feel the prickling up my spine that told me the sun was rising. It raised my desolate spirits. Once the sun was well past the horizon, the stinging sensation stopped. Even though I desperately wanted to see the rays of light blanketing the Earth, I waited. I wanted to see them alone, so I needed to make sure Halina was asleep. I had nothing to go on except what I knew of her patterns. She usually stayed up for an hour or two after sunrise, having quiet conversations with Gabriel, or with me, if we were buried together. I figured she would stick to the same pattern here, so I gave her several hours to fall asleep before I rose from my bed.

I was exhausted, and even though I yearned for sleep, I knew I wouldn't be able to get to that peaceful state this early in the day. My body still hadn't adjusted, even after all this time, and it took me hours to fall asleep every morning. But today, that was okay; I wanted to see the daylight anyway. I left my room and stealthily crept down the hall until I realized I didn't need to. While the entire floor was soundproof from up above, each individual room was also soundproof. I supposed that was for privacy of an intimate nature, but it also made it easier to sneak upstairs. I couldn't wake Halina even if I tried.

When I pushed open the gilded doors that soundproofed the entire bottom floor, noises rushed in on me. Snoring. Cooking. Humming. Roosters. Cows. All of it assaulted me, and it took me a few seconds to push it away to just a dull buzz in the background. Excitement and trepidation grew inside me with every step I took toward the secret exit that led to the main portion of the house. I didn't think I'd ever been so excited for anything in all my life. As I pulled the door inward, light cut like a knife through the darkness. I sucked in a breath and didn't move. I waited for the pain that the golden rays would surely give me, but I felt nothing. Smiling, I experimentally held up my hand in the crack between the door and the wall. The light that touched me bothered my skin no more than an incandescent bulb. Giddy, I opened the door wider.

It took a few seconds for my eyes to adjust to the brightness of natural light, and I blinked a few times as I stepped into the room. So eager I was shaking, I turned to face the wall of windows. My breath caught. Bright, orange-red sunshine streamed over the hills and valleys, leaping up to the glass, and pounding against it with all its glory. The room was bathed in heavenly light, and I timidly stepped toward it, sure I would ignite at any moment, even if I hadn't felt an ounce of pain yet.

When I reached the glass, I tentatively placed my palm against it. It was glorious. It was awe-inspiring. It was everything I'd been hoping for and more. I wasn't sure how long I had, but I knew I wasn't moving from this spot until I absolutely had to.

Nika

I MUST HAVE fallen asleep at some point last night, because the next time I opened my eyes, sunlight was streaming into Julian's room. Sunbeams, hazy with dust particles, brightened an old chair sitting in the corner of the room. It was beautiful, and I blinked a few times to see it clearer. As I recalled using that sturdy piece of furniture to build a fort in this room with Julian when we were younger, the peaceful silence was broken by a loud snore.

Curling my lip, I looked over at my zonked-out brother. He had most of the sheets twisted around his body, and was lying in a pretzel-like position that didn't look comfortable. Mouth open, he was snoring louder than most chainsaws. Smirking, I whispered, "Arianna's in for a surprise if you two ever do spend the night together."

"Good morning, Nika," a voice sounded from downstairs.

Biting my lip, and wishing I hadn't said that out loud, I looked down at the floor where I could feel Alanna. "Morning, Grandma. Is anyone else awake?" I felt for all the other pinging positions in my head, but they were still.

"It's just Grandpa and me right now. Hungry?" she asked, ever mindful of my stomach.

The mention of food reminded me that I hadn't eaten a single bite last night. Just like Hunter. My stomach growled as noisily as Julian's reverberating snore. "Um, I guess so. I'll come down."

"Bring your dress, sweetheart. I'll fix it for you while everyone is sleeping."

Stretching, I mumbled an okay and stumbled back to my room to get my bag. Grabbing my prom dress, and the shoes I planned on wearing with it, I plodded into the hallway. I didn't feel like I'd slept a wink, but I also didn't feel like I could go back to sleep. As I streaked downstairs to join my grandmother, patches of sunlight washed over my skin. While overwhelmingly beautiful, it was also a heartbreaking reminder—Hunter was hiding for a different reason now. If the sun was visible, he wouldn't be.

I choked back my pain as I blurred into the kitchen. Alanna didn't react to the speed of my arrival, just smiled at me when I finished phasing, and pointed to a plate already waiting for me at the island counter—two perfectly crisp pieces of toast coated with cinnamon and sugar. Next to the plate was a glass of orange juice and a steaming mug of blood. Breakfast of champions.

I dug into my toast, chasing it with a swig of blood. I wanted to ask Alanna if she had any news on Hunter, if he'd come back upstairs after I'd gone to bed, if he'd eaten ... if he'd mentioned me ... but I didn't want to appear lovesick, so I kept my questions to myself. Alanna probably didn't know much more than me anyway.

After breakfast, I blurred out of my pajamas and slipped on my prom dress. A deep red color, it had a plunging neckline, a wrapped waist, and a flowing hemline that needed a couple of inches taken off. Alanna wanted to see how the silky fabric moved in the sunlight, so she was going to hem it in the living room. Floor-to-ceiling windows in there flooded the room with light, and it was filled to the brim with plush couches and lounge chairs—the perfect spot to grab my tablet and settle down with a good book; the peaceful room was one of my favorite places here at the ranch.

While Alanna zipped away to get her sewing supplies, I pulled my hair into an updo. Securing it with a pencil lying on the kitchen counter, I debated if that was how I should wear it at the dance. Then I wondered if I should even still go. It seemed like a waste of time with everything else going on. Maybe I'd cancel and come out to the ranch that night. I'd be safe here while my parents looked out for Julian. And I'd be near Hunter, assuming he stayed.

Just when I was about to head to the living room, I felt something that pierced my heart. Hunter was awake, and he was coming upstairs. I froze in shock and surprise. Why was he still up? Why was he coming up here? When the sun was out? He'd burn to a crisp. As the shock of his moving presence wore off, I remembered that Gabriel had recently vampire-proofed the windows in the living room. They'd give a pureblood a few minutes of sun tolerance, and Hunter must know that.

I placed my hand over my heart to try and calm the wildly beating organ, while I felt Hunter emerge from downstairs and head to the windows. He hadn't said anything yet, hadn't acknowledged my presence or my rapid heartbeat; he must be so caught up in what he was seeing. He probably would when I moved. Taking a deep breath, I quietly walked into the living room. Seeing him standing there broke my heart. He had his back to me, his hand on the glass, as he stared at one of the things that had been ripped away from him the moment he'd converted—the sun.

As I'd predicted, moving toward him had broken the spell of the sun, and alerted him to my presence. Hunter tilted his head, listening to my heartbeat, but he didn't run away, and he didn't look at me. It seemed like he couldn't tear his eyes away from the view. Voice pained, he whispered, "Gabriel told me about this. I didn't think I'd ever get to see sunlight again, and I've missed it ... so much. This is incredible ... ."

Moved by him, worried for him, I cautiously approached the windows. "Did he also tell you it was temporary?"

As I stepped to his side, Hunter let out a sigh full of resignation. He glanced my way without really looking at me. A long, blood-red tear rolled down his cheek, staining his shirt when it fell from his skin. "Yes." His mournful eyes returned to the sun. "I know my time is short."

I wasn't entirely sure what he meant by "time," and it terrified me. Needing to comfort him, needing to touch him, I reached down for his free hand. He was freezing cold, but I curled my fingers around his anyway. I thought he'd pull back, yank his hand from mine, but he didn't. Instead, he hummed, "You're so warm," and clenched me tight.

Hunter's eyes rimmed with more bloody tears waiting to fall as his gaze drifted back and forth over the sunlit countryside. He didn't look any more fed or rested than he had last night. If anything, the light of day upon his gaunt face made him look even sicklier than before. Stroking his hand with my thumb, I gently asked, "Why are you awake?"

His mouth fell open before he spoke. "I couldn't sleep."

He turned his head to me. "I still can't get used to sleeping during the day. You'd think I would have by now, but I just ... can't ... and I'm so tired."

His eyes locked onto mine, and for a moment, he seemed mesmerized, like I was more absorbing than the sun. My heart picked up intensity under his gaze, and my nerves spiked. I longed for him to make some move toward me—brush a strand of hair away from my forehead, touch my cheek, put his arm around me ... anything. I'd take *any* moment of connection I could. The redness in his eyes dissipating, his gaze shifted to my dress ... my prom dress. "You look beautiful," he murmured.

With every place his eyes flashed over, I became increasingly more aware of the cut of my dress—how low the front plunged, the fact that it was sleeveless, the fact that my hair was still up and my neck was exposed. I was showing him a lot of skin, and he liked it. It warmed me; I wanted him to see me as attractive for more than just my heat and heartbeat.

"Thank you," I told him. Feeling courageous, I took a step into his side and moved our joined hands behind me, so his fingers were resting near my backside. It was the closet I could get to him embracing me. My heart was thudding in my chest, which only made Hunter pay even more attention to me. And I loved it.

Hunter's thumb brushed against the silky fabric of my dress, and a trickle of desire seeped into me. I wanted to kiss him ... so much. Would he let me? Or would he run away? Hunter's gaze slid up my body to focus on my neck. "You're gorgeous in the sun. You ... glow, like an angel." His eyes lifted to mine. "Why are you wearing a dress?"

I took another step into him, so that our sides were pressed together. Even through our clothes, I could feel his chill. "Prom ..." I whispered, silently begging him to kiss me, to tell me he still loved me, and we could still be together.

His hand released mine, but instead of pushing me away, his palm ran up my back. I shivered under his touch as he pulled me closer. "You're going to prom?" His lips parted as he stared at my mouth. "Who's taking you?"

"A friend." I chewed on my lip to control the pleased noise I wanted to make. His fingers on my skin were driving me crazy, in a really good way. I was so incredibly grateful that Julian was still sleeping.

"Just a friend?" he asked, his face inching closer to mine.

"Just a friend ..." I repeated. Excited, eager, but still being careful, I reached up and wiped the bloody remnants of his tear from his cheek. Or tried to. Blood wasn't easy to wipe away. Eventually I gave up and cupped his cool, course skin, since that was what I'd really wanted to do anyway. Half closing his eyes, Hunter nuzzled against my hand like a cat. He even made a deep rumbling noise in his throat.

"Your heat ... God, it feels so good. You feel so good ... you sound so good ... you smell so good." His eyes burned with desire and need when he fully opened them. "Your dress ... that color ... it does something to me." His fangs crashing down, he breathed, "I've never wanted you more than I do right now."

I had no idea which way he wanted me, and I really didn't care, I wanted him, too. The longing in my body extinguished any amount of caution left in me, and I pulled his mouth to mine. We collided in a blending of warmth and coolness that was absolute bliss. As my fingers ran back to thread through his hair, Hunter pushed me into the windows. His body pressed against mine, and I trembled with the freezing heat. As our mouths voraciously worked together, I was aware of his teeth nicking me. I didn't care though. His hard body against me, his soft lips, his searching tongue lightly touching mine ... I just couldn't find it in me to care about his teeth. When I tasted blood in my mouth, my own fangs crashed down, but I didn't care about that either.

Hunter cared.

He groaned in a whimpering way that had little to do with desire. I gasped for breath when his mouth left mine. His lips worked their way down my neck, and all I could think through my haze of desire was—*Yes, please ... bite me.* His cold mouth latched onto my neck and his jaw tightened. I tensed, waiting for the pain that I knew was coming, waiting for him to puncture my skin. It didn't happen though. Panting, Hunter turned away from me. "No, I can't do this. You should get away from me, Nika. Right now, before I do something we both regret."

Grabbing his face, I turned him back to me. "No, I want to stay with you." His fangs were down, his eyes hooded. A trace amount of blood was on his lips. *My* blood. Realizing my fangs were down too, I quickly pulled them back up. In as soothing of a voice as I could muster, I whispered, "It's okay. Whatever you're feeling right now is okay."

Narrowing his eyes, he shook his head. "What I'm feeling? I want to tear into your skin. I want your blood in my mouth. How is that okay?" He looked ill, just from admitting that to me.

He immediately started to pull away, and I could tell he was about to blur from the room, from whatever it was that he was feeling—guilt, disgust ... desire. "Don't. Don't leave ... don't run away again." Just wanting him to feel okay being close to me, I laced my arms around his neck, and held him tight against me. "Stay ... talk to me. Tell me everything you're going through. I know you're hurting."

His hands came up to remove my arms, but I wouldn't let him go. "What more is there to say, Nika? I want you in all these ways I shouldn't. You're not safe with me."

Holding his face right in front of mine, I made him look at me. "Yes, I *am* safe with you. Wanting my blood doesn't mean you'll take it. You've already proven that. Trust yourself ... I trust you."

"Nika ... I ..."

His eyes lowered to my lips. Feeling that spark rekindling, I started to pull his mouth back to mine. A voice interrupted our connection. "Everything all right in here?"

Hunter turned from me as Alanna stepped into the room with her sewing kit firmly in her hand. She was tense, sizing up Hunter like he might lunge for my jugular at any moment. Feeling her unease, I dropped my arms from around him, and finally let him leave my side. I thought he would vanish in an instant, but surprisingly, he stayed. It gave me hope.

Her wizened eyes focusing on me, Alanna murmured, "You've got a little blood there, dear." Reaching in her pocket, she pulled out a tissue and blotted the corner of my mouth; I could feel the sting from where my lip was cut. Her gaze flashed back to Hunter as she said, "Wouldn't want a drop to stain that beautiful dress."

Swallowing, Hunter looked away, back toward the sunshine that had drawn him to this room in the first place. He discretely wiped his mouth with the back of his hand and shoved it into his pocket, out of my grandmother's sight. I was sure she already knew though. She knew everything that had just happened.

As Alanna knelt and began pinning up my dress, silence fell over the room. Just as I was wondering how much longer Hunter had before the sunlight eventually bothered him, he spoke. Still staring out the windows, he said in a quiet voice, "I didn't mean what I said earlier."

My heart sank as I wondered what he was referring to. Wanting me? Thinking I was beautiful? My lips still burned from where his had been pressed against me. Was that scorching kiss what he was now regretting?

I turned my head to look at him, to question him with my eyes. He turned to me at the same time, then glanced down at my grandmother adjusting my dress. "When I said I wanted to tear into her skin ... I didn't mean it. I wouldn't ever hurt her."

I felt a flush of heat run up my chest as I remembered that part of our encounter. Alanna had most definitely heard him. Thank God it was early and Dad was still asleep. He probably would have thrown Hunter across the room if he'd walked in on us. He possibly would have thrown him out the window if he'd heard him say that.

Alanna paused in her pinning and looked up at him. Her expression was one of patience and firmness. It was a look I'd seen on Dad countless times when he was about to tell us something he knew we wouldn't want to hear. "Yes, Hunter, you did mean it." Hunter turned from the windows to face her, his mouth opening in protest. Alanna anticipated his remark and beat him to the punch. "No, you're wrong. As much as it disgusts you, blood is what you really want. It's a simple truth, one you're trying desperately to deny."

Alanna stood up and pricked her finger with a pin. A red bead formed on the top of her finger—a perfect ball of blood. With just that small exposure, a burst of fresh, blood-scented fragrance filled the air. A low growl escaped Hunter's chest for a second before he shook his head and looked away. Alanna sucked the blood off her finger, then pointed at him. "The ironic thing here is that you don't want to hurt anyone. I can see that, clear as day, but by doing what you're doing, denying your body what it needs, you're actually making yourself *more* dangerous to others. Dangerous to Nika. And that is why my son doesn't trust you with her."

Hunter hung his head, then peeked up at Alanna. Face forlorn, he sounded like he was defending a losing argument when he answered her. "I stopped myself from biting her. I would *never* bite her." His eyes, soulful and apologetic, shifted to me. I wanted to hug him, but I knew he wouldn't let me get that close, not with Alanna watching us.

As if sensing what I wanted to do, Alanna approached him and gently placed her hand on his arm. "You stopped yourself this time, but as long as you keep starving your body, you're a threat to her. To Julian. To Linda. To my husband. To *all* humans. You're making yourself into the very monster you fear."

Hunter shook as he stood in a bright patch of sunlight, then he cringed like he had a white-hot spotlight shining in his eyes. He looked over at me while Alanna whispered, "You're holding on by a very thin thread, Hunter. How long before it snaps?"

Hunter immediately returned his eyes to hers. "I don't want to be like this ... but ... I don't want to be the alternative either. I don't know what to do." Flinching, he took a step away from the windows, and rubbed the arm that was getting the full force of the sun upon it.

Alanna shrugged. "You're either going to be one or the other, Hunter—a starved vampire who's a threat to everyone, or a full vampire who has better things to do than dream about blood all day. You have to choose which 'evil' you can live with." She said evil with a small twist to her lip. None of us truly felt we were evil. We were just ... us.

Seemingly deep in thought, Hunter stared at Alanna without even blinking. Then his face cracked in pain, and he hissed in a sharp breath. Backing away, he glared at the sunlight that was now starting to cause him pain.

"It's time for you to go," I told him, taking a small step forward. When he looked at me, I indicated the windows. "The light is getting to you."

Keeping his arm up as a shield, Hunter peeked out at the countryside, then back to me. "I hate to go ... it's so beautiful." His eyes slid down my dress as he spoke, and I wasn't entirely sure if he meant the sunshine, or me.

Watching my grandmother warily, hoping she didn't stop me, I stepped in front of Hunter. "Please go downstairs. I don't like to see you in pain." I maintained my distance from him, but extended my hand—in support, in friendship, and in love.

Face contorted in discomfort, Hunter hesitated a moment, then grabbed my hand. It made my pulse quicken to feel his icy touch again, but knowing I was being watched, I shoved aside the feeling as best I could. "Come on," I whispered, leading him forward.

Together, we approached the secret entrance to the light-proof underground layers where the purebloods waited out the day. The bookcase that hid the entrance was already swung inward, open and waiting for Hunter's return. Hunter darted through the opening and sank back into the darkness of the hallway with a relieved sigh. As I hovered at the edge of daylight and darkness, Hunter clenched my hand tight, not pulling me with him, but not letting me go either. The peaceful glow of his eyes radiated warmth back to me as he leaned against the wall, recovering. Hypnotic or not, I could have stared into those eyes all day.

Even surrounded in darkness, I could tell he was still in pain. Giving his hand one last squeeze, I told him, "You need to go ... get some sleep. I'll see you when you wake up."

Exhausted, he nodded. "Thank you, Nika," he whispered. "For caring about me, even when you shouldn't."

Conscious of my grandmother approaching, I shook my head and tenderly said, "No matter what happens, I'll always care about you." Wishing he could stay, wishing I could go, I darted into the tunnel and did something reckless—I quickly tossed my arms around his neck and pulled his lips to mine. As before, he didn't pull away. He kissed me with as much passion as I kissed him. With his fangs safely pulled up, the kiss was better, sweeter, softer. I wanted to kiss him forever, but I heard him whimper in pain, felt him cringing beneath my fingertips as I caressed his cheek. The scant amount of sunlight still reaching him in here was hurting him. I needed to let him hide.

Breathless, I stepped out of the tunnel, pulling the hidden door closed behind me. As I leaned against the bookcase, catching my breath, I heard Hunter let out a long, smooth exhale. "Goodnight, Nika," his voice rumbled out to me.

Smiling to myself, I whispered back, "Goodnight."

When I turned around to face my grandmother, she was eyeing me with a sad, compassionate expression. "I hope ..." She started to say something, then she shook her head and gave me a soft smile. "Things will get better. He just needs time."

I nodded as I longingly looked back at the bookcase separating Hunter and me. I supposed, if anything else, that was one bright spot for the two of us ... we had an endless amount of time. Indicating the wide windows streaming with sunlight, Alanna soothingly said, "Let's finish fixing your dress before everyone wakes up."

I thought that was probably a good idea, and walked back into the natural lighting so she could finish her work. Staring at the windows kept Hunter forefront in my mind, not that he usually wasn't there anyway. I could still feel his body against mine, still see the hollowness of his cheeks, the colorlessness of his skin. I wondered if our meeting had brought him any sort of peace, wondered if he was sleeping now, or still wide awake.

Hearing the rest of my family start to stir, I looked up at the ceiling, then back down to Alanna. "Grandma ..." Her pale eyes lifted to mine.

Pointing up, I shook my head, pointed to where Hunter had disappeared, then brought my finger to my lips. Alanna tilted her head, but I knew she understood—*Please don't tell my parents what happened with Hunter*. I wasn't sure what she would say, if she would keep my secret or spill the beans. I wasn't sure if it really mattered either, but I didn't want my dad to freak out and make us go home. I didn't want him to forbid me from ever coming back here. And he might, if he knew just how close Hunter had come to drinking from me.

Alanna continued to stare up at me, then minutely nodded. Hearing Dad laugh with Mom, she cheerily said, "Good morning, son. Good morning, Emma."

"Morning, Mom," they both said, almost at the same time. Alanna smiled and went back to work while I let out a sigh of relief. Good. She wasn't going to say anything. We wouldn't have to leave. I'd get to see Hunter again in a few hours. I closed my eyes, and his voice echoed through my mind. *Goodnight, Nika*. I couldn't wait to see him again.

CHAPTER SEVEN

Hunter

I WAS AN idiot. I let things with Nika get too heated, go too far ... much too far. I should have left the room the moment she entered, but I hadn't been able to find it in myself to pull away from that glorious sunlight—a sight my damned eyes had no right to see.

But then I'd looked at her, and the sun had seemed insignificant in comparison. Where the sun glowed, she beamed. Where the sun lit the Earth, she ignited it. But both were unobtainable to me, and I was a fool if I believed otherwise. And while my father had done a lot of things, he hadn't raised a fool.

I stormed downstairs to the cooler, underground layers while Nika carried on a conversation with her grandmother. I could hear the resignation in the older woman's voice as she told Nika that I just "needed time." I could tell from her tone that she didn't truly believe that. She didn't think I'd come around. And she was right. I didn't plan on embracing this lifestyle, embracing my life ... embracing Nika. My only plan was to get away. From there ... who knew where my road would take me.

Even still, the memory of Nika's lips on mine burned me more than the acidic feeling of the sunlight as it had finally penetrated the window and seared my skin. Feeling her kiss again had lifted me in a way I'd never expected to be lifted. Our last goodbye kiss was soft, sweet, tender, but full of so much passion. But even it paled in comparison to the taste of her blood in my mouth. The memory wasn't leaving me. That sensuous liquid had absorbed my every thought and desire. Her heartbeat raging in my ears had drowned out all reason. Clamping onto her neck had felt so natural to me, so right. I'd wanted nothing more than to tear through her skin and feel that burst of warmth course down my aching throat. Oddly enough, I had a feeling Nika would have *let* me bite her; I thought she'd even wanted me to. But I wouldn't hurt her in that way, regardless of what the demon inside me wanted.

Once I was inside the lowest level, I breathed a sigh of relief. Shutting the soundproof doors meant shutting out Nika's honey voice, a voice that plagued my dreams, made me ache in ways that reminded me that a man still lived inside this body of a monster. The way her dress had clung to her, the way my hands had felt running over her body, her warm breath washing over my face, the desire in her eyes, the fire in her kiss ... I hadn't expected her to undo me as quickly as she had. I was putty in her hands, and I'd nearly lost control. But I couldn't afford to. I wouldn't snap. Now, or ever. I would remain in full control of this lust. And that meant I had to stay away from Nika. She was too desirable to me. All I would bring her was pain. Or death. And I couldn't handle either of those scenarios happening.

I would tell her. Tonight, I would tell her. We couldn't be together, not like we were before. I needed her to stay away from me. I needed her to let me go. *Please, Nika, let me go.*

I ran into Gabriel in the hallway. He was exiting his lab with a pleased smile on his face. I took that as a good sign, that he was making progress. "I can't sleep. Do you need anything from me right now?" I asked, eager to do something besides dwell on things I couldn't have.

His smile evened, and he extended his hand toward the door of his lab. "Come inside. I'll show you the progress I've made."

His aloof attitude lightened as he explained the various studies he was running on Halina's and my blood, but whenever he spoke directly to me, his expression darkened. The more time I spent with him, the less I believed he was doing this purely for the sake of freeing his girlfriend. A part of him simply wanted me gone.

Examining a petri dish on the table, I asked, "You don't much care for me, do you?"

Not one to beat around the bush, Gabriel shook his head. "No, I don't. If it were up to me, you would have been staked immediately upon your conversion."

His blunt honesty was brutal, but kind of refreshing. I could only think of one reason why he wanted me dead. It was much the same reason I had wanted him dead—opposite sides of the same coin. "Because I killed your kind? Because of what happened in L.A.?"

Inhaling a deep breath, Gabriel folded his arms over his chest. "You and your father set traps for my brethren. The pair of you were single-handedly responsible for killing several members of my nest. Some of them were newly turned vampires. Children, trying to find their way in a new life, many of whom, like you, never asked for it. You killed them in cold blood."

Remembering the many vampires father and I had staked while posing as willing blood donors, I raised my chin. "We were protecting people. They were killers."

Gabriel smirked at my arrogance, or perhaps, naivety. "Were they? Did you follow their every move? Did you see them kill *anyone*?"

I frowned. We'd staked whoever had arrived—young, old, male, female. The only requirement for execution had been that they were vampires. "Well ..."

Seeing my reluctance, Gabriel's expression turned smug. "Halina kills humans. Did you know that?" A strange icy swirl of unease twisted my gut. *She* ... was important to me, I didn't want to put her on the same level as the beasts I'd coldly assassinated. But then, I shouldn't put her on any pedestal. She was an evil monster, as were we all.

Gabriel's voice cracked the sudden silence. "She has absolutely no compunction about taking human life." He lifted a finger. "But ... she makes sure that whomever she kills actually deserves the death." He pointed his finger at me. "Can you say the same?"

Not able to answer his question, I said, "It's a shame you didn't finish us off in L.A. All of this ... wouldn't have happened if we hadn't gotten away."

Gabriel nodded once. "Agreed."

A phantom pain went up my leg as I remembered the attack that had driven us out of Los Angeles. We'd been doing a routine bait-and-stake, only the intended victims had known what was going on. They'd ambushed us, trapped us in the house, and then blown up the house. Dad and I had barely escaped. "Gas leak" the news had called it. Knowing our tactics wouldn't be safe there anymore, we'd healed our scrapes and bruises, and gone in search of new monsters to hunt. We'd found ourselves here, in Salt Lake, a place I would do anything to be able to leave.

When Gabriel proclaimed that there was nothing further we could do today, I ambled off to my room. Weary to the bone, I collapsed onto my bed and closed my eyes. As sleep blanketed my mind, I let all my miseries tumble through me. Was any of this even worth it? Maybe I should just walk outside right now and give up? Maybe I should just stay and give in? I wasn't sure which thought horrified me more.

"HUNTER? IT'S NIGHTTIME. Wake up."

Halina's voice roused me from a nightmare. Gasping in a breath, I clutched at the blankets in some vain attempt to determine what was real, and what wasn't. Her hands cupped my cheeks as her calming eyes washed their hypnotic glow over my body. I panted as I stared up at her. I'd been dreaming of my father, of escaping Los Angeles. Only, this time, the second we'd weaseled our way out of the tiny bathroom window, I'd turned and sank my teeth into his neck, draining him dry. The last thing I remembered about the dream was my father's screams falling silent as he died in my arms.

Grief overwhelming me, I sat up and wrapped my arms around my benefactor. She held me close to her, shushing in my ear and smoothing my hair. I shook as she held me. I just couldn't stop the tremors. "It's okay, Hunter," she cooed. "I remember having nightmares my first few months too, but those will pass. I promise."

Reality crashed into me, and I pushed her away. What were bad dreams compared to the nightmare of my existence? "I'm fine."

She reached out for me again, looking like she wanted to pull me close once more, but then her hand dropped. As her timeless eyes studied my face, I could clearly see her desperate need to connect with me. I felt it too. The guilt raging through my body made me want to open up to her, but I couldn't. I wouldn't. This ... thing ... between us wasn't real, and it would soon be over.

I moved past her to the end of the bed, then stood up. Her sad eyes watched me. "Gabriel and I are going to go upstairs and join the family for dinner. Will you please come?"

A wave of nausea rolled through me at the thought of staring down another bloody meal. I shook my head. "No, I'm not hungry."

My outright lie wasn't fooling either of us, but she didn't press the issue. Instead, she stood and smoothed her tight dress. "Will you please join us after dinner then?" She sighed. "At least try to fit in?"

The pain in her voice constricted my heart like a vice. I couldn't have refused her if I wanted. Holding my hands to my sides, so I didn't reach out for her again, I whispered, "Okay."

Her face brightened, and my spirit soared. Her eyes flicked over my features, and even though I knew she was constantly disappointed in me, all I saw radiating from her was love and patience. It was ... confusing. I stepped toward her, wishing ... hoping she would hold me. She didn't though. She only rested her palm on my chest and smiled up at me. "Come up when you're ready."

She started to turn away and panic seized me. *How long did I have with her?* I clenched my hands into fists, refusing to cave into this absurd desire to ask her to put her arms around me ... to stay with me a little while longer. Noticing my turmoil, she paused mid-turn. "Are you all right?"

Now concerned, she fully looked at me. Horror and embarrassment flashed up my spine. Was I actually seeking comfort from a creature of the night? One that I knew had killed before? One that, in my other life, I would have killed without a moment's hesitation? Turning from her, I walked toward a chest of drawers on the other side of the room. "I said I was fine. Please leave."

She did. And it hurt so much I had to close my eyes and lean my forehead against the dresser.

After changing my clothes, I looked around my room and wondered what I could busy myself with while I waited. Nothing was coming to mind, and the decorative touches in the room weren't sparking any ideas. And really, there were only three things I wanted, and they were all upstairs. Halina. Nika. And blood.

Sighing, I left my room and began the long, arduous journey of heading toward the others. Even though they were all surprisingly open to giving me a chance at becoming a part of their family, I'd never felt so alone. Everything I'd known was gone. My entire life swept away in one painful bite, replaced by a life I barely recognized, and didn't want. And my only hope of escape was a man who wouldn't shed a tear if I died. He'd probably throw a party.

When I opened the soundproof doors, Nika was the first thing I heard. I paused in the open doorway, savoring the melody of her voice. She was asking her family why they weren't waiting for me to join them before they started eating. Her thoughtfulness made me smile. The thought of sitting at that table churned my stomach, but the thought of sitting next to her gave me butterflies. The contrasting feelings made my head swim.

Staying as silent as possible, I continued my trek upstairs. Halina answered Nika by telling her that I was planning on joining the family after dinner was over. I heard metal scraping on porcelain, and food being torn into. The visual made me want to gag, but the thought of Nika hurrying through her meal just to see me ... warmed me. And that was *not* how I should be feeling before seeing her. Not with what I had to tell her tonight.

I paused in the hallway in front of the exit. The wooden door behind the bookcase gleamed in my phosphorescent vision. Wondering if I would be able to break Nika's heart tonight, if I had the strength, I heard her brother let out a disgruntled sound. "Hey, Nick, I wasn't done with that!"

I heard water running, then a garbage disposal, then dishes being put into a dishwasher. Nika really was hurrying through the meal, hurrying everyone through their meal. As a smile erupted over my face, I heard her ask, "Grandma Linda, Grandpa Jack, are you guys done?" She definitely wanted to see me.

Leaning against the wall, I heard Nika's dad tell her to sit and wait until everyone was finished. Teren Adams didn't like me. Or trust me. I didn't blame him. I'd attacked his family after all. And shot him in the chest. He probably wasn't too thrilled about the fact that I was now living here, under the same roof as his family, and his infatuated daughter.

Nika made an annoyed sound and a rhythmic tapping started that could only be her foot smacking against the floor. She was riled up, waiting to see me. I wondered what she'd done today to pass the time? Our last kiss seared my lips, and my smile grew even wider. She was so soft, so sensual. Making love to her would be ...

No. Making love to her wasn't *ever* going to happen. I wouldn't allow it. She was still too young. And I ... wasn't the right man for her. Steeling my resolve to end things once and for all, I calmly waited in the hallway until I heard voices and footsteps entering the living room. I closed my eyes, mentally preparing myself for Nika. I had to do this. I couldn't let her continue to think there was an "us" here. There wasn't. There was her, and there was me, and we were too entirely different to be anything more than that.

Pushing Nika from my mind, I instead shifted my focus to Halina. I pulled the image of her face into my mind, drawing strength from it. The vision of her helped me open the door, and the room hushed as I stepped from the hidden entrance. Even though I didn't mean for it to happen, my eyes found Nika first. Or maybe my ears did. She was sitting on a loveseat next to a long couch, her hands twisting in her lap, longing clear in her soulful eyes. Her pulse raged through her veins in a fast, heavy rhythm. It appealed to every part of me, and I couldn't help but stare at her. A ghost of a smile touched my lips as I watched her swallow a bundle of nerves. Somehow, I knew she was wishing she could control her heartbeat, slow it down, so things would be easier for me. If she only knew how much I enjoyed listening to it race ...

The smell of fresh blood burst into the room, and my smile faded. I twisted my head to watch Halina saunter around the corner, a steaming crystal glass in her hand. Pain, desire, and disgust assaulted me at the same time. Against my permission, a low growl rumbled from my throat. My eyes stayed locked on the deep red in the glass as she walked by me. My knees buckled, but somehow, I remained standing.

"Again?" I croaked, my dry throat cracking with need. I didn't think I could handle being in a room with blood right now. I was too weak, too conflicted, in too much pain. "Why are you doing this to me?"

Halina's eyes were compassionate as she set down the blood on a coffee table in front of the couch. "Because I care about you. I will make blood available to you every day, Hunter. I will offer it to you every chance I get." Sighing, she indicated the couch. "But the decision to drink it or not will still be yours."

I wanted to run away. I wanted to be strong. I wanted blood to stop having such a powerful hold on me. With wooden, choppy steps, I managed to walk over to the couch. I felt like I'd run a marathon I was so depleted, emotionally and physically drained. As I lowered myself to the plush leather awaiting me, Nika blurred to my side. She put a hand on my back as she encouraged me to sit down. Her touch helped pull my focus from the open container of blood in the room. Her heartbeat diverted my attention. I leaned into her side, grateful.

Her father shot me a deadly glance as he sat next to Julian. His entire body was tense as he watched me, and I was positive that he'd be on me in a second if I did anything wrong. My attention drifted back to the glass in front of me. Bloody vapors were drifting into the air. I inhaled and exhaled in long, slow draws, trying to control my breathing, trying to accept the vile, heavenly smell. It took every ounce of will power I had to not reach for the glass. My stomach was in knots, and I was positive I was going to be sick.

Then Nika's hand touched my thigh. It relaxed me, fractionally. Her hand drifted down to cover mine. The heat from her skin seared me, soothed me. I turned my palm, and we interlaced our fingers. I could do this. With her by my side, I could face down my inner demon, and win.

Maybe hoping to distract me, or him, Halina started a conversation with Teren. His voice was crisp as he answered, and I was sure he was staring at me like a hawk watching its prey. Halina too for that matter. Everyone was probably watching me, but I was too fixated on the blood to care. Why did it have such control over me? Why couldn't I ignore it? Why couldn't I just drink it?

The remembered taste of Nika's blood in my mouth hit me, and I felt my fangs slowly extending. I couldn't pull them back up; my body refused to cooperate. I licked my lower lip, remembering Nika's sweet nectar on my skin. My free hand moved forward an inch. I immediately pulled it back to my knee as bile rose in my throat. No. I wouldn't do it. I wouldn't drink.

Nika's thumb stroked my skin in silent support. I drew the strength of her heat into me, fortifying myself with it. I wouldn't cave.

So silent, I almost believed it was subliminal, I heard Halina, whisper, "Drink, Hunter, it will ease your pain."

A whimpering groan escaped my scorched throat. God, yes, it would. It would soothe the rawness in my mouth, the empty ache in my stomach, the fatigue that made every movement an effort. I could stop suffering, if I just ...

My hand reached out for the glass, and I couldn't pull it back this time. I touched the stem, and imagined the relief that warm liquid would provide me. It had been so long ... so very long. I was dying to have it again. Blood. I wanted it, I needed it.

No!

I shot to my feet, tipping the glass over in my haste. The crystal cracked as the blood inside of it spilled over the tabletop. Halina and Teren jumped to their feet as well, but all I could focus on was the ever-expanding pool of deep, red blood. A need-filled rumble erupted from my chest as Nika slowly rose beside me. She placed her other hand over mine, subtly prying my fingers loose, and it was only then that I realized we were still holding hands, and I was squeezing her palm tightly, probably hurting her.

I blinked out of my trance as guilt pummeled me. Releasing her, I scrambled over the back of the couch, eager to get as much distance from the blood as I could. All eyes followed me as I pressed my back against the wall. Halina moved toward me, and I held my hands up to stop her. "Please, don't."

Trying to ignore the hollow ache in my soul, an ache that was quickly filling with disgust, I said, "I can't do this. I'm sorry, I just ... can't." I scanned the room full of disappointed and distrustful faces. "I know what you're all trying to do for me. You've taken me in ... when nobody else would." My eyes settled on Nika's. Hers were watery as she watched me struggle with the necessity of life that I was denying myself. Meaning much more than just blood, I held her gaze and told her, "But I can't do *this*."

Her brow bunched in confusion, like she didn't understand my sudden mood shift, and I supposed she wouldn't. I'd been very misleading today. "Hunter?" she asked, extending her hand to me.

I sighed as I stared at what she was offering me. In truth, I wanted her hand, her love, as badly as I wanted to drink the blood pooling over the tabletop, but I wouldn't let myself be a dickhead monster any more than I would willingly become a vampiric monster. Seeing her emotions on her sleeve, her eyes begging me not to reject her, tore me to pieces, but I knew I had to do it anyway, for both our sakes. She was too attached to me. I was too attached to her.

Bringing my hands to my sides, I shook my head. "I'm sorry, Nika, I can't do this either."

Her hand dropped from the air like it weighed a thousand pounds. "What?"

Unable to keep looking at the torment in her eyes, I averted mine. "What happened earlier today, shouldn't have happened. I had a weak moment. It won't happen again."

Her father immediately asked, "What happened earlier today?"

Ignoring him, since Nika was my main concern, I stepped as close to the couch as I would allow myself. Feeling like I'd aged a thousand years in the span of a day, I told her, "I care about you, I do, but we're not meant to be together. I don't want to hurt you by letting you believe there's a future here. There isn't." In a whisper, I added, "I don't think there ever was."

I could tell that every word I was saying was a blade slicing off sections of her shredded heart. I hated myself even more for letting it get this far. I never should have returned. I never should have let her kiss me. I never should have kissed her back.

With tears in her eyes, she shook her head and lifted her chin. "You don't mean that, you're just going through a rough time. I know you want to be with me as much as I want to be with you." Glancing around the room, she lowered her voice, "I felt that when we kissed."

Teren started to take a step toward me, but his wife grabbed his arm. Nika's words sliced me as surely as mine had sliced her, and I turned my face from her. "Like I said, I care about you. I ... I lost control for a moment." Thinking of the hopeless life she'd have with me, thinking of my secret plan of escape, I strengthened my resolve, and shifted my gaze back to her. "But I'm not the right person for you. I'm not who you should be with."

Her jaw started to tremble, and I knew I needed to leave. If she cried, if she fell apart, the desire to sweep her into my arms would be too much. I wouldn't survive it. I'd cave, and pledge my undying love and devotion to her. Needing to hide from her as much as the blood, I started walking back to the doorway leading to my room. She blurred in front of me, blocking my path. "Shouldn't *I* decide who the right person for me is?"

Her spirit made my lip turn up into a small smile, but it instantly faded as our impossible realities crashed around me. "If I leave it up to you, I know you'll choose wrong." Leaning in close, so close I could smell the warmth of her skin, I whispered, "I don't love you like you love me. I can't. So, I won't let you choose me." Straightening, I made myself look into her watery eyes, at the destruction I had just created. Then I finished tearing out her heart. And my own. "I don't need you to save me, Nika. Just let me go."

Looking too stunned to do anything else, she stepped aside and let me walk around her to my escape. When I was gone from her sight, I heard a choking sob escape her. I couldn't listen to it. The wound I had just given myself was too raw, it hurt too much. Using up what little energy I had left, I ran toward the soundproof doors. Slamming them shut behind me, I sank to the floor and dropped my head to my knees.

God, I really was a monster. I didn't love her as much as she loved me? What a laughable joke that was. It was *me* I didn't love. Nika ... was perfect. But I needed to push her away, and claiming I didn't feel for her like she felt for me was the easiest way to do that. And now I hated myself even more.

I felt Halina coming and thought to run even farther, but my legs refused to carry me. I was down, and I wasn't getting back up for a very long time. Halina slowed as she approached the soundproof doors. Knowing she was about to enter, I sat up straight, leaned my head against the wall, and pulled my knees into my chest. I could at least pretend I wasn't losing it.

The door cracked open slowly like she didn't want to spook me. Arguing assaulted my tender ears. Nika was telling her parents that I was depressed, that I didn't mean anything I'd just said. Her parents were saying it didn't matter ... they were going home. I sighed as I slumped against the wall. What a mess I'd made.

"I'm not depressed," I told her, once she shut the door and blocked out the sound of people bickering.

Halina dropped to her knees in front of me. "I wish I could believe you." She laid her hand on my arm. "I know you probably won't believe this, but I went through something similar after my conversion. Granted, it didn't last nearly as long as what you're going through. Or should I say, what you're putting yourself through."

Sniffing, I ignored her implication that all this turmoil was my own fault. I looked away. "And how did you get through it?" I risked a look back at her. "Start killing everything in your path?"

She smirked, dark humor in her crystal eyes. "I had a child who depended on me to be strong, to survive. Not eating was never an option. But I found something that helped me overcome my misguided conscience."

Knowing she was going to tell me that love could set me free, or something equally flowery, I gritted my teeth. "Let me guess ... love saved your life?"

The humor in her face completely faded as her expression turned chilly. "No. Hate saved my life. I held on to the hatred of what was done to me, of what was done to my child, of what was done to my husband. That was what got me through the dark times. That was what kept me sane, kept me focused, allowed me to stay strong."

She stared at me coolly, for once completely compassionless. Surprise washed through me. "Do you want me to hate you, like you hated your creator?"

Tilting her head, her dark hair flowing over her shoulder, she calmly stated, "I'll be that for you, if you need me to be, if that will keep you alive, but truly ..." Her cold mask evaporated into the worried mother that I knew her to be. "... am I really the one to blame for what you are? Am I really the one you should hate?"

I knew who she meant—my father—and I did see the point in her question; I just wasn't sure if I was capable of hating him. He was my *father*. He'd shaped me into the person I was. He'd raised my sister and me on his own after Mom had passed away. He'd loved me. And he'd also forced this abhorrence upon me, and then abandoned me. For all the positives he'd given me, I knew I couldn't overlook that mountainous negative. He'd betrayed me. And I *did* hate him for that.

CHAPTER EIGHT

Julian

MY SISTER HAD started out the day in a much better mood than she'd been in lately. I'd noticed it immediately when I'd woken up; she was practically glowing as she sat on the couch in the living room, staring out the window. When I'd asked her why, she'd only responded that she loved it here at the ranch. I'd bought that about as much as I bought it when Trey told me he was sober. I'd started to ask her more, but she'd tossed a pointed glance at Mom and Dad and I'd fully understood—*Not here, you idiot ... I don't want our parents to know.*

I figured it had to do with Hunter. I'd groaned in protest when she'd volunteered us to help the ranch hands for the afternoon, but I'd been too curious about what was going on to say no. She'd confessed about her rendezvous with Hunter while we'd been slugging through the fields, checking the health of the cattle with Peter Alton and his team. Peter hadn't even batted an eye when Nika and I had knocked on his door and offered to help him for the day. He was used to strange things when it came to our family, and he never questioned anything. That was a major reason why he still ran the crew after all these years.

Nika had gushed—and I mean *gushed*—about Hunter the entire time we'd been working. I was thankful when Dad had retrieved us for dinner. One, so I could get out of the muddy, poop-filled pastures, and two, so Nika would stop telling me how wonderful her sort-of boyfriend was. But I would have rather listened to her go on about him for another sodden afternoon, than feel her heart being removed from her chest and ripped into thousands of tiny pieces. Again. Hunter was no prince. Hunter was an asshole.

Nika was devastated as she stared at the space where Hunter had been standing just seconds ago. Her grief was swelling, slowly crushing her from the inside out. I rushed to her side, to lend her support in case her body gave out on her. She didn't move when I grabbed her hand; she just kept gazing at the empty space and breathing in through her nose and out through her mouth. Her eyes were brimming, ready to pool over.

"Nick," I whispered, squeezing her hand. She turned to look at me and a tear rolled down her cheek. "I'm sorry." I didn't need to say it, since she could feel it, but I wanted to verbally acknowledge her pain.

Nika swallowed and nodded, and I could tell she was seconds from breaking apart. I wrapped my arm around her just as the sob came out. As I rubbed her back, Halina frowned and took off after Hunter. I was sure she was going to speak with him, but I had no idea if she'd tell him he'd made the right decision or not. I hoped she agreed with what he'd done. My sister deserved a better future than being with a pureblood vampire who despised vampires.

Alanna and Imogen tried to offer Nika encouraging words, but she was too far gone to hear them. Mom eventually pulled her from my arms. Kissing her head, she held her tight. Wrapping his arm around Mom and Nika, Dad told me, "Why don't you go get yours and Nika's things, Julian. I think it's time to go home."

Nika raised her head, her eyes puffy from crying. "No, I don't want to leave." She made a strangled cry while saying it.

Dad put his hand behind her head and smoothed her hair. "I know, but space is what you both need right now."

Nika was still arguing with Dad when I left her side. I could hear her debating her reason to stay at the ranch while I packed up her stuff. "He didn't mean it, Dad. He's just depressed, confused. He needs me more than ever!" I wasn't sure if her argument was right, and I also wasn't sure if it was relevant. Even if Hunter was depressed, and even if he hadn't meant the words he'd said, the words themselves were still true. She shouldn't choose him. She should choose someone who hadn't spent their entire life trying to kill our kind. That would be a good starting point for a healthy relationship.

The ride home from the ranch was silent. Nika had thankfully stopped crying, but she was in a state of numbness that was almost worse. Hardly even blinking, she just stared out the window. Mom and Dad glanced back at her every few minutes, but neither of them spoke to her. They'd already said all there was to say. I tried holding Nika's hand, but she pulled away from me. It broke my heart to see and feel how upset she was, and I really wished Hunter had just stayed where he'd been hiding. My sister would be better off if he'd never returned.

Nika wasn't much better Monday morning at school. I tried talking to her on the car ride there, but like the ride home from the ranch, she just stared out the window, ignoring everyone and everything. I felt her pain though. *That* she couldn't help but share with me. Her ache was my ache.

Trey and Arianna met us by the steps, and my mood picked up considerably when Arianna—*my girlfriend*—put her arms around me. I hadn't left Nika's side once we got home, hadn't called Arianna to tell her I was home early. Making sure Nika was okay had been my priority. But now that Arianna was in front of me again, I was struck by how much I'd missed her.

Threading my fingers through the softness of her hair, I greeted her with my lips. Arianna giggled as her warm mouth moved across mine. I'd *really* missed kissing her.

Nika sighed, and I felt her sadness deepen. I tried to push Arianna away, for my sister's sake, but she slipped her tongue between our lips, and I ended up pulling her into me instead.

Luckily for Nika, Trey ended the moment. Smacking my shoulder to knock us apart, he muttered, "Dude, get a room." When I looked over at him, he added, "Save it for Saturday."

Trey grinned at me from under his stocking cap, then turned to my morose sister. "Speaking of Saturday ... I thought we could go to that new pizza place for dinner? You know, the one by the library that you like."

Looking out of sorts, Nika blinked and asked, "Saturday?"

Trey stuck a finger under his knitted hat and scratched his head. "Uh, yeah ... the dance? Prom? We're still going, right?" Face confused, he looked over at me.

I nodded, since I was still planning on going. I wasn't sure about Nika, though, not after everything she'd gone through this weekend. But surprisingly, Nika nodded too. "Oh, yeah ... we're still going. Sounds great."

Trey didn't usually notice a whole lot, because he was usually stoned out of his mind, but he seemed a little clearer today and narrowed his eyes in speculation. "You okay, Little A? You seem a little whacked out."

Nika turned away from him. "I'm great. Not a problem in the world." Her voice drifted off as her throat tightened. The slice of fresh pain that went through her nearly made me cringe, and I took a step away from her. It didn't help very much, but sometimes space diminished our emotional bond.

Trey, for once, didn't buy Nika's answer. Still studying her, he asked, "You sure? You look worse than when that older guy ditched you a while back."

Fast as lightning, Arianna struck out and smacked Trey's arm. "Trey!"

He cringed away from her. "Hey! Hitting is against the school's zero tolerance policy."

Nika's emotional void seemed about to crack. Seeing her distress, Arianna grabbed her elbow and started sympathetically leading her away. Trey sighed and raised his hands in the air. "I'm sorry, Nika! I didn't mean anything by it."

Remorse on his face, he turned to me once the girls were gone. "I wasn't wrong, was I? She does look just like when that guy dumped her. I've never had my heart ripped out, but shouldn't she be over that dude by now?"

I wasn't sure what to say and what not to say, since Trey didn't remember anything that had really happened with Hunter. When Nika had stopped seeing him, we'd just told Trey they'd broken up, which was basically the truth. Shrugging, I told him, "Well, she would be, except ... the guy kind of broke up with her again over the weekend."

Letting out a low whistle, Trey started walking to class. "Wow, that would definitely mess a person up. How the heck did that go down?"

Adjusting my backpack, I felt Nika's emotions start to even out. Not lift, but settle. "He showed up at the ranch—"

Lifting his head, Trey cut me off. "Dude, I gotta see that ranch someday. I want to wrangle something. What the heck does wrangle mean anyway?" I rolled my eyes at Trey's lack of focus. Before I could respond, Trey redirected himself. "What the heck was Nika's ex doing at your family's place? I thought your mom didn't even know about him?"

I sighed. How I wish that were true. "He's sort of ... involved ... with another family member now. She showed up, and he came with her." I guess that was a simple enough way to describe Hunter and Halina's relationship.

Trey whistled again. "Damn ... drama."

Closing my eyes, I let out an unamused chuckle. "You have no idea ..."

SATURDAY ARRIVED SOONER than I thought it would. I was so excited for the dance that the entire week went by in a blur. I couldn't even remember what I'd been taught in class, a fact my parents weren't going to like when report cards came out. Currently, though, I didn't care about my grades, because it was Saturday ... and I might be having sex tonight.

While my week had sped by, Nika's week had been the opposite. She'd drudged through every day, usually in a bad mood. Or even worse, she'd been numb. Trey did his best to make her laugh, but not a whole lot was making her laugh lately. She hadn't seen or spoken to Hunter since last weekend, but I knew he was on her mind. Try as she might to not think about him, Hunter was always on her mind.

As I tried for the hundredth time to adjust the tie I was wearing, Nika curled her hair into ringlets. The long brown locks fell into perfect curlicues as she released them, each strand bouncing off her shoulder blade before relaxing. I thought she might sweep the ringlets up into some complicated hairstyle that all girls instinctually seemed to know how to do, but she surprised me by leaving her hair down. She even fluffed her tresses around her shoulders so they hid her neck. A wash of sadness went through her after she did that.

"You look great, sis," I told her, pulling apart my tie again.

Nika glanced over at me, and a faint smile touched her painted lips. "Need some help?"

Frustrated over the tie and nervous about the potential sex, I tossed my hands into the air and gave up on the impossible task of tie tying. "Yeah," I mumbled. Nika walked over to me, and I couldn't help but smile at how pretty she was. With the deep color of her dress, the way it flared out at her hips to swirl around her ankles, she reminded me of an old-time movie star—Grace Kelly or something. It suited her. Nika was sort of an old soul.

"I mean it. You really do look great," I told her again.

Grabbing my tie, she made a couple of adjustments, then pushed it up into a perfect knot. Patting it down, she responded, "Thanks. So do you. You're like James Bond." I was wearing solid black everything—shirt, jacket, tie, pants. The combination had been Arianna's suggestion. She said the monochromatic look was dramatic, and suited my coloring. She said it made my eyes pop.

Thinking about Arianna reminded me what was going to happen in a few hours ... and the fact that I hadn't really talked to Nika about it yet. She knew Arianna was officially my girlfriend, but she didn't know what was possibly going down tonight. "So," I began, conscious of the fact that my parents were behind their soundproof door, but they wouldn't be for long. "Arianna wants to ... come over tonight, after the dance."

Nika nodded, like she wasn't too surprised. "Okay," she murmured.

Biting my lip, I ran my hand through my hair. "Later, after everyone's sleeping ... she wants to ... she thought it would be a good time to ..." I sighed, then closed my eyes. "She wants to have sex," I bluntly stated. Embarrassment poured through me, and I kept my eyes tightly sealed.

Surprise burst through Nika, followed by sadness. "Oh ... I thought you'd wait longer."

Cracking open an eye, I risked a look at her. Seeing the resignation on her face made me sigh again. "I thought we would too ... but Arianna says she's ready now, and if she's ready, then I'm ..." Pressing my lips together, I halted the admission. Nika didn't need to hear me say I was emotionally and physically ready to have sex with my girlfriend; she knew exactly how I felt about Arianna.

A small weary smile graced Nika's lips, and she gave me another small nod. She was giving me permission, or at least her blessing. And with all the crap she was going through right now, that meant a lot to me. *This could actually happen.*

My stomach was in knots just thinking about it, and I began to get really anxious. Could Arianna and I pull this off without my parents finding out? Could we do it without Nika waking up and feeling it? It was Arianna's first time too ... would it hurt her? What if I messed it up? What if I completely sucked at it? What if it was so incredibly bad that Arianna never wanted to see me again? What if, what if, what if ...

Nika lightly thumped my chest. "Stop worrying, it will be fine." She smiled at me encouragingly, even as a trace of horror flashed through her at the thought of me sleeping with her best friend.

Releasing a quick breath, I nodded. "Thanks." Peeking up at her, I whispered, "Thank you for being so cool about this. I know it's not easy for you."

She shrugged. "One of us should be happy." Her smile diminished, swallowed by sadness. "I wish we'd had a chance to talk to Gabriel about our bond. But ... other things ... sort of ... came up."

Feeling her pain like a knife to my chest, I wrapped my arms around her and held her tight. I tried as hard as I could to radiate warmth and caring into her. She was loved. She wasn't alone. Everything would be okay, someday. Nika sniffled, then pushed me back. "I'm fine. Stop worrying so much about ... everything."

Smirking at her, I grabbed my jacket off the bed. "Not gonna happen, Nick."

Nika gave herself one last look in the mirror. Thanks to her artfully applied makeup, nobody at school would be able to see the dark circles under her eyes or the paleness of her cheeks; she hadn't been sleeping well lately. Truthfully, she hadn't been sleeping well since Hunter's conversion. When she seemed satisfied with her appearance, she turned to me and frowned. "Guess we should get this over with, huh?"

Mom and Dad exited their room the same time Nika and I left ours. They were dressed to the nines in formal wear that was going to top every other couple there—the coat of Dad's tux even had tails. Mom and Dad claimed chaperoning was for our protection, but I had a feeling getting dressed up was the real reason they'd wanted to go. I scoffed at Dad's outfit when he walked by. "Where's your cane and top hat, Dad?"

Mom gave me a disapproving frown. Her white gloves went all the way up her arms. She was even wearing a freaking tiara. Were they intentionally trying to be embarrassing? "Be nice. He looks amazing."

Dad bowed and kissed Mom's hand. "As do you, my dear." Nika let out a soft laugh, and I groaned. God, they *were* trying to be embarrassing.

The doorbell rang then, momentarily saving me. I was just about to blur downstairs to answer it when Dad grabbed my arm. "Trey is with her," he admonished.

With a sigh, I hopped down the steps at a normal, human pace. In my excitement to see my date, it had nearly slipped my mind that Trey had offered to pick her up. When I pulled back the heavy front door, I saw them waiting with smiles on their faces. I couldn't take my eyes off Arianna. She looked like a vision. Her dress was solid black, just like my outfit, with six thin spaghetti-sized straps that crisscrossed across her exposed back. It was super tight, and emphasized every God-given curve in such a way that my own clothes were starting to feel a little tight. Wow ... she looked amazing.

With a drink in her hand and a smirk on her lips, Starla walked around the corner. "Well, son, are you going to let your date in, or mentally undress her at the door all night?"

I flushed with color as I shot Starla a wicked glance. Since Trey believed Starla was our mom, we'd called her over to see us off. Starla had been a little irritated about the inconvenience, but she seemed to be enjoying herself now. Taking a sip of something that smelled strongly of alcohol, she waved Arianna into the room.

Trey stepped inside a second later. Pointing at Starla with both hands, he told her, "Hey, Mrs. A ... lookin' hot."

Starla gave him a genuine smile as she sank back into her hip in a pose that was both casual and seductive. "Why, thank you, Trey. You're not so bad yourself."

She eyed him up and down as Mom and Dad walked into the room. Mom frowned at Starla's inappropriate remark, and told her, "Starla, want to get some pictures of the kids before we leave?" Twisting her head to Mom, Starla shrugged like immortalizing the moment didn't much matter to her.

Trey, for once, wasn't wearing his signature stocking cap, and my sister did a double-take when she saw him. He was tall and a little gangly, but he cleaned up all right. While I didn't think my sister would ever develop feelings for Trey, I hoped against hope that maybe tonight would start something between the pair. At this point, I'd take Nika being with *anyone* other than Hunter.

Trey's eyes lit up when he saw Nika. Not wanting him to push her away by saying something stupid, I elbowed him and murmured, "Behave." He rolled his eyes at me, then put one hand behind his back and extended the other to Nika. He reminded me of a butler, and I forced myself not to laugh.

Starla took a half dozen pictures of our group, then the four of us kids headed out to eat. My parents were skipping that part since eating wasn't something they could do anymore. They could fake it, of course, but I had to imagine that was really annoying. I think they'd declined out of politeness as well. They were giving Nika and me some tiny moment of privacy with our dates, and that was probably all we would get tonight, unfortunately.

As I escorted Arianna to Trey's car, a ratty Ford Escort that he was borrowing from his parents, I told her, "You look amazing. No, amazing isn't strong enough. You look …"

I wracked my feeble brain for a word that beat amazing, but I blanked. An adorable smirk on her lips, Arianna supplied the answer for me. "Edible?" she said.

I tripped on my own feet, making Trey laugh as I stumbled. Feeling my embarrassment, Nika patted my back as she climbed into the front seat. "Goodnight, Mrs. Adams!" Trey yelled, starting the car.

Starla waved from the door and murmured, "It's *Ms.* Adams. Won't you ever get that right?"

Mom sniggered at Starla's sullen comment as she cuddled into Dad's side and waved goodbye to us with a gloved hand. Trey closed his window, then ran his hands back and forth over his knees, apparently as excited about this as I was. "This is gonna be awesome," he mused.

Grabbing Arianna's hand in the backseat, I silently agreed with him. Yes, this was definitely going to be awesome. I hoped. *God, please don't let me mess this night up.*

After eating at a noisy pizza place downtown where we were all seriously overdressed, the four of us headed to the dance. Right on time, Mom and Dad pulled into the parking lot seconds behind us. Trey thought that was pretty miraculous, but Nika and I knew better. It was easy to coordinate timing when the people you were meeting were constantly pinging their location to you.

The gym was thumping and alive with music and gyrating bodies by the time we got inside. My parents checked in and disappeared into the throngs to observe the student body. Their main job here was to separate couples who were dirty dancing, and to check the punch for alcohol. Basically, safeguard the virtue of the innocents. That was what the school expected from them at any rate. In actuality, what they would most likely be doing was slow dancing with each other while keeping mental tabs on Nika and me all evening.

Doing my best to forget that they'd be watching my every move, I turned in my tickets and stood in line for photos. Arianna and I were practically glowing in our picture, arms securely wrapped around each other, but Nika's smile was clearly forced when it was her turn to pose with Trey; she stood at least a foot and a half away from him too. I gave her a good dose of empathy, but she shooed me off with her hand, whispering, "Stop worrying, go have fun."

I nodded at her, then turned to my date. Practicing the gallantry that effortlessly oozed from my father, I extended my palm to Arianna and inclined my head over to the packed dance floor. Arianna giggled as she accepted my hand. Just holding her fingers warmed me. *She* warmed me. She accepted everything about me—my true nature, my family, the odd connection I had with them. There was only one thing I hadn't told her about yet.

My emotional bond with Nika. It was an odd thing to describe to someone, and I wasn't sure how Arianna would take it. Would it freak her out to know that Nika felt every moment of joy I felt? That Nika knew when the joy I was feeling slipped into something more? A part of me really wanted to confess it to her, especially before we had sex—*tonight*—but the larger part of me was scared. Arianna had been really accepting up to this point, but if it ever got to be too much and she broke up with me, Halina would erase her mind and I'd lose her forever. That wasn't a risk I wanted to take right now. I'd tell her ... later.

A dazzling amount of colored lights swirled around the room in haphazard patterns. The bass of the music reverberated in my chest, rattling my sensitive ears. Streamers littered the floor, crinkling under my feet. Stranded silver and white balloons were being popped by pointed heels and heavy shoes. Everywhere I turned there was another dizzying burst of color as the twisting and turning outfits around me clashed with each other. It made the solid blackness of Arianna's dress a source of refreshment. The room was sensory overload for a vampire, but she was my solace.

By the time we settled into the middle of the packed crowd, a slow song was playing. Arianna laced her arms around my neck while mine slid around her waist. Pulling me tight, she gazed up at me and threaded her fingers through my hair. The entire world fell away as I stared into her love-filled, hazel eyes. They were the perfect mixture of sea-green flecked with golden brown, and as I got lost in them, I stopped caring about the swirling colors and deafening music. I stopped worrying about my sister, my parents. I stopped thinking about Hunter. I stopped caring about Hunter's father, the vampire hunter who knew about my family and would one day come back to finish us off, once he recovered from the horror of what he'd done to his son.

All of it faded away as I held my girl in my arms. Wishing we were alone, I lowered my lips to hers, and let her feel how much I cared about her, how much I loved her. And I knew it was love. It was too intense to be anything else. I would do *anything* for her. I would die for her. Over and over again, I would die for her.

It was easy to feel how much she cared for me in the way her mouth moved against mine. There was meaning in the softness. A declaration of *I'll never hurt you* in the tenderness. The gentle melding of our bodies was a physical proclamation of our mutual pledge to never hurt each other. We were safe together. Complete.

I fully expected my parents to pull us apart, but they never did, and we remained lip-locked for the rest of the song. Most of the next one, too, which was sort of odd, since it was a fast song. Finally, laughing, Arianna pulled away and told me, "Shouldn't we be dancing at a dance?" Whispering in my ear, she added, "We can do that stuff later."

I instantly wished it was later, but I did as my girl asked and attempted some form of awkward dancing. I wasn't as seamless at it as she was, but I soon lost myself in the beat. We turned, dipped, shimmied, and grooved for the longest time—it felt like hours, although it could have just been minutes. I wasn't sure. Even though I knew the night was only going to get better afterward, I never wanted it to end. Nika was moderately happy too. I could feel her on the other side of the gym, and she seemed to be having a good time for once. I was grateful for it, and glad that, if anything, Trey was keeping her mind off Hunter.

Then I felt something that made my heart drop. Nika's too.

Looking at the far wall behind me, I muttered, "Damn it."

Arianna didn't hear me, but me suddenly standing still got her attention. "What's wrong?"

Sighing, I looked back at her. "My grandmother is here with ... Hunter." Sighing again, I scoured the gym for Nika. She was staring at the same far wall. Her eyes were wide; they shimmered in the rotating lights.

Arianna glanced over at her friend. "Oh ... Nika." Looking back at me, she asked, "Why is he here?"

Curling my hands into fists, I glared at the wall separating my sister and me from Hunter. "I don't know. He told her they couldn't be together, told her she should let him go. He broke her heart, again, and now he's *here*?" Fire in my eyes, I looked back at Arianna. "What an asshole," I hissed.

So much for letting my sister move on.

CHAPTER NINE

Nika

THE LIGHTS WERE disorienting, the music was loud, and my brother's emotions were soaring into a heightened state of bliss. I didn't really want to be here, but I'd promised Arianna I'd go, so here I was, dancing to a song whose lyrics were—I kid you not—*bite me and I'll bite you back.*

But as I watched my date move around the floor, I started relaxing and having fun. Not wanting anyone's arms around me tonight, I'd made sure Trey and I sat out the slow song that had been playing when we'd first hit the dance floor, but I was feeling better now, and I let Trey grab my hand and twirl me around.

Trey was sort of awkward, like an oversized puppy who hadn't quite grown into its body yet, but he was surprisingly graceful as he danced. He was also surprisingly sober. His eyes were clear, and there was only a faint odor of cologne about him—a scent I much preferred to pot.

He kicked a couple of stray balloons into the air. One of them smacked some poor, dancing girl square in the face. Trey quickly spun back around toward me before her date could figure out who'd assaulted her. It was then, while Trey was laughing, that I noticed something that I hadn't before: he had a really nice smile.

He was also sort of cute without his signature stocking hat in place. Since he wore that damn thing practically all year long, even when it was ninety degrees, I rarely ever saw his hair. While some longer strands hung down almost to his shoulders, the bulk of it was a mess of short, shaggy, blond layers. I imagined he generally did nothing to arrange those layers, but tonight he had some sort of gel or spray holding each piece in place. It was really kind of ... attractive.

Attractive was such a difficult word for me to associate with Trey. I'd never seen him that way before. I wasn't getting butterflies or anything, not like when I was around Hunter, but I *was* enjoying the view.

By the time another slow song started playing, I was feeling comfortable enough with Trey that I didn't push him away, or tell him we had to go sit down. He had just pulled me into his body when the song changed tempo. A look of disappointment crossed his features, and he started to point to the bleachers, where a group of kids were sitting. In answer to his silent question, I ran my fingers up the stiff fabric of his tuxedo jacket, and looped them around his neck. In the car, Trey had given me a red rose corsage that matched a flower pinned to his jacket. The smell next to my nose was heavenly, and I smiled at Trey as I looked up at him.

He swallowed, like he was suddenly nervous, then he placed his hands on my back. I expected him to grab my butt, since he could be an obnoxious flirt, but he didn't. His fingers stayed at a respectable level.

While he looked down at me, I reminisced about his reaction to finding out what my brother and I really were. He'd instantly accepted us, thought what we were was "cool." He hadn't been afraid, not for a second, not even when we were in the middle of real danger. He'd been so brave that night, and I suddenly wished Halina had let him remember just how courageous he'd been.

Leaning down a little, he told me, "You're really pretty."

Compliments from Trey were nothing new. He joked that I was hot at least three times a day. Resisting the urge to roll my eyes, I replied, "Thanks."

Trey's brows creased, like my nonchalant answer bothered him. "No, I mean it. I know I tell you stuff like that all the time but ... I'm not joking, or doing whatever it is you think I'm doing when I tell you you're hot." Looking me directly in the eye, he said, "You're the prettiest girl here tonight."

My cheeks felt overly warm, and I wanted to look away, but couldn't. Somehow, his words made me instantly aware of just how close our bodies were. It felt odd to be in such a romantic position with him, but, it felt sort of nice too, and it had been a while since I'd felt simple niceness.

Maybe feeling bolstered by the fact that I hadn't run from the room screaming, Trey straightened and added, "That dude's a dick for dumping you."

That made me finally look away. A giant slice of pain tore up my spine; I was surprised the sting of it didn't crumple me to my knees.

"Ah, shit. I'm sorry, Nika. I shouldn't have said that." I looked up at Trey's adorable, remorseful face. He shrugged, his eyes apologetic. "I'm sorry," he repeated.

Even though I felt hollow, my momentary happiness gone, I gave him a smile. "It's fine." With an empty laugh, I added, "You're right, anyway. He is a dick." I wasn't sure if I believed that—Hunter was just massively confused—but it felt good to say it. Brightening, I told Trey, "The biggest dick I've ever met."

Seeing my humor, Trey grinned, and I was again taken aback by the attractiveness of his smile. "A supersized dick!" he exclaimed.

Some of the dancers around who were busy having a "moment" gave Trey annoyed glances at his outburst. It made me laugh in a way I hadn't laughed in a long time, and it felt great. As my levity returned, Trey gazed at me with soft eyes. "You have a great laugh," he said. "You should use it more often."

A feeling settled over me as Trey and I locked eyes. It was … warm. Comfortable. Tightening my arms around his neck, I told him, "You have a great smile."

His reaction was, of course, to smile, but then he started leaning down. At first, I thought he was just moving closer to tell me something, but his eyes were glued to my mouth, and I knew no words were going to be involved here. My heart started to race and nerves shot through every inch of me. *Oh my God. Trey, my brother's flirtatious, stoner best friend, is going to kiss me.* I almost couldn't comprehend it. I definitely didn't want him to kiss me, but how did I turn him down without hurting his feelings?

When his lips were just inches from completing the connection, I felt something that chilled my entire body like ice water. I jerked back, releasing Trey. Thinking he'd gone too far with me, Trey immediately started apologizing again. I didn't know how to tell Trey that, while I wasn't interested in kissing him, it wasn't him that had made me move away. He wasn't the one making my blood run cold. I didn't know how to tell Trey anything. I wasn't sure if I could even speak right now.

Hunter was here. Right outside. Why?

Stepping away from Trey, I stared at the wall separating Hunter from me. Halina was out there with him, but that barely registered. Why was Hunter here? I needed to know. I needed to see him. I needed to go ...

Not looking at Trey, I told him, "I'm sorry ..." and started striding through the crowd. I wanted to blur so badly, but not using my gifts was too ingrained in me, and I shoved my way through the dancing couples at a regular pace. I felt my parents and my brother moving toward me, but I ignored them as I bullied my way through the annoyed students to get to the doors. I managed to get away from my parents—they were behind me, and couldn't catch up unless they phased in a room full of humans, something they would never do unless it was absolutely necessary—but I couldn't escape my brother. He was between me and the exit.

I tried to avoid him, but he cut me off. "Out of my way, Julian," I snipped, annoyed at the obstruction.

I moved to the side, but he moved over too. "No, Nick. Let it go. Stay here."

"I have to go. Please move." Glaring at him, I stepped the other way. He moved over to block me. Frustrated didn't even begin to describe how I felt. And feeling Julian's compassion didn't help me one tiny little bit. Tossing my hands in the air, I told him, "You owe me." I gave Arianna a meaningful look after I said it. If Julian and Arianna were really going to have sex tonight, the least they could do was let me have a few minutes with my wayward boyfriend.

Julian glanced at his date, wrestled with his conflicting desires for a second, and then stepped aside. Feeling my parents getting closer, I grabbed Julian's arm and whispered in his ear, "Do whatever you have to do, just give me time ..." Pulling back, I indicated Mom and Dad with my head. Julian sighed, but nodded. He'd play along. Arianna looked confused as I ran past my brother. I'd let him fill her in, since I didn't have time. Julian would only be able to delay Dad for so long.

Knowing time was of the essence, I crashed through the doors like a woman possessed. Adrenaline, fear, and hope pounded through my body. I think the hope was the hardest one to deal with. Why was Hunter here? Had he come here for me? To patch things up? And if he had, could I forgive him for what he'd done? For lifting me up, then tearing out my heart?

The second I was outside, Hunter's form streaked to the roof. Disappointment hit me like a wall. Was he running from me? Why come here if he didn't want to see me? Halina approached while I debated if I should run after him or not. Leaning against the cold metal door of the gym, I gulped in air while Halina tried to look through the window my back was pressed against. "Was there a fire?" she asked, a smirk in her voice.

Shaking my head, I stepped forward. The night air made goosebumps burst up and down my arms, but I didn't care. All I cared about were answers. Had Hunter changed his mind? Was he starting to accept who he was? Was hope returning to him ... to us? "What are you guys doing here?" I asked in a pant.

Grabbing her wild mess of black-as-night locks, Halina swirled her hair into an updo. Pushing out her hip, she murmured, "It's been a while since I've gone dancing. It sounded like fun." I glanced down at the tight, party dress she was wearing, the thigh-high boots. I was certain she really would enjoy a night of dancing, but I was also certain that wasn't why she was here with Hunter.

"Why is Hunter here?" I watched her eyes as intently as a hawk watched for movement in the grass, ripples in the stream. Did she know something?

Halina sighed as she dropped her hair. It fell down her back in loose waves. "We didn't mean to disrupt your evening, Nika. Why don't you go back inside?"

Her words didn't sound encouraging, and grief threatened to drown me, but I pushed it back. "Not until I talk to him," I told her. Turning, I stared upward, to the roof. After a brief squat, I jumped straight up into the air. I used every supernatural muscle I had, but even so, I wasn't sure if it was enough; I wasn't quite as enhanced as the purebloods, and it was a bit of a leap to the roof. I made it to the ledge, but I forgot about my heels. My ankle twisted on the unstable footing, and I cried out in pain as my knees buckled. I could tell I was going to fall backward, straight off the ledge, and I instinctively reached out for something to hold onto. What I found was an ice-cold hand reaching for me.

I locked eyes with Hunter right as he pulled me safely away from the lip and onto the flat, stable part of the roof. He held me in his arms while I tried not to cringe in pain. My ankle throbbed and standing on it hurt, but being this close to him again sliced me open. "What were you thinking?" he asked, anger in his voice.

My grandmother sighed, muttered, "Good luck," and entered the gym.

"What are you doing here?" I responded, shoving him away from me. I put too much weight on my injured foot and stumbled to the ground. Hunter was right there, kneeling over me. His eyes scoured my body, then focused on my feet. His soothing hands wrapped around my ankle, and I nearly purred in relief. Vampire hands. Nature's ice packs.

"You're hurt?" he whispered, concern replacing his anger.

"I'll be fine."

His dark eyes peeked up at me again. There was a decent amount of light pollution in the sky, so his eyes weren't glowing at me, but I could see the subtle phosphorescence highlighting the whiteness. He looked just as frail and sickly as before, and I wondered if he'd had anything at all to drink since I'd seen him last. Probably not, nothing more than a sip or two, not enough to sustain him and keep him strong.

"What were you thinking, making a jump like that in an outfit like this?" His gaze lingered on my curves, and I suddenly didn't feel cold anymore.

Ignoring his question, I repeated, "What are you doing here?"

Not answering me, his eyes shifted to his hands on my ankle. So, he was going to ignore my question too, huh? Sitting up, I placed my warm hands over his. "Hunter? Why did you come here?"

Silently, I begged him to tell me that he was here because he just couldn't bear to be apart from me anymore, that he'd found a reason to go on: me. That he didn't mean it when he said he didn't love me like I loved him.

Like he could hear my inner thoughts, and he wished I wasn't having them, Hunter let out a weary sigh. "I'm just keeping an eye on things. Large gatherings usually attract a vampire or two." He looked up at me. "I didn't want anybody to get hurt tonight." He lifted his lip in a sarcastic smile as he gently squeezed my ankle. "Guess I failed."

My hope evaporated in a puff of smoke. "You were just ... doing your job? Even though you're a ... ? Even after everything that happened to you?"

His mouth tightened into a firm line. "I'm still a hunter. It's who I am." Just as I was wondering if he would still hunt *me*, he lowered his eyes and quietly added, "I won't hurt your family, Nika." He let out a sound that was full of pain. "They're all I have now ..."

There was so much heartache in that sentence that I couldn't stand it anymore. I had to comfort him, and I gently placed my hand on his back. "I'm sorry about what happened to you. I'm sorry about your father."

Hunter's eyes snapped up to mine. "He abandoned me. He just...left. We've always had each other's backs, always, and he walked away. No ... he ran away." Bitterness and hatred surged though his voice. Whatever bond had been between father and son was broken now. Hunter would never forgive him for leaving in his moment of greatest need. But I wasn't his father, and I wasn't leaving him. Ever.

I rubbed a circle into his rigid back. "I'm here for you, whenever you need me. I'll never abandon you."

Giving me a confused look, Hunter whispered, "Were you going to kiss that boy?"

By the chill that flashed through my body, you would have thought he'd shoved an icicle through my heart. "You saw ..." My gaze slid behind him, to the ground. He'd been watching me through the gym doors, and his sharp eyes had seen that misleading moment with Trey. My eyes returned to his. "No, that wasn't what it looked like."

Hunter's gaze returned to my ankle. "Doesn't matter, Nika. You and I aren't together, so if you want to kiss him ... it's okay."

His hands pulled away from my numb skin, and I knew he was seconds from leaving. Scooting forward, I grabbed his jacket. "It does matter, because you and I ..." I didn't know how to voice what we were; I wasn't sure how to classify us. But I knew we *were* something, and so long as we were, I wouldn't let another boy kiss me.

Hunter's dark eyes focused on my lips, much like Trey's had earlier. Shaking his head, he murmured, "I meant what I said before. I can't love you like you need me to. Don't waste your life waiting for me." He cupped my cheek, and my breath increased. Leaning closer, so our lips almost touched, he whispered, "I'm never going to be who you need me to be. I'll never be anything but a monster."

"That's not true," I whispered back, closing the space between us.

I thought he might move away, but like every other time, he didn't. As our mouths worked together, Hunter's hand on my cheek slid through my hair to rest at the back of my neck. Exhaling in a groaning growl, he held me to him. Sitting up on my knees, our lips never pausing, I held his face in my hands, then carefully repositioned myself so I was straddling his lap. Hunter melted under my heat. The rigidness left his body as his free hand trailed down my back. I reveled in our reconnection, hoping it lasted.

"Why are you really here?" I murmured between our lips. It couldn't just be for vampires.

Hunter's breath was faster, his eyes hooded. "I was jealous. I had to see for myself ... who this guy was ... your date. I know I shouldn't be here ... I'm sorry. I couldn't stay away."

My heart started to race. Jealousy ... over me? He was sorry? He wasn't apathetic ... he *did* care. He did love me. We could get through this. We could be together again. "Trey's a friend, nothing more," I told him as my fingers ran back through his hair.

"He wants more," Hunter murmured, his eyes flashing with covetous anger.

Wanting *him* more than I'd ever wanted anyone in my life, I laced my arms around his neck. "I want you," I whispered, before pressing my lips against his, hard and fierce. He loved me, and I loved him too. I wanted to show him just how great we could be together.

Hunter responded instantly. Blurring us, he changed our positions so my back was flat against the gritty roof and he was lying on top of me. I couldn't believe this was happening. I couldn't control my excitement, how much I wanted him, how much I needed him. Julian, and what he was feeling from me now, was only a faint concern in the very back of my head, and I thanked God for the thumping bass in the gym. There was no way my family could hear what was happening over that noise. Whatever my brother was doing to distract Mom and Dad, I hoped he could keep it up for a little while longer. I didn't want Hunter to stop touching me ...

As Hunter pressed his hips against mine, I wrapped my legs around him. I couldn't even feel the pain in my ankle anymore. It didn't even matter. I gasped as I physically felt Hunter's need for me. He did want me ...

he couldn't deny what we were both feeling. As his lips moved down my neck, I cinched my fingers into his hair. His tongue ran along my jugular, and I moaned his name in his ear. Oh God, I wanted him so much. I'd missed him so much.

One of his hands ran up my legs, under my dress. Once his hand was at my hip, his fingers slipped under my underwear. I wanted him to touch me. I thought I might die if he didn't. In the back of my mind, disgust flooded through me, but it was coming from Julian, not me—all I felt was fire. I pushed Julian's emotions away as I ran my hands down Hunter's chest to his jeans.

When I started unbuttoning them, Hunter's hand left my hip, and he grabbed my wandering fingers. His face returned to mine; his fangs were down and long as multiple desires flooded through him. "No," he growled.

I yanked my hands away from his grasp and returned to his jeans. "Yes ..."

Hunter grabbed my wrists and brought them above my head. He leaned over me, his weight crushing every inch of me. It felt ... amazing. "No," he murmured again.

My control long gone, I squirmed beneath him. "Please? I love you. I want more."

He stilled my hips by pressing his against mine; we both let out low groans. I could tell the animal inside him was begging to be let out. I felt the same. Irrational as it was, as much as we'd both probably regret it later, I wanted him. Pulling one of my hands free, I grabbed Hunter's neck and pulled his mouth to mine. "Please ... don't stop. I want you."

His voice was strained as our hips moved together in a seductive rhythm that was slowly driving me toward the brink of something ... amazing. "No, Nika, the ways I want you ... aren't right."

Feeling his fangs against my lips, I knew exactly what way he wanted me. I wanted it too. The last time he'd nearly bitten me the idea of it had driven me crazy. Now, when I was feeling completely unrestrained, it couldn't be any other way. This *had* to happen. I needed him to bite me. I needed him to drink from me. I needed it ... now.

I removed my fingers from his hair, and trailed them down his chilly cheek. Nearly purring with need, he leaned against my hand as our hips continued rocking together. I felt like my entire world was spinning as several different cravings pummeled me at once. I never wanted this to end.

When Hunter's eyes fluttered closed, I rubbed my wrist across his lips, encouraging him to open his mouth and take me in. The veins there were close to the surface; he could probably feel the pulse of my life against his skin.

Hunter's mouth opened on instinct, his lips conforming to my shape. I felt his tongue trace my vein, and I gasped. His eyes sprang open, and he automatically released me. Our lower bodies froze as Hunter's gaze locked onto the blood he could see surging beneath my flesh. "Do it," I begged, my voice breathless with desire. "It's okay. You need it, and I want it."

He immediately flew off me. Panting, eyes wide, he stood five feet away from me. The loss of his chill made me shiver. I looked up at him as I lowered my wrist. Oh God, why had I pushed him in that way? I knew how he felt about it. How disgusted he was by the desire to drink. I'd just never had a longing like that ... ever. But it was a part of who I was too. I was a vampire. Vampires bite. Vampires shared blood. It was in both of our natures.

Backing away, he shook his head. "Don't ... *ever* ... do that again." As he examined my wrinkled dress, my heaving chest, my tousled hair, his face instantly turned remorseful. Even before he said it, I knew our moment was over. "That shouldn't have happened. That's not why I came here."

Anger shot through me as I struggled to my feet. I was so tired of hearing him say that to me. "Right. You only came here to protect the humans. From what though? You're the biggest threat out here tonight, and you won't bite anything!" I tossed my hands into the air. "So, I guess you did your job. Congratulations!"

I hadn't meant to say any of that, but his hot and cold behavior was really starting to piss me off. Hunter hissed at me, then retracted his fangs. He inhaled a deep breath, composing himself. "I'll help you get back down, since your ankle is still injured."

Ignoring his offer, I limped past him. "I can make it by myself just fine, thank you."

He harrumphed at me and grabbed my elbow. "Don't be dramatic. How are you going to get down when you can hardly walk?"

My eyes flashed to his, and even though I wanted to hold onto the anger, pain was starting to leak in. I'd just thrown myself out there, and he'd just rejected me ... again. And it stung. A lot. Yanking my arm away, I sniffed back the tears that were building. "I'll find a way. I don't need you."

My voice hitched, and I knew that wasn't true. I *did* need him. I only felt truly alive when I was with him. Hunter's voice softened when he heard my pain. "Nika, I'm so sorry. I don't know why this keeps happening between us."

Straightening, I lifted my chin. "It keeps happening, because you can't accept yourself. You can't accept what you are now, so you can't accept me, can't accept us. Because you're giving up. You're throwing us away. The only problem here ... is you."

Hunter's eyes lowered, and he responded with silence. I was tired of silence. With an exhale that felt a lot like defeat, I told him, "Every time I see you, you break my heart. You know that, don't you?"

His eyes snapped to mine. "I'm sorry. I'm not trying to hurt you. I'm just ..."

Just as he was about to say something—something that was surely going to be deep, profound, and possibly start to heal this massive gap between us—I smelled something on the breeze that immediately caught my attention. Blood. Fresh blood. Fresh human blood. Hunter stopped talking as he smelled it too. Fangs crashing to full length, his head snapped in the direction of the heavenly smell. A low growl erupted from his chest, a primal growl, full of interest.

"No, Hunter—"

I tried to grab him, but I wasn't fast enough. He blurred away from me, leaping off the roof and disappearing into the night.

"Shit."

Hunter had shown an enormous amount of control at the ranch, and Halina said he wasn't drinking, even when she exposed blood in the air ... but he was so hungry. I could see it every time he looked at me, every time he listened to my heartbeat. I wasn't sure if he was at his breaking point yet, but I knew I couldn't just sit here and let Hunter stare down a bleeding meal all on his own. He would never recover if he lost control and hurt somebody. I'd lose him forever.

I tightened my jaw as I prepared to jump off the roof and run after him. This wasn't going to feel good. Testing my ankle, I braced myself to take a supernatural leap. Cringing as the dull ache radiated around my swollen joint, I noticed a less painful option—there were stairs on the corner of the roof. Stairs would hurt a loss less than asphalt. Ignoring everything my body was feeling, I phased toward the staircase and hurried down them.

I was on the ground and blurring toward the smell of blood—toward Hunter—faster than the human eye could even begin to process. My foot felt better as I moved it, as the blood and adrenaline surged through me. Hunter's supersonic exit from the roof, followed quickly by mine, alerted every single one of my family members. Already on edge from feeling my pain when I twisted my ankle, Julian was spiking with concern. Along with Mom, Dad, and Halina, he was slowly moving toward me. They were all still in the gym, still surrounded by humans, and they had to move and act normally. I was the only one who could get to Hunter in time, before he *truly* did something he regretted.

When I approached the source of the blood, I froze in shock. It was just a few blocks from the high school in a parking lot for a doctor's office. The back wall of the lot had a chain link fence, the kind with plastic slates between the metal links to make it look a little more elegant than it really was. It was secluded back here, dark, but my sharp eyes could clearly make out a young girl lying on her stomach in front of the fence, arms stretched in front of her. She was dressed in a formal gown like I was, so I had to assume she'd come from the dance. Dark hair covered her face, masking her identity, and her pale pink dress was splattered in blood. She was alive; her heartbeat was slow and thready, but still beating. Deep gashes down her arms oozed dark crimson rivulets of blood that dripped onto the cold pavement beneath her. The splashing droplets were ominously loud to my sensitive ears. While there was no evidence of it around her, she looked like she'd just run head first through a plate glass window or something. It didn't make any sense. There was nothing sinister around her. Nothing but Hunter.

He crouched down as he stalked her, and the look on his face was no longer conflicted. He was hungry. She was food. It was that simple. The smell of blood was overwhelming this close, and I had to consciously keep my fangs up. Hunter wasn't concerned about his anymore. They were fully extended, gleaming in the dim parking lot lights. I knew by the predatory way he was moving toward her that Hunter wasn't going to pass this test. Resisting reheated cow's blood was one thing. Resisting biting me, the person he loved, another. But this? A fresh, bloody stranger who was offering no resistance? This was too much for any starved vampire to resist.

Just as I screamed at him to stop, Hunter blurred to the comatose body and clamped his mouth around a gaping wound in her arm. She didn't even react when he bit down and started draining her. Knowing he was hungry enough to kill her in seconds, before he even comprehended what he was doing, I stuck my shoulder out and plowed into him. The impact hurt like hell, but it knocked him backward. I landed on top of him, and quickly pressed all my weight into his chest, hoping beyond hope that my tiny body could hold him down. At least for a few more seconds, until the calvary arrived.

Fresh blood streaming from his mouth, Hunter snarled at me in a starvation-induced fury. His piercing eyes were wild with hunger and desire. He was completely out of control, and even though he was weak, he was still strong. It took everything I had to keep him on the ground. My heart pounded in my chest. If I let go of him, that girl was going to die.

As he growled and snarled, twisting beneath me, I tried to reason with him, tried to return him to his senses. "Hunter, stop! Stop fighting me! You don't drink blood! You don't want to hurt anybody! You're a good person. You don't kill! Snap out of it!"

My words made zero difference to him. Leaning up, he hissed in my face, then his eyes locked onto my neck. His expression changed, and ice washed through me. He was looking at me in a way he'd never looked at me before. Like he suddenly realized ... I was food too. I'd been expecting him to try and get away from me, but I hadn't ever expected him to attack me. When he lunged, his fangs aiming for my throat, I did the only thing I could think to do ... I head-butted him. It hurt so bad I saw stars. My stomach clenched like I was going to vomit, but the force I'd used was enough to make Hunter's head snap back and hit the concrete. He stopped moving, and I collapsed against him, feeling ill, sore, and really tired.

And that was when my family finally showed up.

CHAPTER TEN

Julian

HOW DID MY sister always manage to talk me into letting her do things I didn't want her to do? Either I was a sucker, or Nika had an uncanny gift for manipulating me. I supposed the damn bond was to blame. It was hard to refuse someone when you could feel their need for something, even if it *was* a stupid need. But Nika had asked to be alone with Hunter, and I'd agreed. And now I had to stall my parents to give her that time. Super.

Perplexed, Arianna looked up at me and grabbed my hand. "What was all that about?"

Sighing, I looked down into her brown-flecked green eyes. "Nika won't rest until she talks to Hunter."

Arianna stepped closer to me, like she was a little frightened. Purebloods still unsettled her. "Is that … wise?"

I scoffed as I felt my parents nearly upon me. "You're asking me if my sister is wise?" As far as I was concerned, she'd stopped being wise the minute she'd met Hunter.

Seeing my parents breeze past me as they made their way to the doors, I hurried over and grabbed my dad's arm. "Hey, can I … talk to you? Both of you?"

Dad glanced from me to the doors, then back to me. "We'll be back in a minute."

He patted my shoulder, then twisted to leave. "It's about sex!" I blurted out. Embarrassment heated my body. I might owe my sister for giving me the okay to sleep with my girlfriend, but after this little mortifying distraction, she was the one who owed me.

Arianna gaped at me as Mom and Dad stopped dead in their tracks. Some students around us had heard me say that and were sniggering. I tuned them out as I locked eyes with Dad. "Nika is fine. Halina is out there with her." I indicated Arianna by my side. She was white as a ghost. "You've always said I should wait until I'm older, and I was just wondering ... why?"

Dad seemed torn. This was something I knew he wanted to seriously discuss with me, but I also knew he wanted to check on my sister. He looked over to Mom, like he was going to tell her to go ahead while he had a chat with me. Beating him to the punch, I asked Mom, "What do *you* think?"

The music blared in the gym as my parents open and shut their mouths, trying to come up with a reasonable, responsible answer. For a moment, Nika was forgotten. Mission accomplished. As Dad fully turned to me and said, "Well, it's just ..." I felt Nika's mood shift, and her location. She was on the roof now, following Hunter, while Halina was strolling through the doors. A sharp pain shot through Nika and I did my best not to cringe as I felt it too. I was concerned for a moment, but her pain faded quickly. Whatever had happened to her must have been minor.

As my parents felt Halina approaching, they stopped talking. I knew detaining them for long while Nika was alone with Hunter was going to be even more difficult. As Halina stopped beside us, she gave Arianna and me a onceover. "Aren't you two adorable."

Dad looked up to the roof and immediately said, "You left Nika alone with Hunter?"

Not wanting the conversation to shift to Hunter, I stepped forward and asked Halina, "Do you think I'm too young to have sex?"

Arianna covered her face with her hand. Oh yeah, Nika owed me big time. Halina gave me a wide smile. "Are you going to become a man tonight, Julian?"

Mom and Dad responded simultaneously. "No."

Halina turned to Dad. "Why not? He loves her, she loves him. She's already accepted us. Why delay it? They might as well start giving us heirs." She sighed as she tilted her head. "I miss having babies around the house."

Arianna started choking and sputtering. Smirking, Halina gently patted her back. "What? Heirs? Babies? I'm not ..." Arianna turned to look at me, her eyes as wide as her gaping mouth. "I'm not having kids right now."

I wanted to rewind to about five minutes ago, and smack myself into unconsciousness for *ever* agreeing to delay my parents. It was working, but oh my God ... I did *not* want to be having this conversation. "Uh ... of course not ... now ..."

Crossing his arms over his chest, Dad stared Halina down. "They're not having children at sixteen. And they're under no obligation to continue the line. Don't push them like you pushed me."

Halina stepped up to my father, staring right back. I felt a familiar tension building between the pair. While they loved each other more than anything, there was a battle of wills between them when it came to certain topics. Nika's and my sex life was one of those topics. Nika's current situation on the roof was all but forgotten now. Except by me. I was feeling something from her that was making me a little nauseous. She was ... turned on ... *really* turned on. I guess things were going well with Hunter. Maybe I should stop distracting my parents now. While they bickered about my virginity, Nika was about to lose hers.

Oh God, I was going to be sick.

Halina's eyes narrowed. "He asked for her memories to remain intact, and in return he agreed to have children with the girl. Why not get a jump on it?" As Arianna beside me gasped, my grandmother's expression softened. "Think of Ben, Teren. True humanity is possible. It's *actually* possible. We can't stop now. We're so close."

Dad sighed. It was a long-standing wish in my family for the vampirism to be "bred" out. With each generation the side effects lessened, and the recent discovery that Ben, my father's completely human best friend, was a descendent of a vampire had given my family hope. Our line could be human again. All Nika and I had to do was have children to keep it going. To say it was weird to have my great, great grandmother fighting for me to have sex was an understatement.

The entire conversation was suddenly too much for Arianna. She turned to Halina with wide eyes. "Whoa ... get a jump on it? I'm sixteen." Maybe realizing who she was talking to, Arianna shifted her eyes to me. "I don't even know if I want kids, but I definitely know I don't want them right *now*. You agreed to this, Julian? Without even asking me how I felt about it?"

People around us were starting to pay attention to our wildly inappropriate conversation. As I tried to convince Arianna that I hadn't signed her up for some weird vampire breeding program, Halina started "telling" people to forget what they'd just heard and go back to dancing.

"It's not like that," I told her, shaking my head. "I agreed to *maybe*, I agreed to *one day we might have kids*, if we were ready. But really, I just wanted a chance to see if that was our future. I wanted you to remember me." My heart was breaking, but then I realized it wasn't my pain I was feeling. It was Nika. *Her* heart was breaking.

Trying to remain focused on my problems, I was about to tell Arianna how much she meant to me, when Halina snapped her head to the far wall—Hunter was leaving the roof, in a hurry. Halina's brow furrowed as she tracked him, and she hastily began making her way to the door. Mom and Dad glanced at each other, then started following. Sighing, I shifted my attention back to Arianna. "I'm sorry. I was going to tell you about that, but it doesn't—"

I cut off when I felt my sister streaking away from the gym roof. I knew she was in pain, physically and emotionally, so her leaving in such a rush was alarming. Switching my words, I told Arianna, "Something's wrong ... I have to go. Stay here with Trey."

I didn't have time to explain further. Gently moving her aside, I ran toward the exit. Arianna asked what was wrong, but I couldn't answer her. Nika was worried—no, panicked. I sensed the streaks of my other family members rushing away once they were outside, and my concern leapt even higher. What was going on? When I burst outside into the chilly night air, I knew instantly. I smelled it. Blood. Human blood. It was heavy on the breeze. More confused than ever, I hurried over to a dark corner of the school, then zipped toward my family. Whatever was going on, I wasn't about to let them face it alone.

When I arrived where Nika was, I slowed to a human run. Then I stopped in my tracks. Nothing about the scene I was witnessing made sense. An unconscious woman was lying in front of a fence, bleeding all over the ground. Nika was lying on top of Hunter, looking dazed. Halina was beside Nika, asking her if she felt okay enough to stand up. Hunter had his fangs fully extended, and a stream of blood was trickling out of his mouth as he stared up at the sky; his expression was completely void of emotion.

What the hell had happened here?

My parents had stopped a fraction of a second before me, and were taking in the odd scene with equally bewildered expressions. Then Dad blurred over to Nika and helped Halina get her to her feet. Nika stumbled, and I felt the ache in her leg and the throb in her head. Dad looked enraged as he examined her skin. "Did he bite you?" he snapped.

Nika was still disoriented and confused. I didn't feel any pain coming from her that matched a bite, but Dad seemed to take her mumbling speech as an affirmative. His jaw tight, he handed Nika to Halina. Then he reached down and snatched Hunter lightning-quick. Yanking him to his feet, he yelled, "What did you do?"

Halina snarled at Dad; I thought she would have ripped him away from Hunter if she wasn't holding Nika. "He did not hurt her."

Hunter seemed just as dazed as Nika, but Dad's aggressiveness woke him up. Scowling, he batted Dad's hands away. "Nothing." Then his eyes turned to my sister. She was blinking and shaking her head like she was trying to focus. Looking like he'd just remembered something awful, Hunter's face shifted into remorse. "Nika, I'm so sorry ..."

He took a step toward her, but Dad pushed him back. I wasn't sure what Hunter was sorry for, but I didn't think it had anything to do with biting. Looking back at the poor girl bleeding on the ground, I thought *she* was more likely the reason for Hunter's contrition. Her arms were sliced open, and she was bleeding pretty badly. Had Hunter scratched her up like that? What the hell?

Mom was tending to the girl, flipping her over and cooing in her ear that everything would be all right. When Mom twisted her, exposing her face, my heart leapt into my throat. I knew that girl ... knew her very well. The shock coursing through me was powerful enough to clear Nika from her mental fog. Her eyes shot over to me as I shouted, "Raquel!" and rushed to her side.

Brushing Raquel's dark hair from her face, I frantically whispered, "No, no, no." Even though I could hear her slow heartbeat, I checked her pulse. Feeling the light beat of life under my fingertips, I lifted my gaze to Hunter. "What the hell did you do to her?"

Looking sicklier than I'd ever seen him, Hunter clenched his stomach. "I didn't …"

By the way he looked like he was about to vomit, I knew he was lying. He *had* done this. Jumping to my feet, I blurred over to him. "I'm going to kill you, you sick son of a bitch!" Hatred shot through my veins like liquid fire. He'd sliced her open and fed on her like some twisted psychopath. He couldn't deny that the blood on his lips was hers. Not with the guilty way he was wiping it away with the back of his hand.

Nika yelled at me to stop, but I ignored her. If my father wasn't going to end him, then I would. But as I lunged for Hunter, Halina blocked me. Fangs lowered, I growled at her. Leaning into my face, she growled right back. She wasn't going to let me hurt her child, even if he deserved it. Frustration grew in me as I stared her down. I knew I couldn't take her. She was a pureblood, I was a fourth-generation mixed vampire … practically human. I didn't stand a chance against her. Not that I wanted to fight my grandmother. But Hunter had to be punished for this.

Stepping between us, Dad forced my grandmother and me apart. While he didn't seem to disagree with my statement, he obviously didn't want me to follow through with it. Fighting was against the rules in our house, so murdering someone was definitely off the table. Maybe he'd help me kick Hunter's ass to the curb though. He shouldn't be allowed to remain in our nest. Not after this. This went way beyond losing control and biting someone. He'd practically torn her apart.

As I glared at Hunter, burning him to ash with the heat of my eyes, my sister stepped up to him and put a comforting hand on his stomach. Of course. Of course, she would side with *him*. A growl burrowed its way out of my chest as my disappointment flowed into her.

"Julian, it's not what you think," she implored, her eyes and emotions begging me to calm down.

I couldn't calm down, not knowing what Hunter had done to Raquel, how he'd brutally tortured her. Not with how he was casting her shameful, apologetic glances. With everything I had inside of me, I wished him dead. And that was when a crossbow bolt thudded into his chest.

Thinking I'd wished a weapon into existence made icy shock run through me. Understanding came next, quickly followed by fear. I hadn't magically assaulted Hunter ... we were being attacked.

Everything happened at once after that. Hunter dropped to the ground. Nika shouted his name, then dropped to her knees beside him. Halina crouched in front of them, scanning the skyline. Dad pushed me back into the shadows of the doctor's office while Mom scooped up Raquel and joined us in the darkness.

Another bolt whizzed through the air. Listening intently, Halina tilted her head, then twisted to snatch the arrow out of the sky; it would have hit my sister right in the back if Halina hadn't grabbed it. Much to Nika's relief, Hunter was still alive, but he was screaming like someone was pouring acid on top of him. I didn't understand why until Halina hissed and dropped the arrow she'd just caught. There was a familiar metallic gleam to it as it shone in the parking lot lights. Silver. The arrows were made of silver.

Dad ordered me to stay with Mom, then zoomed toward Halina and Nika. Just then, two more arrows sailed into the sky. Halina grabbed the one heading for Hunter, but missed the one heading for her. She cried out in pain when it lodged into her side. Dad shifted his attention from Nika to Halina when she fell to her knees. Nika, still struggling with a writhing Hunter, yanked the arrow out of his chest; it must have been just an inch or two away from his heart.

All of this happened in a minute, at the most.

Once the arrow was removed from Hunter's body, he stopped howling in pain. He wrapped his arms around Nika and blurred with her into a nearby patch of trees. Dad lifted Halina and jumped over the fence with her. I could tell Dad had removed Halina's arrow when her screams stopped. An eerie silence fell over the parking lot, and terror shot up my spine as I held myself as still as possible. I had no idea what to do—run to Nika, run to Dad, or stay with Mom.

A light moan at my feet reminded me that Mom and I weren't alone as we huddled near the dark corner of the building. I sank to Raquel's side, wondering what I could possibly do about her injuries, especially when I was too scared to do much more than breathe. I could feel Dad and Halina's presence moving away from me, systematically scouting the area. I could hear my sister whispering for Hunter to come back. He was scouting too. Mom's worried eyes took in everything around her, and I could tell she didn't know what to do either. It didn't help her anxiety any that Nika and I were on opposite sides of the parking lot.

I could feel Nika's fear as sharply as my own, but I wasn't sure if she was scared for herself or scared for her boyfriend. Knowing her, most of her trepidation was for him. "Nika," Mom whispered, "are you okay?"

"Yeah," she breathed back, her voice almost inaudible.

Eyes focused on the trees where Nika was hiding, Mom told her, "Stay where you are, don't try to cross the lot. We don't know how many are out there ... and we don't know where they are."

Nika murmured that she would sit tight while Raquel groaned again, a little louder than before. Brushing the hair from her face, I shushed her as quietly as I could. Now was not the time for her to wake up and start screaming. Her eyes stayed closed, but her head made slight jerking motions, like she was having a nightmare. I supposed she was ... we all were.

Knowing I was ruining any chance of getting back the deposit on my tux, I pulled off my jacket and ripped off the sleeves. As carefully as I could, I wrapped the black fabric around Raquel's bloody arms. I just couldn't stand to look at the open wounds anymore. She flinched in pain, but her eyes remained sealed shut. I wondered if she'd been drugged. Drugged, cut apart, and left out in the open. The perfect bait for a vampire.

The longer we waited, the tenser Nika became. I figured she would wait about five more minutes, and then she'd dash off after Hunter. Mom was anxious too. She didn't like us being separated, and she kept watching the trees around Nika, looking for any sign of danger. We could hear noise, scuffles that sounded like fighting, and even muffled cries of pain. Not knowing who they belonged to only amplified the anxiety.

I could tell the second Dad started heading our way, and not because of my bond with him. Mom's eyes fluttered closed, and she let out a long exhale. Dad strode into the parking lot with Halina and Hunter right behind him. He looked a little roughed up, his tuxedo jacket torn and splotched with mud, but that was about it. Of course, he healed super-fast, so any injury he might have received would have been gone by now.

Looking my way, he called out, "It's safe."

Nika had moved from her hiding place even before Dad finished speaking. She blurred to Hunter and tossed her arms around his neck. "I was so scared," she murmured, nuzzling her head in his neck.

Dad frowned at the pair, but kept walking toward Mom and me. Halina had a scowl on her face as she examined the hole in her clothes from the arrow. "I just bought this dress," she huffed. Her expression softened as she glanced down at where Mom and I were trying to comfort Raquel. "How is the child?"

I shook my head. "We need to get her to a hospital."

Halina nodded as I scooped up Raquel; she weighed next to nothing in my arms. She moaned as I held her to my chest, but she still didn't open her eyes. *What the hell did they do to you?* Looking over to where Dad was embracing Mom, I asked, "What happened? Did you ... did you get them?" I didn't really want to know if my father had just killed someone, but I needed to know if they were still out there.

Dad looked over at Hunter and Nika. "There were two of them ... but they aren't a problem anymore."

That was all I needed to know for now. Fixing my face into a mask of firmness that no one would be able to argue with, I informed my father, "Raquel needs help. I'm taking her to the ER." By my look and tone, it was clear I meant—*I'm getting her there in the fastest way possible.*

Dad grabbed my arm to stop me from blurring away. "No. Her wounds aren't life threatening. We'll go back to the high school and drive her."

My mouth fell open. "That will take forever. I could get her there in three seconds flat."

Dad's face was resolute. "We've done enough supernatural things this evening." He again looked over at Hunter; he had separated from Nika, and was watching with haunted eyes as my sister picked up the silver arrows. He had blood on his shirt, but it was gone from his mouth. Good thing, because I might have had to punch him if Raquel's blood was still on his lips. Twisting back to me, Dad said, "We do this the human way."

Jerking my arm away, I muttered, "Fine."

Dad twisted back to Halina. "We'll probably need your help. Her injuries will attract attention."

Halina gave him a curt nod, then looked over at Hunter. "Take him with you. I will clean up this mess; he will clean up that mess." My guts roiled as I considered all the possible things she meant when she said "clean up." Was she hiding dead bodies tonight?

Hunter shot her a look. "I don't think—"

Halina clenched her fists as she took a step toward him. "No, you don't think. If you did, you wouldn't have been so starved that you fell for one of the oldest traps in the book." Gritting his teeth, Hunter averted his eyes. In a firm voice, she continued. "We have two situations here that need to be addressed. I cannot be in two places at once, so you will pick up the slack and start doing your part. You're a member of this family, whether you like it or not." She brushed past him, bumping his elbow as she went.

Hunter swallowed as he looked over at Raquel's limp body in my arms. I held her tighter to me and resisted the urge to growl a warning at him. He didn't get to look at her with remorse, regret, or pity. He didn't get to look at her at all. Nika admonished me through the bond, but I didn't care. I wasn't sure what had happened tonight, but I knew it was Hunter's fault.

As Halina zipped away to take care of ... whatever mess we were leaving behind, our group started heading back to the high school. I went as fast as I could "humanly" go while carrying an unconscious woman. When we got back to the school, we avoided the gym and skimmed the shadows until we got to the parking lot. We were almost to Dad's car, when I heard someone yell, "Julian!" I turned around to see Arianna running toward me, with Trey right behind her. Damn it. In all the chaos, I'd completely forgotten that I was on a date tonight. A date that was not supposed to end this way.

Sighing, I slowed so she could catch up. She was huffing and puffing when she did, and her face was a picture of concern. I hadn't explained anything when I'd run away from her. "I've been looking everywhere for ..." Her voice trailed off as she stared down at Raquel's limp body in my arms. The flush in her cheeks instantly faded to pale white. "Oh, my God ... what's going on?"

Arianna couldn't see Raquel's wounds, not with how I'd bandaged them in my jacket sleeves. I wasn't sure what this looked like to her, but I was sure it looked bad. "She's hurt. We're taking her to the hospital." I indicated my father over my shoulder; he'd unlocked the car and was waiting for me by the open backseat door.

Turning back to my girlfriend, I grimaced and said, "I have to go ... but I'll call you later?"

Gaping at me in shock, she nodded. Wishing I could stay and explain, I turned my attention to Trey. He was staring at Hunter and Nika, and I swear he looked angry. "Trey." When he didn't respond, I kicked his leg. "Trey!" He finally looked back at me, and I tilted my head at Arianna. "Will you drive her home?"

"Sure." He nodded, then his eyes returned to my sister. Nika was rubbing Hunter's back, while his gaze remained firmly locked on the doctor's office parking lot we'd just left.

Not able to worry about any of that right now, I hurried to the car and got inside, Raquel still tight in my arms. When Dad closed the door behind me, I risked a glance at Arianna. She still looked concerned, but there was an underlying hurt there too. The one person in the world who she felt insecure around was currently cradled in my arms. Arianna knew I loved her and only her, but even still, I had to imagine seeing me hold another woman—someone I'd once cared a lot about—wasn't easy for her to process. I'd have to make it up to her as soon as I could.

Dad started the car as Mom got in the front seat. When Nika didn't get in the car with us, Dad rolled down his window. "Hunter can walk. You get in," he told her.

Reluctant to leave him, Nika clung to Hunter's side. I thought Dad was going to fling open the door and drag her into the car, but Hunter twisted her to face him. Tucking a strand of hair behind her ear, he said, "I'll meet you there."

Nika raised her chin, defiance in her eyes. "You promise you're not going to run away on me?"

Hunter let out a sad exhale, then rested his head against hers. "Yes, I promise. I have a job to do."

My sister seemed satisfied with that, and finally hurried around to get inside the car. I wanted to smack her for taking her sweet time, but I was too concerned about the bleeding girl in my arms, and snapped at Dad instead. "Can we go now? Please?"

Dad stepped on the gas and shot out of the lot, and I finally felt a bit of relief. We were finally getting Raquel some much needed care. That was probably the only good thing to come out of tonight's multiple debacles.

True to his word, Hunter arrived at the hospital almost at the same time we did. He was swiftly walking across the parking lot when Dad stopped the car in front of the emergency room doors. Nika immediately hopped out and rushed over to him. She hugged Hunter like she hadn't seen him in days, and her mood overflowed with relief that he was there. It made me nauseous. We were only *here* because of him.

Dad opened my door so I could get out. A nurse standing near the door noticed our arrival, and immediately came our way. "What happened?" she asked our group.

Hunter inhaled a deep breath. Walking up to the nurse, he calmly said, "Don't ask any more questions, don't take down any information. Just ... fix her."

The nurse gave him a blank look, then turned to me. "Bring her inside."

I'd seen my grandmother trance people, I'd even seen her wipe minds—my best friend Trey included, but I'd never seen Hunter do it. From the surprised look on his face, I didn't think he'd ever done it before. Motioning with his hand, he indicated for me to follow the nurse through the sliding doors. I glared at him as I passed. I wasn't two years old ... I could follow directions without guidance. Especially his.

Nika's irritation spiked in response to my prickly mood, but I didn't care about what she thought right now. Bypassing everyone waiting, the nurse strode us right past the registration desk, and through the doors that led to the exam rooms. A few people looked our way, but nobody stopped us. And it wouldn't have mattered if they had. We had our own personal Simon Says leader. Everyone in here was or could be under Hunter's control. And that did not sit well with me.

Stepping around a privacy curtain, I placed Raquel on the fresh white sheet covering the bed; it smelled like antiseptic in here, and it stung my sensitive sinuses. Raquel's normally tanned cheeks looked pale to me, even more so against the stark fabric. "Her arms are pretty cut up. She probably lost a lot of blood. And I think she's been drugged."

The nurse peeled off the strips of my jacket that I'd wrapped around her arms. She didn't say anything, didn't ask any questions about the slashes on Raquel's arms. The smell of blood thickened in the room as her wounds were exposed. Hunter groaned, then turned away.

"If you can't handle it, why don't you leave?" I quipped.

Nika slugged me in the shoulder, which Mom reprimanded her for. Standing tall, Hunter twisted back to where the nurse was cleaning the blood away. "I can handle this," he stated.

Under my breath, I muttered, "If that were true, we wouldn't be here."

Nika slugged me again, and this time Dad pulled her away from me. "He didn't have anything to do with this, Julian. We found her cut up like that," Nika told me.

Tired of getting smacked, I turned to face Nika. "So, he didn't cut her. But he drank from her, right?" Leaning around my sister, I hissed at Hunter, "How close did you get to killing her?"

A low growl echoed around the room as Hunter took a step toward me. Even though he looked weary enough to drop at any moment, he was an intimidating sight with his fangs fully extended and fiery heat in his eyes. He was also taller, older, and more muscular; I suddenly felt about ten years old standing next to him. Reflexively, I took a step back. His expression cautious, Dad stepped in front of me while Nika stepped in front of Hunter. I shot Nika a cool glance. We'd always been on the same side before, a united front. But now that Hunter was in the picture ... Was this how we were going to be from now on?

Perhaps feeling the tension in the room, the nurse tending to Raquel looked up. Her eyes widened and her mouth dropped when she saw Hunter's fangs. He immediately noticed the nurse's reaction and said, "Don't scream."

She closed her mouth, but she still looked terrified. Pulling his fangs up, Hunter sheepishly told her, "You didn't see any of that. You didn't hear any of that. Just keep working on her."

Dad put a hand on my chest and lightly pushed me back. "I'll think we'll wait outside." Hunter nodded, and, grabbing my bicep, Dad started pulling me away. I resisted at first, but Dad eventually won the battle. At the door, he stopped, turned, and walked back to grab Nika's arm. She squeaked as he pulled her toward the door too. "I think we'll *all* wait outside."

A satisfied smile finally stretched across my lips. Feeling my vindication, Nika looked like she wanted to go all Mom-zilla on me again. Since I was in a bit of a mood too, I welcomed it. Mom followed us out into the hallway. Mom and Dad glanced at each other, and some silent conversation passed between them. Nodding, Mom said, "I'll take the kids home. You stay here with Hunter and the girl."

Dad sighed, then leaned over and gave her a soft kiss. Cupping her cheek, he whispered, "I love you," in Russian.

Mom melted as she smiled up at him. "I'm so glad they didn't hurt you," she told him.

Her words reminded me just what had happened tonight. Some of my anger faded as I watched my parents. I couldn't imagine losing either of them. I couldn't imagine losing anyone in my family. And it could have happened tonight. Because of Hunter, it could have happened. My anger instantly returned.

After a few more tender words and kisses, my parents finally separated. Nika instantly started objecting as Mom pushed us toward the exit. I joined her. "I need to stay, Mom. I can't leave until I know Raquel's all right."

"Your father will make sure she's fine," she answered, her hands firmly on our backs.

I looked over my shoulder at Mom; the white gloves up her arms were smeared with blood now. "What if she wakes up? She'll panic, and she'll be with strangers." I started turning away. "She needs me."

Mom adjusted my position. "Hunter will calm her down."

When we got to the doors, Nika shook her head. "Hunter can't handle this yet. He needs me there for support."

I twisted my head to her. "How are you going to support him? Slap his wrist when he starts biting the nurses?"

"He's not going to—"

Mom pushed us both forward, cutting off Nika's objection. "Enough! Your father will keep Hunter in line, and Hunter will calm Raquel. The two of them can handle this. The two of you being there will only make it worse."

There was an awkward silence in the car on the drive home. Nika was irritated, I was irritated, even Mom seemed upset. I picked up one of the bloody arrows that Nika had tossed on the floor in the back. I hoped Raquel was okay. How the heck was Hunter going to explain away her injuries? He had to tell Raquel something. Her parents would have to be told something as well. I hated leaving without knowing those answers. I felt like I didn't have any answers about what had happened tonight. Just questions. And disappointment. And anger. Tonight just royally sucked.

I stormed to my room the minute we got home. I didn't want to talk to Mom or Nika. I wanted to talk to Raquel or Arianna. Pulling my phone from my jacket pocket, I debated calling Arianna. What would I say? How could I make up for this disastrous evening?

Sighing, I put the phone on my dresser and laid down on my bed. My head was spinning, and if I talked to her now, I'd probably screw up and say something stupid. No, I would wait, talk to her tomorrow. Maybe, by then, some of my anger would have faded away.

CHAPTER ELEVEN

Nika

WHILE I FELT my brother fuming next door, I paced my bedroom. We were feeling the same edgy, antsy emotion, just for entirely different reasons. Julian wanted to know if Raquel was okay, I wanted to know if Hunter was okay, but both of us were stuck here with no answers. It was beyond frustrating.

Julian was also angry because of Hunter. I understood why, but it was still aggravating. Hunter wasn't to blame for what happened tonight. It wasn't his fault that Raquel had been hurt and used as bait. He couldn't have controlled that any more than we could have controlled it. Julian needed to back off.

I thought about sitting down and trying to have a serious, grown-up conversation with Julian about Hunter. That was what Dad would have done. But Julian's mood made it difficult to approach him. I just didn't want to deal with him right now. Walking into our mutual bathroom, I closed the door on his side. I didn't feel like looking at him right now either.

His bad mood surged higher. As I washed my face, I couldn't help but think about how excited and nervous Julian had been for tonight. My frustration and annoyance slipped some as I patted my skin dry. Julian had been hoping to share something truly intimate with Arianna, and instead he'd carried an unconscious woman to the hospital.

After I was finished, I whispered, "I'm sorry." As I left the bathroom and closed the door on my side, he sighed in answer, but his mood calmed.

Quickly changing my clothes, I crawled into bed. Sleep was impossible, and I stared up at my ceiling, waiting. Dad had to come home eventually, and when he did, I'd be able to find out if Hunter was okay. If Raquel was okay.

When I opened my eyes some time later, I hadn't even realized I'd closed them. Everything was dark and silent, and I knew before I looked at the clock that it was the middle of the night. Dad's presence was safely tucked in his room. Sitting up, I silently cursed. Damn it. I'd fallen asleep and missed my chance to interrogate my father.

Since I was up, I took a half-second to locate the others. Halina was still in the city, but nowhere near the house. Hunter though …

My head snapped to the window just as a pair of legs walked in front of the ledge, and a body ducked down in front of the glass. My eyes widened at seeing the low glow of Hunter's eyes staring at me through the windowpane. Tossing my blankets aside, I rushed to open the window and let him in.

He looked awful as he stepped into my room. He still had the weariness of someone who was moments away from dropping of exhaustion, but now, on top of that, he was wearing the expression of someone who was on the verge of an emotional collapse. Even before he spoke, I knew Hunter was at a breaking point.

"Nika," he said again, his voice cracking. "I can't …"

His hand came up to cover his mouth, and he stopped talking. Not knowing what else to do for him, I led him to the bed and urged him to sit down. When he did, he leaned over his knees and dropped his head into his hands. Reaching my hand under his jacket, I rubbed small circles over the T-shirt chilled by the coolness of his skin.

"What's wrong?" I whispered. Without including what had happened tonight, there could have been a half-dozen things bothering him.

Hunter shook his head in his hands. "I … I knew those men …" When he looked up at me, his eyes were ringed in red. "The hunters … the ones who shot Halina … and me. I knew them." He swallowed a knot in his throat before he continued. "My father worked with them all the time. Brett, I didn't know very well, but Sam was like a second father to my sister and me ... and he tried to kill me."

Hunter stared at the ground while I said the only thing I could think to say. "I'm so sorry."

"I'd known Sam my entire life, and he didn't even give me a chance. He said I was an abomination, a monster ... evil. He said for the safety of humanity, I needed to die." Pressing his lips together in a firm line, Hunter returned his eyes to mine. "And the weird thing is, up until he said it, I agreed with him. But ... the way he looked at me ... he just assumed I'd been out slaughtering people. And I have tried *so* hard." The words caught in his throat, and he had to stop speaking. When he continued, his voice was shaking. "I have done everything in my power to not hurt anyone, to not hurt any*thing*. I've gone weeks at a time without blood. I'm so hungry, sometimes I can't even see straight. And I'm so tired. I feel like every move I make takes *so* much effort. I've been trying so hard to remain who I was before ... and it didn't even matter to Sam. I had to die simply because of what I was. What I'd done, or hadn't done, didn't matter to him."

I didn't know what to say to that. This had been a point of contention in Hunter's and my relationship. He couldn't see past the species, to the person beneath it. In silent support, I grabbed his hand and squeezed it.

Hunter's eyes softened as he watched me. "I understand now how wrong I've been about your kind. About ... *our* ... kind. And I think that hurts more than anything else."

I scrunched my brows. "What do you mean?"

Hunter's gaze returned to the floor. "I was the same as Sam. I killed vampires without hesitation, simply because they *were* vampires." He looked back up at me, pain in his eyes. "How many did I kill that didn't deserve to die? How many strangers did I pass judgment on? I have so much blood on my hands, Nika ... How could you ever love someone like me?"

My free hand went up to cup his stubbled, exhausted cheek. "How could I *not* love you?"

Hunter's forehead compressed with tension. "I killed him. Sam, the man who was as much a father to me as my own, I'm the one who ended his life." He lifted a brow. "Still love me?"

I knew he was goading me, trying to lead me into some sort of admission that he was a bad person. I didn't respond to his question. Instead, I asked my own. "What happened tonight?"

Hunter ran a hand down his face. When his fingers brushed over mine on his cheek, he paused his hand. Our temperatures were opposite—fire and ice—but somehow it was a complementary difference. We soothed each other.

When Hunter was ready, he opened up about his traumatic evening. His low voice rumbled around the room. "Halina, Teren, and I ... we hunted them. I've hunted vampires before, but that was the first time I'd ever hunted a human. It ... appealed to something in me. It excited me ... and disgusted me. I didn't know what we were going to do once we found them, but it was never my intention to kill them." He looked over at me, his eyes begging for understanding and forgiveness. "I swear."

I nodded, encouraging him to continue. He stroked the back of my hand with his thumb, then pulled our hands into his lap. "Halina and Teren took off one way, I went the other. I smelled Sam first, then I heard his heartbeat. It was pumping so fast, like he knew I was coming for him. You get one chance to surprise a vampire, and he'd blown his. He missed my heart." Shaking his head, he peeked up at me. "Missing is a death sentence in our line of work." He frowned. "In my old line of work."

I gave him a sad smile, and his eyes got a faraway look. "Sam didn't hear me coming. He was prepping for one last shot." His gaze refocused on me. "He'd spotted where you were hiding in the trees. He was going to shoot you. I acted before I even realized who he was ..."

My eyes widened. I hadn't realized I'd been that close to being shot again. Absentmindedly, I pulled a hand away and scratched the scar on my shoulder that suddenly itched. Hunter's eyes followed my fingers as he continued his confession. "I yanked him backward. He recovered fast, trained the crossbow on me, but I was faster. I grabbed it before he could fire ... I turned it on him." His eyes met mine again. "That was when I recognized him."

Hunter's hand in mine hardened into a fist. "I asked him what he was doing—why he was here. He told me I was a monster, and I needed to be put down. He said he was just doing his job." Hunter's eyes reddened. "I was going to let him go. I was going to wipe his mind and send him on his way. I even lowered the bow." Hunter sniffed back the emotions swirling within him. "Then he told me that ... my father sent him here."

Hunter's jaw trembled. His obvious pain made my eyes water in sympathy. "My father sent him to kill me. He couldn't stomach doing it himself ... so he sent his friend to finish me off." He turned his head and ceaselessly scanned my room like every object he looked at burned his eyes if he stared at it for too long.

I could feel him hovering on the precipice of falling apart, and I wrapped my arms around his shoulders. "I'm so sorry, Hunter." I couldn't even imagine the pain of having your own family wanting you dead.

Hunter sniffed again, and I heard a thick, tension-filled knot travel down his throat. "He tried to kill me. My dad tried to kill me. I was so ... I couldn't deal. I was stunned stupid. That was when Sam threw a knife at me. I barely caught it in time. I didn't catch the second one. He got me in the side, and I fell to my knees. The knife was silver, like the arrows ... it felt like acid ripping my insides apart, but I couldn't pull it out because he lunged at me. He tackled me, driving the knife in deeper. Then he pulled the first knife out of my hand. He was going to jam it in my chest. I didn't have a choice. I still had the crossbow. I raised it, shot him in the gut. And when he fell back, I pulled the knife out of my side and staked him in the heart with it ... like he was the monster." He dropped his head into his hands. "Jesus, Nika ... what did I do?"

As tears flowed down my cheeks, I squeezed him as tightly as I could. "You defended yourself. You defended me. You didn't do anything wrong."

Hunter nodded but didn't lift his head from his hands. Long minutes passed before he looked up at me. When he did, his eyes were clearer, but his pain was still evident. "Can I stay with you tonight?" he whispered. "I just ... want to be near you."

I looked outside, to where I could sense Halina's presence. She'd come closer, but she was staying a respectful distance away. "What about Grandma?" There was a hint of jealousy in my tone. I hated that it was there, but there was no denying the connection between Halina and Hunter. She would always have something with him that I couldn't have.

Hunter's cold fingers came up to touch my chin, retuning my eyes to his. "I'm drawn to her because of the bond, but she's not the one who gives me peace."

The jealousy immediately faded as I stared into his dark eyes. A different emotion surged through me, and the bed we were sitting on suddenly felt like red-hot cinders smoldering under my body. "Yes, you can stay." I knew no one else could hear me, but I still barely breathed the words.

I pulled back the covers while Hunter took off his shoes and jacket. Looking at his clothes, he whispered, "I'm filthy."

I knew there was no way I could sleep beside him if he was half-naked, so I ducked into my brother's room and rifled through his clothes to find a shirt and some sweats. Julian was tangled in his sheets, blissfully snoring away. I prayed he stayed that way for a while. I gave the clothes to Hunter when I popped back into my room. As I slipped into bed, I heard him undressing. It took everything in me to not turn and watch.

"Do the clothes fit okay?" My voice came out tight, and I cleared my throat.

"Yeah. A little small, but they'll work for now." The mattress compressed beside me, and my heart started racing. "Thank you for doing this," he said as he rested a cool hand on my hip.

I let out a low exhale before turning to face him; my heart was thudding against my ribcage. God, why couldn't I slow the stupid thing down? "I would do anything for you. You know that, don't you?" I slid closer so that our bodies were only an inch apart. I could almost feel the chill radiating from him. Timidly, I put a hand on his chest.

In the darkness of my bed, Hunter's glowing eyes unblinkingly stared at me as we faced each other. My heart finally started to slow as his gaze lulled me into peace. Even though he couldn't compel me, I would do anything he asked of me. Hunter broke the connection by looking down. "I know. I don't know why ... but I know."

Closing the distance between our bodies, I curled my leg around his and buried my head in his shoulder. "Because I love you, that's why."

He exhaled in contentment as my heat seeped into him. His hand on my hip ran up my back, and he kissed my hair as he pulled me against him. "I ... I love you too. I'm going to be better. I'm going to be stronger, healthier. I don't know how I'm going to stomach eating, but I will *never* let hunger get the best of me again. I will never attack a human again." His voice was strong with conviction and determination.

I smiled into his skin as I kissed his neck. "I'll help you ... if you'll let me." I pulled back to look at him. "Will you let me?"

His hypnotizing eyes drank me in for a minute, then he nodded, and lowered his lips to mine. Our kiss was slow and easy for several minutes. It felt completely natural to have him in my bed with me, like this was where he belonged. When I ran my hand up his back, he rumbled, "Your heat ... is so incredible."

Pushing him to his back, I laid my body down on top of his, giving him as much of my heat as possible. A shiver ran through me, but I didn't care. Returning my lips to his, I murmured, "Is that why you like me? Because I'm warm?"

He laughed, and my heart nearly tore open. It had been forever since I'd heard him laugh. His arms wrapped around my torso. "Yes, that's exactly why." He sighed between our tender kisses. "But your warmth has nothing to do with your temperature."

I pulled back to stare down at him. There was love in his eyes, and desire. As our bodies laid flush together, I felt that desire in other places on him. It grew in me too. I tried to be rational, to remember that he was going through a lot of changes, and advancing our relationship now probably wasn't the best idea, but it was hard to hold onto that logic when he was staring at me with those tranquil but burning eyes. Especially when I also knew that everyone in the house was either asleep, or behind soundproof doors.

Wondering what he was ready for, I experimentally rocked my hips against his. He sucked in a breath while I contained a groan; he felt so good beneath me. This was right. I knew it was.

I pressed my hips against him again, harder. I couldn't contain my groan that time. Hunter either. But instead of ravishing me, his hands slid down to my hips, and he shifted me off him. "Stop, Nika. That's not why I came here."

Bringing one leg back to curl around his, I sighed in disappointment. Hunter smiled and tucked a strand of hair behind my ear. "I just don't have the energy for that yet." The humor in his eyes shifted to seriousness. "And you're still too young."

I shook my head at him. "You're seriously still going to turn me away because of my age?" Smiling, I added, "See, becoming a vampire hasn't changed you at all."

He laughed again. "Maybe. I just ... I'm not ready to go there yet." He lifted an eyebrow. "Let me get past the fact that your heartbeat is driving me insane first, before we start in on your body, okay?"

I smirked at him, then cuddled into his side, content with snuggling. For now. As sleep drifted over me, I mumbled, "I'm sorry your father did that to you, Hunter."

I thought I heard him say, "Thank you," before I succumbed to the darkness.

Hunter

I WASN'T SURE how I'd ended up here, in Nika's bed. I could tell from her stillness and the light, gentle thudding of her heartbeat that she was sleeping. I should leave, let her get her rest. But her body was so warm tangled with mine, and I couldn't quite make myself move. For the first time in a long time, I felt at peace, and I didn't know how much longer that feeling was going to last. It was certainly a far cry from earlier in the evening.

Smiling, I kissed her hair and remembered the heated look in her eyes when our quiet moment had turned toward the intimate side. Lately, that always seemed to happen around her. Turning away from her body was almost as hard as turning away from her blood. I didn't know if she was doing it intentionally, but she was driving me absolutely crazy, in several different ways. Between her heart, her blood, and her body, I swear I was slowly being torn apart with all the various ways I wanted her. But she was healing me too. I wanted to be a better man for her, a man who didn't attack unconscious teenage girls. Not my finest hour.

Sighing, I shifted my eyes to the ceiling. Tonight had been an absolute disaster. Nothing about this evening should have happened. I should have stayed at the ranch with Halina and the others. That had been my plan when I'd woken up. I'd had no desire to leave the nest. But Nika had been on my mind all night ... Nika and that damn red dress. All I'd been able to think about was her looking so incredible for another man. It had boiled my blood ... driven me crazy. I'd made up some excuse about needing fresh air, then I'd run off toward town. Halina had followed me, of course, and she hadn't seemed surprised when I'd eventually wound up at the high school. She'd just been curious. I think Halina wanted me to connect with Nika. Because if I could connect with Nika, then maybe I'd fight to live. Did I want to live?

That troubling question reverberated around my brain, giving me a headache with its intensity. I wasn't sure anymore. Something had changed inside of me tonight; I just couldn't put my finger on what it was yet. There was something brewing, though, something I wanted to hold onto, but ... it was bothering me too.

My mind swirling with chaos, I gently removed myself from Nika's arms. Before I could figure out what we were, if we were even anything, I needed to sort out my own shit.

Standing, I looked back at Nika alone in her bed. Even though my temperature was much cooler than hers, she shivered without me underneath her. I wrapped the blanket more tightly around her, hoping she was warm enough. She smiled in her sleep, and I wondered if she was dreaming of me. Marveling at her beauty, I tucked a strand of hair behind her ear.

She had stopped me from killing that girl tonight, I was positive of that. I'd gone over the edge, let the monster inside completely take over. I hadn't been thinking. I'd caved to instinct and desire, and once I'd tasted her blood, I'd had no intention of stopping myself from drinking it all ... every last drop. The thought of what I'd done, what I'd taken into my body, still made my stomach clench, made me want to heave. But it could have been so much worse. And Nika was the reason it hadn't gone that way.

She'd tried to knock some sense into me, tried to tame the beast, but the beast had almost turned on her. No, the beast *had* turned on her. I'd turned on her. I'd tried to attack the love of my life. I wasn't okay with that, and I knew I needed to change.

As much as the thought of blood repulsed me, I couldn't keep denying myself. I was no good to anyone like this—weak and starving. I'd foolishly told Nika that I didn't need her to save me, but that was a lie—possibly the biggest one I'd ever told her. I did need her. I couldn't do this without her. I needed to be healthy, and I needed her help to get me there.

And when I was healthy, and Gabriel freed me ... then I would leave her.

That thought chilled me to the bone, almost brought me to my knees, and I turned away from Nika, no longer able to look at her. Was I still leaving? If I could somehow stomach eating the only food source left to me, could I stay? Could Nika and I be together? I'd told her no so often, I wasn't sure if I could even see another scenario in front of me ... a happy scenario, where we worked out, where we rode off into the proverbial sunset together. All I saw in my future was bleakness and death, and this one nagging idea in the back of my head that was screaming at me to pay attention to it.

My dead heart squeezed, and I risked a glance at Nika's sleeping form. Staying with her sounded so nice. But ... no ... didn't she deserve better? Someone ... alive? Like that boy who'd almost kissed her tonight. Surely, he could give her things I couldn't. She wouldn't have sunlight with me, or children, or normal friendships, or a future. She'd be as far away from a normal life as she could get. On the flip side, if she took Gabriel's shot, she could live and die a normal, human life.

But with me ... nothing would be normal. And I wouldn't let her throw away a chance at humanity. Not for me.

Sighing, I removed Julian's clothes that she'd let me borrow. I was fooling myself by thinking there was a future here with her. Best to end it now, while we still could. Before we stupidly crossed that last line of intimacy. Before we made love. Because I was positive I wouldn't be able to walk away if we ever went there. And I needed to let her go. As soon as I was strong enough, I *would* let her go.

After I slipped on my dirty clothes from last night, I folded Julian's into a neat pile. My dad had drilled cleanliness into me from an early age. He'd always told me it was easier to take off at a moment's notice, if you knew exactly where everything was. That advice had always stuck with me. Thinking of my father instantly brought Sam to mind. The confrontation with him was almost too fresh to think about. I'd already purged the pain by talking about it with Nika, but the wound of betrayal was still inside me, still dripping with fresh blood. How could my father send him?

Shaking off the dark memory, I wrote Nika a quick thank you note, and left it on the pile of Julian's clothes. Then I walked over to her window and put my hands upon the ledge. I peered out into the dark night as Sam's voice echoed in my ear: *I don't want to do this, but you know I don't have a choice.* My fingers curled around the wood, and a section of the ledge cracked under the pressure. Sam's next words swirled around my head. *Your father sent me ... asked me to finish you off, since he couldn't.*

My father had tried to kill me. And he would try again. And again. And again. He would try to kill me, and every vampire around me. So long as I stayed here, they were all in danger. I had to leave to protect them. But no, not just to protect them. To avenge them—them and myself.

That thought awakened me to a truth that had been buzzing in my brain. A truth I'd been avoiding dealing with. Straightening, a new resolve filled me, a resolve born from duty. It burned away every doubt in my head, every disgust in my body. I *had* to embrace this life, I *had* to drink, and I *had* to become as strong as I possibly could. Because ... I *had* to kill my father. That was what I'd been avoiding, that was what had been burrowing inside my brain ever since Sam's confession. I knew my dad. I knew how he worked, how he thought. There was no way my father and I could occupy this planet at the same time; he wouldn't allow it. He wouldn't stop sending hunters after me. And I wouldn't allow him to harm Nika. Or her family.

The only way I could keep Nika safe, keep Halina safe, keep them *all* safe, was by hunting Dad first. In this battle of father versus son, I had no choice but to be the victor.

As new determination filled me, I looked back at Nika one last time. Fortifying my mind, I drew in all the peace and comfort she'd given me, all the love she'd shown me. I had a feeling there would be dark times ahead—times when I would need the reminder of what I'd once had. After filling myself with her serenity, I turned back to the window and opened it. I stepped through, closed the glass behind me, then easily landed on the lawn several feet below me. Halina met me a few seconds later. Looking up at her granddaughter's window, she asked, "Do you feel ... better?"

I glanced up at the dark window, then looked back at her. "Much better." A smile lit my face as the words left my lips. I was telling the truth. I did feel better. I had purpose now. I had a goal, a mission, something to live for. Halina had used hatred to get her through her conversion. I would use justice. Putting my hand on her arm, I told her, "It's going to be light soon, we should go home."

A bright smile exploded over her face at hearing me call the ranch home. Before anything could happen that would change my mind, I quickly added, "I want you to know, I'm going to eat. Nika is going to help me. And if it's all right with you ... it would be easier for me if it were just the two of us."

You would think I'd just given Halina the gift she'd been waiting for her entire life. Nodding, she tossed her arms around me. "Yes, whatever you need, Hunter. Whatever you need to get through this is fine. You don't know how happy you've made me."

As I wrapped my arms around the tiny woman embracing me, contentment again overwhelmed me. Safety. Home. Solace. Love. Instead of pushing the feelings away, I welcomed them. Maybe they had been manufactured emotions in the beginning, but they were genuine now. These people were important to me, and I would fight with every cell in my body to keep them safe. I would clean up this mess I'd made. That was what my father had always told me anyway—*Clean up your own mess. It's good for the soul.*

Before Halina and I streaked away, I looked back at Nika's dark room where I knew she was peacefully resting. My new path in life was sort of a double-edged sword when it came to Nika. I was going to enjoy spending time with her while Gabriel worked on breaking the bond, but I was going to miss her even more when I left. It was for the best though. I expected the showdown with my father to be a bloody one, and regardless if I won or lost, I wasn't planning on walking away from it. If my life didn't end at the hands of my father, I would continue with my original plan and find someone to finish me off. Either way, once my mission was over ... so was I.

Because what I couldn't deny was the fact that I was a monster. To protect those I loved, I would embrace the horror within me, but only for a short time. I had no intention of living like this forever.

CHAPTER TWELVE

Nika

WHEN I WOKE the next morning, I had a miniature heart attack. My first thought was *My parents are going to walk in and see me with a boy in my bed and ground me for the rest of my life!* My second thought was *Oh God, it's morning. Hunter fell asleep and is now a pile of ash beside me!* Much to my relief, though, neither of those things had happened. My bed was empty, but clean. Hunter's dirty clothes were gone, and my brother's clothes had been neatly folded into a pile on my dresser. A note on top of them said *Thank you for last night*. I wanted to kiss that note.

As I clutched the paper to my chest, an irritated grunt nearby reminded me that not everyone had had a great night last night. I was assuming, since Julian had been alone when I'd walked in and borrowed his clothes, that he hadn't had any late-night visitors. His big night had completely fallen apart ... because of Hunter.

When I heard Julian stumble and curse, and I felt a jolt of pain running through him, I asked, "You okay?"

"Peachy," he responded, sounding anything but.

Feeling bad for him, I walked through our bathroom and knocked on his door. "Come on in, I'm dressed," he sighed.

He was sitting on his bed, massaging his foot when I entered. He glared at the edge of his dresser, like it had purposefully reached out and attacked him. I hid my smile, but I couldn't hide my buoyant heart. "Why are you so cheery? Last night was a disaster," he said.

I nodded as I sat beside him. "I know. Are you sure you're okay?"

He started to answer me, but then his eyes slipped down to the note in my fingers. "What's that?"

I'd forgotten I was still carrying Hunter's message. I tried to hide it by folding it, but Julian snatched it from my hand. "Thank you for last night? What happened last night?"

His pale eyes snapped to mine, and irritation flowed into me through our bond. Feeling my parents still safely tucked in their soundproof room, I told him the vaguest form of the truth that I could. "Nothing," I said, taking the note back. Okay, maybe calling that the truth was a stretch.

Julian's face agreed with my silent omission. His lips curled in disbelief. "He came to the house, didn't he?"

I shrugged one shoulder. "For a little bit."

Shaking his head, Julian looked away from me. His gaze snapped back to mine as curiosity spiked in him. "What did he say about Raquel? Is she okay? Did she wake up? What did he tell her? What did he tell the hospital? What did he tell her parents? Is she still at the hospital, or did she go home?" His questions came out like shotgun blasts, powerful and insistent, and with no space between them for an answer.

All I could do was shake my head. When he finally paused, I blurted, "I don't know. I didn't ask." I instantly felt bad that I hadn't. I should have. In a quieter voice, I added, "It never came up."

Floored, Julian gaped at me. "It never came up? Our friend was sliced, diced, and left as bait, and how she was doing ... never came up?"

I wanted to say something about calling Raquel our "friend," which was a stretch at best, but I knew that wasn't the point of his question, so I didn't comment on his choice of words. Julian glanced at the note in my fingers. "What *did* come up?" His eyes widening, he leaned past me to look into my bedroom. "Oh my God!" His eyes returned to mine. "Did you sleep with him?"

"No!" In a quieter voice, I added, "Not really."

Julian's face contorted in confusion. "What does that mean? Or maybe I don't want to know." His face shifted to stare in front of him. "Thank God I was asleep."

I considered smacking his arm, but resisted. Trying to rein in my embarrassment, I told him, "Hunter spent the night, but we didn't do anything. He was having a hard time. He needed me ... for comfort."

Julian looked back at me, and I felt the turmoil within him. Hunter wasn't his favorite person, but he understood how I felt about him. Putting my hand on his forearm, I told him, "You can't hate him for what happened with Raquel. The fact that she was laid out as bait wasn't his fault."

Julian sighed and stared down at his injured foot. His tumbling emotions shifted into a frustrated form of resignation. "Why him, Nick? Why did you have to fall for *him*?"

I sympathetically rubbed his back. "Trust me, sometimes I wish I hadn't fallen for him either."

The door to Mom and Dad's room cracked open, and Julian immediately sprang off his bed. Blurring to his door, he looked down the hall. Skipping morning pleasantries, he asked, "How is she?"

I felt Dad walking toward us, heard his deep sigh. "She's fine. The wounds, while messy, weren't overly dangerous. She was cleaned, treated, and the sedative was flushed out of her body. When she woke up enough to realize what was going on, I called her parents. They took her home."

Julian hung his head as Dad appeared in the doorway. Putting a hand on his shoulder, Dad told him, "She's okay, and she doesn't remember what really happened to her."

Standing, I walked toward them. "What does she remember?"

Edging past Julian, I stood in the hallway across from Dad. His eyes scanned my face and then Julian's. He looked reluctant to tell us. I didn't take that as a good sign. "You need to keep in mind that while we can hide her memories, we can't hide what was done to her. We can't hide her injuries. We had to come up with something believable ... so ..."

Julian's head snapped up. "What does she think happened?"

Mom stepped into Dad's side. Her long brown hair was pulled into a ponytail that bobbed around her shoulders when she shook her head. "She was told that she made the cuts herself. That a staff member at the school found her passed out in a hallway, and rushed her to the hospital."

Julian's emotions dropped to the floor, as did his jaw. "You told her *she* made the cuts? She's going to think ... It's going to get around school that she ... Why would you do that to her?"

Dad shared a look with Mom before returning his eyes to Julian's. "It was the only way, Julian. If we told her someone else did it, everyone would be looking for the attacker. A young, pretty girl getting sliced up at a high school dance would draw national attention. We can't risk that. Especially since ... *we* took care of the attackers. No one can know that she didn't do this to herself. Do you understand me?"

Julian clenched his jaw; he was furious. "Yes," he seethed.

Dad put both hands on his shoulders and ducked down to look him in the eye. "Do you understand?" he repeated.

Julian's eyes flashed up to his. "I said yes."

Dad released him, then squeezed him in a tight hug. "I'm sorry. I wish it could be another way. I really do."

Sniffing, Julian looked away from him. A well of sadness burst through him, and I reached for his hand. He pulled away from me, and from Dad. "I need to go for a walk. That okay?"

Dad nodded, and Julian stepped back into his bedroom. He slammed the door, and we all flinched. Sighing, Dad looked at the floor. The guilt on his face was crystal clear. He hated what he'd done to Raquel, what he'd made her believe she'd done to herself, but he was right, there was no other choice. Julian would understand that, eventually.

After Julian left the house, my cell phone rang. It was Arianna. "What happened to Raquel? Is she okay? What is she going to tell people? How did Julian find her? How did he even know to look for her?"

I wanted to tell Arianna the truth, but I wasn't sure how much it would freak her out. I mean, a vampire slayer sent by Hunter's father to kill him snatched Raquel from the dance, drugged her, then sliced her open as bait, wasn't exactly the most comforting thing to hear. And while Arianna had fully accepted Julian, she was still a little freaked out about our world. I didn't want to push her over the edge. I also didn't want to make her lie to everyone, so, I made a hard choice, and decided to lie to my best friend, for her own sake.

"Raquel cut herself. A custodian found her passed out in a hallway. He ran into Julian, and asked him for help getting her to the hospital. When

Julian saw her, well, you know how he is about helping people." I bit my lip, hoping she bought my jumble of half-truths.

After a silent moment, Arianna whispered, "I know how he is about helping Raquel ..." I tried to say something to that, but there was nothing to say. She kind of had a point. "Is Julian there? I'd like to talk to him."

"No, you'll have to call his cell ... He took off a little bit ago."

"Okay." Her voice was quiet in my ear. "Hey, can I talk to you about something?"

"Of course," I instantly told her. "I'm always here for you."

"Well, it's about your brother ... and, you know ... and I don't know if you want to hear about that."

Knowing she meant sex made me cringe. No I didn't want to hear about that, but Arianna was my friend, and I'd always known there would be certain sacrifices I'd have to make when she started dating Julian. "It's okay, go ahead."

I listened for my parents. They were downstairs, having a conversation about last night. They seemed pretty absorbed in each other, so I didn't think they were listening, but certain sentences might get their attention.

"Julian and I were going to ... do stuff last night, but after everything that happened, that plan sort of fizzled."

I let out a short exhale. "Oh ... I'm sorry ... that didn't work out."

"Yeah ... me too. But ... we had a really weird conversation about it at the dance. With your grandmother and your parents."

I sat up straighter from my lounging position on the bed. "What? Why would you guys discuss it in front of my family?"

Arianna sighed. "I have no idea. It was right after you left. Julian just out of the blue asked your dad why we shouldn't have sex. It was ... beyond mortifying." I wanted to slap my hand over my eyes. Oh God, he'd done that for me, so I could have a few minutes alone with Hunter. Damn it. I owed him big time. Arianna continued while I wondered how I could possibly repay him. "And as if that wasn't weird enough, your grandmother said ..." she stopped to sigh, "well, she basically said she wanted us to have kids as soon as possible. Kids! Why the hell would she say that?"

I was suddenly very uncomfortable. I tried fidgeting into a new position, but it wasn't helping. How in the world could I explain this to her?

"Umm ... Grandma's got a thing for children, but it's not like she's going to force you to—"

I knew the second the words left my lips that it was the wrong thing to say. "Oh my God, could she force me? Could she do that hypno thing and make me have kids? That's so ... wrong."

"No, no," I quickly said. "She would *never* do that. Ever. I promise. If you do or if you don't, it will be *your* choice."

"Good ... because I'm only sixteen, Nika. I don't even know if I want kids. That's something I'll figure out in the next decade or so, but I don't want to be pressured in the meantime. I just want ... to be sixteen."

"That's what Julian wants too. All he cares about right now is being with you, Arianna. You mean everything to him." I poured as much sincerity into that as I could. Even if Julian was driving me crazy lately, I wanted him to be with Arianna. They were a good couple, and I could see them having a really great future together. If my brother didn't completely mess it up, of course.

Arianna sighed at my statement, then shifted the conversation toward how I was doing. I told her what I could, which wasn't nearly enough. I wished I could have taken my phone into my parents' bedroom so I could tell her everything, but I couldn't, so instead I was vague with my best friend. I hated it, and I felt unsettled when the phone call ended.

When Julian returned, he kept to himself the rest of the day. He didn't even voluntarily come down for dinner. Dad forced him to sit at the table and be a part of the family, but it was obvious Julian didn't want to be there. His sullenness threatened to ruin my good mood, but I managed to hang on to my happiness. I wasn't 100 percent sure, but I suspected that Hunter would be dropping by tonight so I could help him get through a feeding. I was edgy and nervous, but most of all, excited. If Hunter could just accept this one aspect of himself, I knew he could accept the rest. Then he'd feel a lot more positive about his life, about us.

After being silent for most of dinner, Julian headed to his room, shut his door, and called Arianna. She had a lot of questions for him, mainly about why Halina wanted them to have children. Julian, ever conscious of so many listening ears, did his best to explain that the family wanted children to dilute out the vampirism, and stressed that while it was important to *them*, it wasn't necessarily important to *him*.

Arianna asked about Raquel next, about how she was doing. Julian hesitated, then told her Raquel was going to be fine. After a long pause, Arianna said, "Well ... that's good. I'm glad you were able to be there ... for her ..." While her words were encouraging, her tone was sad, full of unease.

Julian did his best to brighten her spirits, but their conversation dwindled to nothing shortly after that. Julian's mood was dour when he hung up the phone. I sent him supportive feelings, but Julian wasn't in the mood to receive them. He was only interested in stoking his misplaced anger toward Hunter.

After getting ready for bed, I sat up and waited for everyone to fall asleep. It felt like it took a hundred years for me to hear Julian start snoring. My eyes grew heavy as I stared at the curtains framing my window. Hunter had to show. He just had to. We'd had such a great moment yesterday, but sometimes that wasn't enough with Hunter. His moods could spin on a dime. All I hoped was that he didn't push me away again. I didn't think he would, since he'd been the one to ask me for help, but it was really hard to tell with him.

I must have dozed off while I was waiting, because I startled to alertness when icy fingers touched my skin. When I opened my eyes, Hunter was standing beside the bed, leaning over me, a half-smile on his face. His eyes cast the room in a warm, faint light; they highlighted the hollowness of his cheeks, the paleness of his face. His chilled fingertips swept across my cheek, then ran along the length of my jaw. Frowning, he pulled his hand away. "I shouldn't be back here."

Sensing his mood shifting again, I sat up on my knees and wrapped my arms around his waist, symbolically preventing his escape. "Yes, you should. You're exactly where you're supposed to be." When his dubious face didn't respond, I asked, "Are you ready?"

Already distressed over what he was about to do, Hunter ran a hand through his hair. "No." Exhaling in a slow, controlled way, he nodded. "I don't think I'll ever be ready, but I know I need to do this. It's the only way I'll be strong enough to ..." His lips compressed as his sentence died off. "I need to do this. I'm choosing my evil." He lifted an eyebrow as he referenced my grandmother's warning.

Detaching myself from him, I patted the bed beside me, then stood up. "I'll be right back." I gave him a stern look as I pushed my finger into his hard chest. "Don't go anywhere."

A small laugh escaped Hunter as he sat down where I'd indicated. Tilting his head to the window, he murmured, "There's really nowhere for me to go."

I glanced outside, to where I could sense Halina hovering. She was giving us privacy by not entering the house, but she was definitely keeping tabs on Hunter. If this went badly, she could be here in a heartbeat. It wasn't going to though. It was going to be fine, and Hunter was finally going to be well fed. In the same way he'd touched me earlier, I slid the back of my finger over his jaw. The light stubble was rough under my sensitive skin—a wonderful sort of rough.

With an encouraging smile, I turned and left him alone in my room. I'd debated dragging him downstairs and having him eat in the kitchen, but I thought the preparation process might disturb him. It would be best to have the blood just appear in his hands. Less to think about.

I blurred to the kitchen, hoping that the scent of fresh blood didn't wake my brother. It shouldn't bother my parents at all, not locked away like they were. Soundproof was also smell-proof. Finding a large container of cow's blood in the fridge, I opened it and poured some into an extra tall coffee mug. Normally I'd heat it on the stove, but time was of the essence here, so I nuked it. I didn't want Hunter to change his mind and run away. He needed this.

When it was ready, I hurried back upstairs, careful to not spill any. A low growl echoed in the hallway as Hunter smelled what I was bringing him. As much as he denied it, he wanted this. My grandmother's presence moved forward, but just by a few feet. She wanted this for Hunter just as badly as I did, and if me feeding him was the secret to him eating, then she'd gladly let me do it. She'd probably even hide all of this from the rest of the family if we asked. Anything to get her child to drink.

Hunter was standing when I walked into the room. He was partly turned toward the window, like he was going to dive out of it at any moment. I hoped he didn't. I stepped forward tentatively, my free hand extended palm out, like he was a wild animal I was trying to tame. And, in a way, he was. His eyes flashed from mine to the cup and back again. His fangs were already extended, and he clenched and unclenched his hands in an obsessive-compulsive sort of way.

"Nika ..." His voice was strained, aching with need. Even though I knew the blood was the source of his tone, it sent a surge of excitement through me.

"It's okay ... just relax," I cooed, approaching him.

His eyes locked onto the steaming mug in my hands. "I don't know if I can do this. It's wrong ... but I want it so much ..."

I offered the mug to him. "You *can* do this. I know you can."

He swallowed a lump in his throat as he took the mug from me. "Okay. I can do this. I can do this."

He repeated it over and over like a mantra as he brought the mug to his lips. His fingers were shaking as the blood inside the cup touched his mouth, then he clenched the mug so hard I had a momentary fear he'd accidentally break it. "Relax, it's okay."

His grip eased just fractionally as a small stream entered his mouth. He immediately pulled the mug away and looked like he might be sick as he gagged. I knew it wasn't because of the taste. The taste, to a vampire, was pure heaven. It was the knowledge of what he was drinking that was killing him, making eating so incredibly difficult. His mind couldn't accept what his body wanted. Stepping into him, I rubbed my hand over the rigid arm I could feel beneath his jacket. "Don't think about what it is, just enjoy the taste. Let yourself swallow it, Hunter. Let yourself enjoy it."

His eyes locked onto mine as he struggled with something that was as natural to me as breathing. With obvious difficulty, he finally swallowed the small amount in his mouth. His eyes fluttered closed as he sucked in a deep breath. "God, it's so good," he murmured.

Not wanting him to lose that feeling, I urged the drink back to his mouth. "It is. Have more."

A brief look of disgust crossed his face, as the battle of wills inside him waged on. Hunter's determination won out, though, and he tilted the mug back and gulped down huge swallows. The more he accepted drinking, the more ravenous he became. A purr escaped his throat as the bottom of the mug rose toward the ceiling. His expression changed from revulsion to euphoria. The look of pure contentment on his face was making me hungry, but I pushed aside the feeling and embraced the joy I felt instead. He was eating, of his own free will. It was a beautiful thing.

When the blood cocktail was gone, Hunter's eyes burned with desire. He shifted them to me, and a shiver went up my spine. Maybe I was imagining it, but I thought his cheeks looked a bit fuller already. He was breathing heavier as he handed the mug back to me. "More," he panted.

Nodding, I grabbed the mug and rushed downstairs to heat up more. When the timer dinged on the microwave, Hunter appeared beside me like he'd teleported there. It surprised me, and a tiny squeak escaped me. Hunter stepped into my body, pushing me back into the counter. He was cold, hard, and rigid with tension, but my body contorted to his like he belonged there. He reached beside my head to open the microwave door, and my breathing sped up to match his.

While he grabbed the mug and brought it to his lips, I placed my palms on his chest. I felt the rumble of a growl beneath his skin as he guzzled down the liquid life he'd so long denied himself. When he was finished with his second serving, his eyes seemed glazed, like he was buzzed. "More," he repeated.

I twisted as best I could with his weight pressed against me, trying to reach the container of blood on the counter. Hunter's heavy gaze slid to the jug and he blurred over to it. Setting his cup on the counter, he tore the lid off the jug and drank straight from the container. He gulped down the cold blood like it was just as good chilled. I cringed as I watched him. It wasn't as good cold.

When the container was almost empty, he finally set it down. Groaning, he put his hands on the counter and leaned back with his head hanging down. "Too much," he muttered, sounding a little sick for an entirely different reason.

Smiling, I put my hand on his back and rubbed a circle on his jacket. "I think you're finally full. How are you feeling?"

He peeked up at me; a small amount of blood trickling from the corner of his mouth was the only evidence of his gorgefest. "Okay. Tired ... but okay."

Feeling shy for some reason, I indicated my bedroom upstairs. "Do you want to ... lie down? Stay with me again tonight?"

Hunter wiped the blood from his mouth, then straightened to his full height. I held my breath as I watched strength and confidence return to his visage. Weak was not a word that would ever be used to describe this man right now. Resisting the urge to feel his chest again, I whispered, "Please stay." I couldn't look him in the eye. My heart was racing a million miles an hour.

Hunter's hand came out to grab my side. "Nika, I don't know if that's a good idea. A part of me doesn't feel right being here. I should stay away from you." Instead of retreating from me like his words suggested, his thumb brushed back and forth along my ribs, igniting me.

Stepping up to him so that our hips touched, my restraint fell away and my fingers trailed down the T-shirt exposed between the opening of his jacket. "Don't. Don't do that thing where you pull away for my own good." I stared him in the eyes, his phosphorescence gone in the faint lights emanating from under the cabinets. "You get to choose your path, your evil, and I get to choose mine."

Hunter's lips twitched. "Am I your evil?"

"Sometimes …" Leaning into him, I pressed our chests together and slid my hand up to his neck; his eyes locked onto my jugular. I tilted my head, flicking my hair over my shoulder and giving him a better view of the blood rushing through my body. Almost like he was tranced, his head started lowering, his fangs still fully extended. As before, all I could think was *Yes, take a bite*.

When his teeth were almost to my skin, an irritated voice broke the silence. "What the hell is he doing here? It's the middle of the night?"

I spun around to see Julian standing in the doorway, a scowl on his face. Knocked back to reality, Hunter took a step away from me. "Nothing, I was just …" He looked over at me, his brows furrowed. "Nika was helping me out with something."

Protectiveness oozed from my brother as he stepped into the kitchen. "Helping with what?" Mood prickly, Julian moved so that he was standing between Hunter and me.

Rolling my eyes, I stepped out from behind him. "He asked for my help, so I gave it to him."

Julian held out his hand in expectation. "Help with … ?"

Hunter looked uncomfortable as he answered. "I needed to eat. She helped me get through it."

Julian's eyes flashed to mine. "Are you crazy? What if he lost control and ate *you*?"

At the same time Hunter said, "I wouldn't," I shoved Julian's shoulder.

"Knock it off, Julie."

Julian gave me an irritated expression which matched my own. He needed to get over this beef he had with Hunter. Face contrite, Hunter told him, "I'm so sorry about what happened to your friend, Julian. And what we had to tell her ... if there had been any other way, I would have taken it. I hope you believe me."

Julian took a step away from Hunter. "You made her sound suicidal. You'll excuse me if I have a hard time forgiving you for that." Hunter gave him a brief, accepting nod. Julian's anger flared at Hunter's lack of a rebuttal. Julian had too much anger in him; it needed to be vented somewhere. Poking a finger into Hunter's chest, he snapped, "Those hunters ... were they friends of yours?"

Hunter's eyes flicked to mine. "I knew them, yes."

Julian narrowed his eyes as his mood spiked even higher. "You knew them? Okay, then maybe you can tell me ... is it common practice to drug and slice up an innocent human girl as bait? You don't see vampires doing that, so who's really the bigger monster here?"

Hunter clenched his jaw and averted his eyes. "No, that's not common." His gaze returned to Julian. "What Brett and Sam did to her ... that practice isn't something my family condones. It's one of the reasons Dad and Sam parted ways a few years back. Sam started leaning toward the 'anything to get the job done' line of thinking. Dad had a problem using unwilling bait."

Julian smirked. "Right, he used his children instead."

I bristled at Julian's remark, but Hunter raised his chin. "His *willing* children."

Hunter and Julian defiantly stared at one another for a moment until finally, Hunter lifted his hands. "I just wanted to tell you, for what it's worth, I'm sorry. And I took care of Sam, so you don't have to worry about anyone else being used as bait again."

Some of Julian's anger faded as he saw the pain flashing over Hunter's face. A trace of compassion washed over him, and hope sprang in me that Julian might finally see that Hunter wasn't to blame for any of this. He gave him a brief nod, and Hunter added, "If it makes you feel any better, I told the girl that she would be stronger from now on, and she'd never do anything like that to herself again."

Julian blinked. "You did? Well, thank you."

Hunter smiled, then turned to me. "Thank you for everything you did for me. I should go, though. She's waiting." He glanced behind him to the wall separating him from my grandmother. When his eyes returned to mine, there was a longing in them that I knew had nothing to do with me. "I'm still drawn to her, even when I'm with you, and I feel like I should apologize for that too."

I shook my head as jealousy crept up my spine. "It's the bond. It's not your fault."

Hunter nodded as he leaned down. His fangs retreated into his mouth as our lips met—cold and warm, soft and fervent. The best of both opposites. When he pulled away from me, I clenched my hands into fists to resist the urge to grab him and hold on. He would come back to me, I was sure of it. Almost sure of it. His moods were so unpredictable, but maybe they would stabilize now that he was eating. That was my hope anyway.

Walking around me, Hunter murmured, "I'll see you later."

I was smiling when he left the room. Julian gave me a blank stare, then he rolled his eyes and headed back up to his room. He was less upset about Hunter than earlier, but he still wasn't about to act happy about my relationship with a former vampire hunter.

CHAPTER THIRTEEN

Julian

MY SISTER WAS being stupid. She just couldn't seem to help herself when it came to Hunter. It was like all common sense flew out the window when he was around. And why? Because he was tall, dark, and, according-to-her, handsome? There was no way he was the only brooding, attractive man in the world, and I was sure I could find her a half-dozen other guys to fill the void. Guys who didn't have an innate desire to destroy our species.

Freaking Hunter Evans.

Maybe I was being too hard on him, but he *really* got under my skin. Sure, he was going through an enormous, life-changing event, but he'd starved himself nearly to the breaking point. Idiot. How was making himself even more dangerous to the human population helping anything? He should have sucked it up from the beginning, and accepted that he lived on blood now. And what was the big deal about drinking cow's blood anyway? It just went to waste. At least we were making some good out of it. Hunter was being stubborn just for the sake of being stubborn, and that didn't sit right with me.

While I stewed in bed, I listened to Nika popping open frozen containers and slopping them into the jug. I almost told her that she should heat it up first, so it wouldn't be half-slush when Mom and Dad woke up, but I wasn't in the mood to help her cover up her covert relationship with a vampire hunter who was also a vampire.

Freaking Hunter.

Arms crossed over my chest, I stared at the ceiling and fumed. All of this was his fault. Raquel being used as bait was a trap for *him*. And now she was under the impression that she'd created the wounds herself. On prom night. The student body was going to have a field day with that. And I couldn't tell anybody what really happened. Dad was right about that. I wanted to call Raquel, talk to her, but I felt torn about it. Arianna wouldn't be happy if I reached out to Raquel. Not with our history. Or, *my* history, I guess I should say.

Damn Hunter and his stupid vampire hunting friends.

I awoke to the sounds of Mom and Dad shuffling around downstairs, making breakfast. Guess my turmoil had calmed enough at some point that I'd zonked out. I'd had really weird dreams though. I couldn't completely remember the details of them, accept that Hunter was there, laughing his ass off as more and more pieces of my life fell apart. Even in my dreams he was a dick. God, I hated him.

As I stood and stretched, I heard Dad ask Mom, "Why is the blood in the fridge half-frozen?"

I smirked as I stood up. *Good question, Dad. Maybe you should check the stash in the freezer. Do a quick inventory. Then maybe you should repeat that question to your daughter. I'd really love to hear her answer.*

Nika was in the shower, her mood still elated from her secret rendezvous with Jerk-hole, so I tossed on some clean clothes and ambled downstairs to eat. Dad was stirring the blood when I entered the room; it smelled amazing, and my stomach growled. Peeking up at me, he asked, "You know anything about this?"

I shook my head. "I just got up." Even irritated at her, I wouldn't throw Nika under the bus.

Dad knew I would always protect her, so his expression was one of disbelief. Ignoring him, I grabbed a box of cereal and emptied it into a bowl. Dad poured the blood from the jug into a pot on the stove; the chunky parts splashed the red liquid everywhere. The shower shut off, and Dad looked up at the ceiling. "Nika, you wouldn't have any clue why the blood suddenly turned to slush overnight, would you?"

I felt the slice of panic rip through Nika, and I couldn't contain my smile. Served her right. There was a lot of banging and clanging upstairs while she got ready for school. "Uh, maybe the temperature of the fridge is off? Sometimes things in the back get icy when that happens." Without waiting for a response from Dad, she immediately turned on the hairdryer.

Dad looked back at the fridge, murmuring, "Maybe."

I had to give my sister props for her lie. Dad looked somewhat convinced. Opening the fridge to grab the milk broke Dad's train of thought. As I filled up my bowl, he asked me, "You doing okay? I know the weekend was hard for you."

I nodded as I grabbed a spoon for my cereal. "I'm fine, Dad. But thanks."

Dad gave me an encouraging pat on the back before returning his attention to his breakfast, and I had to give myself props too. He'd bought both lies his kids had just told him. Nika and I were getting better at fooling our parents. That probably wasn't a good thing though. We were supposed to be a team.

I let Nika drive us to school. The closer we got to the campus, the edgier I became. I bounced my knees, tapped my fingers. My restless energy buzzed through the car. I could tell I was irritating Nika, but she didn't comment on it. Maybe she figured she owed me a little quiet time.

When we got to school and parked, I immediately hopped out of the car and searched the grounds. I wanted to see both Arianna and Raquel, but for completely different reasons. I didn't see either, though, so I waited for my sister to get out of the car, and we walked to the main building together.

While my sister oozed compassion and sympathy, I kept an eye out for Raquel. I didn't see her, but I heard about her. Even before I'd officially set foot on school grounds, I heard about her. She was on the tongues of every single student: *Did you hear what Raquel did? She tried to kill herself! Bled all over the hallway near the gym storage closet. Janitor found her and took her to the hospital. Wow. I never pegged her as the suicidal type. Do you know why she did it?*

Why, why, why. That was all anyone was asking. Why she did it. What was wrong with her. Not a single person asked if she was okay. Not a single person asked if she was at school today. They just wanted to know what happened. They just wanted the gossip. My mood was particularly bitter when I ran into my girlfriend.

Without meaning to, I vented my frustrations on Arianna. "Everyone is talking about Raquel, and there's nothing I can do about it." I glared over at a couple of freshmen who were huddled together debating if Raquel was abused at home. God, I hated this.

Examining my face with narrowed eyes, Arianna adjusted the backpack on her shoulder. "Of course there's nothing you can do about it, Julian. Raquel is the one who sliced herself up at a dance. I feel horrible that she felt compelled to do that, but it was clearly a cry for help. She wanted the attention, and she got it. You can't blame people for wanting to talk about it now."

I grit my teeth as I stared at her. Nika had told me after my walk yesterday that she'd told Arianna the lie, that Raquel's wounds were self-inflicted, so that Arianna wouldn't be scared. I wasn't sure if that was the best decision—I wanted an honest relationship with Arianna—but it did make sense. I didn't want her living in constant fear of potential attacks either.

Seeing my blank expression, Arianna shook her honey hair. "I'm not condoning the gossip, I'm just saying it's ... expected ... after something like that."

I sighed and looked away. Yeah. Expected. And my fault. No ... *Hunter's* fault.

Just because there was nothing I could say after Arianna's comment, I glared at my sister. Her compassion died a little as a spark of anger flickered through her.

Arianna's next sentence returned my attention to her. "Everyone's saying the janitor took her to the hospital though, and not you. In fact, no one seems to realize you were involved at all." Her inquisitive eyes flashed between Nika and me. "Was that intentional? To keep you out of the gossip?"

Nika nodded. "Yeah, Dad wanted Julian left out of it, so he had Hunter tell the hospital and Raquel's parents that was what happened. We try and keep a low profile, you know?"

Arianna nodded, then bunched her brows together. "Do I know everything that happened?"

I opened my mouth to tell her no, to tell her the truth ... maybe ... but Trey walked up to our group before I could say anything, and I immediately snapped my mouth shut. I couldn't explain whacked-out vampire hunters in front of Trey; he didn't remember the truth about what we were.

Silence fell over our group as Trey joined us. He looked a little worn around the edges, and smelled like he'd slept in a giant bong. Stocking cap pulled low over his ears, he fixated his gaze on my sister. "Craptastic weekend, huh?" he told me, his eyes never leaving Nika.

I nodded. He had no idea.

MY CRAPTASTIC WEEKEND turned into a craptastic week. Raquel didn't return to school, and I was bombarded with more gossip about her. I hated every second of being at school; I felt so guilty about everything she was going through.

On top of that stress, things between Arianna and I were different, strained, and I didn't know how to fix it. I couldn't shut off my concern for Raquel, and I knew that had a lot to do with how awkward my relationship with my girlfriend was. She was concerned, she was unsure, she was ... hurting. She was quiet and withdrawn; it felt like an eternity since I'd heard her laugh.

On Friday morning, when I was going through my daily routine of searching the grounds for Raquel, Arianna finally lost her patience with me. "She's not here, Julian. You can stop looking for her ..."

She spun on her heel and immediately started walking away from me. Catching up to her, I grabbed her elbow and turned her around. "What's wrong?" I asked, searching her face.

She lifted her chin, but I saw her jaw trembling as she tried to keep it together. "I really thought you were over Raquel, but now ... I'm just not so sure."

"Because I'm concerned about her?" I asked.

Arianna shook her head. "No ... because you haven't touched me since she ... did what she did. You haven't touched me, and we hardly talk anymore. And when we do talk, it always seems to be about *her*. I feel like something has changed, but I'm not sure what. I just ... I can't stand that we're not as close as we used to be."

She turned away from me, and I let her go. She was exaggerating. I had touched her. I'd touched her a lot. And I didn't talk about Raquel *all* the time. Maybe more often than I should, but it definitely wasn't all the time.

Just when I was about to run after Arianna, whispers on the breeze caught my attention. Normally, I wouldn't have paid attention to what the student body was talking about, but they were whispering Raquel's name, saying she was here. She was back.

Turning around and around, I tried to find the source of the conversations. I spotted Nika hurrying after Arianna, Trey watching after Nika, but no Raquel. Then I caught sight of a group of kids pointing and whispering, and a lone dark-haired girl, walking with her head down and her arms crossed over her chest like she was struggling to get through a hurricane. Raquel. I hesitated, wondering if I should go to Arianna, or go to Raquel. But Nika was with Arianna, and Raquel was alone. And it was my family's fault she was alone.

My mind made up, I jogged my way over to Raquel's side. When I caught up to her, I realized I had no idea what to say to her. She didn't know what had happened to her any more than the rest of the student body. And she didn't know my part in it. All she knew was what Hunter had told her—that she'd done it to herself.

Raquel looked up at me when I encroached on her personal space. Her eyes were wary, her expression guarded. I saw the remnants of dark circles under her eyes. She probably hadn't been sleeping well. I wondered if reality was seeping into her dreams. Did she have nightmares about a strange man abducting her, drugging her, cutting her? The words gushed out of me before I could stop them. "I'm so sorry, Raquel. So very, very sorry."

A line formed between her dark brows. "What are you sorry about? You didn't have anything to do with ..." She bit her lip and forced herself to stop talking. The wind blew a dark strand of hair across her face. She tucked the strand away, and my eagle vision saw the fading pink lines hidden under her jacket. At least she was healing.

I looked down. "I ... I know ... I'm just ..." Floundering, I looked up at her face again. "For whatever reason you felt you had to ... I just want you to know that I care, and I'm ... sorry."

She locked gazes with me for a long time. Her dark eyes filled with tears, and it took everything in me not to hug her. Damn those hunters for hurting her. She didn't deserve what they'd put her through. "Thank you," she whispered. Looking around the school grounds, she quietly admitted, "I was scared to come back today. I was scared of what people would say. I feel like ..." Brows creased, she returned her gaze to my face, "I feel like they're going to want to know why, and I honestly don't know what to tell them. I don't know why." Her expression hardened. "But I do know it will never happen again. I won't ever let myself ..." Her voice trailed off. "It won't happen again."

I felt horrible as I looked at the lost, confused girl before me. "I'm glad to hear it, Raquel. I really am." I put a hand on her shoulder, squeezing it in support. Everything that had happened to her was directly or indirectly my fault. The least I could do now was comfort her.

From behind me, I heard a curt voice say, "What the hell?"

Spinning around, I pushed Raquel behind me. Russell was in front of us, eyes blazing. If there was anyone I hated more than Hunter, it was this guy. He pointed a meaty finger at Raquel. "You ditch me at prom, and now there's all these rumors about you being a cutter. You don't take my calls, and now you're slumming around with this lowlife. What the hell's going on, Raquel?"

It took everything in my power to not rip out his jugular. I started to take a step toward him, to defend her, but Raquel didn't need me to. Stepping around me, she calmly replied, "You and I are done, Russell. For good this time. Don't call me again. Don't come over again. Don't talk to me again."

A crowd was watching us. They gasped at this "shocking" turn of events. I wanted to tell them all to get a life, but I was too intently focused on Russell. He wasn't going to like this new and improved Raquel. As she started walking away from him, he sputtered something unintelligible and lunged for her elbow. I, discretely, socked him in the stomach. To the crowd, it looked like I'd barely touched him, but I'd used a great deal of my extra strength and he doubled over, gasping for breath. While he slowly recovered, I placed my hand on Raquel's back and led her to our first period class.

Raquel glanced back at Russell bent over in pain. "Um, I'm not sure what you did, but thank you for doing it." She looked over at me, gratitude in her eyes. "I may not know exactly why I did what I did on prom night, but I have this sinking feeling in my gut that Russell had a lot to do with it." Shaking her head, she stood taller than I'd ever seen her. "I won't ever let a man walk all over me again. I'm worth more than that."

Slinging my arm over her shoulder, I said, "Yeah, I know. I've been telling you that for a while."

She grinned at me. "Yeah, yeah you have. But I finally get it now. For some reason."

She laughed, and I marveled that one small subliminal phrase from Hunter had pushed her into the confidence that I'd been waiting to see from her for a long time. I guess I couldn't stay angry at Hunter after all.

I held Raquel tight to my side as we walked down the halls. I hated people staring, gossiping. Nobody here knew the truth. All they were spreading were lies. Protectiveness surged through me as I scanned the halls. I just wanted my friend to be left alone today. She deserved better than being bombarded by those lies.

As we rounded the corner to our classroom, I stopped dead in my tracks. Nika was waiting at the door … with Arianna. Shock, surprise, and pain were clear on Arianna's face as she stared at me. I was so stunned at seeing her there, waiting to talk to me, that I couldn't even remove my arm from Raquel's shoulder; I was still stupidly glued to her side. This looked bad, even I knew that.

Arianna's cheeks flamed bright red as she clamped her jaw shut. Through trembling lips, she said, "Julian? I can't believe … I trusted you … How could you … ?" Not finishing that, she twisted to run off down the hall. I felt like a wrecking ball had just smashed through my stomach. Shit. I needed to fix this, fast.

I separated from Raquel to run after Arianna, but the moment I moved, the wolves descended. A crowd formed around Raquel as she tried to enter the classroom. They were being polite, courteous, but they were overdoing it. They were all asking her if she was okay, but in the way you asked mentally unstable people if they felt all right. Their voices were giving me a headache, and I wanted to push them all away and tell them to give her space. I also wanted to mend things with my girlfriend. I had no idea what to do. And to make my choice even harder, the bell rang.

Snapping my gaze to Nika, I silently begged her for help. Feeling my need, Nika tossed her hands into the air. "I don't know how to fix that, Julian," she whispered. "What were you thinking, holding Raquel like that? When you know Arianna has insecurities …"

After watching Raquel make it through the bubble of people to get inside the classroom, I walked over to Nika. "Please try, Nick. It's not how it looks, you know that."

Nika closed her eyes. Under her breath, she told me, "Yes, I know that, Julian. I know what you're doing, and I know what you're feeling. But if you give in to this obsessive need to protect Raquel, you're going to lose Arianna."

"I know," I muttered, angry at myself. I couldn't just abandon Raquel right now though. My family was to blame for what happened to her. She needed me.

Nika

JULIAN SURE KNEW how to make a mess of things. I wasn't sure why I ever thought it would be a good idea to have my best friend date my brother, because now I was the official fixer of all their relationship problems. And I didn't know how to fix this one. I didn't know how to convince Arianna that she hadn't seen what she'd thought she'd seen.

Leaving Julian on protection detail for his ex-crush, I hurried after my friend. I thought I'd fixed this situation already, by convincing Arianna to come back and talk to Julian some more ... but, no, Julian had to go and make a mountain out of a molehill. As much as Arianna believed she had Julian's whole heart, a small part of her feared she didn't. And in about five seconds, Julian had all but confirmed that her fear was valid. I kind of wanted to kick his ass.

"Arianna, wait!"

Head down and hands balled into fists, Arianna ignored me as she stormed across campus. The warning bell had already rung, but with how quickly Arianna was striding toward class, I knew we'd make it with time to spare.

Sprinting, I finally caught up with her. "Arianna, wait," I repeated.

Twisting her head, her eyes full of tears, she sniffed and said, "I hate your brother."

I shook my head. "It's not what it looked like ..."

"He had his hands all over her. How is that anything but what it looked like? He's always had a thing for her. He's always been obsessed ..." The tears in her eyes dropped to her cheeks, and my heart broke for her.

"Trust me, he doesn't want her anymore; he wants you. He's just being a supportive friend to Raquel, nothing more."

Arianna shook her head as she opened the door to the building. "You can't know that. Not for sure."

I worried my lip. Actually, yeah, I could know that. I *did* know that. I felt what Julian felt when he was around Raquel, and it wasn't the same as it was earlier in the schoolyear. His emotions didn't soar when she was around, his desire didn't rise—thank God. He just felt protective. And guilty.

Arianna tilted her head as she examined my face. "You're not telling me something. And Julian's not telling me something. What exactly are you two hiding from me?" She glanced up and down the hall, making sure the coast was clear. It was. All the heartbeats I heard were behind closed doors. "I thought I was on the inside now. I thought I got to know everything." Her eyes returned to mine. "But I'm not, am I?" Her expression saddened into tragedy. "I'll never really be let in ... will I?"

I opened my mouth to tell her everything, but the second bell rang, and she darted into class. Crap. Did I just make everything worse?

Arianna was truly upset after that, and it didn't help matters any that Julian stuck to Raquel's side for the rest of the day, like he was her life preserver and she'd drown without him or something. He gazed longingly at Arianna whenever he caught sight of her, but he hadn't been able to talk to her yet. From what I'd heard, things between them had been so frosty during the class they shared together, that everyone had noticed. People were starting to talk about them, beginning to wonder if they'd broken up. Raquel's self-inflicted injuries were almost a byline in the story running around school. So, in a way, I guess my brother had successfully shielded Raquel from the gossip-mongering. At Arianna's expense.

At lunchtime, Arianna sat with some other friends, her back to Julian. I could tell Julian wanted to go over to her, but Raquel was sitting with us, and he didn't want to leave her side. Once again, he was torn between two women. While Raquel made small talk with him, I whispered, "You need to fix this, Julie."

He looked over at me, concern all over his face. "I know."

I nodded at Arianna. "Then go over there and talk to her. Raquel won't die if you leave her side for two seconds."

Julian sighed, then looked over at Raquel. "Hey, I'll be right back, I need to—" He was about to excuse himself when Russell plopped down at our table next to Trey. Trey looked over at him, blinked, returned his eyes to his food, then snapped his head back to look at Russell again. He never sat with us. Ever.

Raquel kept a straight face, but I saw her hand clench Julian's under the table. "Go away, Russell. I think I made myself pretty clear this morning."

Russell smirked and pointed at my brother. "You're seriously leaving me for this twerp?"

Raquel shook her head. "We're just friends, but you wouldn't understand that concept, since all women are beneath you."

Leaning in, Russell sneered, "*You* used to be beneath me. A lot. And I didn't hear you complaining about it."

Raquel's cheeks flushed with color, and she averted her eyes. Julian half-stood from his seat. "She said leave her alone."

Every sound stopped in the cafeteria while Russell and Julian stared at each other. Finally, Russell sniffed and rolled his eyes. "Whatever. It took me three years to finally unclench her knees, and then it wasn't all that great." Standing, he added, "You can have her. I've had better."

Julian shot to his feet, a low, inaudible growl escaping him. Raquel tugged on his arm, trying to get him to sit down. I did too. Julian couldn't make a scene in front of the entire school, not when he was this angry. He might ... do something. Russell only laughed and walked away though. In his wake, I saw Arianna staring at my brother; she had fresh tears on her cheeks. She fled the cafeteria seconds after Russell returned to his friends, and Julian sank back down to his seat in defeat. I was sure he wanted to go after Arianna, but not with Russell still hanging around, waiting to pester Raquel. Raquel thanked Julian, but it didn't lift his spirits any. He knew he'd just made things even more awkward with Arianna, and he didn't know what to do about it.

While Julian and Raquel headed off to their next classes, I left the lunchroom with Trey. He was shaking his head, confused. I understood the feeling, I knew everything that was going on, and even I was struggling to make sense of it all. The only thing I was sure of was that Julian needed to get his act together, quick, or he was going to lose the best thing he'd ever had.

Trey cleared his throat, and I looked over at him. He had a scowl on his face. "So, I saw how cozy you and that Hunter guy were at the dance. You two back together? After he dumped you on your ass? Twice?"

I nearly tripped on my own feet. I'd been expecting Trey to comment on Julian's situation, not my own. Keeping my eyes focused straight ahead, I shrugged. "It's complicated, and I don't want to talk about it." Very complicated, because I wasn't quite sure what Hunter and I were doing. He'd come over every night this week, but only to eat. Once he was fed, he left. Eat and run. I was beginning to feel like my home was a late-night, all-you-can drink buffet to him ... and nothing more.

Miffed, Trey tightened his jaw. He was silent for all of twenty seconds while we walked along the cement pathway. "I just don't get it. I mean, isn't he dating one of your cousins or something?"

I wanted to throttle Julian for mentioning to Trey that Hunter had shown up at the ranch with Halina. He couldn't have known that Trey would fixate on that detail though. "They're just friends ... it wasn't what Julian thought."

Trey scoffed as he kicked a stone on the ground. "Uh-huh, friends. Like Raquel and Julian are friends? Like *we're* friends?"

Surprised he would say that, I stopped and stared at him. There was a telltale red tinge to his eyes, but I didn't think his being stoned had anything to do with his question. "What do you mean? We *are* friends."

Trey's eyes shifted to the ground. "I know. It just seemed like ... at the dance ... I don't know. I thought ... for a second there ..."

I wanted to crawl in a hole for giving him that impression, for not telling him immediately that I didn't want to kiss him. Since I couldn't get away from him now without hurting his feelings, I forced the words to leave my mouth. "I don't feel that way about you. I'm sorry," I quickly added.

Trey was silent for a moment as he stared at me, and my discomfort grew exponentially. Then he laughed and slugged my shoulder. "I know that, Little A. I don't really feel that way about you either. I just didn't want to see you end up with a dickwad like that ... dickwad."

Before I could comment, he added, "I gotta get to class. Maybe I can knock some sense into Julian while I'm there. Catch you later, Nika." He patted my shoulder like we were best buds, then he turned a corner and practically sprinted away. Yet another boy running from me. Super.

Maybe Trey had actually talked some sense into Julian, because by the end of school, he was finally at the groveling stage. Of course, he was groveling to Arianna with Raquel standing right behind him, and that pretty much ruined the entire effect. I wanted to tell Raquel to go home and let my brother patch up his mangled relationship in peace, but she was talking to Trey, and I was sort of avoiding Trey. God, when did my life become so dramatic?

Standing off to the side to give them privacy, I eavesdropped on my brother and my best friend.

"Come on, Arianna, just talk to me?"

Arianna's eyes flashed to Raquel standing by the steps. "About what? You seem to have already decided what you want, so I don't see the point in talking about it"

Julian grabbed her elbows, forcing her to look at him. "I don't want Raquel. How many times do I have to tell you that?"

Arianna lifted her chin to look him in the eye. "If you don't want her, then tell her to go home. Tell her to leave you alone."

Julian sighed, and by the level of guilt exploding in his chest, I suddenly realized we were giving Raquel a ride home today. Great. "Can't you understand what she's been through? How much she's struggling? I'm just trying to be a friend to her, because she really needs one right now."

Arianna's cheeks flushed with color, and her eyes watered. "I know that. And I feel horrible about what happened. I feel awful for whatever was so bad in her life that she felt she had to hurt herself, and I feel like a complete bitch for not wanting you to be around her, because I know you *are* helping her. I just can't stand to watch the two of you be so close. It kills me, Julian. Don't *you* understand that?"

Julian let out a weary sigh. Instead of answering her question, he quietly said, "Raquel didn't do it to herself. What happened to her was my family's fault. That's why I feel like I *have* to help her. In a way, *I* did this to her."

Arianna looked floored; she clearly hadn't expected him to say that. I took a step toward them before deciding to hold my ground. Julian needed to explain this to her, not me. I'd been trying to protect her by not telling her everything up front ... but I guess I should have just told her the truth from the beginning. She might have understood Julian's motives more if she'd known what really happened.

Maybe realizing that something wasn't adding up, Arianna looked my way. "But Nika told me ..."

"Nika told you the 'story' because the truth isn't ... allowed." Julian raised his eyebrows in a pointed gesture that meant "vampire business."

Arianna looked even more confused. "What really happened on prom night?"

Julian tried to cup her cheek, but she pulled away. She was still hurt. "I'll tell you everything, just please, call me tonight? Or come over?"

Arianna chewed on her lip before finally letting out a huge exhale. "Fine ... okay." Like she couldn't stomach any more turmoil, she waved goodbye to me, then turned around and headed for her house on the other side of the graveyard behind the school.

Julian sighed as he watched her leave, then he looked over at me. Feeling his pain, I walked up to him and rubbed his back. "What do I do, Nick?"

Hoping Arianna wasn't too upset to listen, I told him, "Tell her the truth, hope for the best."

Julian closed his eyes. "What if she can't handle it? What if this is finally too much for her?" He looked back at me. "Grandma will erase her if we break up."

Sending him sympathy, I whispered, "Yeah, I know. I'm sorry."

Julian shook his head. "No, you don't get it. She'll erase ... *everything*. Arianna won't even recognize us."

My hand on his back froze. "What?"

Julian swallowed, then told me in a low voice, "Grandma said it was all or nothing. If Arianna and I break up, I lose her in every way ... and so do you."

My heart thudded in my chest. It hadn't occurred to me that Halina would take *every* memory if things didn't work out between Julian and Arianna. Maybe it should have. Since everyone would be wiped when we left town, what would a year or so of memories removed early really matter?

But it *did* matter. It mattered a lot. "Fix this, Julian. Please. I don't want to lose Arianna."

Julian closed his eyes like his lids weighed a thousand pounds each. "Trust me, Nick ... I don't want to lose her either."

CHAPTER FOURTEEN

Hunter

I WOKE UP hungry, but it was a tolerable level of hunger, not the gut-wrenching torture I'd been enduring for months. My glowing eyes fixated on the clock, but I didn't need to look at it; I instinctively knew what time it was—forty-three minutes and fifty-six seconds until sunset. Give or take a few milliseconds.

Leaping from my bed, I marveled at the difference in my energy level. A week ago, just thinking coherently took an extraordinary amount of effort. But now, after a week of eating every night, I felt like I could take on the world. I felt invincible.

Flexing my arms, I watched the muscles bulge and contract. Physically, I felt better than I had in a long time. Mentally, I wasn't quite so healthy. What I was doing to strengthen my body was tearing up my psyche. It went against everything I believed. Drinking blood, like a dirty, disgusting demon. I couldn't deny how much I enjoyed it though. The thrill it gave me was unparalleled. The taste … indescribable. But it still horrified me. There was just no getting around that aspect of it.

Walking into the bathroom, I studied my features in the mirror. I looked more like my old self, not quite so gaunt. Even the circles under my eyes were gone. I was fed and rested, a perfect vampire specimen. Opening my mouth, I let my fangs lower. Disgust flooded me as I stared at the physical manifestation of the beast inside me. These teeth were a reminder of my fall from grace. Or maybe they weren't. Maybe I'd fallen a long time ago.

I ran my tongue over a fang, feeling the sharpness of the ivory point. Now that I was drinking, the desire to puncture something, to hunt, was growing in me. I thought it would fade as I got stronger, but it wasn't. I wanted to sink my teeth into something warm, juicy, tender ... I didn't even care what. Blood was all the same to me. It made being around Nika especially challenging. Her heartbeat tended to rage in my ears, the fragrance of her blood beneath her skin tingled my nose. I daydreamed about biting her. I wanted it as badly as I wanted to make love to her. And because of that, I tried to keep my nightly visits as short as possible. I didn't want to cave into either desire.

Nika wanted me to cave, I could tell. She wouldn't push me, but her body language screamed at me to take her. In every way. She didn't realize what that closeness would do to us, though. Of course, she didn't know I was leaving soon, never to return. I was already going to miss her. Adding sex and ... biting ... into the equation would just make it even more difficult to leave her. And I had to. I had a job to do—a job that was becoming increasingly more important as time went on.

Ever since Sam and Brett's trap for me, I'd been scouting the city while Nika and her family slept, looking for more hunters. Just in the last few days, I'd come across two more that I'd once known, lurking around the Adams' home, waiting for a chance to strike. I didn't give them the opportunity. Sneaking up on them, catching them unaware, I cleared their minds and sent them on their way, never to harm another vampire again. Like most things in my life, I was torn on this as well. I was reducing the number of fighters waging war on the bloodsuckers. We were few and far between as it was, so I felt really shitty about that. But these men knew about Nika, they knew about me, and I couldn't let them go on with that knowledge. Or risk them running back to a social circle that would clue them in on that knowledge again. My only way to protect Nika, for now, was to completely obliterate their minds.

Dressing for my nightly rendezvous with Nika, I wondered if the attacks would continue after I left. I was certain they would stop once I put my father down, but what if he sent someone while I was away? I'd been hiding my activity from Halina, not wanting her to spook the family, but maybe I should clue her in. Let her know what was going on, in advance of my departure, so she could take over watchdogging them. Yeah, I would do that. I would tell her tonight, after my feeding.

When it was fully dark, I walked upstairs to join the rest of the nest here at the ranch. I could smell fresh blood in the air, the intoxicating, heady scent that sometimes drove me to distraction. I considered sitting and eating with Halina and the others, but I just couldn't bring myself to do it yet. Maybe after a few more feedings with Nika it wouldn't be so hard. Right now, though, the smell was making me sick to my stomach, and I just wanted to get away. I went to the only place I could think of going, a place with a scent so pungent, it drowned out all the blood around me—the pool house.

The air was heavy with moisture when I walked into the heated building housing the Olympic-sized swimming pool. The water-laden air felt heavenly on my chilly skin, and the chlorine-filled aroma cleared my senses. Standing near the edge of the pool, I debated going for a swim. I had time. I had to wait until everyone in Nika's house was asleep before I could head over. Much like before, Nika and I were keeping our activity a secret. As I removed my clothes, I wondered if things between us would always be a secret.

Forgoing the pool, I headed for the hot tub instead. I wanted to feel warm, especially now, when I felt chilled to the bone. The water was like liquid fire as I sank into it. It burned its way up my body, igniting my numb bones. "Oh God," I groaned, lying my head back on the padded headrest.

"Feels good, doesn't it?"

I didn't look over, because I knew who was here. "Why aren't you eating with the others?" I asked.

Halina's legs appeared inside the tub beside me as she sat on the edge of it. "I wanted to check on you first. Invite you to join us."

I looked up at my maker. Her dark hair was loose around her body, her pale eyes brimming with hope. "I'm not ready for that. I do feel better, but ... I just can't sit and eat like that. I'll eat later tonight, I promise."

She smiled at me—an easy, carefree smile. "I finally believe you." Her hand came down to touch my cheek. I was so warm from the water, her fingertips felt like ice. "You look so much better. It makes me so happy to see you like this."

Sitting up in the tub, I grabbed her hand. Searching deep into her eyes, I said, "Let me go out on my own tonight then. Give me an evening to myself." I could scour the city so much more effectively if I wasn't constantly worried about her following me. And she usually did. She usually only gave me a half-hour of alone time before she found me. That made hunting very difficult.

She raised an eyebrow. "An evening with my granddaughter? Her parents would be very unhappy with me if I allowed that." She smirked, so I knew she didn't really care if I stayed with Nika.

Seeing an opening, I told her, "She's been asking me to stay all week, and tonight ... I'd like to spend the night with her. Privately," I added, so she wouldn't just lurk outside the window, which was what she normally did.

Halina pursed her lips as she pulled her hand from mine. Brows bunched, she said, "You'll be careful with her? Gentle? She is mainly human, and very important to me. I don't want you damaging her in your eagerness."

I looked away, feeling embarrassed. "I won't ... hurt her. I don't even know if we're going to ... do anything. I just want to stay with her." After the words left my mouth, I felt the truth in them. I *did* want to stay with her. It hurt that I couldn't.

As I sighed, Halina patted my shoulder. "It will be fine. I've bedded many a human in my time. So long as you remember how breakable they are, you'll do great. Better than great I'd say." She chuckled as she stood up. "I'll stay at the ranch tonight. Gabriel will enjoy that anyway. He's been ... testy lately."

Nodding, I thanked her. If Halina stayed here at the ranch, she would only sense that my presence was in town. She wouldn't know that I was darting all around it, not really staying with Nika.

She started to leave me, then paused. "If you bite her—"

I immediately cut her off. "I'm not going to."

She raised a finger at me. "I know how easily it can happen in those situations. I just wanted to warn you, to not take more than a small sip. If it becomes too much, if the desire is too strong, then you have a glass of blood nearby, at the ready. You understand me?"

I blinked, disbelieving that she was giving me tips on how to successfully have sex with a human. This was so much stranger than my dad's birds and the bees talk. And that had been pretty strange.

"I'm not biting her tonight," I repeated. To put her mind at ease, I added, "But we'll keep blood handy ... if it starts to go that way."

Flashing a smile, she ruffled my hair. "Excellent. Enjoy your evening then, and make sure you return well before sunrise." I briefly considered telling her about the hunters I'd been coming across, but I didn't. For one, she'd never leave me alone with Nika tonight if I told her—she'd probably rouse the family and form nightly search parties. Secondly, she'd probably berate me for not killing the potential threats to our nest. But I didn't plan on killing anyone anymore—except my father. He would be my last sin. Well, him and then myself.

Once Halina was completely gone from the pool building, she added on the breeze, "Oh, and don't leave the city, Hunter, or I *will* bring you back."

I clenched my jaw and ducked my head under the water. My chain might have been lengthened, but it was still very much a leash.

When it was time, I headed out to see Nika. It was almost strange to leave the ranch and not have Halina's presence follow me. It gave me a sad, wistful feeling that made me want to turn around and return to her. But I knew that manufactured feeling was from the bond, and I fought against it.

For the first time since my conversion, I ran the entire way to Nika's and didn't feel the least bit drained afterward. I was getting so much stronger, nearly at my peak. Excitement started to build in me as I leapt to the second story. I was about to eat. Steaming warmth was about to be coursing down my aching throat. I almost let out a growl of anticipation as I scrambled to Nika's window. I needed to calm down, but I was so ready for it.

Before I opened Nika's unlocked window, I scanned the evening sky. Inhaling the breeze, I sniffed for any scent that didn't belong. I listened to every noise, letting them all assault me at once. A cacophony of heartbeats filled my ears, but none nearby were beating rapidly; all was quiet tonight. Satisfied that no threats were lurking, I opened Nika's window and crawled inside her bedroom. Not wanting her to freeze, I instantly closed the window behind me. Nika stirred on her bed, but she didn't wake up. As I stared at her, I wondered why I really came here to eat. Surely, I could do it on my own by now. How much of this routine was about food, and how much of it was about Nika?

Sadness filled me, and I ached to lie beside her. We were supposed to be together ... in another life. One where I was still human, and she was only human. Who knows, maybe in that life, I would have given up hunting to be with her. I'd always imagined her joining me in the fight, but maybe I would have retired, and spent a life full of peace with her. Didn't matter now; all of that was gone.

Thinking maybe I should stop coming here, I sat on the edge of her bed. My weight on the mattress woke her up. "Hunter?" she whispered into the grayness.

I turned my enhanced eyes her way. Most of the glow was blocked by the streetlamps filtering light into the room, but I knew there was still an unnatural brightness around the whites of my eyes. Demon eyes. Nika didn't seem bothered by them as she stretched out, then sat up. "Hey," she murmured, lacing her arms around my neck.

Like always, her smell, heart, and warmth hit me all at the same time. I practically purred in her embrace. Caving with need, I wrapped my arms around her waist and buried my face in her neck. God, she smelled so good.

She threaded her fingers through the back of my hair and sighed in a happy way, like she'd been wanting to do this all day. "You're not as cold as you normally are," she breathed in my ear.

I shuddered as I spoke into her skin. "I took a bath. A six-hour bath."

She laughed and pulled back to look at me. One benefit of vampirism, I supposed, was the fact that there were no time limits on hot tubs. I could have spent the entire evening submerged under the near-boiling water and been quite content. Nika's fingers traveled down my cheek. "I love seeing you like this." Her eyes glowed at me, but with love, not phosphorescence. It made me feel even worse. I should push her away. I just ... couldn't.

I tilted my head as I examined her. "Like what?"

She cupped my cheek. "Healthy. Happy."

Not meaning to say anything, I whispered, "Do I look happy?"

Her smile fell. "Aren't you?"

I pulled away from her. I hadn't meant to give her any insight into my emotional turmoil. Best if she thought I was content, or at least becoming content. Then she wouldn't try to figure out what I was up to. But then, it would only hurt her more when my plan came together. When I left her. That was the way it had to be though.

I gave her a half-smile. "I'm still struggling with this, Nika. Eating. Drinking blood. I don't ... I wouldn't say I'm happy." Her face shifted into compassion. The look was so beguiling on her, I couldn't hold back my next words. "But being with you gets me close to feeling happy again ..."

Her eyes filled with moisture as she stared at me. The heaviness in my chest lifted, and I instinctually leaned toward her. She automatically came toward me, and our lips met in the middle. For a second, as her mouth moved in sync with mine, I felt completely at peace. I felt human again. My hand came up to thread through her hair, then slid down to her neck, holding her close to me. Her heartbeat picked up when my tongue slipped into her mouth. The growl that escaped my chest was both from longing and desire. I wanted her, in so many ways.

Not feeling human anymore, I pulled away from her. She gasped, then tried to pull me back to her. "It's okay. The growling doesn't bother me." Breathless, she added, "It's kind of hot."

I wanted to sink my teeth into her flesh. I wanted to strip the tank top off her. Knowing I couldn't give in to either carnal desire, I murmured, "I'm hungry."

Nika instantly stood and held out her hand for mine. "Then let's get you something to eat."

She gave me a shy smile as her eyes flicked to the bed. I knew she was hoping we'd return to fooling around once I'd fed, but that wasn't going to happen. Not wanting her to see my grief, I grabbed her hand and stood. Nika beamed at me as she led me downstairs. I hated the hope in her eyes—hope for us. God, I was a selfish son of a bitch for coming here every night. I needed to end this. I was strong enough to eat on my own. I didn't need her holding my hand anymore. I clasped her fingers tighter after that thought.

Nika released me when we got to the kitchen. Tucking her long hair behind her ears, she set about making me my nightly meal. Now that my hunger wasn't so dire, she warmed a large batch of blood on the stovetop, instead of the microwave. I preferred it that way; the blood's temperature was more consistent. I sort of hated that I had a preference now.

Feeling eager and anxious, I gripped the counter behind me as I leaned against it. I couldn't peel my eyes away from the blood she was pouring into the pot. Another growl escaped me, a hunger-filled growl. With a chuckle, Nika murmured, "Calm yourself, I'm working on it."

Her humor broke the blood's hold, and I glanced up at her. A charming grin lit her face as she watched me, and a very human laugh replaced my primal noise. Embracing it, I eased my stance. "Sorry. Guess I was hungrier than I realized."

Once all the blood was in the pot and Nika had the stove on low, she turned to me. "That's because you need to eat more than once a day. You're not a five-year-old, you're a newborn."

She crossed her arms over her chest like a mother scolding her child. The disciplinary posture would have been more effective if her lounge pants weren't disastrously low on her hips, exposing a good chunk of her waistline. The blood suddenly wasn't the only appealing thing in the room.

Eyes on her bare stomach, I walked over to stand in front of her. Her hands dropped to her sides as her heart spiked at my nearness. "I'm not a child," I whispered, dragging my knuckles over her exposed abdomen.

She swallowed, hard. "I know."

Her breath picked up. It pulled me toward her. Our hips touched, then I pressed her into the counter behind her. Placing my hands on the counter, on either side of her, I trapped her there with my body. She tentatively placed her hands on my chest, slowly rubbing them up and down. The movement sent shockwaves through my body. It was better than the bloody aroma filling the room.

Overwhelmed and unthinking, I started lowering my head to hers. Before our lips touched, she whispered, "Grandma's not with you?"

I paused, my lips brushing hers. "No. She gave me a night to myself, since I'm eating."

Her hand came up to my neck, digging into my skin as she tried to pull me closer. "Are you staying with me tonight? Please?"

Her voice. Her actions. Her obvious need. It woke a very human part of my body. I wanted her so much. The ache overriding my common sense, I adjusted our hips so I could press my desire against hers. My name falling from her lips, she moaned and dropped her head back. Her neck was now directly touching my mouth. I groaned as I leaned down to suck on her skin. Her hand tangled in my hair, holding me in place. Her leg wrapped around my hip, squeezing us together again. It was too much for my body. I needed so much more. I needed all of her.

My hand came down to pull her leg farther up mine. It gave me a better angle to press against her, and she gasped. My other hand ran up her side, my fingers brushing past the bottom of her breast. She squirmed, panting. I sucked harder on her neck, wishing I could drop my fangs and sink even deeper.

Nika rocked her hips hard against mine in a rhythm that was quickly making every last speck of reason leave my body. God, I loved her. I wanted her. I wanted inside of her. I wanted to possess her. I wanted to pierce her skin. I wanted to drink from her.

I lifted my lips from her neck right as my fangs crashed down. I barely pulled them away in time. Nika snapped her head down to stare at me; her eyes blazed with lust. "Don't stop," she whispered, rubbing herself against me. My eyes closed as the sensation of her body gyrating against mine warmed me more than the hours of hot water.

"Nika ... I won't drink from you." I said the words through clenched teeth, my fangs still fully extended.

Then another growl filled the kitchen, this time from her. My eyes sprang open as the desire in me tripled. Something about that sound ignited me. She was right, it was hot. As I watched, Nika bared her teeth. My breath picked up as I watched her fangs extend. While I should have been revolted, some part of me was excited by what she was showing me. Her eyes still locked on mine, her hand ran down to pull the neck of my t-shirt open to expose my shoulder. An ache unlike anything I'd ever felt before filled me.

"Yes. God yes," I murmured, tilting my head to give her complete and total access to my skin. I had never wanted anything more in my life, than for her to bite me. God, was this what she felt when I teased her? Was this what it could be like for us? "Please," I croaked, marveling that I was begging her to bite me.

Her tiny fangs ran across my tender flesh, scratching me, and I convulsed under her touch. "Please do it," I whispered, my breath fast with need.

She paused with her lips against my skin. "I never have before. Do it with me?"

She angled her head so I could bite her while she bit me. The aching pulse of need flushed out every other sensation in my body. Ready, overwhelmed, I moaned, "Yes," and clamped my teeth on her skin.

My hand across her back held her tight as I drove my hips against hers at a frenzied pace. I had lost control on every single level. So had she. We were both poised and ready for the bite, to bury ourselves in each other, but another need was escalating first. Nika's teeth retreated from my skin as she dropped her head back. Her movement changed my focus, and I watched her face instead of her neck.

"Oh God, Hunter ..." she moaned, before letting out a noise that was so erotic, I almost couldn't remain standing. Her arms and legs clenched around me as the explosion rocketed her body. It was mesmerizing to watch, by far more interesting than the blood rushing through her veins, or beginning to bubble on the stove.

I slowed my pace, letting her down easy. Like pliable putty, she collapsed into my arms. I released her leg and held her tight to me while both of our breaths stabilized. I still wanted her, but reason was returning to me now, and I wouldn't go any further with her tonight.

Regret filled me as my body calmed down. That shouldn't have happened. She was too young for something that intense. And I couldn't be out of control with her. I almost ... Several things almost happened that shouldn't have.

When she could stand on her own again, I stepped away from her. She was all flushed and giggly, happy. I ... was not. Averting my eyes, I whispered, "I'm sorry. That shouldn't have happened."

She grabbed my elbow, making me face her. "Don't. Don't ruin this by saying stuff like that. You just gave me something ..." she beamed as she smiled, "... amazing. Don't feel bad for that."

I pointed at her neck. "I also almost took something."

She shook her head. "No. I wanted to give that to you." She looked down. "I wanted to share that with you. I want to share everything with you."

Needing to get my mind off what had just happened. I grabbed the pot of blood on the stove. "Don't tempt me yet, Nika. I might not be able to stop next time." I poured the blood into my mouth straight from the pot. It was wonderfully disgusting. It burned my lips, my throat, but I didn't care.

The pain was momentary, and it was better than the guilt and nausea I was feeling.

As I swallowed large gulpfuls, Nika told me, "I don't want you to stop next time. I'm ready for you ... whenever you're ready for me."

I paused in drinking to stare at her. Swiping my hand over the back of my mouth, I shook my head. "You don't know what you're saying. Sex permanently complicates things, and you can't ever go back to the uncomplicated times." I knew she didn't just mean sex, but that was the only thing I could focus on right now. I couldn't think about biting her.

Nika crossed her arms over her chest, again resembling a scolding parent. "When have you and I ever not been complicated? The only thing sex will do to us is ..." she reached out and ran her hand down my arm, "... is bring us closer. And sometimes ... I feel so distant from you."

Closing my eyes, I turned away from her. The distance was my fault. It was also intentional. It would be easier for her, in the end, if we didn't get any closer. "I can't go there with you, Nika. I'm sorry." I finished the pot of blood without pausing again. Nika was silent as she watched me.

When I was full, I felt more level-headed, more in control. I faced her, and her grief. She wanted an intimacy with me that went beyond our physical closeness. She wanted me to stay. I owed her some small amount of honesty, I just wasn't sure if I could really give it to her. Cupping her cheeks, I whispered, "You are so important to me. More than you'll ever know. But I can't cave into these desires. I can't bite you. And sex ... will lead to biting. I'm positive of that."

She lifted her chin as her eyes filled. "You won't kill me." She shook her head. "You can't. If you take too much, I'll just ... I'll convert, like all my other family members."

I raised an eyebrow at her. "That's not the story I've been told, Nika. You're too young, your conversion won't happen for another decade. A death for you now, would just be a death."

I started to walk away from her, and, panicking, she grabbed my arm. "Okay. No sex. No biting. But please, stay with me tonight. Don't leave again. Don't eat and run. Just ... stay with me. Hold me."

Everything in me was conflicted. Holding her all night sounded so wonderful. So did sex. So did biting. But weren't they all different facets of the same problem? They would all bring us closer, and I was trying to avoid that. Maybe seeing that I was conflicted, she added, "You're fed now. I won't be as tempting to you."

I smirked at her statement. "You'll always be tempting to me, Nika." Closing my eyes, I felt defeat swell in me. Maybe I could stay for a little while, at least until she fell asleep. "Okay. I'll stay."

She hugged me tight, and I again felt my world shifting. Could I leave her? I wasn't sure anymore. But I had to try. Holding onto the hope of going after my father was the only way I was surviving this hellish life I'd been forsaken with. If I abandoned that mission, there'd be nothing left of me, and I was certain I'd slip back into the melancholy that had made every second of my life excruciating. And besides, I had to leave, to keep Nika safe from Dad's hunters. My father had to be stopped. My father had to be punished for what he'd done to me.

But, maybe if I lived through this battle, I'd return. For her. Maybe. If she still wanted me after that.

Nika sent me upstairs to wait for her while she cleaned up the evidence of my nightly gorging. I listened to her as she pulled some blood from the freezer and reheated it. Her parents hadn't caught on to the fact that she was replenishing the fresh blood with frozen every night, but I was sure they'd notice when their supply unexpectedly ran out. Nika hummed while she worked, perfectly happy since I'd agreed to spend the night with her. Slipping off my boots, I again debated if I was doing the right thing. I didn't think so.

Nika was grinning when she rejoined me. It was her vibrant stunning smile that stole my breath, made me reconsider lying beside her. In a bed. Why did she have to be so beautiful? And warm, funny, sweet, wonderful. Why did I have to be in love with her?

Closing the door, she hurried to my side. I was sitting on top of the covers, my knees in the air, my arms wrapped around my knees. Not exactly a cuddling posture. Nika didn't care. She sat beside me, and curled both of her arms around one of mine. Then she laid her head on my shoulder. A stab of loneliness pierced my heart, and I wanted to sob for the humanity I'd lost. Instead, I kissed the top of her head, then scooted down the bed, so we were lying on our sides, facing one another. Her fingers traveled down to my hands, and she brought them to her lips, kissing each knuckle.

I felt lost as I stared into her eyes. I also felt found. Wrapping my arms over and under her, I pulled her into the safety of my body. She held her arms tight to her chest and let me cocoon her. I laid my cheek on her hair and let every troubling, wondrous emotion tumble through me. I pushed nothing away, and it hurt in the best possible way.

"I love you, Hunter," she whispered.

A fresh shock of pain exploded in my chest. I loved her so much. I wished it was enough. "I love you, too, Nika."

She sighed in contentment, and nuzzled into my chest even more. The feeling was overwhelming. I almost couldn't take it, but I couldn't leave either. Cautious of her fragility, I clutched her closer to me.

CHAPTER FIFTEEN

Hunter

WHEN NIKA'S BREATHING was low and shallow, I gently unwrapped my arms from her body; I instantly filled with loss. Knowing I needed to be stronger, I hardened my heart. I couldn't let her in, not when I was getting out.

Without letting myself dwell over the perfection of her sleeping form, I slipped out the window. The night air was filled with familiar noises that I surprisingly found comforting—crickets, owls, a wolf in the distance. Nighttime had always been an uneasy time for me when I'd been human. A time to be on full alert, as the vampires were free to roam the Earth after sunset. I'd much preferred the middle of the day, when the light kept the monsters at bay, or so I'd thought. But now that I was the monster, forced into darkness, I was beginning to find pockets of beauty around me. The way the moonlight filtered between the trees, the way the black clouds slid across the stars, the way the world seemed simpler, outlined in black, white, and varying shades of gray.

As I stepped to the edge of the rooftop, I paused and inhaled a deep breath. There was something there on the breeze, a faint odor that returned me to my past. A past full of hunters, and hunting. Fangs crashing down, I tensed and squatted low. Someone who should not be here was nearby.

Stealthily moving to the peak of the Bavarian-style roof, I scanned the area, searching for anything out of the ordinary, anything moving. I picked out several small creatures darting among the brush; I ignored them, searching for larger prey. The scent gave me a direction to focus on, my hearing gave me a count—one lone heartbeat was surging in the night, far more rapidly than the sleepy community around me.

Remaining as silent as possible, I leapt to the roof of the nearest neighbor's home. The predator was that way. My enhanced abilities made it easy to skim the rooftops; I made no more noise than a frog hopping across lily pads as I jumped my way across the neighborhood.

When I reached where the scent and heartbeat was strongest, about three houses away from the Adams' place, I dropped to the ground. It was a particular brand of cologne that had caught my awareness. It belonged to a hunter named Markus. I'd chided him on several occasions for wearing any sort of perfume. It was stupid to make your scent even more apparent when you were hunting creatures with capabilities that far outweighed any bloodhound on the planet. Why not spray-paint a target on your chest? Markus had never listened to me though. After tonight, he'd finally understand what I'd been trying to tell him.

The heartbeat was pounding away at the corner of a darkly painted rambler. There were high hedges forming a fence that enclosed the backyard, and I could see the outline of a person hiding in their shadows, walking toward me. Markus's plan had probably been to hide in the darkness as he made his way toward the vampire nest. Since he was alone, I doubted he was here to make an attack. Most likely, he was only scouting. Once he'd confirmed how many vampires were living here, and that *only* vampires were living here, he'd assault the home during daylight hours.

That was Markus's favorite technique—burn the vampires to the ground while they were peacefully sleeping. His tactic was very effective against purebloods. It terrified me some now, since I couldn't protect my nest during the day. It made me feel vulnerable. But we had protection that most vampires didn't have. We had mixed-breed day-walkers. Interesting, how I was suddenly referring to them as "us," like we were a unit.

Quiet as a mouse, I blurred to the end of the hedge, where Markus would soon be appearing. While his heart was fast due to his scrupulous nighttime activity, it wasn't racing in nervousness. He had no idea I was so close to him. His scent was particularly pungent this near, and for a moment, I wondered if his blood would have a perfumed aftertaste. I immediately abolished the thought. If I didn't have it in me to drink from Nika, then I definitely wasn't drinking from a fellow hunter. Well, a soon-to-be *ex*-fellow hunter.

I closed my eyes to mask the glow. I didn't want to alert him to my presence prematurely. The loss of vision didn't hamper my senses any; I could hear and smell him as clearly as I could see him. When he tiptoed around the corner, I phased in front of him, grabbing his hands and splaying them out straight from his sides while I backed him into the hedge. Only then did I open my eyes.

Markus's face paled as I held him trapped in place by my vision and my body. He was wearing earphones, but his trance-inhibiting music wasn't blaring yet. Crooking a fanged smile, I told him, "Don't make a sound."

His mouth fell open, but no words escaped him. An enticing feeling of power coursed through my veins. I could do anything I wanted to him; my body was holding him in place like steel. I could say anything I wanted, and he would do it without hesitation. And thanks to the hypnotic glow of my eyes, he wasn't even nervous about it. That sort of influence was intoxicating, to say the least.

"It's been a long time since we've crossed paths, Markus." Leaning in, I exaggerated sniffing him. "What did I tell you about that freaking cologne? I bet you're wishing you'd listened to me." He flinched, but still remained silent, as I'd ordered. "You're here for me?" I asked, tilting my head as I examined his features. My eyes caught flaws—nicks and scars—that my human eyes would have missed.

Markus nodded, his dark eyes and dark hair emphasizing his paleness. He started to speak, but no speech came out. I rolled my eyes; sometimes the compulsion was as much of an annoyance as it was a benefit. "You can speak, just don't yell out."

"I'm here for you, the vampire who turned you, the half-human girl you love, and whatever other bloodsuckers I can take down." His voice was quiet and calm. The voice of a seasoned killer.

I grit my teeth. "My father sent you?"

He nodded again. "Connor wants Salt Lake cleaned, starting with you."

Closing my eyes, I looked away. Damn him. He had me turned, then ordered our friends to put me out of my misery. Along with my creator and my girlfriend. Hell if I was going to let *any* of them harm a hair on Nika's head. "Today's your lucky day, Markus—"

Markus's knee connected with my groin, interrupting my speech. I might be an undead creature with super-healing abilities, but some things still really hurt. Cursing, I relaxed my grip on his hands as I reflexively curled into a ball. My cockiness had caused me to make a stupid, rookie mistake. And Markus might smell, but he wasn't a newbie. Once his hands were free, he simultaneously switched on his music and reached for his stake. No longer having the advantage of telling him what to do, I only had my speed to rely on.

Markus was good, though; he didn't strike where I was, but struck where he anticipated me to go, and he was spot on. When I dodged, he dodged with me, catching me right above the collar bone. Seeing his miscalculation, he immediately removed the wooden stake. I felt the blood pouring out of the gaping wound before it healed, and I growled at him, hissing in pain. He immediately backhanded me, and I gasped as my cheek was ripped apart by several tiny metal triangles jutting from his knuckles. It stung worse than him kneeing me. The pain went right through my face, ricocheting around my skull. Nothing hurt as much as silver.

Markus took my moment of agony to swipe my legs out from under me, crashing me to the ground. Once I was prone, Markus wasted no time leaping on top of me to make his finishing move; with both hands, he held the stake perfectly poised above my heart for the death blow. I was done. My father was going to win. He would kill me, then Halina. And then Nika. Game over.

No.

Remembering I wasn't a weak human being anymore, but an amped-up, bad-ass vampire, I leaned up and shoved Markus's shoulders away from me right as his hands started their downward trajectory. He flew into the air; the stake never even touched me. Zipping to where he was going to land, I grabbed him from the air and smashed him to the ground. Growling in frustration, I thought of several vile things all at once—breaking his back, snapping his neck, draining him dry. What I ended up doing was ripping out his earphones.

"Do. Not. Get. Up," I commanded as I yanked the stake out of his hand.

Eyes defiant, his body still as stone, Markus spat, "You gonna kill me, Hunter? Feed on me? After I saved your ass in Houston? You remember that night? How I staked that vamp in the back, right before he was about to bite you."

Calming myself, I retracted my fangs. "Why shouldn't I kill you? You were going to kill me." Standing up, I hissed, "And I haven't done anything! Haven't killed anyone! Doesn't that mean anything to him? To you?"

Markus watched me, since it was all he could do. "You don't see it, Hunter, but we're trying to do you a favor. We're trying to right a wrong. You should have died that day. You *did* die that day. This," he lifted a finger to point at me, "isn't natural. It isn't right. And the real Hunter wouldn't have wanted to live this way."

"I *don't* want to live this way!" I snarled. "I want death!" I blinked after I said it. Was death what I still wanted?

Markus narrowed his eyes. "You want death? Then let me give it to you. Why are you fighting this? Why are you fighting *me*?"

I squatted beside him. "Because I care. The beasts who changed me ... I have feelings for them, and I can't—I *won't*—let you, or anyone else harm them. I won't die until they're safe, until they're off the radar." I frowned. "Which means I have to stop my father. Maybe even kill him. And you know what, I don't feel bad about doing it, because *he* made me this. What I am is his fault. And he *will* face justice for that. I deserve vengeance," I growled.

Markus's face softened. "Hunter ... killing him won't change what you are. Let me fix you. Let me set things straight. I can ease your pain."

Sitting on the ground beside him, I considered what he was offering. I stared at the stake in my fingers while I debated what to do. Should I completely wipe Markus like I'd wiped the others, or should I make arrangements now? I could leave him with specific instructions to finish me off once my job was done. He could be the answer to all my problems, if death was what I still wanted.

And it was.

Looking up at him, I said, "Not yet. I *will* let you kill me, but I need to deal with my father first. I need to make sure Nika and the others aren't in danger from him." Tilting my head, I asked, "Where is he, by the way?"

Markus looked like he didn't want to answer, but of course, he did. He had no choice. "Flagstaff ... Arizona." He finished his proclamation by giving me my father's exact address in Arizona. Perfect.

I patted his leg, "Thank you, Markus. Now, I want you to listen very closely to what I'm about to tell you ..."

After I was finished reprogramming Markus, I spent the remainder of the night scouting the city for more hunters. When I didn't find any, I returned to the ranch. I had mixed emotions about several things that had happened tonight. I'd almost bitten Nika. I'd shared an intimate moment with her that wasn't going to help either one of us. And I'd left a ticking time bomb out there. When I finished my mission with my father, Markus would finish me. There would be no happily ever after with Nika, not that one had been going to happen anyway. Not with me like this. But it was for the best.

Why did I feel so sad about it then? I couldn't deal with this right now. I just wanted to take a shower, and go to bed.

When I walked through the front door of the opulent home I was staying in, Halina zipped into the entryway like a worried mother hen. I barely had time to close the front door before she rushed up to me and started examining my body. I was confused as to why she was in such a tizzy, and then I remembered—the front of my shirt was covered in blood from where Markus had staked me. Damn it. I should have changed clothes before I came back.

While Halina ran her hands over my chest, looking for a wound that was no longer there, Imogen and Gabriel trailed into the room; the others in the home were asleep this late at night. "You're hurt?" Halina snapped. "What happened? And why do you stink like cheap cologne?" Her nose wrinkled, and I mentally cursed. I should have showered too.

"It's nothing, please stop that."

Before I could successfully push her away, she found the telltale hole in my shirt and stuck her finger through it. I sighed as her eyes snapped to mine. "Nothing? You were staked!" Her fangs crashed down and a low growl rumbled from her chest. Imogen looked surprised and concerned over the news. Gabriel remained impassive.

Halina's gaze flashed to the front door; the destructive gleam in her eyes reminded me of a blossoming tornado, building strength, about to wreak havoc on an unsuspecting town. I grabbed her shoulders before she could streak away. "I'm fine. I ran into a hunter, but I dealt with him."

Imogen gasped and took a step toward us. "A hunter? In the city? Are the children okay?"

By children, I knew she meant Teren and Emma just as much as she meant Nika and Julian. I nodded. "I was the only one he encountered. They're all safe."

Halina reluctantly pulled her eyes from the front door. "Did you finish him?"

I knew what she really meant was did I kill him, and I kept my expression as neutral as possible. I had to be careful how I answered her. If I said I killed him, she'd know I was lying; I wasn't capable of purposely doing that and she knew it. But if I told her I let him go, she'd be pissed. "He's ... no longer a problem."

Both of her eyebrows climbed up her forehead. "You let him go, didn't you?" Her finger pressed into my chest. "Rule number one, love, we don't let hunters who try to kill us live."

I shook my head. "He's not a concern. I made sure he wouldn't harm any of the others."

Halina's eyes narrowed. "Any of the others? And what about you? Will he still harm you?"

Damn it, she'd caught that slight slip. "You know I don't want this life."

Her face shifted into a mixture of sadness and anger. I wasn't sure which one was going to win out. Her chin quivering, she slowly intoned, "Why did you even fight back then? Why not just let him stake you, since you hate yourself so much?"

I shrugged. "I don't know. A moment of weakness, I guess." That, and I still had a job to do, not that I could mention that to her. I'd already said too much.

She gaped at me, momentarily stunned speechless. "You consider self-preservation a weakness now, do you?" I swallowed, but didn't answer. She shook her head in disbelief. "And just when I thought you were getting better, just when I thought you were actually starting to accept this life."

"You know I'll never accept this," I whispered.

Her pale eyes shimmered with red tears. "Don't think I'm ever leaving you alone again after this." I hung my head. I figured she wouldn't. I'd royally messed up this time, and I was positive the short leash she'd given me had just retracted. Voice heated, I heard her tell Gabriel, "Make sure he stays here while I take care of this."

I snapped my head up. "No! You can't kill him."

Halina leaned into me. "I can, and I will. I protect my family ... every single member. Whether they want it or not."

She radiated power and confidence, and I was struck with an overwhelming feeling of humbleness as I stood before her. As much as I hated to admit it, Halina was the leader of our group, and a part of me wanted to fall on my knees and do whatever she asked. But I had a plan too, and I couldn't let her mess this up for me. "Please, don't kill him. I've done everything you've asked of me—everything. I've eaten, I've stayed here with you ... I've lived for you."

"And you'll remain alive," she immediately responded, her voice soft. She inhaled a deep breath of my clothes, memorizing Markus's scent, then she looked over at Gabriel. "With this stench, he shouldn't be hard to find. I won't be gone long."

Gabriel frowned. "I do not like you going alone. I'll go with you."

Seeing an argument about to go down, I prepared myself to leave. Maybe I could get to Markus and hide him somehow before Halina could track him. Before I could move, though, Halina's viselike grip cinched around my wrist. "No. He will bolt at the first opportunity. Only you are strong enough to handle him. I'll take Imogen with me."

Gabriel ground his teeth. "You do not have long until the sun rises."

Halina smirked. "Like I said, this won't take long." She patted my chest. "Especially since he ordered the hunter not to harm us. That makes the task almost ridiculously easy. Starla could probably do it."

She smiled a little wider at her joke. Gabriel's frown increased, along with my struggles. It was useless, though; I couldn't remove myself from her grasp. Then Gabriel stepped behind me, locking my arms behind my back as effectively as shackles. He might be a mixed vampire, but his age made him stronger than all of us.

Halina released my wrist when it was clear Gabriel had a firm hold on me. "Don't do this!" I pleaded, but she was gone, and a hazy ghost image of her was the only thing that remained.

Her daughter took off a second later, then it was just Gabriel and me standing alone in the entryway. I struggled against him, but he didn't move a muscle as he held me. I could feel Halina's presence getting farther and farther away. It made my bones ache to have her rushing away from me. I hated that it did.

So that was it. Markus was as good as dead now, and my backup plan for finishing myself off had just gone up in smoke. A part of me was relieved that the time bomb was being defused. A part of me wanted to create another one. But first, I had to get to Flagstaff. My father was my priority, my mission, and I had no idea how long he'd stay there. I needed to act on this. I needed Gabriel's concoction now more than ever.

When I could feel Halina in the city, tracking poor, clueless, helpless Markus, I growled at Gabriel, "You can let me go now. There's nothing I can do to stop her. I won't run."

Gabriel squeezed me tighter instead. My shoulders were stretched more than was comfortable, and a trace amount of fear went up my spine. He wouldn't hurt me, though. He wouldn't dare. "If something should happen to her tonight ... I will be very displeased."

"If something happens to her, you'll finally be able to kill me. I would think you'd be happy about that," I murmured.

He let out a short, humorless laugh. "Double-edged sword."

He let me go, and I rolled my shoulders to relieve the discomfort. "Thanks." By my tone, it was clear that what I really meant was, *Go to hell.*

Gabriel gave me a brief, understanding smile. Tilting his head, he said something unexpected. "This was not your first solo encounter with hunters. How many have you run into since prom night?"

I froze, not sure what to say. Since Gabriel was the one vampire I didn't have any secrets from, I shrugged and told him the truth. "Including tonight, there have been three."

Gabriel nodded, expecting as much. "By your reaction to his impending death, I'm assuming you know these hunters?"

I eyed him warily. I'd only confessed that to Nika and Julian. "Yes, I knew them ... in my other life."

Gabriel's gaze penetrated my very soul. "This city has been relatively quiet prior to your arrival. Five hunters this close together tells me something ... is your father sending assassins to kill you?"

His question stung worse than I thought it would; it hurt more than the silver that had grazed my cheek earlier. "Yes," I whispered. "And those five won't be the last he sends. When my father wants something, he stops at nothing to get it."

Gabriel frowned. "Then what Halina is doing tonight is only a patch, and won't solve the larger issue. The only real way to stop these killers is to stop your father. He should be our primary focus."

I nodded. "I know ... that's one of the main reasons I want to be away from her. I'll find my father, and I'll stop him. Permanently. I want vengeance for what he did to me, and it's mine to have—mine and mine alone. You okay with that?"

He thought for a moment, then gave me a slight incline of his head. "So long as you can give me your word that you *will* end him, and quickly, I will let you have your revenge."

"Good. Now, before any of that can happen, I need you to free me." I looked around the elegant home that was my prison. "I need out of here, Gabriel. Now."

Gabriel lifted a cool eyebrow. "Agreed. And I have made a tremendous amount of progress in the last two weeks. I believe the shot is nearly ready for you to take. Unfortunately, I have no real way to test it, since Halina will be alerted to what we're doing the second you inject it."

I walked past him, toward the entrance to the lower levels of the home. "Just give it to me when you feel it's ready. I know where to find my father. I'll get there as soon as possible, and deal with him once and for all. And hopefully the shot will last long enough that Halina won't have any idea where I am when I ..."

"When you die?" he asked, following me.

I glanced back at him. "That's the plan."

He only nodded in response. Once we were in the lowest level, we headed to his laboratory. There were a ton of things bubbling and percolating down there. I only knew what one of them was—the shot that kept mixed vampires as alive as humans for an indefinite amount of time. The rest? No friggin' clue.

Gabriel led me over to a beaker full of something puce colored. It smelled awful, like sulfur. My nose crinkled as I stared down at the opening. It was smoking a little as it sat atop a bright blue flame. "That's not the one I have to take, is it?"

Gabriel lifted the beaker and swirled the purple liquid around, making the smell even worse. "Yes. This is the one you will need to take." He looked around the beaker to study me. "And as bad as it smells, it will hurt infinitely more."

My mood sank as I stared at my liquid freedom. Of course it was going to hurt. I wouldn't be surprised if he'd engineered it that way. "Okay. What do I do? I want to be prepared, when the time is right."

Setting the glass back upon the burner, Gabriel grabbed my arm. I flinched a little at him grabbing me, but made myself relax. He could probably kill me with about three dozen things in this room if he really wanted. He'd just have a lot of explaining to do to his girlfriend if he did.

Pushing my shirt up, he exposed my arm. "It's quite simple. Puncture the skin anywhere on your body and inject the liquid. The results are nearly instantaneous, so don't use it until you're ready."

I yanked my arm away, nodding. His jade eyes studying me, he added, "The bond is hard to break, and will return without constant interference." He pointed to the bubbling liquid. "I've enhanced the original version of this, but you will still need to take a shot every twenty-four hours. I wouldn't go past twenty if I were you."

I frowned at this new information. "I have to inject myself with a painful shot every day? You failed to mention this before. Can't you make one that breaks it forever?"

His lip curled into a smile. "Of course I could. It would just also kill you in the process." His expression turned inquisitive. "Would you like that one? Maybe you could take it with you?"

Not answering, I looked away from him. Trancing hunters to hunt me down was one thing. Injecting myself with poison, quite another. Just like facing the sun or staking myself … I couldn't take my own life. And that fact was truly my greatest weakness.

Gabriel silently mused over my response, then said, "I'll include a vial in your pack. It will be clearly labeled. Then, if you find that this life is just too much for you to handle, you'll have a reprieve available to you."

I looked back at him. Reprieve? Interesting way to phrase it. Shrugging off the moroseness of our conversation, I asked, "How will I get more ... of the other shot? I can't exactly call in an order."

Gabriel tilted his head. "I'll send some to L.A. every few months with instructions that you are to be allowed to pick it up." He narrowed his eyes at me. "I assume you remember where that nest is?"

Sniffing, I told him, "Yeah." That nest had been the first domino in the chain of events that had killed me. And now it was going to be my source of freedom. Great. "I don't expect to need the shot for long, but I don't want to suddenly pop up on Halina's radar if things with my father take some time." I knew where Dad was now, but if Gabriel took too long, I'd lose him again.

Gabriel smiled. It wasn't comforting. "I suggest you handle that situation expediently, otherwise, your supply may *all* be the lethal shot one day. Just something to keep in mind."

Double great. Well, surviving this had never been my intention anyway. If Gabriel slipped me a shot that would instantly kill me and I unknowingly took it, that wouldn't necessarily be killing myself. He was simply another sleeper agent working for me. One who would kill me when I least expected it. I could live with that. I returned his smile. "I'll keep that in mind every time I stick myself."

His expression turned genuinely pleased. "I appreciate the fact that we understand each other perfectly. That simplifies things a great deal."

I nodded again. Yes, it certainly did.

I was lying on my bed in my dark bedroom, watching the way the glow of my eyes reflected on the hills and valleys of the white plaster above me when Halina returned. Closing my eyes, I both cherished and hated the feel of her approaching. When she was downstairs, she hesitated beside my door. I held my breath. Right would take her to Gabriel's lab, where I knew he was still plugging away at my cure. Left would take her to my room. I wasn't sure which one of us she wanted to see, and I couldn't help but hope it was me.

Since the individual rooms were all soundproof, I couldn't hear her until she cracked open my door. "Hunter?" she softly asked. "Are you still awake?"

Even though a flush of relief coursed through me that she'd picked my room, I considered leaving my eyes closed, not exhaling my breath ... acting asleep. Unfortunately, I couldn't stop myself from answering her. "Yes," I whispered, opening my eyes.

I turned to look at her as she stepped into the room and closed the door. She seemed the same as before—tight dress in a deep purple color, knee-high boots in shiny black vinyl. No apparent injuries, tears, fresh blood. No sign of a struggle. Of course, there wouldn't be any. I'd made Markus as docile as a lamb. No challenge for a predator like Halina.

"So, he's dead then," I said, as she sat on the bed beside me.

Giving me a soft smile, she grabbed my hand. "No."

Sure I'd heard wrong, I sat up. "You left him alive? Why?"

She ran the back of her fingers down my cheek. "It was important to you that he lived, and you're important to me." She cupped my cheek, her thumb stroking the rough stubble along my jaw. "We're not as bad as you think we are, Hunter. I want you to see that."

I was dumbfounded. I'd truly believed she would rip him apart and bury the pieces. "Thank you," was all I could think to say.

She nodded, removing her hand to her lap. "I did, however, wipe his mind completely blank and give him the distinct impression that his life would best be spent cataloging the mating rituals of penguins in the Antarctic. I hope he doesn't mind the cold," she laughed.

Surprisingly, I laughed with her. Her content expression grew at seeing a trace amount of mirth on me. Then a wistful sigh escaped her. "I hope ... I hope you come to find peace, Hunter. I would hate to see you do something ... rash ... to yourself. I've grown rather fond of you." She rolled her eyes. "Even if you do give me gray hairs and worry lines." She added something in Russian that I was pretty sure was very descriptive profanity.

I had a lump in my throat that I couldn't get rid of. I hated how she could reduce me to an emotional wreck with just a few tender words. Her parenting style was much different from my father's. His was duty wrapped in steel. Hers was warmth wrapped in steel. I'd wanted to please my father for his approval. I wanted to please Halina because I couldn't stomach the thought of letting her down. It made what I had to do that much harder.

She spoke more foreign words to me as she kissed my head. These words were soft, tender. I wanted to know they meant, but I also feared what they meant. I was already struggling with guilt; how much more could I add to the pile. "Halina?" My voice quavered, and I swallowed past the knot.

"Hmmm?"

I met her eyes; her face was content, at peace. Would I ever look like that? Not able to ask what I wanted, not able to give her tender words in return, I could only instead say, "I know I messed up tonight, but I would still like my freedom."

Disappointment immediately replaced her happiness. She sat up straighter on the bed, and her lips shifted to a frown. "No. I cannot trust you to not harm yourself, so I will not leave you or let you leave me. You will just have to suffer through my presence." She immediately stood and stormed from the room.

I exhaled a stuttered breath once my soundproof protection was back in place. "I care about you too," I whispered into the darkness. Eyes glued on the door, I added, "But I can't stay."

CHAPTER SIXTEEN

Nika

MY BROTHER WAS pacing his bedroom, anxious. The family was getting ready to head out to the ranch. I was ecstatic—I'd get to see a lot more of Hunter than our short, secret, midnight rendezvous. Julian, however, didn't want to leave town. He was acting like being away for a couple of days was the end of the world. And all because of the women in his life.

Arianna hadn't called him last night. She hadn't come over either. He'd called her at least four dozen times, but her phone was always off. He'd even tried calling her mom, but all she'd told him was that she'd gone out with friends. Julian was gutted.

I was worried. If we didn't fix this fast, I was going to lose my best friend forever. And all because of freaking Raquel Johnson. I couldn't believe it. I also couldn't believe it when Julian called *her* after he couldn't get a hold of Arianna. They'd still been talking when I'd fallen asleep. My brother seriously needed an intervention.

I silently watched him wearing a circular pattern into the floor as he paced. He looked up at me, his face and mood distressed. "Why didn't she call me? I told her I would explain what happened on prom night if she called me. So why didn't she call? Or come over? Why would she ... go out?" He tossed his hands into the air.

Folding my arms across my chest, I leaned against the doorframe. "I don't know, maybe she's making you sweat it out. You know, because you basically ignored her all week."

His feelings turned droll as he stopped and stared at me. "I didn't ignore her. I was just ... a little preoccupied."

I raised an eyebrow. "A little? Talking to you was like talking to a wall."

He ran his hands back through his hair. "I just felt bad for what happened to Raquel. I felt responsible. I still feel responsible."

I lowered my gaze. It wasn't Julian's fault, and I told him as much. "You didn't have anything to do with what happened to her."

His voice hardened. "I know." He sighed. "I can't shake the feeling though. It was a member of my family who caused the situation. That kind of, sort of, makes it my doing."

My heart skipped a beat and surprise washed through me. Julian bunched his brows as my emotions flowed into him. "What?" he cautiously asked.

I couldn't contain my happiness, or my smile. "You just called Hunter family."

Julian looked away. "Well, he is ... isn't he?" Getting a mischievous grin on his face, he looked over at me and added, "Which means you can't date him. Incest and all."

I grimaced at his words, then chucked a hairbrush at his head. He easily dodged. Heat flashed through my body as I remembered the explosion Hunter had given me last night. Epic didn't even begin to describe it. And while it had been exceedingly satisfying, it hadn't been enough. I wanted him, body and soul. I wanted to share every last intimacy with him, which was yet another reason why I wanted to go to the ranch. Hunter had a soundproof room ...

Julian's mood turned curious while he examined my flustered feelings. When he figured out what I was thinking about, his curiosity instantly shifted to horror. "Nika, did you ... ?"

Our parents were downstairs, so he didn't finish his question. Instead, he acted out the movement with his hands. My face flamed brighter than the sun, and I wished I had another hairbrush to throw at him. "No!" I hissed. "And stop asking me that question."

Julian turned over my words with disgust on his face; he was filled to the brim with disbelief. He knew we'd done something last night. Thank God he'd been asleep. I bit my lip as Hunter's hard body swept over my thoughts. Julian held up his hand. "Whatever you're thinking about, please stop."

Clearing my throat, I tried changing the subject. "Why don't you try calling Arianna again before we go? I'm sure she's done tormenting you by now."

Julian was just as ready to redirect the conversation, so he nodded and pulled out his phone. Exhaling a cleansing breath, he sat on his bed and called her number. His nerves spiked while he waited for her to pick up. He looked over at me, fear in his eyes. He didn't want to lose her, any more than I did.

He shot off the bed the second she said hello. "Don't hang up!" he implored.

I could hear Arianna's sad sigh. "I wasn't going to. If I didn't want to talk to you, I wouldn't have answered the phone."

Julian frowned. "Like last night?"

"I just needed time to think about things," she said.

Julian sighed, his mood sinking. "And ... what do you think ... about us?"

"We have a lot to talk about ... but, I don't want to give up on us just yet. I'm still in love with you, Julian." She didn't sound entirely pleased as she confessed that.

Julian went straight to ecstatic though. "I love you, too. I'm so glad to hear you say that, Arianna. I was really freaking out."

"I'm sorry ... that wasn't my intention. I just ... needed space."

Julian's voice was impassioned when he spoke again. "I don't want to do this over the phone. I want to talk to you face-to-face. Can you come over?"

"Aren't you going to the ranch today?"

Julian swore under his breath. Without even asking for permission, he told her, "Come with us? Just for the day. Or night. Have dinner with my family?"

My dad's voice immediately drifted up the stairs. "Julian, can I talk to you for a moment?"

Julian ignored him, and concentrated on Arianna. "Please?"

She made a hemming and hawing sound. "Dinner? With your entire family?"

Arianna knew that would involve a lot of blood drinking. She still wasn't overly comfortable with that, but she wanted to be, so after Julian begged her a few more times, she finally relented. "Okay, I'll ask. I'll call you back in a few minutes."

Julian was joyful as he told her goodbye. His glee faded a bit when Dad snapped, "Julian! Get down here. Please."

Julian groaned as he looked my way. I gave him a supportive smile, but he'd kind of brought this one on himself. His mood petulant and reluctant, he walked downstairs at a slow, human pace. I heard a rapping sound downstairs and imagined Dad tapping his foot while he waited. Before Julian was even in the room with him, Dad said, "I know you and Arianna are close, but you can't invite her along without clearing it by us first. Especially with Hunter staying there. I'm not sure that the ranch is the safest place for Arianna to be right now."

I instantly glared at the floor. "Hunter's eating now, Dad. He's not a threat to her. He's not a threat to anyone."

Silence stung my ears. Even Julian stopped moving. I cringed. I hadn't meant to give away that much information.

"How do you know Hunter's eating, Nika?" Dad asked.

Closing my eyes, I cursed. Damn it. Hearing me swear, Dad gruffed out, "Why don't you come downstairs, too. I think we all have things to talk about." I trudged down the stairs even slower than Julian.

We both looked equally guilty when we were finally standing before our parents. Dad's sky blue eyes narrowed to pinpoints as he studied us. He shared a glance with Mom, then said, "You two want to tell me what's been going on around here?"

Like we'd rehearsed, Julian and I answered at the same time. "Nothing's going on."

Dad looked like he believed that about as much as he believed that Hunter was no longer a threat. "Right. Want to try that again? But with a little honesty this time? What have you two been up to?"

Julian filled with resignation while I filled with panic. My brother could totally throw me under the bus right now if he wanted. I didn't think he would, but I beat him to the punch anyway. "I've been talking to Hunter on the phone every night ... when you guys are asleep." Surprised flashed over Dad's face. He opened his mouth to talk, but I beat him to it. "Eating is really hard for him. He finds it helpful for me to be there ... talking him through it." I crossed my arms over my chest. "And you're always telling us to be as helpful as we can to people. I was just following your example."

Dad didn't seem to know how to counter that. A flash of pride went through me that I'd actually stumped my father. Seeing that I'd sort of won, Julian grabbed the reins. "Yeah, and I made a pretty monumental mistake with Arianna this week, and I'm trying to correct it. You always say to do everything you can to set right a wrong. That's what I'm doing."

Julian and I looked at each other, matching glee in our bellies. Dad couldn't argue against his own teachings. "We're just practicing what you preach," I said with a shrug.

Dad scratched his head, at a loss. "Well, okay, I guess I see your point." Sighing, he looked at me. "Phone conversations are fine, but Hunter is still too dangerous for you to be around right now." I kept my face smooth and hoped I didn't look guilty; I hated lying to my parents. Dad's gaze swung to Julian. "I appreciate what you're trying to do with your girlfriend, but the ranch—"

"Is a perfectly safe place for her to be," I interrupted.

Dad looked over at me with forced patience on his face. "Nika ..."

Mom looped her arms through one of Dad's. "There are going to be a lot of people there watching out for her, Teren. And Arianna is aware of the danger. I think it would probably be okay for her to come to dinner." She looked over at Julian. "Every man should get a chance to set things right with the woman he loves."

She looked back at Dad with a soft smile on her lips, and Dad practically melted as he stared down at her. "All right ... I guess it will be fine." Mom's smile grew, and she leaned up to give Dad a warm kiss.

Julian clapped his hands together while they tenderly kissed. "Okay, perfect. I'll just ... go wait for Arianna to call back."

Dad pulled away from Mom's mouth, and Mom started nibbling his ear. Grimacing, I fled the room. As I did, I heard Dad tell Julian, "Just dinner, she can't spend the night."

Julian left the room a split-second after me. "Sure thing, Dad, no problem."

As we met up on the stairs, the sound of kissing and giggling drifted out to us from the kitchen. And Dad murmuring, "You make it very hard to be a stern parent."

Mom's voice was low when she responded, "I'm sure I make several things hard for you."

A low growl rumbled the air, and Julian and I both made faces like we were about to throw up before we zipped back to our rooms. God, they were mortifying.

After Arianna called back and agreed to meet up with us for dinner at the ranch, we headed out. Julian was in a much better mood when we left, and for once, we were both sort of hopeful about things. Even our parents were in bright spirits as they sang along to songs on the radio. Yep. The school year had started out rocky, but we were on our way now.

My mom's spirits dwindled a little when she noticed a certain shiny BMW in the garage. Looking over at Dad, she cringed. "Starla's here."

Dad looked over at Starla's car, then looked back at Mom. His smile was amused. "Great-Gran will be thrilled."

I immediately scanned my internal radar for Hunter's location when our group walked into the living room. He was downstairs, though, not basking in the sundrenched room. Starla was draped across the couch with an expression of complete and utter boredom on her face. She perked up a little when she saw us. "Vamp Boy! Vamp Girl! Vamp Kids! How fun that we're all going to be staying in the middle of nowhere together."

Dad forced a smile to his lips as he greeted her. "Starla. What a nice surprise. You don't come out to the ranch very often."

Starla hopped off the couch. Rubbing a spot on her shoulder, she sighed, "Yeah, well, Father insisted that Jace and I visit him for a while, so …" She shrugged at the end of her sentence, like it was a foregone conclusion that she would do whatever Gabriel asked. And she generally did.

A concerned look crossed my father's features, but Starla ignored the implied question on his face. Instead, she blurted out, "Jace! I need your magic hands!"

Her blonde counterpart rushed into the room mere seconds after she bellowed for him. Tilting his head, he examined the spot on her shoulder that she was furiously rubbing. "Still bothering you?" he asked in a soft voice.

Biting her lip, she nodded and turned her back to him. He placed his cold hands on the area that was grieving her, and she instantly sighed in relief. "You okay, Starla?" Mom asked.

Starla gave her a lopsided grin. "Yeah. Jace and I were just trying out some bondage techniques. He tied my arms a little too tight, I think I pulled something." Her smile grew. "So worth it though. You two should try it? Spice things up a bit."

She shimmied her hips against Jacen's pelvis as he concentrated on her shoulder like it was the only thing left in the room. Equal parts disgust and curiosity blossomed in Julian. My mood matched his. God, those two were so much worse than my parents when it came to private information.

Irritated, Mom sputtered, "We have the perfect amount of spice, thank you very much. We don't need whips and chains to—" Dad grabbed Mom's arm, stopping her from finishing that sentence. He flicked a quick glance at Julian and me. Our mouths were probably wide open. I never wanted to hear my mother say 'whips and chains' again. Mom stopped talking. Thankfully.

Starla laughed as she looked at the discomfort on everyone's faces. "Oh, this weekend is going to be so much more fun than I'd originally thought." Grabbing Jacen's hand, she started pulling him from the room. "Come on, Jace. I've got a better idea of how you can help me." The pair, who looked more like mother and son than boyfriend and girlfriend, giggled as they left.

In a whisper, my mom muttered, "Gabriel soundproofed their room, right?" A smirk on his face, Dad gave her a quick nod in response.

When the living room quieted, Julian started laughing. Mom shot him a look, and he tossed his hands up. "Sorry."

He was still chuckling over the encounter when we ran into the rest of our family in the kitchen. I thumped his arm, and he only shrugged. He couldn't help it. He was just in a really good mood. I hoped it lasted.

I waited out the day by doing mundane things with my family—helping Alanna bake, playing a card game with Grandma Linda. Julian spent the afternoon on the phone. He alternated his conversations between

Arianna and Raquel. It irritated me, but I did my best to let it go. Arianna was the one coming over tonight. She was the one who had Julian's heart. His obsessive need to help Raquel would eventually fade.

When the sun finally set, I was antsy. Julian too; Arianna would be here soon. My father had already left to go pick her up. Arianna getting a ride was one of the conditions Arianna's mother had given. She didn't want Arianna driving out to the ranch all by herself. She was probably still a little upset about the time Arianna had stolen the family car and driven out here. She would be even more ticked if she knew what had really happened that night.

I bounced my legs while I waited for Hunter to come upstairs. Julian and I were playing Gin Rummy. Pausing his hand, he glared at me. "Will you please stop that. You're giving me a headache."

I wasn't sure if he meant my nervous tick, or my emotional anxiety. I could only stop the tick, so I stilled my legs. "Sorry, I'm just—"

I felt Halina coming up the stairs and shot to my feet. Julian shook his head at me and put his cards down on the table. Halina came out of the tunnels, followed closely by Gabriel. I expected to feel Hunter approaching next, but he was still downstairs. Halina greeted everyone in the room, and I gave her a half-hearted hug. Was Hunter not coming out; was he still hiding from me?

Just when I thought he'd stay tucked away the entire weekend, I finally felt him move upstairs. Mere seconds later, he stepped out of the hidden hallway. All heads turned in his direction. Hunter's dark eyes scanned the room of people watching him; they ended on me. "Hey," he finally muttered.

I giggled as I stepped toward him. That was probably an immature thing to do, but I didn't care. I was just so happy that he was willingly joining us. He looked good as I wrapped my arms around him—healthy, strong, more alive than he'd looked in months. Drinking was bringing him back to some form of normalcy. He still needed to do it more often though.

His arms loosely circled my waist as I squeezed his chilly body. "I'm so glad you're here," I whispered in his ear.

A shudder passed through him. "I … I'm not joining you for dinner, but I thought I'd say hello."

Disappointment washed through me as I released him. "You're not?"

He shook his head. There was a sadness in his piercing eyes that I was getting used to seeing on him. It was almost difficult to remember a time when I hadn't seen a trace of despair on him. "I'm getting better, but I still can't handle eating like that. I need to do it in my own way. Privately." He glanced at the many grandmothers in the room. "I'm sorry."

Halina stepped forward. "You have nothing to apologize for." She lifted her hand toward the glass doors leading out back. "Go. Do what you need to do. I'll find you later."

Hunter nodded and stepped away from me. I grabbed his hand. I'd really wanted some time with him. He smiled back at me. "I'll be close. I just … I can't be in the house for this."

Sighing, I leaned up and kissed his cheek. "I'll find you before she does."

His lip curved into a half-smile that was disastrously attractive, then he said his goodbyes to the room and headed outside. Even though conversations blossomed around me, all my focus was on Hunter; he'd gone to the pool house. I tried to listen for him, but he was too far for my diminished abilities to make out any noise.

I attempted to go back to my game with Julian, but I couldn't, not with Hunter awake. Feeling that Dad was still moving toward the city, and would be gone for at least another hour, I turned to Halina. "Would it be all right if I brought him something to eat? He shouldn't have to wait since he's not eating with the rest of us."

Halina nodded, but my mom instantly objected. "No, I don't want you around him when he's eating, Nika."

I kept my expression smooth as I faced her. "We're constantly telling people that we're not dangerous. That just because we drink blood, it doesn't mean we go out slaughtering people. Is that true or not?"

Mom sighed. "You know it is, but Hunter—"

"Is drinking everyday now. He's not starving anymore, and he's not going to lash out in hunger. He's also not going to drain me dry because he's a psychopath. He cares about me, and I care about him. And I would like to help him do something that he finds disgusting. Please." I was pretty proud of myself for saying all that. And I'd managed to not use that whiny tone that drove my mom crazy. Maybe she'd relent.

With another long exhale, she muttered, "Teren is going to kill me." In a clearer voice, she told me, "Okay. Half an hour, and then I come check on you."

I nodded and darted away to the kitchen to make Hunter a tall thermos of blood. He'd probably need it. When I got to the pool house, I found him lounging in the family's super-large hot tub. His back was to me, his arms resting along the sides of the tub, his head laid back on the cushion. His clothes were in a pile next to the tub. Oh my God … was he naked in there?

Swallowing a nervous lump, I made my way over to him. Feeling me approach, he turned his head my way. "Should you be in here? Alone with me?"

He looked up at my face when I stepped beside the tub. "Mom gave me thirty minutes before she's going to loose the hounds." I cocked an eyebrow as I purposely avoided looking at his bare body; my cheeks warmed. "Is this how you spend dinnertime? In the tub?"

His eyes skimmed over my features, a faint smile on his lips. "I like being warm."

My eyes accidentally dropped to his waist, only slightly hidden beneath the shimmering water. Thanks to my enhanced sight I could tell that he was indeed not wearing a swimsuit. He brought his legs up and wrapped his arms around his knees before I really saw anything, but I knew he was naked, and the knowledge was enough to steal my breath.

"What are you doing here, Nika?" His eyes were glued on the thermos in my hand, his fangs just slightly elongated. He was hungry.

I held it out to him. "I know you're not ready to eat with the others, so I thought I'd bring you something to eat in private."

He smiled and looked down. "You're too good to me." His smile slipped, and sadness again leaked into his features. Setting down the thermos on the cement, I did something impossibly stupid. I streaked off my clothes, well, down to my bra and underwear, and hopped into the water with him. Hunter jerked up straight. "What are you doing?"

He tried to politely keep his eyes off my chest, but they kept drifting back. Some mature, feminine part of me liked him looking at my body. I kept my breasts above the waterline as I settled beside him. "Joining you for a dip while you eat. I like being warm too."

He smirked. "You're already warm, and I don't think your family would approve of this."

I sat right beside him, timidly putting my hand on his knee. Since my mom hadn't rushed out here, I had to assume she was being kept busy by the family, and wasn't paying a great amount of attention to me; this building was a strain for Mom, but if she tried hard enough, she could hear us. "Well then," I quietly said. "We won't tell them."

Hunter grabbed a section of my hair; the ends of the long strands were completely soaked as they floated on top of the water. "Good luck with that," he murmured.

Reaching behind me, I grabbed the thermos. Hunter's gaze shifted from my body to the carafe. He wanted two things right now. I'd be happy to give him both. He shifted how he was sitting so he was facing me; it left his lower body exposed, but Hunter didn't seem to care. He just wanted to eat. Since he was often a gentleman, I did my damndest to not sneak a peek while I handed him the thermos. I succeeded for the most part. His fangs crashed down before he even brought the container to his lips. His eyes closed as he tipped it back, and it made me smile to watch him eat without hesitation. Or even a grimace. This was getting easier for him. Finally.

As he gulped down his meal, his free hand came out to clutch my thigh. Gently squeezing and releasing, he slid his hand up my leg. I was sure he wasn't even conscious of what he was doing right now. *I* was sure conscious of it though. Every section he touched ignited my flesh more than the steamy water. I wanted him to keep going. I wanted him to give me another moment like last night. Julian was awake, though, and he'd definitely put a stop to this if it went that far. We'd have to wait. Maybe I could sneak down to Hunter's room later?

When Hunter's hand wrapped around my hip, I forgot all about my brother. He pulled on me, like he wanted me closer, so I straddled him. Finished with his drink, he lowered the thermos and stared at me with hooded eyes. My heartbeat raced, and he tilted his head, listening to it. "You shouldn't be here. You shouldn't be so close to me," he whispered. His hand slipped underneath my underwear though, to rest on my bare hipbone.

Desire blossomed through my core, and I scooted up his lap. I needed to know if he was feeling this too. When our chests were flush together, I could tell that he was; his body was fully ready for me. All he'd have to do was rip my underwear away and he could have me. Breath heavier, I told him, "Quit trying to push me away."

He had blood on his lips, and I leaned down to lick it off. His grip on my hip tightened, his hips moved beneath mine. "Stop. We can't."

I could hear blood sloshing in the thermos still in his hand. My words full of double meaning, I indicated his meal. "Do you want more?"

He understood the double-entendre and seemed unsure how to answer me. Finally, he nodded and whispered, "Yes."

I rocked my hips against him; the feeling of his body so close to mine made the ache almost unbearable. I didn't think I could wait until tonight. I didn't think I could wait another second. I needed him, body and soul. Containing the moan I wanted to make, I said, "Then have some more."

Instead of caving, Hunter pushed me off his lap. I wanted to whimper at the loss of him. "Nika ... you should go."

He set down the thermos, not partaking in that desire anymore either. I had to resist the urge to straddle him again. "I'm not going anywhere, Hunter, can't you just accept that?"

His face aged as he closed his eyes. When he reopened them, the sadness I saw there broke my heart. "And I'm not going to accept this life. Ever. So where does that leave you?" He looked away. "You deserve better."

Grabbing his cheek, I made him look at me. "You keep saying you won't accept this life, but I see you acclimating. Day by day you're getting better. You *can* get through this, Hunter, I know you can. And I want to help you. I'm not leaving you ... like he did."

Pain and betrayal flashed over his features, and I wanted to cry for him. If his father had just stayed, just accepted him, Hunter's pain wouldn't be nearly as great. But instead of his father's unconditional love, he had mine. I leaned into him and placed my lips against his, letting him feel how much I loved him, how serious I was about this. He wasn't alone.

His kiss was reluctant at first—he still wanted to push me away—but like he did so often, he melted under my touch. His hand came up to cradle my head as we tenderly moved our mouths together. I could tell his fangs were up as he kissed me, and I smiled against his lips. I could taste the residual blood in his mouth. He'd retracted his fangs despite that fact ... and that took a great deal of effort. He was getting so much better at this.

Being respectful of his wish to go slowly, I didn't jump back onto his lap, and that took a great deal of effort for me. I did run my hand down his chest though. And I might have placed it low on his firm abdomen. Low enough that the back of his straining body touched the back of my hand. It killed me, in the best possible way. It affected him too. The longer I held my hand there, perfectly still against his belly, the more heated his kiss became. He was breathing heavier in no time, and his hand tangled into my hair, holding me against him.

When he finally broke apart from my mouth, he could barely speak. "Do you know ... what you're doing to me?"

I knew what *he* was doing to *me*, so I had to imagine that the fire raging through him was very similar. "Can I touch you?" I breathed in his ear.

He dropped his head to my shoulder as a low groan escaped him. "Please," he begged.

I rotated my wrist so my fingers could wrap around him. He fell apart under my caress. "God, you're hotter than the water." He let out a groan that was far too loud for how close we were to the main house. I didn't care though. I also didn't care that I was about to explode and Julian would surely feel it. As my fingers traveled up and down his body, I breathed in his ear, "Please touch me too."

His head came back up, and he stared at me so intensely, I thought I would die if he didn't do it. "Nika," he murmured, his lips seeking mine again. I didn't think he was going to honor my request, but then I felt his hand up my thigh again. My body pulsed with need, and I leaned back in the water, giving him a better angle.

His fingers snuck inside my underwear, and his tongue darted into my mouth. I ached so badly I could hardly think straight. My fingers caressing his body squeezed and pulled. He moaned in my mouth, then his finger ran between my legs. Oh. My. God. Lost in the moment, I laid my head back in the water as a long cry left my lips. It was the most wonderful, intense feeling having him directly touch me, so much better than everything we'd already done. I didn't want it to end. I wanted to go all the way. Right now.

"Nika ... get back in the house. Now."

Reality crashed down on me like ice water as my mother's voice shot through my brain. She was right outside the pool house, and I didn't need to see her to know she was pissed. Her words woke up Hunter, too, and he blurred to the other side of the tub, as far away from me as he could get. He was panting, and his eyes were still heavy with desire. The lingering sensation of him touching me was still with me, and I had to rub my legs together as I cursed under my breath. Damn Mom.

"Yeah, okay. I'll be right there," I yelled at her.

"I'll wait," she replied.

Hunter ran a hand through his hair. "You should go," he told me again.

Groaning, I hopped out of the water and grabbed a towel on a nearby rack so I could dry off enough to redress. Crap. My mom was gonna kill me if she'd heard all that. And then Dad was going to kill me again when she told him. Great.

CHAPTER SEVENTEEN

Julian

MY SISTER WAS trying to send me straight to the loony bin, I was sure. What I'd felt coming from her in the pool house was more than anything I ever wanted to feel again. Mom was handling the situation now, but there was a residual amount of disgust in my stomach that wasn't leaving. Gabriel was standing to my right; he seemed deep in thought while he watched Halina laughing with her daughter. I hated to butt in on his thoughts, but I couldn't take this anymore. Nika and I needed help.

"Gabriel … please tell me you've found a way to break my bond with Nika."

His green eyes widened as he looked down at me. I couldn't be sure, but I thought he looked alarmed. Maybe he thought I meant the familial bond. No, that one I wanted left in place. Strange as it sounded, I liked always knowing where Nika was. It was comforting.

I shook my head and clarified what I meant. "The emotional bond. Please tell me you can break it." I looked around the room and lowered my voice, not that it mattered; they could all still hear me. "We're too old to keep sharing this connection."

Amusement lit Gabriel's eyes as he looked in the direction of the pool house. He, and probably every other member of my family, could probably guess what Nika had been doing in there. Thanks to my squirming, sighing, and grimacing, they'd all figured it out pretty quickly. Nika was going to kill me for unintentionally tattling on her.

When Gabriel looked back at me, the smile was gone from his eyes. "Unfortunately, I've had a lot on my plate, Julian, and haven't had much time to devote to that particular problem." He indicated the windows. "I'm still working on giving the purebloods a bit more freedom." He switched his finger to Starla. "And allowing Starla the chance to successfully go through her conversion."

Jacen heard him, and squeezed Starla a little tighter. Sometimes I forgot that she was aging because she had to. She wouldn't survive the process of becoming an undead vampire. Some strange flaw in her blood.

I hung my head while that sunk in. Those were pretty big problems to deal with first. Gabriel patted my back. "I have other ... side projects, as well, but when I'm able, I will find a cure for the two of you. I give you my word."

I looked up at him, grateful that he was going to try to help us. "Thank you."

Starla exhaled in a puff. "Better help him quick, Father. They shouldn't have to feel each other getting busy."

Every vampire in the room had been politely ignoring my conversation with Gabriel, but they all stopped and stared after Starla said that. I dropped my head into my hands. God, the lack of privacy in this family was mortifying. Nika looked just as embarrassed as me when she entered the room. Her hair was soaked, she reeked of chlorine, and her shirt and jeans were damp from her underwear. I lifted an eyebrow in question. Were they almost having sex in the pool? I'd have to remember to never use it again.

Mom pointed to the cushion beside me on the couch. "Sit. Stay."

Nika huffed, but did what she was told. I looked over at her and mouthed, *Sorry*. Her feelings had just been too strong to ignore. Color rushed to her cheeks and she stared straight out the window. Her mood flooded with horror; my mood matched hers. This couldn't keep going on. We'd both die of shame.

Nobody said anything until Dad returned. When I felt him in the driveway, I shot up off the chair, nervous and excited. Arianna was with him. Nika started to rise too, until Mom pointed a long finger at her. "Stay." Nika rolled her eyes and crossed her arms over her chest. She silently fumed, but did as Mom commanded.

I hurried into the entryway to greet my girlfriend. Well, I hoped she was still my girlfriend. She was here, so I took that as a good sign. Unless she'd refused to go and Dad had come back alone. Nerves sizzled through me at that thought. Was he coming back alone?

I paced back and forth until Grandma Alanna put a hand on my shoulder. "Relax, Julian. Everything will be fine." I inhaled and exhaled a deep breath, hoping that was true. Once my nerves settled a little, I heard Arianna's voice outside and smiled. She was here.

I opened the front door right as Dad approached it. He grinned at me. "Thanks, son."

I told him, "You're welcome," but my sight was already locked onto the person right behind him. "Hey, I'm glad you came."

Dad walked through the door while I held my hand out to Arianna. She bit her lip, and looked hesitant to take it. I held my breath. She had to ... I couldn't lose her. Eventually, she exhaled in frustration and grabbed my fingers. It wasn't exactly a romantic gesture, but it was better than her refusing to touch me.

Arianna's green-brown eyes surveyed my family's fineries while I surveyed her. There were slight red, spidery veins in her eyes, and a bluish discoloration under them. While she was covering it well, she looked exhausted. Had I done that to her? I hadn't meant to. I hadn't meant for anyone to get hurt.

Dad was already walking into the living room, his bond to Mom naturally pulling him that way. I tugged on Arianna's hand. "Hungry? Dinner's just about ready."

Some of the color left Arianna's cheeks, and she swallowed. "Yeah, a little." I could sense the unease in her. I hoped Halina wouldn't tease her. Sometimes Halina liked to test people's fortitude—see if they would stay or run. I wasn't sure which one Arianna would do right now, and I didn't really want to find out.

When all of us were in the living room, everyone waved a greeting at Arianna. Nika gave her friend a brief smile; she was still pretty irritated.

The tense mood in the air hadn't alleviated in the short amount of time I'd been gone. Dad noticed. After giving Mom a tender kiss, he asked, "Everything okay while I was gone?"

Mom looked over at Nika on the couch. "We need to have a talk with our daughter. Privately."

Nika laid her head back on the couch. "You're overreacting, Mom. Nothing happened." By the look on her face and her tone of voice, she was clearly disappointed about that fact.

Mom narrowed her eyes. "That didn't sound like nothing, and the look on your brother's face didn't seem like nothing." Arianna bunched her brows and looked up at me. I glanced back at her, nervous. Arianna didn't know about the emotional bond yet. I wasn't eager to tell her about it, either.

Dad narrowed his eyes as he looked over at Nika. "What happened?" He sighed and looked toward the pool house, where Hunter was.

Nika shot up off the couch. "Nothing happened. I brought Hunter something to eat, because he can't do sit-down meals yet, and we … kissed. That's it."

I cleared my throat and looked away. Some kiss, if that was all they'd been doing. Mom and Dad both looked at me, then back to Nika. "For some reason, I don't quite believe that," Dad murmured.

Nika shot me a glare, and I raised my hands. "Sorry. I tried, but I'm sure you can imagine how … weird it was for me." Arianna looked even more baffled, and I clamped my mouth shut. Damn bond.

Dad's mouth compressed into a firm line. "Nika, would you please join your mom and me upstairs for a minute?"

Nika exhaled in a rush. "This is totally unfair. I'm sixteen, practically an adult. If I want to fool around with my boyfriend—"

Cringing, Dad held his hand up. "Upstairs. Please."

Furious, Nika brushed by him. I was enormously grateful there were soundproof rooms upstairs, because I was sure they'd be talking about things I never wanted to hear. Halina stepped forward when Dad turned to follow Nika. "Wait, Teren. Before you go off to chastise your daughter for something *you* actively participated in at her age, I need to tell you something."

Nika and I exchanged a victorious glance while Dad closed his eyes. He didn't like being called out for being a hypocrite, but hey, if the shoe fits ... .

"What is it?" he asked, his eyes still closed.

"Hunter stopped a predator in your neighborhood last night. Hunter was injured in the fight ... but the man he stopped won't be a problem anymore. Even still, you should be cautious."

Concern flashed through Nika, and Dad's eyes sprang open as Halina's words sunk in. "A hunter? In our neighborhood?" Then his eyes narrowed, and he twisted to look at Nika. "And Hunter stopped him? What was Hunter doing in our neighborhood?" All good questions. I knew the answer to one, but not the other. Vampire hunters were near our home? While we were sleeping? I didn't like that thought at all.

Nika couldn't have looked guiltier if she tried. Dad snapped his head to the doors leading outside. "Hunter? If you can hear me, get your ass in here now!"

Halina folded her arms across her chest. "You're sort of missing the point of my warning."

Dad pointed a finger at her. "You're supposed to be watching him. Where were you?"

Halina lifted her chin. "I was here." Her tone fully implied that she wouldn't tolerate Dad questioning her decisions. Dad clenched his hand into a fist, but didn't say anything more.

Hunter appeared at the door. When he opened it, the scent of chlorine wafted into the room. He was just as wet as Nika. Yep. They'd definitely almost had sex in the pool. Never swimming again. Hunter's eyes scanned the group, then he glanced toward the kitchen, where blood was warming for dinner. "Could we do this outside?" he asked. "I'd rather not be in here right now."

Irritated, Dad walked over to him. "And I'd rather you not ever touch my daughter again. But I have a feeling that's not going to happen either. Unless I stake you in the next twenty seconds."

Nika stormed across the room toward him. "Dad!" she snapped. Dad ignored her as he glared at Hunter.

Halina rolled her eyes and looked over at Arianna. "Men," she muttered. "Everything's a pissing contest." Arianna clenched my hand and stepped into my body as she tittered nervously. Halina made her a bit uneasy. I wrapped my arm around her shoulder. At least the excuse to snuggle with her was one positive in all this drama.

Hunter lifted a corner of his lip at Dad. "You're still mad at me for shooting you, aren't you?"

"It didn't feel good," Dad stated. "But I'm more concerned about what you found last night than what you're doing with my daughter." He glanced back at Nika. "Just fractionally more concerned."

Hunter glanced at Nika. Pain washed over his face, and Nika's mood slipped. Whatever was between them was still rocky at best. Looking back at Dad, Hunter shrugged. "I was in the neighborhood. I smelled him, followed him, and took care of him."

Dad raised an eyebrow. "You killed another hunter? The first time was self-defense, but this? You're hunting hunters now? Isn't that ... against what you believe?"

Hunter gave him an unflinching stare. "He was hunting your family. *My* family. I wasn't okay with that."

Dad appraised Hunter, then asked him, "And what exactly were you doing in our neighborhood in the middle of the night?"

Practically broadcasting his intentions like a flashing neon sign, Hunter flicked a glance at Nika. "Uh ... I ..."

Something clicked into place for me while I waited for Hunter to think up an excuse for stalking my sister. "Did you know this hunter too? Like the last ones?"

Hunter sighed and looked my way. Dad's concern spiked. "You knew them?" he asked.

Hunter's gaze drifted around the room, finally locking on Gabriel, for some reason. "It's not that significant. Hunting is a small world. I'd say I probably know most of them."

I took a step forward. "Really? If that's true, and you're all so tight, then why didn't you know about mixed vampires? Wouldn't that have come up sometime?"

Hunter seemed peeved by my question. Well, too bad. It was a valid one. "There aren't that many of you, and you hide what you are ... very well."

Dad studied Hunter carefully. "So many hunters in such a short period of time is concerning. I've been watching the ads closely, but I haven't seen or heard anything about your father. Do you think he has something to do with this?"

My eyes widened. I hadn't considered that possibility. If Hunter's dad was sending assassins out to kill him, then we were all in danger. A flash of mixed emotions went through Nika—guilt, fear, concern. I wasn't sure what that meant, but I was sure it meant something. Hunter kept his expression the same. "I haven't seen or spoken with my father since I died, so how would I know if he had anything to do with this. If I had to guess, I'd say no." Swallowing, he looked away. "If he wanted me dead, he'd do it himself. We clean up our own messes."

Nika frowned for a second before fixing her face. Her mood shifted to curiosity, confusion. She knew something Hunter wasn't saying. Looking back at Dad, Hunter pointed to the kitchen and said, "I really can't stand the smell of that anymore. Are we done here? Can I go back outside?"

Dad nodded. "For now." Hunter turned to leave, and Dad grabbed his elbow. Hunter tensed under his grip. "You might be a part of this family now, but I don't trust you. Stay away from my daughter."

Hunter glanced over Dad's shoulder at Nika. Pain flashed over his face again. "I'm not trying to start anything. I just needed help transitioning ... and she was there for me. And I'll be forever grateful for that." He returned his eyes to Dad. "But if you really don't want me around her, then I'll stay as far away as I can."

"No!" Nika immediately interjected.

Dad held his hand up to her. "Just ... for now. I don't want the two of you alone anymore." He looked between Nika and Hunter. "Okay?"

Hunter nodded. Nika fumed, then finally sputtered, "Fine. Whatever."

Hunter looked around the room. "I should go. Enjoy your ... meal."

He left the same way he came in. Nika didn't waste a minute to let her distaste be known. "Unbelievable. Thanks, Dad."

Dad sighed. "You're sixteen, Nika. You're too young for that ... kind of intensity."

Nika raised her chin. "I know what I can handle. If you don't trust him, that's fine. But trust *me*."

Dad looked down, then peeked back up at her. "I do. I do trust you. I just ..." He raised his hands. "You're my little girl."

Nika tried to maintain her stubbornness, but she melted at the look on Dad's face. Exhaling, she walked over to him and laced her arms around his neck. "I'll always be your little girl, Dad. No matter what happens."

Mom sniffled, while Dad and Nika hugged. They both looked over at Mom as she wiped her eyes dry. "What?" she muttered. Dad laughed and wrapped his arm around her shoulder.

Nika headed upstairs to change into dry clothes, and the rest of us headed into the kitchen for dinner. All conversations about Hunter and Nika were momentarily dropped. They lingered with me though. Hunter had lied about something, I was sure of it. Nika knew the truth, and I was going to get it out of her. Later, after my girlfriend left.

My sister was pensive during dinner, deep in her own troubled thoughts. My family took it as sullenness and gave her space. My curiosity grew even stronger, but Nika ignored me, wouldn't even look at me. I stopped worrying about it when the blood arrived.

Halina placed a glass in front of me, and I stared at it in contemplation. I'd never drank blood in front of Arianna before, but if she wanted to see all of me, this was a part I couldn't leave out. I could feel her eyes burning into me as glasses were set in front of all the vampires. I figured it was just easier for her to focus on me, since I was the one she was the most comfortable with. Well, she was pretty comfortable with Nika too, but Nika was off in her own world at the moment.

I glanced over at Arianna sitting beside me. She had her fork half-raised to her mouth as she stared at the steaming red glass in front of me. She was still ignoring the rest of the vampires in the room, and that was probably a good thing, since I could hear light growls filling the air as they reveled in their bloody cocktails.

Me staring at her broke her focus, and she looked up at my eyes. She smiled half-heartedly, then she glanced around the table. She sucked in a quick breath, and I could smell the burst of fear. Halina raised her lip, exposing a fang tinged in red. "Problem, dear?"

Arianna's eyes widened, and she started trembling. I put my hand on her arm, and she jumped. "No, no problems," she muttered, slipping her fork into her mouth.

She chewed while my family sipped. Her heart raced a mile a minute. Eventually, even Nika noticed. "You sure you're okay, Arianna?"

Arianna swallowed a huge chunk of food; she had a little trouble getting it down. "Yep, this isn't a big deal. It's just what you need to live." She looked over at me. "You can trust me with stuff like this. I'm not going to run."

My sharp ears caught Halina muttering to Imogen, "Too bad. I like it when they run." Luckily, Arianna didn't hear her.

I smiled at Arianna, rubbing her arm encouragingly. She glanced at my still full cup. "Go ahead," she whispered. "Don't hold back because of me."

I looked back at my glass. I really did want some, but I didn't want to freak her out before we'd even had a chance to talk. "It's okay. I don't need it like the others."

Arianna set down her fork. "This is you not letting me in again. Deciding for me what I need to know, what I need to be included in. Just take a drink, Julian."

Halina chuckled. In Russian, she said, *"I like her, she's feisty. She'll give us good babies."*

My dad lowered his glass and snapped, "Stop it. We talked about that."

Halina rolled her eyes. "I was kidding. Relax." By her smile, it was obvious she wasn't kidding.

Arianna glanced between the two of them. "What are you guys talking about?"

Distracting her, I grabbed my glass. "Okay, I'll drink in front of you if you want. If you're sure you're okay with it?"

Arianna turned away from my family and again focused on me. "I'm sure." She was jittery with nerves; I hoped she was serious.

Steeling myself for all sorts of different reactions, I brought the glass to my lips and tipped it back. My fangs dropped the instant the tangy treat hit my tongue, and a content noise escaped me as the warmth traveled down my throat. My eyes fluttered closed. God, this stuff was so good.

When I was satisfied, I righted the glass. I'd probably downed about half of it in just a few gulps. A little afraid, I slowly opened my eyes. Arianna was staring at me with her mouth open. I wiped my mouth with the back of my hand, waiting for her to say something. When she didn't, I got even more nervous. "Arianna?"

She blinked, then twisted to her food. "Yeah, not a big deal. It's fine." Grabbing a knife, she started cutting her chicken into bite-sized pieces. I wanted to believe her, but her hand shook so much she could barely cut her food.

"Here, let me help you," I whispered.

She held her knife up to me. "I got it. Just ... let me do this. Please."

I nodded and left her alone. She needed to process this by herself.

Arianna stuck it out for the rest of dinner. She seemed a lot less nervous by the end of it, like she was slowly getting used to the gory sight in front of her. After dinner, I felt really good about telling her everything I'd been holding back. She'd handled so much already, and she hadn't fled, so maybe she really could handle it all. I was still nervous about talking to her, though, and didn't want to do it around my entire family.

So, after a leisurely dinner, I indicated outside. "Want to go for a walk? We have a lot to talk about." I couldn't quite look her in the eye.

Arianna sighed, the reluctance clear on her face. "Yeah, okay."

I looked up at Dad. "We'll be back in a little bit. Okay?"

Dad was preoccupied with watching Nika, but he looked my way to answer my question. "Stay close," he warned. "And don't be gone long. I need to take Arianna home soon." He turned back to Nika. "And you're coming with me this time."

Nika groaned, her face and mood exasperated. I needed to talk to Nika tonight, too, but now wasn't the time. Now was for Arianna. Grabbing her warm hand, I led her out back. Her eyes darted all over the darkened landscape, maybe searching for other creatures of the night. "I want to show you something, and it's a little on the far side. Do you mind if we go fast?"

I held my arms out, like I was going to pick her up. She eyed me warily, then nodded. I scooped her into my arms, savoring the feel and smell of her. It had been far too long since I'd really held her. I didn't like that fact. "Hang on," I whispered. She obediently squeezed me, and I took off into the night.

I didn't have the glowing headlights that my family had, but I knew the terrain well enough that I didn't stumble or fall. Thank God, that would have been really embarrassing. Within seconds, we were at a large pond. The water was pitch-black, but the light of the moon showed ripples where small creatures were breaking through the surface. Tall grasses lined the edges of the pond, and there was a long wooden dock jutting out into the water. Nika and I had learned to swim here, and had spent several summers jumping off the dock into the frigid water. We'd always challenged ourselves to see who could hold their breaths the longest. Nika had always won; being under the water made me too claustrophobic.

Setting Arianna down, I walked to the end of the wooden walkway with her. We swung hands as the sounds of crickets and frogs filled the air. Sitting down on the edge with her, I quietly said, "I'm really glad you came out tonight. I'm glad you gave me a second chance."

Holding my hand with both of hers, she was silent for a moment. Then she asked, "Do you still have feelings for Raquel?"

My head snapped up. "No. Not like that." Arianna bit her lip. The moonlight reflected in her watery eyes. "Not like that, Arianna," I repeated.

She swallowed, then nodded. "Okay ... so tell me what really happened that night. And why did you lie to me about it?"

My eyes drifted to her small hands holding mine. "Nika didn't want to frighten you, so she told you what we were telling everybody else. I went along with it, because I was scared. Scared you'd freak out and leave." I looked up at her. "I don't want you to leave me."

She squeezed my palm. "I won't. Tell me what happened."

I looked out over the blackness around us. "Vampire hunters. They caught Raquel, drugged her, then slit her arms up and left her as bait. Vampire bait for Nika's boyfriend, Hunter. Raquel was hurt because of my family, and then we had to make everyone believe she'd done it to herself. And now the whole school thinks she's suicidal." A weary sigh escaped me. "Everything that happened to her was my family's fault. I owe her."

"Oh," she whispered. "Well, now I feel like a jackass. You were just so obsessed with her ... but I see why now."

I returned my eyes to hers. "I never wanted to hurt you, I just didn't want you to worry or be scared. I didn't want you to think that being with me was dangerous. Nika didn't want that either."

She looked down. "I get it." After a moment of reflection, she looked back up and asked, "Hunter found another one by your house. *Are* you in danger?"

I pressed my lips together. I wanted to tell her no, to ease her mind, but I knew honesty was important right now. "I don't know. I need to talk to my sister. Hunter's hiding something, and I think she knows what it is."

Arianna looked back toward the direction of the house. "Maybe we should go back and ask her?"

"I can't ask yet. I have to wait until we're alone." Arianna looked back at me and I shrugged. "We don't narc each other out to our parents, and if I ask her where they can overhear ..."

Arianna nodded. "I don't like the idea of you in danger."

I ran my thumb over her cheek. "I don't like the idea of you being mad at me. Do you forgive me?"

Her cheek heated under my caress. My sensitive skin could feel it. "Yes, I guess so. But ... I feel like there's more. I feel like you're keeping other things from me. And I want to know everything. Even if you think it's going to make me mad."

I shifted to face her. "The children thing. My grandmother wants them. It's important to her. I told her we might give her some one day ... but I only said it so she wouldn't wipe your memory ..." My voice trailed off. I couldn't tell her that a breakup between us would be permanent. I just ... couldn't say it. "Because I like that you know my secret. I like not having to hide who I am."

Her hand came up to cup my cheek. "Is that all you've been hiding? That you were attacked? That your family expects kids from us?"

Her lips were so close to mine, my heart started surging. It had been even longer since I'd kissed her. I really *had* been ignoring her. God, I was a bastard. I nodded, and leaned in for her mouth. "Are you still mine?" I asked. "Are you still my girl?"

Her eyes locked onto my mouth as her hand drew me closer. "I never stopped being your girl, Julian. I'll always be your girl."

Her mouth found mine in the darkness and the sweetness of her kiss stole my breath. Our lips worked together soft and light at first, but the week of separation hit us, and we moved together with more intensity. The stillness in the air was punctuated with the sounds of our breath, our lips. After a few passionate minutes, Arianna pulled away from me. "We never got to have our moment on prom night. It's so beautiful out here, so peaceful, so perfect ... do you want to ..." She gave me a shy shrug. My body instantly went into overdrive. Yes, yes, I did want to.

In answer, I laid her back on the dock. Her breath increased when I moved over the top of her. I couldn't believe this was happening. Thank God, I still had our prom night condom in my wallet. Thank God, I still had my wallet with me. My mouth lowered to hers as our bodies rocked together. It wasn't long before I was ready for her, but I wasn't sure if she was ready for me.

"Oh God, Julian, I've missed you so much. I want you so much."

I groaned as I worked my mouth down her throat. "I want you too. Just you." In the back of my mind, I could feel Nika's disgust rising. I understood, as I'd felt the same way earlier, but like Nika when she'd been with Hunter, I couldn't stop this. I wanted it too much. I pushed her feelings away and focused on the sensation of Arianna's body under my fingertips.

Our hips rocked together at a faster and faster pace. She moaned beneath me, squirming as her hands tangled in my hair. "Oh, Julian, I'm glad this is happening. I was so disappointed after prom."

I groaned as my ready body rubbed against hers. "I know, me too."

Her hands worked up my shirt, wanting it off. I helped her, pulling it up over my head and throwing it up the dock. Her mouth pressed against my pecs, and I shuddered. Her lips on a part of my body that was normally hidden sent a jolt of electricity through me. My shaking hands went up her shirt, needing to feel her soft curves. She groaned when I touched her bra. Adjusting herself, she ripped off her shirt and tossed it up by mine. She was panting when she grabbed my head and led me to her chest. I slipped the cup of her bra to the side, and nearly lost it at the sight of her bare breast. She was still pulling me into her, so I closed my lips around her nipple. She cried out, and I didn't think I was going to make it to the actual act of sex. She was soft, rigid, sweet. It was unlike anything I'd ever felt before. I needed more. My hands went to her jeans, unbuttoning and unzipping them. I ran my fingers down the inside, my heart nearly exploded. I just ... needed to feel this.

My fingers ran between her legs, over her underwear. "Oh my God, Julian," she groaned. "That feels so good." Grunting, I released her breast and removed my hand. Quick as a flash, I worked on pulling down her jeans. I needed her. I couldn't wait any longer.

Her hands stilled mine. "Wait. Before we ... is there anything else I don't know. I don't want any secrets between us when we do this."

It thrilled me that she said *when* we do this. Nika's mood simmered in the back of my head. She was flipping through annoyance, irritation, understanding, and nausea. Arianna's hand came down to rest on my rock-hard body. I gasped, "Yes. There's ..." my train of thought left me.

"What?" she asked, her hand running up and down the length of me through my jeans. "Um ... I ... Oh, God that feels good."

"I know," she whispered. "It feels really good."

She unzipped my jeans, then slipped her hand inside. I sucked in a breath as I felt her touch the most sensitive part of me. "Oh God," I panted. I ran my hand back inside her jeans, inside her underwear this time. When I reached her, she was wet, warm. She cried out again, clutching me tight. Then her hand slipped inside my underwear. It was incredible. I was going to explode.

"Tell me," she moaned. "Please tell me."

My head spun. What was I telling her? What did she want to know? I'd tell her anything. I'd tell her everything. "Oh God ... it's just ... Nika and I share feelings."

She froze underneath me. Realizing what I'd just said, I froze as well. "You ... what?" she asked, removing her hand from my jeans. I ached with the loss of her touching me, but the shock of ice water running through my veins helped cool my fire; I hadn't meant to tell her that. I slowly withdrew my finger from her underwear. "Nika and I ... have a bond unique to us." My breath was still fast with passion. I tried to temper it, but couldn't. "We feel what the other person is feeling."

Arianna wiggled out from under me. "So Nika is feeling this ... right now?"

I cringed. Nika was going to kill me for doing this, for confessing our largest secret to her best friend. Arianna would never look at us the same. "Yeah. She's ... horrified, but she understands. I have to put up with it when she's with Hunter. We deal as best we can."

Arianna sat up and crossed her arms over her chest like Nika was physically out here with us. "So, it's not just that your family has super-hearing ears, Nika can feel you ... she can feel *us* ... when we ... Oh my God!" She looked around like she was looking for her clothes. "I can't have sex with you."

Leaning up, I grabbed her shirt and handed it to her. "Yes, you can. Nika understands."

Arianna threw on her shirt. "No! Ew! I can't go there knowing she can feel it. I'm surprised you can."

I grimaced. "Well, I don't like it, and I'm not happy about it, but at a certain point, I just don't care if she can feel it." I ran my fingers down her arm. "I want you."

She pulled back from me. "I can't have sex with you! Ever!"

Sighing, I sat up. "She doesn't feel anything when she's asleep. We can wait until then if you'd feel better about it."

Arianna gaped at me. "Asleep? We have to wait until your sister falls asleep before we can … for the rest of your life? Does the bond ever go away?"

Wrapping my arms around my knees, I sighed. "No. It's permanent. Unless Gabriel can find a way to medically break the bond, we'll always be connected to each other. And trust me, nobody wants it broken more than we do."

Arianna stood up. "I'm sorry, Julian. I just can't … deal with this right now. I'd like to go home."

Grabbing my shirt, I stood up with her. Crap. Was this her breaking point? I hoped not. "Okay, I'll take you back to the house."

CHAPTER EIGHTEEN

Julian

I WAS MOROSE on the way back to the ranch, and for once, my mood matched Nika's. We'd both had disappointing nights, and for fairly similar reasons. Arianna was silent as she reentered the house. She wouldn't directly look at Nika, who wouldn't directly look at her. The air was thick with tension. I'd said it before, and I had to say it again: Damn bond.

Nika must have done a better job hiding her disgust than I had; no one in the room appeared to be suspicious about what I'd been doing outside with my girlfriend. I wondered if Dad would have the same reaction with me as he'd had with Nika. Probably. Dad had multiple other concerns when it came to Hunter and Nika, but I knew he didn't want me to have sex either.

Gabriel was gone. Hunter was downstairs. Starla and Jacen were now occupying the pool—I'd heard them splashing around on the way back to the house. Definitely not swimming anytime soon. Grandma Linda and Grandpa Jack were having a quiet conversation with Imogen and Alanna about all the other ranches around the country. Mom and Dad were having a conversation with Halina about the vampire hunter Hunter had caught near our place.

Nika stayed quiet and stared at her hands on her lap as she listened to them talk about Hunter. Whatever she was thinking about, it was troubling her, and I was sure she wasn't ruminating on my near-sex experience. I needed to talk to her alone, and I needed more time with Arianna. Actually, the three of us needed a talk. Maybe Nika could convince Arianna that the bond wasn't as horrific as she thought. Yeah ... that conversation wasn't going to be the least bit awkward.

Clearing my throat, I walked up to Mom and Dad. "Hey, since you guys are busy talking and stuff, is it okay if *I* take Arianna home?" Dad narrowed his eyes, and I quickly added, "Nika wants to come, too, so you know, we're not gonna be alone or anything."

Surprise washed through Nika, but she kept her expression level. She was so much better at hiding her emotions. She glanced over at Arianna who flushed with color. Arianna wasn't very good with hiding how she felt either. We were peas in a pod.

Dad scratched his jaw. "Ah, I don't know, Julian. That's a long way for you to drive. I'd feel better if I took her back."

I shook my head. "It's not a problem, Dad. And it would just be straight there and straight back. I won't even stop the car. Well, except to let her out, of course." I laughed at my own joke, and a slight tremor of humor ran through Nika.

Dad smiled too. "Well, I'm glad some of my manners have kicked in. All right, you can take her back. But no speeding, no passing traffic, no scenic routes, no pulling over to help people, no music playing, and no cell phones."

I gaped at his list of commands. "Can I *breathe*?"

Dad smirked. "I would prefer it if you did. And you return here the second after you've dropped her off."

I nodded as Dad handed me his keys. He clenched them before turning them over. "I'll be tracking your progress. If you're taking too long, I'm coming for you."

Rolling my eyes, I snatched the keys away from him. "Was Grandma as unrelenting with you as you are with us?"

Dad shared a look with his mother. "You have no idea."

After turning away from Dad, I looked over at Nika and nodded my head toward the garage. "We'll see you guys in a little bit," I told the room.

Nika glanced down at the floor, to where Hunter was. She bit her lip, obviously not wanting to leave him. Grabbing her elbow, I whispered in her ear, "He'll be here when we get back."

She grudgingly let me pull her away. It wasn't like she could meet up with him again while Dad was awake anyway. I grabbed Arianna's hand with my other one. She took it, albeit loosely. To my family, she politely said, "Thank you for having me for dinner. It was good to see you all again."

Halina gave her a wide, amused smile. "Ah, we didn't have *you* for dinner, dear. Maybe next time." She winked at Arianna, and I glared. Sometimes Halina's sense of humor was a little too much.

Arianna gripped my hand, hard, and was all too eager to follow Nika and I out of the room. Once we were in the garage, I told her, "Don't worry about Grandma. She was just messing with you."

Knowing Halina could hear her, Arianna only gave me a tight smile in answer. Everyone remained silent as I drove the car away from the house. When we passed through the gate topped with the large letters of my family's name, Nika's eyes locked onto mine in the rearview mirror. "What's up, Julie?" she asked.

I didn't answer her right away. I waited until we were on the main road and about a mile from the ranch. "You know something," I said. "What is it?"

Her face twisted into sourness. "I know whatever you two were doing tonight, it was a lot more than talking."

Arianna and I glanced at each other, then she stared straight ahead. "How could you both not tell me about the bond?" she asked.

Nika's eyes flashed to me in the mirror. "You told her?"

I opened my mouth, but Arianna beat me to it. "Yes, he did. Why didn't you? I mean, this entire time Julian and I have been fooling around, you could feel it?" Arianna twisted her body around to face Nika in the back seat. "We were going to have sex on prom night! Sex! And you would have felt it! Why didn't you say something?"

Nika held her hands up. "We had a plan ... I was going to be asleep for that."

Arianna glanced between the two of us. "You and your sister had to come up with a plan so you could have sex with your girlfriend. That's so ... messed up."

Sighing, I ran a hand through my hair. Dad would probably faint if he saw me taking a hand off the wheel. "Trust us, we know how messed up this is. But it's the hand we were dealt, so we're just trying to deal."

"It's a pretty crappy hand," she said, sympathy in her eyes.

From behind us, Nika murmured, "It's not always bad." She locked eyes with me again. "When I give Julian a gift that I know he likes, I *really* know he likes it. When someone does something to hurt me, and it makes him mad, I feel how much he cares about me. When we're together, hanging out, and neither one of us is talking, I know he's content and happy, because I feel it. We're closer, because we don't have to guess. We know. I can't imagine what it would be like to not know exactly what Julian felt about something. That sounds … lonely to me. But I know that's the way it's going to have to be someday."

I smiled at my sister, but didn't say anything. I didn't have to. She felt all the love and warmth I had for her, and she felt how much the idea of separating our emotions hurt me too. But it was inevitable, and we both knew it.

Then, remembering my original question, I frowned. "And I feel it when you're holding something back from me. I felt your emotions when Hunter was talking to Dad. You know something about Hunter that you didn't want to talk about. What is it? What's going on?"

Nika sighed. "He lied to Dad … about his father. He told me after the first attack that Connor had sent those men to kill him. Now I'm wondering if Connor sent the other man to kill him too. And maybe there have been more instances that we don't know about. I don't know. I need to talk to Hunter, but I'm not allowed to be alone with him."

My eyes bugged out. "Jesus, Nika. If that's true, if his father is sending assassins after him, we're *all* in trouble. We can't sit on this information. Even if this latest guy was a coincidence and Connor only sent the jerks who hurt Raquel, we have to tell Dad."

Nika looked at her lap. "I know. I didn't realize until tonight that it had happened more than the one time." She closed her eyes in defeat. "We'll tell Dad when we get back. We'll tell them all."

We were silent for the next twenty minutes, each of us absorbing the knowledge learned tonight. Hating that my life was more complicated than Arianna deserved, I held my hand out for her. I wasn't sure if she'd take it, and I was greatly relieved when she did. Kissing the back of her hand, I asked, "Did dinner weird you out?"

She smiled at me. "A little. I want to be okay with everything that comes along with dating you, but ... it's a lot to take sometimes."

"I know. But just the fact that you were sitting down with me and trying to be okay with it means a lot." And hopefully she'd keep trying, and I wouldn't have to let her go. Nika and I both.

Nika laughed a little in the back seat. When I met eyes with her, she shook her head. "Quite a night, huh? We both almost lost our virginities, we told lies, we exposed lies, we got a 'talking to' from the parents." She laid her head back on the seat. "I'm glad today is almost over."

That was when I felt something ... odd. One of the blips in my head that belonged to my family members disappeared. It struck me so hard and so fast that I groaned and grabbed my head. Nika did the same. Arianna's eyes were wide as she looked between us. "What's wrong?" she asked.

Struggling to keep driving, I looked at Nika in the rearview mirror; panic was flaring through her. "I can't feel him," she whispered. "Why can't I feel him?"

Keeping my eyes locked on my sister, I answered Arianna's question. "Hunter's gone."

My simple statement didn't help Arianna fully understand the severity of the situation. "Gone? What do you mean he's gone? And how do you know?" She looked around, like he was outside in the darkness. Problem was ... he could be, and we'd never know it.

As I quickly explained to Arianna that Hunter had dropped off our internal radar, Nika's phone rang. She instantly grabbed it from her jacket pocket. Glancing at the screen, she quickly brought the phone to her ear. "Dad, what happened? Where's Hunter? Is he okay? I can't feel him anymore ... can you?" There was so much hope in her voice, it broke my heart.

Dad's words confirmed what I already knew. "No ... nobody can feel him anymore. Everyone is searching the house, but it's doubtful he's still here. I just wanted to make sure ... you were okay."

Nika's face contorted in confusion. "How is this possible? Does it mean he's ... ? He's not ... ? Dad, please tell me he's okay." Fear rolled through her body in waves. It made it hard to drive.

Dad's voice was soft in her ear. "I'm sure he's fine, honey. Don't worry. It's just some ... glitch in the bond. We'll figure it out, and we'll find him."

Nika's eyes started to water. "The bond doesn't glitch, Dad."

Dropping the placating tone, Dad said, "I know. Just get Arianna home as quickly as you can, then come straight back to the ranch. We'll figure it out when you get here. We'll find him, Nika. I promise."

Eyes disastrously full, Nika whispered, "Okay."

Dad sighed. "Be careful. Both of you."

Nika disconnected the phone and put it back in her pocket like she was tranced. Concerned, Arianna said, "Nika, I'm so sorry. Are you okay?"

Nika flashed her eyes up to me. Even though I'd heard everything Dad had just said, she told me. "No one knows where Hunter is." She looked out over the countryside around us, like he'd miraculously be beside the car or something.

I furrowed my brows, confused. "How did that happen? The bond is permanent. There's no turning it off, and you're right, it doesn't glitch. This shouldn't be possible."

Nika nodded, then she gasped and snapped her head to mine. "No, that's not true."

"What's not true?" Arianna asked, trying to follow along.

Nika looked over at her. "The bond *can* be turned off. It happened to Julian when he was younger."

Arianna's eyes swung my way. "What? How? Why?"

She sputtered on more questions while I glanced her way. I hadn't told her about my abduction yet. It was just one of those things that didn't come up in casual conversation, and ... I didn't talk about it much. "A man ... kidnapped me when I was three. He injected me with something to shut off the bond so my family couldn't find me."

Nika leaned forward to place a hand on my shoulder. "He couldn't shut off *our* bond though. I felt everything Julian went through."

Arianna's eyes widened to capacity. "I had no idea. Julian, I'm so sorry."

I shook my head. I didn't need to be reminded of that night right now. "It was a long time ago, and the man who gave me that shot is dead, so I doubt he gave it to Hunter."

Nika slowly shook her head. "No, *he* didn't, but someone else could have given it to Hunter."

It took me exactly a millisecond to realize who was smart enough to develop something that could shut off the bond. "Gabriel? But why would Gabriel want to shut off the bond?"

Nika sank into the seat. "It wasn't his doing. Hunter took the shot because he wanted to." She looked out the window again. "Because he wanted to run away, and he didn't want anyone chasing after him."

My mind spun as I tried to work out the complexities. "Because his dad is trying to kill him? Because he wants to hide ... from us?"

Nika shook her head. "I don't know. I don't understand why he'd ..." Her thoughts trailed off as her face twisted into a look of extreme concentration. Her eyes widened as she was struck with some realization. "Pull the car over," she said.

I blinked in confusion. "What? Why?"

She grabbed my shoulder, digging in with her nails in her haste. "I know where he is, but he won't be there long. Pull the car over."

Absolutely bewildered about what we were doing, I broke Dad's command and pulled the car over. Nika opened her door and shot into the night before I could even ask where she was going. "Nika!" I called out the open rear door. "Damn it!"

I sat in my seat, torn about what to do. Nika was zipping toward town much faster than I could drive. The only way to catch her was to get out and zoom after her on foot. But I'd have to leave Arianna behind to do that, and I didn't want to.

Seeing my turmoil, Arianna pushed on my shoulder. "Go. Go follow her, make sure she's okay."

I turned to her. "What about you?"

She pointed to the keys in the ignition. "I'll drive myself home. It's not a big deal."

My decision made, I shut off the car. Putting the keys in my pocket, I opened my door and sped around to her side. Opening her door, I held out my hand. "I'm not leaving you behind anymore. We'll go get her together."

Arianna beamed at me as she stepped into my arms. "Are you sure? That's a long way to run carrying somebody."

Reaching down, I scooped her up. "You're like a feather to me." I adjusted her so she was on my back, then I locked up Dad's car. He'd be furious if it got stolen because I'd left it unlocked. He was probably going to be ticked that we'd left it alongside the road, but then again, he *had* told us to get Arianna home as quickly as possible.

I started rushing after Nika while I felt the rest of my family disperse from the ranch in every direction; they were systematically searching for Hunter. I wasn't sure why Nika thought he was back in Salt Lake, but right now, I really didn't care about Hunter. I wanted to make sure my sister was safe.

While I could run farther and faster than most humans, I was winded when I got to Salt Lake. Surprising the hell out of me, Nika had gone back to our house. I'd been expecting her to go to some secret rendezvous spot or something. But, then again, I guess our house *was* their secret rendezvous spot. Wondering what the heck we were doing here, I set Arianna down. Nika was in the front yard, staring up at her bedroom. Her curtain was sticking out of the open window, and I could hear someone moving stuff around inside. Surprise washed through me; I really hadn't expected Hunter to be here.

"What are we doing here, Nick?" I asked, glancing around to see if any of our neighbors were paying attention. All was quiet though.

Eyes glued on the second story, she told me, "If Hunter *is* skipping town for good, there's one thing he won't leave behind. But only I know where it is, so he has to talk to me to get it."

Before I could respond, she did a quick squat followed by an inhuman jump, and easily landed on the roof.

I turned to Arianna. "You want to wait here or—"

She laced her arms around my neck and jumped into my arms before I'd even finished asking my question. "Hold on tight," I told her. Squatting, I made the same leap my sister had.

Not having my hands free to balance myself, I stumbled a bit on the roof. Arianna held onto me even tighter, but she didn't make a peep. I eventually righted myself and ducked into the window. Hunter was rifling through my sister's closet like a man possessed, and I gaped at his frenzied search as I set Arianna down.

Nika blurred to his side and grabbed his arm. "Hunter, what happened? Are you okay?"

Hunter jerked his arm away. He looked worried, frantic, and eager to be anywhere but here. "I don't have a lot of time, Nika. Where's my sister?"

Nika took a defiant stance. "I hid the urns, but I'm not telling you where they are until you tell me what happened."

Hunter groaned and ran his fingers back through his hair. "I don't have time for this. I should be a hundred miles from here."

Nika shook her head. "So, you *are* running away. After everything? After all the progress you've made? You're running? Why? I thought you liked my family?"

Hunter started pacing. "I do. I do like them. I don't know when it happened, but somewhere along the way I started to ... care ... about all of you." He flashed a brief smile. "Even your dad, and I'm pretty sure he hates my guts." His face darkened. "You all mean something to me, but I can't stay. And I don't have time to sit and chat about why I have to go." He pointed out the window. "She's looking for me, and you two will lead her straight to me."

I knew he meant Halina. I also knew she was too far away to be able to pinpoint our exact location. "She went north, looking for you. She can't tell exactly where we are, and our parents think we're taking Arianna home. They won't be suspicious." For now. If we stayed here long enough they would be.

Hunter didn't look any less concerned. "Regardless, I need to go. Where are the urns, Nika? Please, you have to tell me. They're mine."

A knot of guilt went through Nika, but she held her ground. "If you're taking your sister, then you don't plan on returning, so I think I have the right to ask why you're leaving me."

Hunter slumped and closed his eyes. "Don't do this, Nika. Don't make this even harder for me."

"Why should I make it easy? If you want to leave me, then be a man and tell me why."

Hunter's head snapped up. "That's just it. I'm not a man anymore. I'm a ... a ..."

Nika crossed her arms over her chest. "You're a vampire. Just like me. And I'm tired of you acting like that's such a bad thing. What have I done to make me such a bad person in your eyes?" She lifted an eyebrow. "What have you done, for that matter?"

Hunter swallowed, and looked around the room. "It's not that simple. It's not just because of what I am. It's also ... because of *who* I am."

I tilted my head, trying to understand. "Your dad wants you dead?"

Hunter locked eyes with me. "Yes. And he'll destroy all of you to get to me. The only way to keep you safe, is to get to him first. I know where he is, but he won't stay there long. I need to go."

Nika shook her head. "If this is about your dad, then let's go back to the ranch. The entire family will help you deal with him." She put her hand on his arm. "You don't have to do it alone."

Hunter glanced at her hand, then his lightly glowing eyes settled on her face. "This is my mess. I'll clean it up."

Nika clenched her jaw. "Because you're hoping he'll get you at the same time. You're hoping this ... curse ... you hate so much will end with your father."

Hunter shrugged. "He started this nightmare for me. He should be the one to end it."

Grief washed through Nika, and a tear rolled down her cheek. "So that's it? You're done trying. You're just going to let him kill you?"

Hunter looked away. "Nika, I don't expect you to understand. You say you know what being a vampire feels like, but you don't. Not really. What you are is so diluted ... you have no idea what being a pureblood means." He looked back at her. "I'm different from you. My desires are different. My urges are stronger. I have to fight a lot harder. And I'm tired of it."

He sighed. "But I won't let my dad remain a threat to you. I'll take care of him first. It's the least I can do to repay your family for their kindness."

Nika moved to block him, trapping him in the closet with her body. "I'm not going to let you do this. I'm not going to let you commit suicide." She talked to me over her shoulder. "Julian, call Dad. Tell him we found Hunter."

Hunter's eyes flashed to me. They were dark, menacing. I knew if I picked up my phone, he was going to be really ticked off. "I wouldn't do that, Julian. I'm eating regularly now, and I'm a lot stronger than you."

Arianna clenched my arm. I could smell the fear on her. Looking over, I saw that fear reflected in her eyes. She shook her head. "Let's just go. If he wants to run away, we can't stop him."

Nika's voice brought my attention back to her. "He's not going to hurt us. And I *can* stop him."

Hunter growled and bared his fangs at her. Arianna shook like a leaf. Nika only smiled. "I'm not scared of you. I'm in love with you. And I'm not letting you do this."

Hunter rolled his eyes, which made his appearance a lot less intimidating. "You're really getting on my nerves, Nika."

"Join the club, Hunter."

She lifted her chin, and a small smile touched Hunter's lips. Then he frowned. "Fine. If you won't tell me where my sister is, then I'll leave her in your care. That's probably for the best anyway."

He started to move past Nika, but she shoved him back. He hadn't been expecting it, and she successfully pushed him. I knew she wouldn't be able to trap him on her own, though, not with his strength. Making sure Arianna was safely to the side, I blurred over to stand by my sister. Hunter growled at us. "Back off, and let me go."

Menace blossomed in the air, but I ignored it. Nika wanted him to stay, wanted him alive, and it was my duty to help her. I put my hands up to his chest. "No. You need to stay here until our dad comes ... and that shouldn't be too long now, since your disappearing act put everyone on high alert."

Hunter shifted his snarl to me. "I don't want to hurt you, Julian, but I will if you don't get out of my way. Please," he added, his voice strained.

His expression was conflicted, and I knew he didn't want to injure us, but like a wounded, trapped animal, he would. I didn't like this. Not one little bit. "How did you break the bond?" I asked, hoping to distract him long enough that Dad would figure out there was a problem.

Hunter clenched and unclenched his fists. "How do you think? I had help from a very intelligent person."

Anger and betrayal washed through me. "Gabriel? Why would he betray my grandmother by helping you? He loves her."

Hunter nodded. "He does. And he also hates me. I killed more than a few of his nestmates in L.A. He can't kill me directly because of Halina, so this was the next best option for him. Break the bond with her and kick me out of the house to sink or swim on my own."

"Does he know about your father sending killers after the family?" Nika asked, her mood just as shocked as mine.

Hunter shifted his gaze to her. "Yes. But I assured him that my first task once I was free was dealing with him. And that is exactly what I should be doing right now."

Hunter was wearing a large black backpack. One of his hands deftly reached around and slipped inside the pack. I had no idea what he had in there, but I really didn't want to find out. "Hey, stop that ... whatever it is you're doing."

Hunter sighed. "I don't want to do this, but the two of you aren't leaving me much of a choice. I have to go, and I can't have you two homing devices following me, or keeping me here until your family shows up." Pulling something out of his pack, he locked eyes with my sister. She was finally nervous, but she bravely held her ground. "I'm sorry, Nika. I never wanted any of this to happen, and if there was another way ..."

Nika held out her hand. "There is another way. Come back to the ranch with me. Stop fighting what you are and join my family."

Hunter's face grew heavy with sadness. "It's too late for that."

His hand came around then. He passed something into his other hand, then crouched to the floor. Something crashed just above his head, and I twisted to see that Arianna had thrown a lamp at him. I had one second to be impressed, and then something stabbed my leg and liquid fire burned throughout my body. I screamed in pain at the exact same time that Nika did. Whatever he'd done to me, he'd done to her too.

I crashed to the ground, holding my leg. I saw Hunter dash past me, but I really didn't care about him anymore. The fire was quickly spreading over my entire body. It hurt, and yet, it felt oddly familiar. I saw two empty syringes on the ground, and with horrifying clarity, I suddenly knew exactly what Hunter had done to us. It was confirmed a heartbeat later, when I could no longer sense my sister beside me. Or anyone in my family.

Hunter had just injected us with the thing that shut off the bond.

Nika stood up as I still writhed in pain. She was gasping, wobbly, but she managed to stay standing. I didn't even want to try yet. My nerve endings felt on fire. Arianna was by my side in an instant, running her hands through my hair. "Julian? Are you okay? What did he do to you?"

I couldn't answer her. It hurt too much. Curling into the fetal position, I rested my head on her lap. God, this sucked even more than I remembered it sucking. Out of the corner of my eye, I saw my sister look over at the open window. Hunter was gone, fled into the night while we were momentarily incapacitated.

Clutching her stomach, Nika grit her teeth and spat out, "No." Then she jumped out the window to follow the bastard. Panic alleviated my pain. I couldn't track her. If I lost her, I'd never know where she was, not until this damn shot wore off, and if memory served, that took forever.

"Nika! Wait!" I scrambled to my feet. It was difficult, my legs felt like rubber. When I was standing, I darted to the window.

Arianna grabbed my hand at the last second. "Don't go!"

I looked back at her, fear filling me instant by instant. "I have to. I can't sense her anymore. If I lose her trail, I lose *her*."

Arianna frowned at me, not following. Realizing she didn't know what Hunter had just done, I quickly told her, "Hunter broke the bond. I can't feel her. I can't track her location. She's ... gone."

Arianna's eyes widened as she looked back to the window. She knew how annoying—and important—the bond was to us. Snapping her gaze to me, she said, "Take me with you."

I wasn't sure if I could handle that at the moment, but I needed to go to my sister before the wind wiped away her scent. It was the only way I had to find her now. And I really didn't want to leave Arianna behind anyway. She was safer with me than all alone.

I pulled her onto my back. My knees shook, and I felt tremors run up and down my body. The sensation would pass, though; I just had to wait it out. Placing my foot on the window ledge, I stepped out onto the roof. I had to find to Nika, and fast.

Closing my eyes, I smelled the air. Arianna's scent clouded my mind, but I shoved hers aside and focused on my sister's. I had to get to Nika. I caught a trace of it to my right, and leapt to the ground to pursue her. My body wasn't ready for the landing, though, and I fell to my knees. Arianna squeaked, but I was able to reach back and stop her from falling off.

"Sorry," I murmured. "I'm not at my best right now."

She patted my chest. "It's okay. Just find her."

I could hear the concern in her voice. I shared it. Nika was following a clearly unhinged person, and I had absolutely no way to track her. Well, except her cell phone, but I didn't know how to track her like that. I could at least give my freaked-out parents some relief though. Over my shoulder I told Arianna, "Reach into my pocket and grab my phone."

I felt her weight adjust and felt her fingers dig into my jeans. Then she switched to my jacket. I frowned. My phone wasn't in my jacket. "I can't find it, Julian. It's not there." She was silent, then, she said, "Mine's gone too."

I cursed under my breath. "He took them." That son of a bitch made us untraceable, then he'd stolen our cell phones, making us unreachable too. Asshole.

CHAPTER NINETEEN

Hunter

THINGS WERE ALREADY not going as planned. I never should have made a pit stop at Nika's house for my sister's urn. I should have run straight to Flagstaff. Dad should have been my priority, not some emotional connection with an inanimate object.

Cursing under my breath, I turned south and headed toward my destination. I hadn't meant for Nika to be involved. I hadn't meant to hurt her by giving her the shot. And I knew how much that shot freaking hurt. I swore Gabriel made it burn more than necessary, just for me. My injection site still ached.

After the family had grilled me at the ranch about the hunter I'd captured, I'd slunk outside for a while. I hadn't felt like soaking in the tub after my heated moment with Nika, so I'd returned to my room while they were finishing up dinner. A surprise had been waiting for me. A backpack, holding a case of filled syringes. The shot was ready.

I'd debated whether I should still go through with my plan and take it, but I knew it wasn't really a choice. I had to finish what my dad had started. Actually, going through with the plan was harder than I'd anticipated. Once I'd decided that my mission took priority over everything else, the next painful decision had been *when* to take it. Did I wait? Have a few more tender moments with Nika before saying goodbye? Remembering touching her in the tub had helped sway me. We were getting too intimate. The longer we spent together, the closer we got to sex. And I couldn't ...

Once I went there with her, I wouldn't be able to do what I needed to do.

I'd decided right then and there to take the shot. I'd grabbed the backpack, headed out to the backyard, as far from the house as I could go without alarming Halina, then I'd pushed up my sleeve, closed my eyes, and injected myself. The pain had almost brought me to my knees, but I hadn't had time to cave into the agony. I'd had to move, had to get as far from the house as possible.

Grunting and groaning as acid poured through my veins, I'd stumbled through the brush, nearly falling every other blurred step. I'd headed north. My goal had been to lead Halina away from the direction I really needed to go. My nerves were as shot as my body by the time I'd looped around and started heading toward the city. The formula Gabriel had created was powerful, and the bond broke almost instantly. It was unnerving to not know where Halina was. It punched a hole through my heart. I'd expected the breaking of the bond to remove the emotional connection to her, as well, but it hadn't. I still cared about her. Of course, my connection to her had nothing to do with the bond anymore. Tears had burned my eyes as I'd run away from her, but my mission had given me the strength to keep going.

Then I'd run into Nika, and my resolve had almost faltered at seeing her. Pure panic had made me act out in a rash, stupid way. But I couldn't feel Halina, or her family, and I knew they were looking for me. I couldn't be found, not until I'd dealt with my father.

The wind swirled around me, and I caught something on the breeze that sent a spark of anger up my spine. Nika. She was following me. I could lose her; I was by far faster and stronger than her, but that would mean leaving her on her own in the middle of the city. I was sure she could take care of herself, but Nika wasn't super-healing like her relatives, and I didn't want her to face something she couldn't handle because of me. And besides, I didn't know if any of Dad's hunters were around tonight. That was a threat she definitely couldn't face on her own.

I stopped in the shadows of a warehouse and waited for her to catch up to me. It only took a couple of minutes. She was really pushing herself.

Her heart was racing when she stopped right beside me. "Stop following me, Nika," I snapped.

She was still shaky on her feet from the shot. Internally, I cringed at what I'd put her through. I kept my face stern as she stubbornly shook her head. "I'm not letting you run off without me."

I could be equally stubborn. "Go back to your family. Where I'm going, you don't need to be."

She grabbed my arm. "*You're* my family, and I'm not letting you do this."

I yanked my arm away. "You don't really have a choice. I'm going, and you're staying here."

Just then, Julian blurred to a stop beside us. He was just as shaky as Nika. He was also carrying his girlfriend on his back. Looked like neither Adams twin was going to leave me alone. Great. I pointed to the direction where I believed the ranch was. "Both of you go home." My gaze shifted to Julian's female backpack. "And take the human with you. It's not safe out here."

Nika cringed in pain, but firmly held her ground. "Where you go, I'm going to follow. If you want me to be safe, then you better go back to the ranch too."

I ground my teeth in frustration while Julian added, "And where my sister goes, I go … and Arianna goes. So, the only way to keep us all safe is to do what she said." He glanced at his sister, and I was positive his concern was only for her. Not for me. Me, he could probably do without.

I ran my hands back through my hair. "You two are infuriating, do you know that?"

Even though he looked to be in as much pain as Nika, Julian smirked at me. "Yeah, we get that a lot." Arianna giggled. It was a very nervous giggle.

Wondering if they were bluffing, and knowing I needed to be farther from the Adams' house, I phased away from them. I didn't stop until I hit the edge of the city. I hovered in the shadows, waiting to see if they'd really follow me. I could take off and leave them in the dust if I absolutely had to, but I couldn't stomach the idea of Nika being alone, cut off from her family, with only her brother to protect her. I cared about her too much to let her fend for herself.

Just when I thought I'd lost them, they blurred into view, Nika first, Julian a few seconds later. I punched a hole in the tree I was standing next to. Damn it! They were ruining my master plan, my perfect escape. What the hell should I do with them now?

They paused in a clearing and looked over at the tree I'd just permanently altered. Nika was by my side in an instant. "You can't ditch me," she said, her tone matter-of-fact.

I was going to tell her that wasn't true, I could easily ditch her, but then I realized it was true. Yes, I could ditch her, but I couldn't leave her, so ... I was going to have to take her with me. This was going to seriously complicate things.

I exhaled a long, drawn-out sigh. "Okay, fine. You two don't want to leave me alone, then you can follow me all the way to Flagstaff. But you better keep up, 'cause I'm not waiting around for you."

Nika twisted her head, curious. "Flagstaff? Arizona? Is that where your dad is? How do you know that?"

I shrugged. "It was the last thing Markus told me before I wiped his mind."

A smile blossomed across Nika's lips that made my breath catch. "You didn't kill him?"

Struggling to remember that I didn't have time to kiss her right now, I averted my eyes from her intense stare. Guilt washed through me as I remembered the one hunter I had killed. "Except for Sam, I haven't killed any of them."

Julian stepped forward. "Any of them? How many have there been?"

I glanced over at him and his piggybacking girlfriend. "Enough that I need to get to my father as quickly as possible. And you're both slowing me down."

Nika shook her head. "We won't. You lead, we'll follow." A look passed between Nika and Julian that spoke volumes to me. They were clearly placating me, and would try and stop me or call for reinforcements every step of this journey. I should just leave them here. Chances were, they'd be fine. Although, now that they both knew I was heading to Flagstaff, they'd show up there regardless of what I did to them. And they'd probably bring the entire nest. No, they had to come with me, so I could make sure they didn't bring in everybody.

"Flagstaff is about five hundred miles from here. We'll go at a pace that you two can maintain for that distance." I again glanced at the slow-moving human in the group. "But she needs to go home. We'll get her a cab or something."

Arianna's arms tightened around Julian's neck. "There's no way I'm leaving him while he goes off on some psychotic mission with you." She lifted her chin in a show of defiance that I was getting really sick and tired of seeing. "Besides, I'll just call Teren and Emma if you send me home. I'll tell them exactly where to find you."

I stepped up to her side; Julian twisted to block me. "Don't forget what I am. I could send you home with a permanent case of amnesia if I so chose."

A growl emanated from Julian's chest. "Speak another word to her, and I'll rip your heart out."

I grunted in frustration, but inwardly a backup plan was forming. I could use the threat of wiping Arianna to keep Nika and her brother in line. That was a handy bit of leverage to have, since I was rapidly losing control of this plan. "Fine, she can come, too. In fact, I insist that she does. And if anybody gives me grief, or tries to stop me when we get to my father, then I wipe her clean." I pointed a finger at Arianna. Her eyes were wide, her cheeks pale as her earlier bravado vanished. "I'll take away every memory that's ever been important to you. I'll leave you with nothing." I switched my scowl to Julian. "Unless you want to go back to square one with her, I wouldn't even try messing with me. I'm not bluffing."

Julian looked hesitant, but he was just as stuck as I was. Nika wouldn't let me go, so he *couldn't* let me go. And now his girlfriend was suddenly important to me, and *I* wouldn't let her go; I'd wipe her in a heartbeat if he tried to take her home now. We were all four stuck in this hellish little boat together. Nika flashed a worried glance at her friend. She knew I'd do it if they pushed me.

I smiled at each of them in turn. "Now that that's settled, we have a long journey in front of us, so I suggest we get started."

I turned and left them without another word. I knew they'd follow me. They had to now.

Nika was beside me in an instant. While we streaked past the countryside at a pace most human eyes wouldn't register, I was running slower than I would have if I were alone. Glancing behind me, I saw Julian trailing behind with Arianna still attached to his back. I briefly wondered if he would be able to carry her the entire way. Then I started wondering what the hell I was going to do with the three of them while I was busy hunting my father. Maybe I could tie them up somewhere.

"You don't need to be a bully," Nika said from beside me. I looked back at her, and she added, "Threatening Arianna? That's not like you."

Her eyes scoured my face, looking for some sign that I wasn't serious. I was. "Sometimes you have to do things you don't want to do to get other things done."

"You don't have to do this. Let my family help."

She started to reach out for me, but I blurred away from her. I hadn't asked her to come with me, and I hadn't asked for her opinion on how I should deal with my family. This was my mess, and I would clean it up.

It took entirely too long to get to Flagstaff with my three tagalongs. Alone, I probably could have run there in an hour. With them, and their perpetually slowing pace, it took over three. I was sure that was intentional on their part, running slower, refusing to let me carry Arianna. Anything they could do to delay me from reaching my father. Resting near the edge of the desert city, I looked up at the sky and contemplated how much longer I had until the sun rose. It was less time than I would have liked. The looming threat of sunlight now felt like an alarm clock ticking in my head. I would have to hide from the sun soon, and once I was underground, nothing would stop Julian and Nika from calling their family. It would be over, and I'd be returned to my plush prison. Time was of the essence.

Julian set Arianna down and they both collapsed to the ground. "I'm so tired," he complained, while she moaned, "My legs ... my back ... my ass ... I'm so sore. And freezing. I can't feel my fingers."

Julian started warming her up, and I rolled my eyes. Their physical discomfort was their own damn fault. They never should have followed me. Nika was to my right, surveying the land. Spindly green trees dotted the dry, dusty earth, and there was a short chain-link fence next to us. The city's water reservoir was on the other side of it. I could smell the brackish pool, could see the edge of the mammoth cement hole filled with liquid so dark, it looked black in the moonlight.

"Now what, Hunter?" Nika asked. She also looked tired from the run. I should find a safe place for her to rest. Especially since I didn't know if my dad was still in the city or not. This was where Markus had seen him last, but that didn't mean he was still here.

I glanced behind me. There were houses sprinkled here and there. Perhaps I could leave Nika and Julian inside one of them while I scoped out the city.

While Nika watched me, an idea started formulating. "You don't have a plan, do you?" she asked, huffing a strand of hair out of her eyes.

Irritation blossomed in my chest. "I had a plan, but it didn't involve you following me. In my plan, I had all the time in the world to find my father. Now, I feel like I'm running out of time."

"Because you're going about this the wrong way, and you know it. We should call my family. The more people on this, the better."

Not wanting to hear her spiel again, I grabbed her hand and dragged her toward the road. I would search every home nearby until I found what I needed. Grunting, Julian forced himself to stand as I passed by him with his sister. "Now where are we going?"

I didn't answer him. He helped Arianna to her feet and followed me, like I knew he would. I walked up to the first house on the other side of the street. It was a surprisingly large home for being out in the middle of nowhere. Even though it was late at night, I banged on the door. I didn't have time to be polite.

It took a while, but eventually lights turned on and loud footsteps clomped toward the door. I could hear the heartbeats accelerating in the others beside me, but I wasn't worried, I wasn't scared. Unless the person on the other side of this door just happened to be a prepared hunter who knew what I was—and what were the odds of that—I wasn't in any danger.

A youthful, clean-cut man cracked open the door. "What is it?" he cautiously asked, shielding his body behind the wood. Seeing cold, shivering girls in our midst, he opened the door a little wider. "You in some kind of trouble?"

I gave him a polite smile. "You could say that. Do you have a room that is completely impervious to sunlight? A cellar or something?"

The man blinked, confused. He looked like he was going to ask a question, and I quickly added, "Don't ask why, just answer my question. Please."

His confusion didn't ease up, but he said, "No. Sorry."

I shook my head. "It's fine. Go back to bed. You won't remember any of this happening when you shut the door. Good night."

His confusion amplified. "Night …"

I turned away from the door when he started shutting it. Julian, Nika, and Arianna were all staring at me. Looking at them in turn, I said, "We need a home base, somewhere I can hide from the sun in a few hours. I figured a home would be much more comfortable for all of you than a grave."

Arianna started backing up. "Whoa! I'm not going anywhere near a grave. And I can't be away this long. My mom is going to flip!"

She started panicking, and irritated, I snapped, "Stop talking." She instantly did.

Julian smacked my shoulder. "Don't trance my girlfriend, asshole!"

A frustrated sigh escaped me. "Then tell her to keep it down. People are trying to sleep." Julian glowered at me, and I turned to Arianna. "Fine, you're free to talk. Quietly."

I started heading toward the next house. From behind me, I heard Julian tell Arianna, "He was kidding about the grave. He wouldn't make us go in one. We'd suffocate."

Her response was in whispered tones. "That doesn't make me feel any better, Julian. I want to go home now."

Over my shoulder, I told them, "No one is going home until I find my father, so stop whining."

The next house we went to didn't have a daylight-proof room. Or the next. It was sixteen houses later before we found one.

It was a secluded, cedar log house. The man who opened the door was older, with gnarled hands, fake teeth, and a weathered cane. By the shape of him, I was mildly surprised he'd heard me knocking at this hour. When I asked him about a light-proof roof, he told me, "Yeah. There's a cold storage basement under the house. Cement walls. No windows."

I smiled, relieved that I was finally having some luck, especially since my reluctant companions were still badgering me at every opportunity. "That is the best news I've heard all night. You're going to invite us in, and let us use it. Indefinitely. No questions asked."

Arianna turned to Julian and whispered, "Indefinitely? We have school on Monday."

The old man opened the door wide; he wobbled on his cane a bit. "Please, come on in. You're welcome to use the room for as long as you like, for whatever reason you want."

I inclined my head in a polite nod as I walked past him. "Thank you for your hospitality."

I looked at the others once I was in the entryway. Nika resolutely met my gaze and walked into the house. She was with me, regardless of what I did. That could be a problem when it was time to face my father; his address festered inside my skull. I just wanted to find him, but I needed to drop off my extra baggage first. Julian frowned as Nika stepped into the house. He was with *her*, regardless of what she did. Arianna let out a frustrated grunt as she followed Julian. She was with him. It was like we were playing a twisted version of Follow the Leader.

Old Man Winter led us to his cheerless basement. I could smell the must emanating from it before he even opened the door. It tripled once he did. It wasn't as nice of a hiding place as my room at the ranch, but it was a step up from sleeping in the ground. And, unlike the earth, Nika and the others could join me here.

The old man flipped on a light switch near the door, illuminating a set of wooden steps that emptied out into a dirt floor basement, then he left us to our own devices. The construction of the basement walls looked solid to me, the seal around the door tight. I thought the room might actually be impervious to sunlight. I wouldn't know until the morning, of course, but an above ground nap seemed more and more likely. That was good; it would be easier to keep an ear on the twins that way.

Arianna started panicking when I stepped on the stairs. "No, no, no! I am *not* hiding out in some random guy's creepy-ass cellar. This has been fun and all, but I want to go home now," she hissed.

Julian tried to calm her down, but I knew this was a job for me. "Arianna." She turned from Julian to look at me. "Relax. There's nothing for you to be scared of. You're going to be fine down here. Just stay close to Julian."

She visibly calmed down as she clamped onto his arm. Julian gave me the evil eye for trancing his girlfriend again, but really, he should thank me. Once she was under control, I turned back to the stairs. Nika followed close behind me. When we got to the bottom and looked around, she muttered, "Are you sure we have to stay down here?"

My eyes flashed around the room, looking for fault lines where the sun could seep in. There were bins full of moldy potatoes, a wall-to-ceiling wine rack with dark bottles covered in dust and spider webs, and about sixty years' worth of old magazines heaped in a corner. All and all, the space had been neglected for a long time. The old man must not feel well enough to come down here anymore. On the other side of the wine rack was a massive trunk with a couple of old, Army cots stacked on top of it. Good, we wouldn't have to sleep on the ground.

I twisted to look at Nika. "I *have* to stay down here. And I need you all to stay with me, so you don't do anything foolish while I'm sleeping."

Julian's expression was dour. "I'd say we're maxed out on foolish today." He turned to Nika. "I don't like this, Nick. Let's just leave him and go home."

"No one is going anywhere," I told him.

He instantly bristled. "This isn't our fight. We won't tell anyone where you are. Let us go."

I studied him in the dim fluorescent lights buzzing in the ceiling. He was probably telling the truth. He wouldn't tell on me, because he didn't care what happened to me. His sister did, though. And I'd be hard-pressed to make her leave me, let alone not tell Halina where I was. "No. I need you here now." I pointed to Arianna clinging to his side, shivering as she held him. Since I'd ordered her to relax, she must be cold. It probably was on the frigid side down here. I'd have to get the old man to toss down some blankets. "And I need her, to ensure that you two don't screw me, at least not until I've finished this."

Julian stepped in front of Arianna, like that would somehow protect her from my voice. "No. I won't let you do anything to hurt her."

I gave him an expression of forced patience. "I'm not interested in harming her, but I also can't have the two of you whistle-blowing on me. Don't push me, and I won't have to push back."

I moved past him, to call for the old man and ask for bedding. Out of the corner of my eye, I saw Julian raise an eyebrow at Nika. I heard her sigh, saw her nod, and I instantly knew they were still planning on turning me in once the sun came up. Well, hell if I was just going to sit back and let that happen. I had leverage on them, and I wasn't afraid to use it. I'd waited too long, endured too much; I wasn't leaving this godforsaken place until I'd dealt with my father. And even then, I might not leave this place.

Blurring to Arianna, I broke her apart from Julian and quickly told her, "If any of you call someone and tell them where you are, or if any of you leave the house without me, all of your memories will vanish, Arianna. You won't remember one ... single ... thing about yourself."

Everyone in the room gasped, and icy dread crawled up my spine. Shit ... did I really just say that to her? The unabashed look of fear on her face told me I had. God, what the hell was wrong with me? And it was too late to take it back. A compulsion was a compulsion. I could superimpose another one on top of it, but I couldn't undo it. Frustrated, angry, guilty, and filled with the desperate need to start my mission, I released Arianna and snapped, "Now, I have an errand to run. I trust none of you will go anywhere while I'm gone."

I felt sick to my stomach as I fled the room. Jesus, what kind of a monster was this vendetta turning me into? It was surely a more horrifying creature than the bloodthirsty demon inside me. So, what should I do? Which monster should I feed?

I blurred outside to feel the fresh air on my face. Once I was on the front porch, I sat down on the steps and stared out into the night. My father was out there, I knew he was. I should be zipping to the address Markus had given me, but all I could think about was what I'd just done to an innocent teenage girl. I shouldn't dwell on my mistake, or worry about how much of an asshole I looked like. I should get up and start fixing what I'd come here to fix. So long as my father was free, Nika's family was in danger.

Duty forced me to my feet. I had a job to do, and I was committed to seeing it through. If anything, my father had given me a solid work ethic.

Not familiar with the city, I stopped at a motel that looked like it saw a lot of foot traffic. I "persuaded" the clerk on duty to pull up the address on his computer. It was much later than I would have liked to start this hunting trip, but I couldn't waste another precious minute. And I was sure things with my father wouldn't take very long to settle. A lengthy debate wasn't what we needed. Speedy action was the only course left to us.

After getting what I needed, I erased the man's memory and left the motel.

I flashed through the city, heading toward suburbia, where my father was reportedly staying. Thankfully, it was clear across town, miles away from where I'd stashed Nika; I didn't want my father discovering she was with me. The guilt over what I'd done to Arianna didn't dissipate while I ran. If anything, it grew. If I found my father exactly where I expected to find him, if he was waiting for me and got the upper hand on me, Arianna would never be able to leave the cabin with her memories intact. I never should have left her in that condition, but I didn't know how else to get them all to stay put. And I needed to do this alone. But, I supposed, eventually the shot would wear off, and Halina would find Julian and Nika. She could fix my grievous error if I didn't make it back to the cabin. They wouldn't be trapped for long.

With the map of where I needed to go firmly in my mind, I easily found my father's address. It was a plain, beige rambler tucked in the middle of a quaint cul-de-sac. It was a completely unassuming, seemingly innocent house with a cheery white picket fence and matching faux shutters. I was positive that none of the neighbors knew that just behind the façade of a brightly painted bird feeder in the front yard, there was a stash of weapons large enough to outfit a small army. An army that would love to drive a stake right through my silent heart.

Standing in the shadows at the corner of the cul-de-sac, I listened for anything out of the ordinary—movement, fast heartbeats, whispers—any telltale sign that someone in the neighborhood was awake. All was still though; only the sounds of sleep met my ear.

Sticking to the darker backyards, I zipped to the house I needed. Speed and surprise were my biggest strengths right now. Deciding that a door was too typical to catch my father unawares, I flashed to the nearest bedroom window and ripped it free—loud and messy, but effective. I hopped through and crouched low, ready for anything. Silence was all I got, though. Silence and emptiness.

All my senses on high alert, I crept through the barren bedroom. Either Dad had never used this room, or he was long gone. Cautiously examining the hallway, I sniffed the air. Also nothing out of the ordinary. Just the scent of lemon, bleach, and carpet cleaner, like the home had recently been deep cleaned. I peeked my head into every dark bedroom, but nothing leapt out at me, nothing disrupted my senses. By the time I got to the stark living room, I knew that my search here was futile. Dad wasn't around.

The rest of the house was just as empty as the bedrooms. I even unnecessarily searched the attic and the crawl space. I spent a lot longer there than I should have, but I just couldn't leave without a clue. I had nowhere else to look once I left here.

Dejected, I opened the slider to leave out the back. No sense in stealth now. The backyard had a small deck with a built-in fireplace. It was cozy, homey, the type of simple home I could have once imagined living in with Nika, while we hunted demons together. How far I'd diverted from my original vision with her blew my mind. My life had been completely turned upside down.

As I turned to go, something in the fire pit caught my eye. Stepping over to the charred logs, I saw the edge of a box sticking out of the recently burned wood. I looked around for any sign of a trap, then I carefully pulled the box free. I recognized it immediately. It was my sister's treasure box. It was one of those wooden contraptions that had to be opened in a specific sequence, by moving certain sections and pressing hidden levers. My sister was the only one who'd ever been able to figure it out. She'd teased me mercilessly over my inability to open it. That had really ticked me off, since she'd only known how because the man who'd sold it to her had shown her. It had been a private joke between us, and I was instantly inflamed that my father had tried to burn it. It wasn't his to burn. It was hers, and now it was mine.

Tucking it into my pocket, I hastily glanced at the sky. I'd stayed for far too long. I needed to return to safety before the sun rose. Maybe my sister would give me the inspiration I needed to find our father ... before he found me.

Disheartened, I blurred back to the cabin. I should have known Dad wouldn't still be at that house. He'd probably fled the instant Markus had fallen off the radar. I would have, if I were him. Now I was back at square one, with no real way to find him and no time to look. Not with Nika and Julian with me. I'd have to lose them when the sun set again. A part of me really hated that thought.

The lights were off inside the cabin, and I could hear people sleeping. A deep rumbling snore came from one of the room's upstairs. That had to be the old man. Walking through the unlocked front door, I headed for the basement. Hopefully they'd all heeded my memory trap and not called in reinforcements. Although, did it really matter if they had? Did I want to keep up this solo act of revenge, now that it was hurting people? Guilt washed over me again. I was such a bastard.

When I went downstairs, surprise overrode my dark thoughts. Julian wasn't there. Arianna either. Only two cots were tucked in a dark corner; one was empty, but for a blanket lain on top of it. Nika was resting on the other, nearly buried in thick covers. I tilted my head, listening. Now that I was paying closer attention, I could hear light breathing filtering through the lumberjack snores of the old man upstairs. Julian was in a bedroom with Arianna? Well, I supposed I hadn't forbid them from leaving the basement. And it *was* freezing down here.

Thinking I'd done enough to them tonight, and I could fix what I'd carelessly done when they woke up, I left them alone. After firmly closing the door behind me, I walked down the steps to my makeshift bedroom with Nika. Why was she still down here, when she could be warm upstairs? And far away from me.

The cots were pushed together in the corner opposite the stairs. With no lights on, the room was pitch-black save for my glowing eyes. As silently as I could, I removed my backpack and shoes, and sat on the edge of the cot. I pulled my sister's box out of my pocket, and felt around the smooth sides for the latches that would open it. It was so perfectly crafted, even my enhanced sensations couldn't feel the proper spots. My sister would die laughing if she could see me now. Sighing, I shoved it back into my jacket and dropped the jacket on the floor. Why the hell Dad was tossing out that little bit of our history now was beyond me. Maybe he was sending me a message. He knew how close Evangeline and I had been. By burning our connection he was telling me—very loudly—that I wasn't a part of the family anymore. He was essentially burning me out of his life.

Abandonment seared my chest as painfully as if I'd had pure silver injected into my veins. I crawled under the blanket left for me on the cot, and turned on my side to face Nika. I shouldn't seek comfort from her, but I suddenly needed it. Only her eyes were visible from under her mountain of comforters. Like she'd been waiting for me, she opened them.

The love I still saw in her gaze broke my heart. I didn't deserve that look. "Hey, you're back. I'm glad you're okay."

Her endless caring instantly brought back the guilt. I wish she hadn't followed me, but ... I was really glad she was here. "You could have gone upstairs with Julian. You didn't have to stay down here ... with me."

She pulled the blanket down to expose her soft lips. "Are you mad that he left the room? Arianna was too cold, and she didn't really want to stay with you after..."

I shook my head. "No ... I understand. And I know he won't do anything. He can't." I frowned, hating what I'd done, and that I wouldn't have a chance to set it right until the sun set again. "I don't know what came over me. I'm so sorry for what I did to her. That was wrong. Really wrong. I'll remove the memory trap as soon as I can. I promise."

Nika sat up on her elbow and smiled down on me. It was warmer than the rising sun that was starting to tingle my spine. "Thank you, Hunter."

I turned away from her. "I almost obliterated your best friend's mind ... and you're thanking me?"

Her soft voice returned my gaze to her. "I know you feel bad about what you did. I could tell you regretted it the minute you did it. It's going to take my brother a little longer, but I've already forgiven you."

I studied her face in disbelief. "How is it that you're not angry with me? Why don't you hate me yet?"

Her hand came out of the blanket to caress my face; it felt amazing against my chilly skin. "Because I love you. And I know you're not really being you right now. You were angry, frustrated, and you said something rash. It happens to us all."

I placed my hand over hers on my cheek. "But bad things can happen when I speak rashly, especially to humans."

Her thumb brushed across my skin, sending tremors through me. "You're not a bad person. You're just confused."

I closed my eyes. That was certainly true. In the darkness, I felt Nika's hair brush against my face, then felt her warm lips upon mine. I couldn't resist the heat, the softness, the sweetness. I never could. Moving my mouth against hers, I savored the connection that always made me feel less like a beast, and more like a man. My hand on hers reached up to feel her silky hair. It slid between my fingers as I rested my palm on the back of her neck; she trembled under my touch.

During a brief break in our kiss, I told her, "You shouldn't be here with me. You should go upstairs with your brother."

Her leg came out from her thick blankets to slide underneath my thin one. "I want to be with you," she breathed.

A familiar zing went up my spine that told me the sun was touching the Earth. I opened my eyes and looked around the dark room for any sign that I wasn't safe. The walls were still dark, though, and the seal around the heavy door leading into the house was unbroken with shafts of light.

Nika paused in her affections to watch me. "What is it?"

I tensed, waiting for the pain from some unknown breach in my sanctuary, as the sensation of sunrise crackled through my body. When I didn't feel anything, I exhaled a sigh of relief. "The sun rose. But I'm okay. The room is light-proof." Nika tucked a strand of hair behind her ear and I turned to watch her. "But now you're stuck in here with me all day."

She cracked a small smile. "We're both prisoners."

Sighing, I sat up. "No, you're not. I won't ever compel Arianna like that again. I won't threaten her. If you guys betray me, then you betray me, but I won't become *that* kind of a monster."

Pulling the blankets around herself, she sat up with me. "Are you still going to hunt your father?"

I exhaled a long sigh as I looked over at her. "I need to finish this, Nika. I *have* to find my father."

Nika sighed. "I'm not leaving here without you, so I'll help you find him."

I shook my head at her predictable stubbornness. "You're impossible."

"As are you," she chided.

A feeling of loneliness overwhelmed me as I gazed at her. It took me a few seconds to realize why I felt it. It was the shot, the separation from Halina. It stung to not know where she was. Was she still north, buried under the earth where she'd been looking for me, or had she given up and returned to the ranch? Was she okay with me being gone, or was she devastated?

"This is going to sound strange, but now that I finally got away, I really miss being connected to your family. To Halina. I thought that feeling would fade with the bond broken, but it didn't. I miss her. A lot." I looked down at the blanket over my knees. "I really shouldn't be telling you that."

When I looked up at her, she had a peaceful smile on her lips. I wanted to kiss them again. "I'm not jealous of your bond with her. Not really. It's an important bond, designed to keep you alive." The smile slipped as her voice trembled. "Are you ... are you still planning on not returning when this is over? Are you still expecting this to be a one-way mission?"

Her voice hitched, and I had to look away. In my answering silence, she asked, "Are we really so awful?"

I looked back at her watery eyes as my dead heart cracked. "I honestly don't know anymore."

Her eyes scanned my face while her hand threaded through my hair. "I think you're unable to fully accept this life not because you can't, but because you *won't*. You're letting your prejudices dictate your feelings."

Frustration soured my tone. "And how do you suggest I get over that? Assuming I live through this."

She showed her wrist to me. "You stop fighting, and you embrace what you are."

I glanced at the vein in her arm, the blood rushing just below the skin. I licked my lips, and forced my eyes away. "I can't. I can't live like this, Nika."

She flipped her hand over and placed it on my knee. "Yes, you can. I'll prove it. What are you most afraid of?"

My expression darkened. "Losing control and attacking someone. Liking it too much. Killing people ... becoming a nightmare."

She nodded, like she'd expected as much. "Okay, let me show you that you're more afraid than you need to be. Drink from me, right now." I shook my head, but she didn't let me verbalize my objection. "I'm not asking, Hunter. If this could make the difference between you living or dying, then I'm going to make sure you at least try it. I'm not going to give up on you simply because you're too scared. Drink. You need to see that this won't change you."

My mouth opened at just the thought of her hot blood in me. "I lost control ... I bit that girl in the parking lot. I almost bit you."

With a patient smile, Nika pulled her hair away from her shoulder and exposed her neck. "You were starving yourself then. You're not anymore. Prove to yourself that you're stronger than you believe, then maybe you can start to accept this life."

I swallowed, my mouth suddenly dry. I had blood in my backpack, taken from the ranch before I'd left, but maybe she was right. Maybe I needed to overcome this fear, before I made another rash decision. A permanent one.

Slowly, I moved toward her skin. Her heart accelerated with every inch, but her breath did too. "I don't want to hurt you," I murmured, my icy breath giving her goosebumps.

"You won't," she whispered. Her hand came up to guide my head down the rest of the way. My lips touched above her jugular, and a low growl escaped me. My fangs lengthened as I fought against the urge to pull away. My head screamed that this was wrong, but my body begged that it was right. Her fingers tightened in my hair, holding me in place. "It's okay," she cooed. "I trust you."

I closed my eyes as pain ripped through me. Consciously biting ... that was the last step to becoming what I hated most. Or it could be the beginning of letting go of my worries. Moving aside her shirt, I brought my lips to just above her collarbone and opened my mouth, taking in her skin. I was nearly panting now, ready for this, and at the same time, I was completely unprepared. "Nika," I whimpered, pulling back so my lips brushed her skin. "I can't ..."

"You can ... we can."

I felt her hand release my head, then felt her pull my shirt to the side. An ache went through me as my skin was exposed. When her lips lowered to my skin, mirror image of how I was touching her, I whimpered in a completely different way. *Yes.* Her heartbeat was loud in my ears. I felt her fangs prick my skin, and I tensed my mouth on her shoulder in preparation. *God yes.* She clamped down, and I flinched at the small amount of pain. My instinct was to pierce her skin in return, and for once, I listened. I bit into her ... and it was heaven.

We both groaned as the life-force of one flowed into the other. Human blood, direct from the vein, was unlike anything I'd ever experienced before, but it was nothing compared to the feeling of closeness I had with her. I knew, in that one moment of clarity, that I would never drink from anyone else but her. This wasn't about food. It was something profoundly intimate that we would only share with each other. I couldn't even imagine biting another person now.

I grabbed her hip under the blanket as I pulled long draws from her. Her blood was warm, sweet, tangy. Unbelievable. Conscious of how much I was taking, and knowing this wouldn't be the last time I bit her, I pulled up my teeth and ran my tongue over the small wounds until the bleeding stopped. Nika was still drinking from me. I pulled her onto my lap while she purred a low growl that gave me an entirely different ache. In a flash, I saw what our life could be like if I did what she asked and embraced both parts of me. It could be glorious. It could be heaven. It could be ... perfect.

When she pulled her teeth away from my shoulder, I pulled her mouth to mine. I needed to complete this connection. I needed all of her. Now.

There was a lingering taste of blood in her mouth as we kissed; it only made it sweeter. With one hand on her back, I lowered us to the cot. Her kiss was fierce with need. The noises leaving her body surged through mine. I was ready for her. Pulling back the mountain of covers, I rolled us onto her cot. Her legs automatically wrapped around me as I pressed against her. She gasped and clutched at my back.

"Oh God," she murmured.

My lips ran to her neck as she clawed at me. "Nika ..." My tongue swirled around her wounds, remembering, savoring. She shivered under my touch, and her mouth sought mine in the darkness.

"Hunter, please ..."

Her fingers dug into my shirt, pulling the fabric up my body. I reached back with one hand and pulled the shirt over my head, tossing it onto the floor. Like hot packs, her hands ran down my chest. They stopped on my jeans, tugging at the button. Rolling off her, I ripped off my jeans. She took my momentary separation from her to blur her shirt and jeans off as well. When my glowing eyes washed over her nearly-bare body, the ache inside me grew painful. She was so beautiful.

She reached out for me, and I rolled back on top of her. Conscious of her temperature, I brought the blankets with me. I couldn't spare her from my chill, but I could spare her from the iciness in the air. With a lot less fabric between us, the sensation of rubbing against her was amplified. It sent shockwaves through my body. It made cries leave hers. I grabbed her hand, clutching tight. God, I wanted her.

I rocked against her in a steady rhythm, and she grew even more restless beneath me. Her legs cinched around mine, her breath came out in pants, and her hands explored my exposed flesh. It was incredible. I wanted more. I wanted to be inside her.

I unhooked her bra, pulled it from her shoulders, and tossed it aside. When my lips trailed down her chest, passing over her sensitive skin, she cried out even louder. When I took her breast into my mouth, she started pulling down her underwear. Looking up at her, I paused her hands.

Chest heaving, her face was a mixture of frustration and desire. "Please don't tell me you're stopping this again. I don't think I can handle that."

Laying over the top of her, I cupped her cheek. "Nika, you're still too young."

Tears pricked her eyes. "Stop saying that. I've waited my entire life to feel for someone what I feel for you. I might be young, but I know what I want, and it's you. I want to share this with you while we have the chance to share it, because who knows what's going to happen to us tomorrow." A tear rolled down her cheek as her voice broke. "I love you, so much. Please, don't stop this."

Sighing, I let her words sink in a moment. Then I shifted her fingers so that *I* was the one pulling down her underwear. The love and pain in her voice; I couldn't resist her, and I couldn't deny her this anymore. She closed her eyes in relief. Hoping I was doing the right thing, I removed mine, then repositioned myself on top of her. Leaning down to her ear, I murmured, "If you change your mind at any time, just tell me."

She turned her head to mine. "Do you love me?"

I couldn't contain my smile. "Yes."

She smiled in kind and pulled on my hips. "Then I'm not going to change my mind. Please, make love to me."

As gently as I could, I pushed into her. She held her breath and closed her eyes. The sensation of being inside her was so powerful, I had to hold perfectly still to stay in control. She was so warm, tight, perfect. When she started breathing again, and I felt she could handle it, I pulled back and pushed forward. A long moan escaped her, "Oh ... God ..."

An equally long groan escaped me. "God, Nika ... I love you."

Her hips started moving in time with mine. The heat, the friction, the sensations ... everything was amplified. It was so much more intense than human sex had ever been. I could smell, hear, taste, feel everything. It was almost too much—sensory overload. I could feel the pressure building, and knew I was getting close to a release. By the sounds Nika was making, I knew she was getting close too. I drove into her harder, wanting her to feel everything as strongly as I was feeling it. God, could I ever leave her now? I could give up this foolish quest, return to the ranch, make love to her every night, drink from her every night. We could be happy like this. Forever. Is that what I wanted?

"Yes," I groaned into the darkness, answering my own question. Yes, I did want this.

Nika started quivering. She wrapped her arms tightly around me as we rocked together. "Don't go," she whispered. "Don't go after him and leave me. Don't die."

Her mind was in line with mine. "I won't. I'm staying with you, Nika. I love you so much. I want this. I want you. I …"

I couldn't finish talking because I was about to crest. All I had time to say was, "Do this with me." I wasn't even sure what I meant by that, but tossing her head back in a long, satisfied cry, Nika finished a half-second before me. And the sight of her climaxing beneath me was simply glorious.

No, I was hers now. My quest was over.

CHAPTER TWENTY

Nika

I FELT DIFFERENT. I wasn't really expecting that. But I definitely felt a little different now that I was no longer a virgin. Physically, I was pretty much the same. I was a little sore down there, but it was a pleasant sore, a nice reminder of what Hunter and I had done together. No, all of my changes were emotional. I felt … bonded to Hunter now. Close to him, in a deeper way than I'd ever felt before. And sex wasn't the only reason. We'd shared blood. I'd lost all my virginities, all in one swoop. And I loved him so much more now. I couldn't stand the thought of him facing his father, of him never returning. I just wanted to take him home to the ranch, and keep helping him get used to his new life. And I was sure he would now. He told me he would stay, assured me he would live, and I believed him. We were going to be together for a very long time. Even though my limbs were chilly, that thought warmed me.

"Are you okay?" his voice rumbled in my ear.

I pulled the covers around me tighter as I twisted to face him. "I've never been better."

His arm was around my bare waist, and his fingers were rubbing patterns across my low back; they felt wonderful. "Again, I feel like I should apologize," he murmured, leaning in to kiss me. "I hadn't meant to go that far with you. I guess I lost control after all."

A low laugh escaped me as I pressed my warm chest against his. Our activities had warmed him up some, and he wasn't as cold as he typically was. "Thank God you did. I was going to explode if you stopped again." He smiled under my lips, and I added, "I wouldn't say you lost control though. I'd say you finally gave up control. You finally stopped fighting against yourself. I'm very proud of you." I pointed to the ache on my neck where his fangs had punctured me. The wounds were nothing. I barely felt them.

Hunter sighed softly, then leaned up and kissed the tender area. His stubble against my skin tingled in an amazing way. "I'll admit, that was amazing, Nika. More incredible than I ever thought it could be, but ..."

He pulled away from me, and I frowned. "If you say we can't ever do that again, I might have to cause you bodily harm."

He laughed, and I delighted in seeing humor on his face again. It had been a while. "No, I was definitely not going to say that." His hand left my hip to travel up my neck. "I was going to say it wasn't just incredible, it was deeper than that. I see what you meant now. That I was more scared than I needed to be." His fingers traced the holes as he whispered, "This was something so intimate and personal, that I know I'll never do it with anyone but you. You're the only one I will ever bite. I know that for a fact. And as strange as it is for me to say that, I've never felt better about anything in my life. I think ... I think I'm actually happy." He laughed again and shook his head.

Tears stung my eyes as I watched the peaceful glow emanating from his. It was a peace that now originated from within him. "And I'm so happy to hear you say that." After a second, I added, "Does that mean we can have sex again?"

Hunter chuckled as he pulled me into his side. "Another time. I need to rest." I tossed my body around his, sharing my warmth. Closing his eyes, he made a content noise in his throat. I shivered, but I knew the longer I held him, the warmer he would become. "You don't have to snuggle with me, if I'm too cold."

I kissed his chest before laying my cheek on him. "You're fine. And I'm hoping my naked body against yours will eventually change your mind."

He laughed again, and I marveled at the change in his mood. "You're going to be a problem, I can tell."

I bit my lip to contain my giggle. After a few moments of silence, I whispered, "Hunter, what are we going to do about your father?"

He didn't answer me. With my head on his silent chest, I could tell that he wasn't breathing. I knew that meant he was asleep. Guess I wore him out. A huge smile on my face, I closed my eyes, and followed him into slumber.

I WAS WOKEN sometime later by someone pounding on the door. Startled, I sat up. Hunter was asleep on his cot, his naked body just barely covered by a corner of one of my thin blankets. The rest were firmly wrapped around me. I wasn't worried about him being cold though.

I could feel my brother's anxiety now, and fear shot through me. "Nika! We've got a problem, I'm coming in."

I panicked for two reasons. One, I was completely naked under the covers, and two, the door couldn't be opened because Hunter would be exposed to the trace amount of sunlight coming in from the interior of the house. Even just that little bit would hurt him. "No, Julian, stay out—"

He didn't listen, and the door burst open a fraction of a second later. The room brightened to a dull grey as light seeped in. Hunter's eyes immediately snapped open. He hissed in a sharp breath like someone had doused him in ice water. Julian instantly closed the door after Arianna stepped through, but the few seconds of exposure was enough to have Hunter panting, his face pained.

Fangs down, Hunter twisted to glare at the door. "Why did you do that?"

Ignoring him, Julian flashed down the stairs; his emotions were brimming with worry, which jacked up my nerves. What the heck was eating him? When he stopped in front of our cot, his mood changed to disbelief and disgust. That was when I remembered what Hunter and I looked like right now. Julian glanced at Hunter's mostly-bare body, then spun around to face the door. His emotions darkened as he watched Arianna head down the stairs. Luckily, it was really dark down here. Her human eyes probably wouldn't see much.

Julian turned just his head in our direction. "Jesus, Nick. You slept with him? After he kidnapped us and held us hostage?"

Arianna gasped and peered more closely into the darkness as she continued her careful progress. Scowling, Hunter picked up his clothes off the floor and proceeded to get dressed. "I did *not* kidnap you. If you remember what happened correctly, I was trying to get away from you."

Julian half-turned to glare at him. "I remember you threatening my girlfriend if we didn't follow you to Flagstaff."

Not wanting the two men in my life to start brawling, I clutched the blankets under my arms and asked Julian, "What's going on? Why did you rush down here?"

He locked gazes with me, and fear immediately flushed out every other emotion in his body. Arianna finally joined us. Hunter's glowing eyes were the only source of light in the room. They highlighted her pale face and trembling body. Oozing nervousness, she clasped Julian's hand tightly as she looked between the three of us; she was so freaked out, she wasn't even impressed by the passionate evidence she'd stumbled across. "There are hunters in the woods," Julian whispered. "Three, from what I can tell."

Hunter paused in zipping up his pants. "What? How do you know? They could just be hikers ... walkers ... regular hunters."

Julian shook his head. "They circled the house. I think they're waiting for the old man to leave. And ... a couple of them have gas cans."

I violently shook my head as I scrambled off the cot. "No, that's impossible. No one knows we're here."

Hunter's mouth dropped, and his eyes flashed to his jacket. "The box. He put a tracker in the box."

I had no idea what he meant by that. "Hunter?"

Hunter closed his eyes like he was cursing himself, then he turned to me. "You and your brother need to get out of here. Now."

Bending down, he handed me my clothes. I reluctantly took them while Julian spun back around. "And you," I told Hunter. "I'm not leaving without you."

Not wanting to waste a minute, I dropped the blankets and blurred back into my clothes. Hunter's sad eyes scanned the basement while I dressed. "I can't leave, Nika."

That reality hit me like a tidal wave, knocking the breath from me. It was the middle of the day. He was stuck here. If they burned down the house … he would burn with it. Gritting my teeth, I fortified my stomach. "This isn't happening. Julian and I will take care of them. We'll protect you."

Julian turned around to face me, his mood unsure and nervous. Knowing he was silently asking me, *Really?* I snapped at him, "He's part of our nest. We don't abandon each other."

I started to storm off, to go wage war on a group of vampire hunters, but Hunter grabbed my elbow. His grip was so tight, I was sure I'd be bruised tomorrow. "No," he growled. "The three of you forget about me and get as far away from here as you can. You run home, and don't look back."

His hard gaze was impassioned, fierce. I knew he would compel me to leave him if he could. "I can't leave you here to die." My voice broke, and my speech cut off.

Hunter cupped my cheek. "I'll be fine, but I can't protect you in here, so I need you to run. Please."

"Hunter …"

Hunter looked past me to Julian. He shoved my shoulder in his direction. "Take her, and get her out of here."

Julian grabbed me and took a step forward. "I would love to, but you made it so my girlfriend can't leave the house without you. Fix her, and we'll happily leave." He indicated Arianna attached to his side.

Hunter closed his eyes, drowning the room in darkness. "I'm so sorry I did that to you, Arianna." Reopening his eyes, he locked gazes with her. "You are free to leave without me, you are free to call for help. Your memories will remain intact." He switched his gaze to Julian. "Now go, please."

Arianna was eager to leave, and pulled on Julian's hand. He, in turn, pulled me. I didn't want to go, but I knew I couldn't help Hunter. As Julian dragged me away, Hunter stood tall and straight, watching us leave with his captivating glowing eyes. I couldn't tear my gaze away from him. I tripped on the steps when we finally reached them. Hunter gave me a sad smile. "Go … I love you."

I twisted to face the doors, and dashed up the steps past Julian and Arianna. Damn if I was going to let a few jerk-holes kill the man I loved. When I got to the door and prepared myself to pull it open lightning fast, it wouldn't budge.

Rattling the knob, I glanced back at Julian. "It's locked."

Like he didn't believe me, Julian reached forward and tried the knob; he couldn't turn it any more than I could. "Did the old man lock us in?" he asked, looking down the stairs at Hunter.

Hunter tilted his head, listening. "No, the hunters are in the house. I can hear them. One is taking the homeowner out the back door, the others are ..." His eyes shot to mine. "You need to get out. Now."

I could smell it then ... gasoline, inside the house. I could hear the fast heartbeat of the hunters, too, could hear shuffling boots and liquid splashing on the hardwood floors. They really were going to torch the place. Julian met my eyes. A simple lock like this wouldn't keep us in. Even a bar across the door wouldn't hold us back. We'd just smash the heavy wood into splinters. But we'd be letting in a lot of light if we did that. It would seriously hurt Hunter.

From downstairs, Hunter murmured, "Nika, hurry. They're preoccupied now, so you can slip out. Save yourselves, and don't worry about me."

Arianna looked down the stairs at Hunter. "But what if they're right on the other side of the door, waiting for us?"

Hunter shook his head. "They're not. I can hear their heartbeats." He nodded at Julian and me. "And so can they."

Julian tightly clutched her hand. "It's okay. They won't even see us."

I knew he was only saying that so she wouldn't be scared. Truth was, they were most likely keeping watch on the door with the vampire locked behind it. They probably didn't expect said vampire to bust out, since he couldn't go anywhere during the day, but they'd surely react the minute they heard the door crack. Plus, if Hunter's dad had sent them, too, then they might know about Julian and me. They might know what we can do, and we could be shot the second we left the room. But I didn't want to think about that, and I definitely didn't want to tell Arianna that.

Julian dropped Arianna's hand and sucked in a deep breath, preparing himself. I gave Hunter one last pain-filled look. My vision hazed and panic started to fill me. I couldn't do it. I couldn't leave him to die in here all alone. Julian grabbed my arm, forcing my attention back to him. "I'll make sure it's clear, and you get Arianna out. Can you handle that?"

By the intensity in his voice, I realized Julian was giving me a mission, so I could get myself under control. Even though I was scared out of my wits, I was impressed. Julian had come so far from the boy who'd had a panic attack in a storage closet. Refocusing on the task at hand, I swallowed and nodded. Calm returned to me as I scooped up my best friend as easily as a child. Arianna needed us. Protecting her came first.

Julian took a slight step back as he wrapped his fingers around the doorknob. I tensed, ready to run. Julian nodded at me, then shoved the doorknob with all his supernatural strength. It took a second, but the wood around the knob splintered and the metal went straight through the door, leaving a fist-sized hole in its wake. Not wasting any time, Julian pulled the door open.

I heard shouts from around the room, and the chaotic shuffle of people reacting. Before I streaked away, I heard a sound that I knew would haunt me for the rest of my life. Hunter crying out in pain as he was exposed to sunlight he could no longer hide from. Tears streamed down my cheeks as I darted toward the front door.

I couldn't feel Julian anymore, but I prayed with every blurry step I took that he was right behind me. I burst through the front door and felt the warmth of the sun on my face. Arianna clung tightly to me, practically cutting off my circulation, but I didn't ask her to ease up. We still weren't clear. As I buzzed down the front steps, I heard a gun go off. I didn't know if it was aimed at me or not, but I dodged anyway. There was a whizzing in the air by my ear as bullets flew past me.

When I hit the lawn, I heard a low, menacing growl. A growl filled with pain. Hunter. Had he run out of the basement? I couldn't even imagine how much pain he was in. The sounds of a scuffle met my ear, furniture breaking, guns firing, people yelling. Then there was a sickening crunch that sounded like bones breaking. But all those sounds paled in comparison to the crackling hiss of flames springing to life.

I didn't stop running until I was at least three miles away. When I set Arianna down, I immediately started looking for Julian. So did she. "Where is he, Nika? Did he get out? Is he okay?"

I felt inside myself for the feelings I knew were his. He was frightened, filled to the brim with adrenaline ... and he was in pain. I could smell his blood in the air nearby, but I had no idea where he was. It was unnerving. Scared beyond all comprehension, I screamed as loud as I could, "Julian!"

From a clump of trees to the right of me, I heard Julian's voice. "Nika!" There was pain in the syllables of my name.

Arianna heard Julian, too, and started running in his direction. While she scrambled around the brush dotting the dry earth, I streaked to my brother. He was sitting at the base of a large tree, holding his leg and rocking back and forth. Blood stained the thigh of his dark denims, coated his fingertips. I hissed in an empathetic, pain-filled breath.

As I rushed to his side, he looked up. "Is Arianna okay?" he asked, fear in his eyes. She crashed through the trees then, and his gaze snapped to her. He smiled and cringed at the same time. "Thank God, you're okay."

Arianna skidded to a stop at his other side and flung her arms around his neck. "Baby, are you all right?"

While Julian told her that he was, I pried his fingers from his jeans. He instinctively fought me. I tried to keep my voice calm, but I was so far beyond calm it was difficult. "Stop it! I need to see how badly you've been hit, Julian."

Arianna grabbed his hand, and he finally stopped fidgeting. He rested his head back against the tree as Arianna cooed comforting words into his ear. I found the hole in his jeans and ripped it open a little wider so I could peer inside. My fangs instantly dropped at the sight of so much blood. I was so stressed it took me a couple of seconds to pull them back up. While he whimpered, and pain from our bond vibrated through my bones, I examined the source of the blood.

My stomach was already queasy by the time I spotted the hole. "They shot you."

Julian clenched his jaw. "No shit."

Ignoring him, I reached inside his jeans, and felt around his thigh for an exit wound. I found it not far away from the entrance wound. Good, a through and through. Even though I wanted to lose my stomach, I exhaled a sigh of relief. "The bullet's out, but we need to get you to a hospital. You need stitches."

Julian shook his head. "Just take me home. I want to go home."

I looked over at him and Arianna. They were both pale, suffering from shock. I supposed I looked the same way. "If I have to carry you both, it's going to take a while."

Julian put on a brave face as he took off his belt and started cinching it around his leg. "I can make it on my own."

Arianna's panicked eyes locked onto mine. "Then let's get started. I want to get out of here."

She looked back toward the direction of the house we'd fled. Another smell on the breeze took precedence over Julian's blood—the smell of burning cedar. Thick, black smoke pierced the skyline, pinpointing the location of the old man's log cabin. It was up in flames. Hunter was most likely dead. And I didn't even have time to grieve him, because my brother needed me. My brother and Arianna both.

Emotion clogging my throat, I helped my brother stand. He looked like he was going to be sick, but he remained upright. "Are you sure you can run?" I had to force out the words. I desperately wanted to run, but not *away* from the cabin.

Julian nodded. "For a bit." He nodded at Arianna. "Take her. I'll make it."

Arianna looked on the verge of a nervous breakdown as I picked her up again. I hoped she held it together for a little while longer. If she broke down, I'd break down, and I couldn't. Not yet. Steering clear of the cabin, we headed north, back to Salt Lake. Julian had to stop and rest every few minutes, and he looked greener and greener with every mile. When he finally slumped to the ground, hanging his head in defeat, we'd only gone about fifteen miles. "I'm sorry, Nick," he panted. "It hurts too much."

I set Arianna down as I looked around. We were at the edge of civilization before we entered the desert sitting between us and Salt Lake. If we were going to contact anybody to help us, it had to be now. "Let's find a phone. Call home."

Hope seeped into Arianna's eyes. "Call my mom. Let her know I'm okay. She's gotta be worried sick." Her eyes scanned the barren landscape. "Maybe she can come get us."

"My family can get here faster," I told her. I spied a gas station nearby and turned back to my best friend; she was breathing heavy and her heart was racing. I grabbed her shoulder. "I'm going to walk over there and use their phone. Stay here with Julian." I rubbed her arm. "He needs you. He's in a lot of pain."

Seeing the pain mirrored on my face, she said, "And you can feel that, can't you?"

I nodded and looked at Julian right as he looked at me. "It's part of the curse."

Julian smirked at me. "Be safe. Scream if you need me."

I raised an eyebrow. "Same goes for you."

Julian scoffed and rolled his eyes, but I could feel the residual fear under his bravado. It matched my own.

As cautiously as I could, I made my way to the gas station on the corner of the street. It was late afternoon, warm, but not overly hot. The station wasn't too busy, one beat-up pickup was at the pumps, one newer hybrid was parked in a stall beside the front door. An electronic beep chimed my entrance, and the clerk on duty looked my way. Changing my expression, I tried to look calm, yet desperately in need at the same time.

"Hey, my brother and I are having a problem with our car and our cell phones are dead. Can I use your phone?" I pointed to a clunky phone behind him that looked as old as my great-great grandmother.

Not looking like he really gave a rat's ass what I did, the guy shrugged. "Sure. Just don't be calling China. The boss would kill me."

He grabbed the phone and plopped it onto the counter so I could use it. I exhaled a steady breath as I dialed Dad's number. He was going to freak out when he picked up. *Please pick up.* Three rings went by before I heard the line connect. Dad's voice was tentative. "Hello?"

"Daddy!" An approaching sob butchered my voice, and the clerk twisted his lips like he was sure I was a crazy, drama queen.

"Nika, thank God! Where are you? What happened? Is Julian with you? Why can't we feel you? Are you okay?" His voice was relieved at first, but tightened with each question he asked me.

I had no idea what to say first. Since I was being watched, I decided all I could say right now was what the human listening to my conversation would expect to hear. "I'm sorry, Julian and I took the car without your permission, and now something is wrong with it. We're stuck just outside of Flagstaff."

There was a pause on Dad's end as he processed that. "Flagstaff? Arizona? Why the hell are you in Arizona?" I was about to tell him I'd explain later when his insistent voice came back on the line. "What do you mean you're stuck? Can't you run home?"

I closed my eyes to banish the heavy moisture filling them. "No. The car won't make it home. It needs to be towed …"

My father understood my cryptic sentence about Julian. "Jesus. Okay, okay, don't worry. Your mother and I are coming to you. Just stay exactly where you are and wait for us."

Knowing he wouldn't be able to find us without help, I asked the cashier, "What's the address here?"

He rambled it off, and I relayed the information to my father. Dad ended the call with, "I love you, Nika. I'll be there soon."

I was sniffling when I hung up. The clerk raised an eyebrow at me. "You okay, kid?"

I forced a laugh. "Yep. Just bringing on the waterworks so my dad doesn't kill me for stealing the car."

The clerk nodded like he completely understood.

I felt better when I left the station to return to Julian. Dad was coming. He'd fix everything. Then my heart sank. He couldn't fix Hunter. He was gone ... nothing could fix that. I made it to the shade of some nearby trees before I broke down into sobs. Hunter was dead. Dead-dead. The first man I'd ever truly loved, the first man I'd ever made love to, and he was gone. Just like that.

Dropping to my knees, I sank to the arid ground. Julian was beside me in an instant; even drained and in pain, he'd blurred to my side. He wrapped his arms around me while I fell apart. Arianna jogged up to us, sat beside me, and put her hand on my back. I clutched Julian's shirt while I cried. "He's gone, Julie. Hunter's gone."

Julian stroked my back. "No, I'm sure he's fine."

"How could he have survived the fire?" I hiccupped. "He couldn't run outside."

"The floor was dirt," he answered.

Blinking, I lifted my head. "What?"

Julian grimaced in pain as he shook his head. "The basement had a dirt floor. It was hard-packed, but I'm sure he was able to dig his way to safety."

Hope sprang through me, muting the despair. Julian smiled at feeling it. "Oh, right. That's what he meant when he said he'd be fine." I looked out over the skyline, to where a faint trail of smoke was drifting toward the clouds. "That's if he got away from the hunters though ..."

I couldn't stop staring at that fading trail of smoke. I watched it the entire time I waited for our parents to show up. Was Hunter under the earth, or was he a pile of ash? While I wasn't watching them, I could hear my brother and Arianna talking. We'd covered up Julian's wound with his jacket so any humans who saw us wouldn't bother us, but more than once, I heard Arianna tell him that he needed to be at a hospital, not slowly bleeding to death in a parking lot. Julian always told her he was fine, that it was barely bleeding anymore. There was some truth to that, I could smell that his wounds weren't gushing or anything, but Arianna was right too. He shouldn't be here. None of us should.

Fueled by pure panic, our parents made it to our location in under an hour. The three of us were sitting, staring at nothing, and then like magic they appeared in front of us. It happened so fast that it took a moment for me to react to seeing them. When I did, the emotion came out in an uncontainable sob.

I shot to my feet and tossed my arms around my father. He clutched me back just as tight. "Nika, thank God. I was so scared."

"Daddy," I murmured, tucking my head under his chin. I never wanted to let him go.

I heard Mom rush to Julian's side. "Teren, he's hurt."

Dad inhaled a deep breath. Catching the scent of Julian's blood in the tepid air, a low growl escaped him. His arms dropped from me as he headed for his injured son. Julian hissed in pain as our parents undid his tourniquet to look at the wound. After inspecting the oozing hole, Dad looked up at Mom; his face was haggard, his pale eyes weary, like he'd aged a decade during our absence. I could only imagine how hard it had been on them to lose us both like that. "This looks like a bullet hole." He looked around at the three of us. "Was he shot? What have the three of you been doing? And why are you here in Arizona? And why can't we feel you?"

I wasn't sure which question was causing him the most distress, but I knew we didn't have a lot of time to answer any of them. I pointed back toward the direction of the log cabin. "We found Hunter. We followed him here to stop him from going after his father ... alone. We were ambushed though. We barely got out."

Dad looked furious for a moment, then his expression softened. Regarding my features, he asked, "And Hunter ... ?"

Barely able to say my fears out loud, I told him, "They burned the cabin we were hiding in to the ground. We're not sure if he got out."

Dad sighed and closed his eyes. Returning his gaze to Mom, he softly said, "I think Julian's wound is stable enough that we can take him back to the ranch." His eyes swung back to me. "Let's go home."

I stubbornly held my ground. Now that Dad was here, now that we were reconnected with our family, I didn't want to run home. Not without Hunter. "You can take Julian and Arianna back, but I want to stay here. At least until nightfall." Dad narrowed his eyes at me, and I bit my lip to hold in the pain. "I need to know if he made it. Grandma would want to know too," I quickly added. "And ... he's a member of our nest, Dad. We can't just abandon him." Hopefully, the bond of family, no matter how loose the connection, was enough to sway him.

Dad seemed at a loss, and a flash of hope burst through me. Had I won? Could I stay? Dad looked up at the sky. It was still a few hours from sunset. "Okay, Nika. We'll go home, rest—" I started to object, and Dad held up his hand. "Then we'll come back at sunset and see if he's okay. Deal?"

No, I didn't want to do it that way, but I knew when to push my dad and when to concede. And besides, the rest of my family was probably sick with worry too. Dad picked up Julian, and Mom scooped up Arianna. Julian was embarrassed to be carried about like a doll, but it would take him forever to get home on his own and he knew it.

Dad looked back at me and nodded. He was trusting me to follow him, and I would. If Hunter was buried beneath burned-out rubble, he wasn't going anywhere for a while.

We headed back to the ranch without pause. Even for the supernaturally enhanced, it was a long run. I was tired afterward, and not excited about the return trip tonight, but I would go three times that distance to make sure Hunter was okay. God, I hoped he was okay.

The front door of the ranch opened as we approached it. Alanna was there with Grandma Linda and Grandpa Jack. They all looked terribly concerned, and I suddenly felt really bad for leaving town without letting them know I was okay. I understood with perfect clarity how horrible that unknown feeling was.

Dad set Julian down in the entryway, and Alanna immediately gave him a fierce hug, then she looked at his leg. Frowning, she said to Dad, "Get him upstairs and undressed. He needs a stitch or two."

Julian's face paled. "Whoa ... maybe we *should* go to a hospital." He pointed over to where I was hugging Grandma Linda. "Nika got to go to a hospital when she was shot."

Standing, Alanna patted his shoulder. "It's a small wound. I can fix you."

Julian's eyes widened as far as they could go. Anxiety rushed from him into me. "You have drugs, right? I won't feel it, right?"

Alanna only smiled, then nodded at Dad. Before Dad could take off with him, a loud squeal pierced the momentary silence. "Julian! You're back!"

His mood sinking, Julian closed his eyes. A young girl dashed into the room and ran toward him. Olivia, Ben's daughter. The tiny girl threw her arms around my brother, burying her blonde head into his chest and nearly squeezing the life out of him. Arianna cracked a small smile at seeing the preteen rival for Julian's affections. I looked around the room. If Olivia was here, then Ben was nearby too.

He came around the corner a few seconds later. "Hey, kiddos. You both had us all pretty terrified."

He held his arms open, and I rushed into them. "Uncle Ben, what are you doing here?"

Squeezing me, he indicated Julian attempting to untangle Olivia from his aching body; Dad had to help him. "Hopped a plane the minute I heard you two dropped off the map. We all did."

Ben looked up at the ceiling, and I followed his gaze. Someone was walking around upstairs, muttering something about vampires not being real. Stunned, I snapped my head down to meet Ben's gaze. "Aunt Tracey is here? And she *knows*?"

I glanced over at Olivia, then back to him. Ben knew what I meant. Tracey knew we were vampires. Mouth in a firm line, he nodded. "Yeah. I couldn't fly out here again without telling her why." He locked eyes with my dad. "The real reason why."

Dad sighed. "I still think you shouldn't have told her."

Ben smirked. "And I still think you shouldn't have tried to wipe me."

Dad rolled his eyes. "You're never gotta let that go, are you?"

Olivia looked confused. "What do you mean wipe him?" She looked back at Julian. "And where did you go? Did you run away? And why is there blood on your jeans." Her eyes widened. "Oh my gosh, are you hurt?"

Alanna patted her shoulder. "He'll be fine, dear. It's just a scratch."

She indicated for Dad to take Julian away. He put his arm around Julian and helped him hobble up the stairs; Grandma Linda went with him. When Olivia started to follow them, Ben grabbed her shoulder. "Leave him be, Liv." She frowned, but remained by his side.

Arianna started to follow, but Alanna stopped her with a sentence. "We should get you home." Alanna patted her arm. "Your parents must be worried sick."

Arianna bit her lip, looking between Alanna and Julian's retreating form on the stairs; he was looking back at her, his heart in his eyes. He wanted her to stay. "I know, and I don't want them to worry. I'll call them and let them know I'm okay, but I want to stay here with Julian."

Julian hesitated on the stairs. Alanna glanced at him, then looked down at Arianna. "I'll get you a phone so you can call them. When they called last night, and again this morning, I told them you had fallen ill and were too sick to travel. You should tell them the same, ask for a few more hours to recover. They might still try to come get you, but at least they won't call the police. We'll set things straight when we take you home."

She winked at Arianna, and I knew she meant she'd have Halina wipe her parents' minds. Arianna understood. She gave Alanna a nervous smile, then turned and darted off after Julian.

Olivia let out a low whistle as she shook her head. "You guys are the coolest parental-type people ever." She looked up at her dad. "How are they related to Julian, again?"

Ben patted her shoulder and pointed to the living room. "Why don't you go play?"

Olivia gave him a full pout that reminded me of her mother; I could still hear Tracey murmuring that her husband was crazy. "By myself?" Olivia asked.

Needing a distraction, I said, "I'll go with her. Keep her company."

I knew my family wanted to talk about what had happened, but I couldn't right now. My mind was spinning. And besides, Julian was filling Dad in on everything. Hopefully he skipped over the part where he'd walked in on Hunter and me after we'd slept together. No need to cause Dad any more grief.

Olivia left the room and I started to follow her. Before I completely left, I turned and asked the room, "Where's Halina?"

Ben raised his eyebrows. I typically didn't ask where my family members were. I usually didn't need to. But I was still cut off from her, and I wanted to know if she was here or still where I'd last felt her—up north. Alanna smiled and pointed at the ground. "She came back right before dawn."

I nodded. Good. I didn't want to waste any time getting her back with us before we returned to Hunter. And I was sure she wanted to know where he was. And if he was safe. I know I did.

CHAPTER TWENTY-ONE

Nika

I GREW ANTSY waiting for the sun to set. It felt like it took a thousand years. I'd already asked Dad numerous times if we could leave before sunset. He'd repeatedly told me no, that we would wait for Halina to be able to go with us. I hated the idea of just what could happen during the time it took us to get down there. The thought of Hunter being attacked while he was alone gave me nightmarish daydreams that left me shaking.

Restless, I discreetly slipped away from Olivia and headed downstairs to wait for Halina to wake up. She was awake when I ran into her, though. She was awake, and she was very, very angry.

I was in the lowest level of the underground rooms. Not only was this entire floor soundproof from the rooms above it, but each bedroom was soundproof as well. I was heading to Halina's bedroom, when I saw Starla and Jacen hanging around Gabriel's lab with their heads down. I was a little surprised they were still here. I also wasn't sure why they looked so glum. Especially Starla, who was never down about anything.

"Hey," I said, getting their attention. "Have you guys seen my grandma?"

Starla looked up. She had bags under her eyes, but she brightened when she noticed me. "Nika!" Stepping forward, she tossed her arms around me. The familiar smell of perfume, gum, and hairspray assaulted me as I hugged her back. "I'm so glad you're okay. We've been looking everywhere for you." Pulling back, I noticed how weary and disheveled she seemed; it was shocking, to say the least. "I haven't slept in ... ages, it seems like."

After her, I hugged Jacen. He was more reserved, but equally affectionate. "We're glad you're safe, Nika. Has your brother returned as well?"

I nodded. "He's upstairs, resting. He was shot." Saying it out loud was strange to me, and I couldn't keep the scowl from my face. We'd been shot at way too much recently.

Starla and Jacen exchanged startled glances. Then Starla bit her lip and asked in a surprisingly timid voice, "And Hunter? Is he ... with you?"

Shaking my head, I swallowed the lump in my throat. "No, he ... we were attacked by a group of hunters. I'm not sure he made it out." My hollow voice resonated through the hallway.

Starla's eyes widened and filled with tears. Turning, she clutched Jacen's hands. "Jace ... if Hunter ..."

Her throat closed, and Jacen pulled her close. "It will be fine, darling. No matter what, it will be fine."

He rubbed her back while a shiver went down my spine. "What's going on?"

Jacen looked to the closed door on his left. "Your grandmother is in there with Gabriel. She's ... unhappy with his part in what happened to Hunter."

My eyes widened, and I moved toward the door. Jacen reached out for my arm. "I wouldn't go in there."

I pulled away. "I have to tell her what I know."

Jacen sighed, then nodded. Rewrapping his arm around Starla, he gave me a sad smile. "Make sure to duck."

I wasn't sure what he meant, or why he and Starla were so upset, until I opened the door. The sound of shrieking immediately met my ear, followed by the sound of glass breaking. The smell of chemicals, acids, sulfur, and blood stung my nose. The tiled floor was littered with debris, shelves were overturned, the refrigerator was on its side. It looked like a hurricane had swept through the space. A hurricane named Halina.

Throwing a beaker full of something blue against the wall, my grandmother yelled, "How dare you! How dare you, Gabriel! You had no right to break the bond! None!"

Gabriel's face was dark as he looked around his destroyed workspace. "I did not force it upon him. He asked. I gave. Do not blame me that he wanted freedom."

Bright red tears streamed down Halina's face as she chucked a garbage can against the wall, just over Gabriel's shoulder. He didn't even flinch. "You didn't have to give it to him! You should have told him no! You should have told me that he'd asked!"

Gabriel cocked his head. "I don't discuss all of my experiments with you."

Halina grabbed a beaker full of a yellow liquid and tossed it at his feet. "He was not an experiment! He was my child!"

Gabriel took a small step backward when the liquid around his shoes started smoking. "He was a *bonded* child to you, Halina. Nothing more. But in case you haven't noticed, your actual, *blood* child has returned." He indicated where I was quietly standing behind her.

Halina raised her chin, but didn't look at me yet. "And what do you know about bonded children, since you've never created one? It felt as real to me as blood, Gabriel. And you took it away from me." Before Gabriel could respond, Halina turned my way. Her momentary grief lessened when she finally noticed me. "Nika, thank God you're all right."

Her cold arms swept around me, and I closed my eyes, blocking out the physical damage of her anguish. Pulling back, she cupped my cheeks; I shuddered under the chill. "Are you okay? Is your brother okay? Is ... Hunter?" Her voice cracked on Hunter's name. Gabriel sighed, but she ignored it.

I nodded as I removed her fingers from my face. "I'm fine. Julian was hurt, but he's okay now." Alanna had numbed him earlier when she'd fixed his leg, so luckily, I hadn't felt him being worked on. He was achy now, but feeling fine. "And Hunter ..."

Halina's eyes bored into mine as she waited for my answer. I could feel the fragile hold she had on her control as she tightly gripped my fingers. "He's safe," I told her.

Her relief was instant. A trace amount of guilt washed through me, but she was so distressed, I needed to ease her into the facts or she might snap.

When she sagged against me, I flicked a glance at Gabriel. Brief guilt crossed his face, too, but he steadfastly held my gaze.

When it seemed like Halina wouldn't explode from any sort of bad news, I filled her in on Hunter's true condition. "We went to Arizona to find Hunter's father. A group of hunters found us. Julian and I got out with Arianna, but Hunter couldn't leave the house because of the sun. The hunters burned the house to the ground, but we believe Hunter was able to dig into the dirt floor to protect himself."

She stood up straighter with every word I told her. When I finished, her jaw went slack. "My God ..." she muttered. Her gaze snapped to Gabriel's. "He was almost burned alive."

Gabriel pressed his lips together but remained silent. Halina started looking around the room. "We need to go get him. We need to make sure he's safe."

I bobbed my head in agreement. "I know. As soon as the sun sets, we'll go to him."

Halina met my eyes, frowning. "No, you and your brother should stay here. Those hunters could still be hanging around."

That was a fear of mine, too. One of many. Giving her my most stubborn expression, I replied, "I'm the only one who knows where he's buried."

Halina sighed, then finally shrugged. "All right." She looked around the room, impatience on her face. "That damn sun is not moving fast enough." She twisted back to Gabriel. "This is all your fault."

Gabriel sighed as Halina tore into him again. Feeling very uncomfortable witnessing their mammoth fight, I slipped out the door to wait in the hallway with Starla and Jacen. Jacen gave me a small smile. "I warned you," he whispered.

Starla sniffled and hugged him tight. "She's going to make him leave, isn't she?"

She looked over at me. I had no answer for her, and shrugged. "She's pretty upset."

Starla nodded, burying her head in Jacen's chest. "I never really felt close to anyone in the L.A. nest ... I'm going to miss it here." Reaching out, she touched my arm. "I might not show it often, but you and Julian are like the children I never had." She frowned, her lips forming a perfect pout. "Or wanted."

Tears stung my eyes at the thought of Gabriel, Starla, and Jacen leaving. They'd been fixtures in my life since birth. They were odd, eccentric, aloof at times, but they were family. Starla had taught me how to put on makeup. Jacen had taught me to always be cautious of my surroundings, and never sit with my back to the door. Gabriel had given my family so many incredible gifts, and he'd always had a soft spot for Julian and me. I think we reminded him of his own children, scattered throughout the world.

Not able to offer any wise words of encouragement, I simply gave her a hug. More emotional than I'd ever seen her, she eagerly accepted it. The sadness radiating from her only made me even more nervous. It filled my soul with trepidation.

When that damn sun finally touched the horizon, Halina emerged from Gabriel's ruined laboratory. She tossed a fierce glance at Starla and Jacen—Gabriel's nestmates—then stormed past them on her way to the exit.

I let out a tense breath and followed. When we reached the living room, my mother and father were waiting with Ben, Tracey, Imogen, Alanna, and Grandpa Jack; Tracey looked really nervous as she sat on the couch beside Ben. Her knee bobbed up and down so fast, it was almost vampiric. Imogen looked ready for travel, wearing jeans instead of her signature long skirt. Dad had filled her in once she'd woken up, and she'd immediately decided that she was coming with us. Upstairs, I could hear Olivia giggling and Julian sighing. Grandma Linda and Arianna were with them. Everything was set, except the sun.

The last rays of sunshine streamed through the windows as we stepped into the middle of the room, but my grandmother was untouched by their harshness. She scowled at the sun, like it was purposely keeping her from Hunter. Gabriel stepped through the secret doorway leading downstairs after us. Halina pointed at him without even looking. "Do not be foolish enough to think that I am going to allow you to come with us."

"I can help," was his calm response.

Halina's emotion sizzled as she snapped her head to glare at him. "Help? You have done quite enough." She switched her finger from him to the backyard awash in golden rays. "You can 'help' by gathering your things and being gone by the time I return."

Gabriel stepped forward, arms outstretched. "Beloved—"

Halina raised her palm to his face. "You betrayed me. I don't want you anywhere near me, ever again. You and the rest of your damn nest need to get out of my home before I kill every last one of you."

I gaped at her coldness, and wondered if she really would kill them. I wasn't sure. Neither was Gabriel. Despair broke over his usually unemotional face. He shook his head, "I only did what he asked, love. I did what he wanted."

Halina's pale eyes hardened into stone. "No, you did what *you* wanted."

Gabriel was clearly at a loss, struggling with deep emotions he usually pushed aside. It broke my heart to watch his turmoil. It took him a minute, but he finally regained control. "My apologies. We'll leave at once." Blankness returning, he inclined his head to her in a polite nod, then headed back downstairs. Halina grit her teeth and turned away.

Mom and Dad shared a glance with Alanna, while Imogen took a step forward. "Mother," she began quietly.

Ignoring her, Halina raised her chin. "We leave the second the sun sets. Nika will show us where Hunter is buried. We will find him, deal with any hunters we come across, then immediately return." Her gaze turned to my honorary uncle. "Ben, if you wish to join us, I will carry you."

Tracey stood at hearing that news. "What! No, no way is he going with you. This is ridiculous." Her icy blue eyes narrowed at her husband. "This entire fantasy you've delved up is ridiculous! Vampires are not real, and you're all freaking crazy!"

Halina blurred in front of Tracey, fangs lowered. Tracey immediately screamed. Halina silenced her with a word. "Quiet. I don't have time for this. My child is being hunted, and I'm not there to protect him. Vampires *are* real. Your best friend is one of them. We've made your mind believe that she's been aging, but she hasn't been. She looks the same as she did when she left California years ago. As do we all. You will not be scared by this information, because I simply can't abide smelling your fear right now."

Tracey was slack-jawed when Halina stepped away, but she did look calmer. Her eyes widened when she looked over at Mom, and I figured she was truly seeing her for the first time in a long time. Mom gave her an apologetic shrug, then glared at Halina. "Was that necessary?"

Halina returned her attention to the window. "No, I could have wiped her clean, sent her home, told her any imaginary story I wanted. Comforting her was definitely *not* necessary."

Ben gave Halina an irritated look, then grabbed Tracey's hand. "Honey, this is what we talked about. Vampires or not, the Adams are my family. If they need me, I'm there."

Tracey pulled her hand free. "Olivia and I are your family. We need you, too. And we need you alive."

Halina opened her mouth to speak, but Ben raised his hand. "I told you when we got back together that I was going to do whatever it took to keep us together, but, honey—"

My mom stepped forward, silencing him. "It's okay, Ben. It was sweet of you to rush out here and help us look for the children. We're forever indebted to you for that. But we can handle this. Stay here with Tracey and Olivia." She half-smiled. "You can keep an eye on Julian for us."

As Ben finally sighed and nodded, Tracey's eyes locked on my mom. "Emma, we're going to have a seriously long talk when you get back."

My mom gave her a quick hug. "I know."

Halina tensed as the sun dipped beyond the horizon; Imogen waited patiently beside her. The faint glow in the sky would follow quickly behind the glowing orb, then we could finally leave. My heartbeat raced, and Mom and Dad protectively flanked me. I could tell Dad wasn't thrilled about me coming along, but I was the only one who knew where Hunter was. Or, knew where he *should* be. Hopefully he would stay put when he dug himself up.

As the seconds ticked by, I heard my brother murmur, "Be safe, Nick."

Feeling his concern for me, I whispered back, "I will."

Dad looked over at Mom. "Em—"

Mom cut him off with a glance. "I know what you're going to say, but I'm coming too."

Her tone was final. Dad knew not to argue, so he merely nodded. His expression darkened though. I hated that once again my family was in upheaval, and it was my fault. The situation might not entirely be because of me, but I was definitely to blame for a large majority of it.

As soon as darkness fell upon the Earth, my grandmother bolted out the door. The rest of us were a split-second behind her. We flew across the ranch, a mere gust of wind to human senses. My feet touched the arid dirt beneath me so lightly, it was almost like I was flying. Halina was the fastest, and streaked ahead of everyone. My parents kept pace with me at the end of the pack. I ran as hard as I could though. I'd never been more motivated to get somewhere quickly.

Even though it just about killed me, I made the long journey for the second time today without resting. I was breathing hard when the group of us hovered outside the edges of the city. Easily remembering where Hunter's hiding place was, I took off toward the direction of the cabin. I thought I might puke I was so tired, but I could still smell a lingering trace of freshly burned wood in the air, and I needed to get to Hunter.

As I knew they would, my family followed me. When we arrived at the cabin, I was shocked at the devastation. The once quaint, two-story home in the woods was now a hodgepodge of fallen, blackened logs. The walls had crumbled in on themselves. The roof was ash. The stone chimney was the only structural support left intact. The land around the home was dark with moisture. Deep tire tracks were in the front yard, and heavy footprints surrounded the home, like someone had tried to save the cabin, but it had been too little, too late. My heart sank for the poor old man who had unknowingly lost everything when he'd given us a place to hide for the day.

"Hunter!" I called out into the night. I tensed, waiting for him to emerge, or for one of our attackers to hear me and lash out. The night was silent, though, with only the sound of crickets answering me. I called out for him again, but no one responded. Desperate, I began to search the home we'd fled earlier today. "He must still be buried ..."

I had no idea how we would find Hunter in this rumble. I didn't even know where to begin. Despair threatened to paralyze me, but Halina leapt into action, and started pulling gigantic logs from the pile. Her determination recharged mine. I picked a spot near her and started sorting through the debris. My parents and Imogen joined us. Getting to the bottom of the pile was all I cared about. Hunter was at the bottom.

We all worked diligently, restlessly, tearing out logs, stones, destroyed remnants of furniture. My fingers were black with soot, but progress was being made. Within a short time, Halina was able to crawl inside the house and start lifting rubble up to us. When she finally leapt into a hole that I knew had once been the cellar, I jumped in after her.

"Nika! It's not safe for you down there!" my dad hissed.

I ignored him and scanned the pitch-black ground with my grandmother. Using her glowing eyes for light, I looked for any section of ground that was unnaturally disturbed. There was crap everywhere, though, and seeing the ground, let alone searching it, was difficult. "Hunter! Where are you?" I yelled into the darkness. Was he still buried? Too weak to dislodge himself? Had he had time to cover himself before the burning cabin fell apart?

Suddenly, Halina snarled and took off to a back corner of the room. I had to squeeze under a fallen beam to follow her, but once I did, I understood her reaction. Beside a half-fallen wall of stone was a pile of freshly upturned earth; even with a floor covered in litter, the disturbance stood out amongst the hard-packed dirt. My heart thudded in my chest. A grave meant Hunter had at least attempted to hide himself from the sun.

The two of us immediately reached into the soil, elbow deep, desperate to find a body. "Hunter?" I called as I scooped out the pungent earth. He didn't answer me, and no bulk the size of a person blocked the path of my fingers. Halina cursed as she dug through the ground. We were both on the verge of losing it.

When we had dislodged a hole large enough to hide three Hunters, it was clear that our search was a futile one. I grabbed my grandmother's arm to stop her frenzied search. "He's not here, Grandma."

She clenched a clump of dirt in her hand, turning it to silt. "Then where is he?" she muttered, looking up at the moonless sky above us.

I swallowed the painful worry crawling up my throat. That was exactly what I wanted to know.

Hunter

AS I STOOD at the top of the stairs, hazy, indirect sunlight scorched me like I was only a few inches from the sun. Every muscle in my body hurt. No, it went deeper than the muscle. It felt like tiny shards of glass had been imbedded into my bones over every square inch of my body, and each movement I made ground the glass deeper. I wanted to lie still, I wanted to rest, but Nika wasn't safe yet.

The hunters clearly weren't expecting me to leave my sanctuary. I'd been classified a non-threat, dulled into submission by the sunlight. Stupid assumption. The door to the cellar opened into a hallway that was just dark enough for me to step into it. A hunter had his back to me, his long arms outstretched toward the front door Nika was escaping through. My body screamed with pain, but I contained the agony as long as I could.

Grabbing the hunter, I slammed him into the wall; the plaster cracked around his body with the force. The gun stopped going off, and, hazy-eyed, the man retrained his weapon on me. I recognized him at once. Collin. We'd done a job together a couple of summers ago. His eyes widened as he took in the sight of me, fangs exposed, ready to strike. His finger squeezed the trigger, but it didn't matter, I had already dodged. Letting out the growling cry of pain I could no longer contain, I lunged forward and snapped his neck. Guilt mixed with my pain, but what choice did I have?

He slumped to the ground with sickening finality. Others in the home shouted his name, but stopped when he didn't respond. I heard the whoosh of flames roaring to life as the sting of gasoline overwhelmed my senses. I risked a glance at the door, to see if Julian and Nika had made it, but the sunlight in that direction was too bright. It seared holes into my brain and obliterated my vision. Through the excruciating agony of my bones feeling like they were turning to ash inside of me, I could feel the heat of the flames upon my chilly skin. Time was running out.

Still blinded by the sunlight, I hastily stepped back into the relative safety of the cellar. I slammed the door shut, but hazy light still shone through the hole where Julian had busted the doorknob. Raw with pain, I stumbled backward and fell down the stairs. It hurt, but I was already so far gone with agony that adding more didn't bother me. When I hit the hard dirt floor, I still couldn't see; it was like my eyes had been burned away. I wanted to curl into the fetal position and scream for hours, but I didn't have time. The home above me was hissing and crackling with hungry flames. As soon as they ate a hole through the walls, I would be fully exposed to the sun. That pain would make my current torture feel like I was back at the ranch, soothing my worries in the family hot tub. At the moment, nothing sounded more wonderful than returning to the ranch, returning home.

Running to a corner of the room that I thought might survive the destructive blaze without too much debris falling on top of it, I shoved my fingers into the ground and started digging. The dirt was so hard it was almost clay. My fingertips were sore and bleeding in no time at all. I healed instantly, but it didn't take long for new injuries to appear, as I continually tore open my skin. Blind, scared, and roiling with pain, I used every supernatural gift I had to open the earth as quickly as possible. I needed Mother Nature's embrace, now more than ever.

When there was a deep enough space that no light would touch me, I crawled inside. Using my hands, I covered the hole as well as I could, then I rolled and burrowed deeper into the earth to completely hide myself. It was difficult in this type of unforgiving soil, and I found myself continually working my way lower and lower, digging, squirming, adjusting. I just wanted away from the sun, away from the pain. It was all I could think about. I squeezed my useless eyes shut tight as I inched my way to safety. *Please, let the dirt hide me. Let Nika be safe. Let this pain go away. Please.*

I wasn't sure when I stopped digging and let sleep overtake me, but when I finally reopened my eyes, they no longer hurt. The soft, glowing light that emanated from them showed me clumps of soil, rocks, the underside of roots. My chest was too heavy to make the movement, but mentally, I let out an exhale of relief. My vision was restored. A definite plus to vampirism was the ability to heal instantly. Although, the effects of the sun had taken a while. The memory of that pain was still with me as I stretched tight limbs as much as I could under the crushing confines of the thick soil.

The natural alarm clock in my body told me that the sun had set, that it was safe for me to reemerge. I was lying on my side, arms still stretched into the earth, trying to dig deeper. I pulled them through the muck back to my chest. Reaching up, I began to push against the wall of soil above me. Freeing myself was easier than burying myself, but the dirt was still uncooperative and difficult to work through. Using my legs as well as my arms, I eventually broke through the surface.

The air was warmer to me than the harsh ground I'd been sleeping in, but it was colder than the basement had been before the fire. As my head emerged from the ground, the clumps of dirt covering me gave way much easier. Sitting up in my hole, I took in the destruction around me. Where a solid wooden floor once was, I could see stars piercing the night sky. Ruined remnants of the old man's life were strewn around me—tarnished metal frames, bubbled, misshapen plastic jugs, loose sheets of paper that had shriveled into fragile, black roses. The cots Nika and I had slept on were buried under rubble, the backpack with Gabriel's shot inside it was smashed, my jacket burned and in tatters, my sister's box in the pocket most likely destroyed. Charred logs above me rested against each other at perilous angles. One shift in the wrong direction would bring the rest of the cabin's skeleton crashing to the ground. Guilt tore at my soul. Without meaning to, I had inadvertently led my father here and destroyed this innocent man's life.

Forcefully tearing my body the rest of the way from the dirt, I crouched in the darkness. It was quiet, only the peaceful serenade of the night's smallest creatures met my ear. I brushed off as much of the filth from me as I could while I waited for an attack that I was positive was coming. Surely those hunters wouldn't leave my death to chance. They would want to see my end with their own eyes, so they could report back to my father that they'd been successful. Then what would he do? Go after my maker? Go after Nika, and the rest of her family? Yes. That was what I would have done, once upon a time.

I wouldn't let him hurt my nest. My *family*. So long as my undead heart still had life in it, I would use it to protect them. They were all that mattered now.

Staring at the moonless sky above me, I determined my best path to exit this hell. As I lightly placed my weight on a fallen log, I vowed to make it up to the old man who'd had his home torched. When I found him, I'd find out what he wanted most in the world, and make it happen. This gift of compulsion was good for so much more than subduing prey and covering up our existence.

When I finally squeezed my way free of the wreckage and placed my foot on solid ground, I immediately looked around for Nika. I still didn't hear anything out of the ordinary as I stood crouched low before the cabin's charred corpse. No odd movement, no unexplainable sound, no errant heartbeats. Nothing. I didn't want to risk calling her name, though. And besides, if she wasn't here waiting for me, then she must be safe at home. She had to be; the alternative wasn't something I cared to think about.

Feeling anxious about her absence, I turned and prepared myself to run. That was when my sharp ears caught a familiar twang of a bow releasing its missile. Not knowing exactly where the arrow would strike, I froze in place. When I sensed it passing through the air in front of me, I quickly stepped back. It lodged into the ground at my feet; its shaft gleamed bright silver in the starlight.

My head snapped in the direction of the arrow's trajectory. I still couldn't hear anything unusual, but I knew someone was out there. I waited for the telltale sound of another arrow loosing into the night, but it didn't come. "Show yourself!"

Just when I thought I should run while I still could, a low voice drifted across the breeze. "Hello, son."

A shuffling sound followed the voice, and a thump, like a body dropping to the Earth. Every part of me tensed at hearing my father's voice. It was the first time I'd heard it with my enhanced ears. Dad had fled from me soon after I'd awoken from my conversion. He'd abandoned me without even giving me a chance.

I straightened as I heard his footsteps approaching. Now that I was listening for it, I could sense his slow and steady heartbeat. I'd been listening for an anxious heart, fast and pulsing. He was so calm that I'd missed him. Foolish mistake.

The groupings of trees surrounding the cabin were widely spaced, with plenty of room between each trunk. I easily spotted my father's lean form as he casually walked my way at an unhurried pace. His crossbow was still in hand, but was dangling at his side. His other hand looked free of weapons. He acted like I wasn't a threat to him. As if he could lift his weapon and end me at any moment. As if I couldn't blur over to him and rip out his throat in the span of one, slow heartbeat.

It took him a couple of minutes to fully emerge from the trees. When he did, I nodded my head at him. "Dad," I stated, my tone businesslike. Seeing that he wasn't wearing any form of mind control protection surprised me. Was he testing me? Or did he believe I was so weak and pathetic, I wouldn't fight him. He should know better than that. I'd eliminated his assassins after all. I could end this madness with just a few words, right now. But seeing him after all this time ... the memories of who he used to be to me overwhelmed me, sapped my desire for revenge. He was my *father*. My last remaining true blood family. That wasn't something I could erase on a whim, no matter how much I'd wanted to for the last few months. I needed answers more than I needed vengeance.

"You tracked me here? Sent hunters after me?" I asked, knowing full well what the answer was. My throat was tight as the pain of his betrayal stabbed me yet again.

Dad sighed and ran a hand through his hair as he stepped without fear right in front of me. His hair seemed even grayer than before; somehow it seemed fitting that a vampire hunter had silver streaks in his hair. "It was my duty to make sure you were dealt with. My only regret is that it's taken me this long to be man enough to do it myself. I should have staked you before you could complete the change." His voice was more gravelly than I remembered it, like stones were grinding together in his throat. "Do you remember what I used to tell you?" he asked.

I eyed him warily, waiting for some sign of attack. "You told me a lot of things. Some true. Some not true."

He'd been avoiding my hypnotic gaze, but at my words, his vision snapped to mine. "I never lied to you." He seemed caught by my gaze, but after a second, he managed to turn away. Quite a feat, since most humans couldn't look away once a vampire had them ensnared.

"You might not have lied, but some things you told me were still untrue." A smile graced my lips as I thought of all the things Nika and her family had taught me, about who I was and who I could be. Their words were truth.

Dad exhaled a weary sigh. "I didn't come here to argue with you."

A flare of anger ran up my spine. "Why *are* you here? To burn an innocent man's home to the ground?" I indicated the destruction behind me. Destruction created on his behalf, if not his hand.

Dad frowned as he glanced at the charred wood. "That wasn't my call. But you know how it is, Hunter. Whatever it takes to get the job done."

I clenched my jaw as my hands curled into fists. "We'll just have to disagree on that. Between this and cutting up that young girl as bait ... what's been done in the name of the greater good has been far more evil than the evil it was meant to end. You can make all the justifications you want, but deep inside you have to know I'm right."

My father closed his eyes. I knew he wasn't a completely cold-hearted man. Like me, he was torn. I could see the conflict so clearly in his worn features. Abruptly, he glared at my chin, still avoiding my eyes. "And you're so much better than me? Killing our compatriots? Our *friends*?"

His heartbeat increased, just fractionally. His cool was fading. Mine was, too, I just didn't have a pulse to give it away. "Friends? None of them were true friends to our family. And I only killed when I had no other choice. Most of them walked away to continue their lives in peace." I shook my head in sorrow as I remembered my days as a human, killing countless vampires that I had known nothing about. How many of those had been innocent? Probably most of them. "That's a mercy we never allowed our victims. How were we any different than what we thought they were?"

Dad raised his bow to my chest, but didn't fire. Heat was in his eyes now. "Victims? Don't pretend that what you are is anything but a monstrosity." His eyes misted as passion filled his voice. "Don't pretend you're still the boy I once knew. That boy died, and I did something so disgraceful to his corpse that I'll never forgive myself for it. But I'm here to fix that, because, like I told you, we clean up our own messes." The bow lowered a fraction. I could easily knock it from his hand, could easily command him to give it to me, but still, I hesitated. "I've been trying to avoid dealing with you, since the memory of who you once were makes this ... so hard." He completely lowered the bow as he almost looked into my eyes. "Please forgive me for what I did to you, Hunter. I can't imagine how awful the last few months have been." Such sadness overcame him then, that I couldn't help but forgive him for everything. For turning me, for hunting me. What would I have done if it were my son?

I lifted my hands in a peaceful gesture. "Dad ... this can end right here. We can be a family, if you just let me in. I'm happy. I don't kill, and I won't ever kill. I've learned to control it. I'm not a monster. I'm still me. I'm still your son. Nothing has changed."

Dad looked up at me, a small smile on his lips. "Everything has changed. You died. You just don't know it yet." With that, he raised the bow ... and fired it.

He was so close to me that I only had a fraction of a second to react. I had just enough time to move my chest so that the arrow didn't pierce my heart. It still torn through my skin though. The cursed metal made it feel like my insides were spontaneously combusting. It hurt so much, all I could do was cry out in pain as I dropped to my knees.

Dad stood over me, face forlorn, a stake now replacing the bow in his hand. "I'm sorry. You understand, this isn't what I want, but it has to be. You must be set free."

I struggled to form the words that would command him to stop. I struggled to touch the shaft protruding from my chest. It was like touching acid, though; I couldn't do it. I couldn't do anything but cry out in agony. *Nika, I'm so sorry I failed you.* As the words reverberated through my mind, my father whispered, "I should have cleaned and gutted that nest long ago, but it's happening now. I'll set all of them free, son. Have no fear about that."

My hazy brain couldn't entirely comprehend what that meant. Gutted? Set them free? Happening now? Nika ... Halina ...

My father's arm came down, his stake poised for the death blow. Through the pain, I found a well of determination. I wouldn't let him harm them. In one powerful move of desperation, I lunged at my father. I knocked him to his back and jostled the stake out of his hands, but he wasn't out of commission, not by a long shot. Reaching up, he grabbed the arrow in my chest and twisted it. Fresh pain burst through my body, and I did the only thing I could think to do. I forced every muscle to move ... and I ran.

I would run all the way home with this arrow in my chest if I had to.

CHAPTER TWENTY-TWO

Nika

I LOOKED AROUND the destroyed basement for some sign that Hunter was okay. What I saw didn't fill me with hope. There were no other patches of churned earth, and the rest of the hard floor was untouched, aside from the rubble on top of it. Across the room were the crushed cots where we'd consummated our relationship. Memories of sharing myself with him pounded through my mind. His cool breath in my ear, the goosebumps across my skin as his hand traveled up my side. The brief sting of pain as he took my virginity. The wash of pleasure as we finished together. Was that moment of connection the only one I'd get with him? It seemed monumentally unfair, but I supposed life was unfair, and this wouldn't be the first time in history a young life had ended all too soon.

As my eyes started to water, I noticed something next to the tangled cots. Hunter's torn and tattered jacket was nearby, but that wasn't what got my attention. It was a scrap of material buried under a section of the basement's roof. The shiny black material looked like the shoulder strap of a backpack. Hunter's backpack.

I pointed toward the cots, and Halina directed her gaze that way. With more of her light to help me define the item, I could see that I was right—it was his backpack stuck under the rubble. Hope lifted in me. If he'd left the cabin, or had been removed from it, and he hadn't taken his bag with him, then he'd be traceable as soon as Gabriel's shot wore off. We could find him.

Halina frowned as she looked over at something that was unremarkable to her. "What is it?"

I smiled up at her dirt-streaked face. "Hunter's bag. If he didn't take it, then he doesn't have Gabriel's shot with him."

Halina's brow furrowed, like she hadn't caught on to what I'd pieced together. My grin widened. "We'll be able to feel him again soon. When the shot wears off, we'll know exactly where he is."

Halina brightened, and extended her hand to me. I took it, and she helped me stand. She looked around the wreckage with worried eyes. "Your father is right. You shouldn't be down here. Let's get you back to the surface."

After a few more minutes, Halina and I carefully left the basement of the ruined cabin. There was no point in continuing our search. Hunter was long gone, that much was clear. Dad had his hand out for me when I made it back to ground level. I took his cool grasp and let him pull me the rest of the way out of the hole. I wasn't sure what to do now, other than wait for the shot to wear off so we could feel Hunter again.

I wiped my muddy hands on my jeans while Dad offered his palm to Halina. She looked at his hand, but hopped out of the hole on her own. Halina stepped beside Dad, and he indicated the sparse trees around us. "We scouted the area, but no one's around." He locked his glowing eyes on Halina's. "There's no trace of Hunter. He could be hundreds of miles away by now. Should we go back home?"

Halina's lips twisted into a scowl. I was sure she was cursing Gabriel in her head. "I'm not returning home without him, but I can't just sit here and do nothing until Gabriel's damn shot wears off. There has to be some trail to follow. We will find it."

Dad looked over at me. I instantly knew what he was going to say, and I hastily beat him to it. "I'm staying with Grandma until we find Hunter." I raised my chin in defiance. He was going to have to drag me back home to get me to leave.

Mom and Imogen walked around from the other side of the cabin while Dad pursed his lips at my stubbornness. Imogen shook her head at

Halina. "There's nothing here, Mother." She glanced at the emptiness around her. "Nothing but questions."

Imogen couldn't have been more correct about that. Questions were all I had. Was Hunter okay? Where did he go? He'd mentioned a tracker … was he still being tracked? Was he being hunted right now? The many questions tumbling around my brain were quickly turning the organ to mush. I needed action to silence the distress. Halina had the same look of mental anguish as she debated our next course of action.

"We split up, search the area. If we still don't find anything, then … we'll wait for the shot Gabriel gave him to wear off. We'll know exactly where to go once it does." Sighing, her pale, glowing eyes searched the emptiness around us. "And hopefully we won't be too late."

Her ominous words rang through my ears, stinging my heart. Halina and Imogen took off in opposite directions. It was strange to not know where they were once they were gone from my sight. Instinctually feeling my family was more a part of me than I'd realized, and I couldn't wait to have that connection back. My parents stayed with me. They didn't seem to want to separate from each other, and they definitely weren't letting me go out on my own. Not while I was untraceable.

Dad nodded his head east. "We'll check out the city. See what we can find."

We took off, heading for some rocky hills comprised of smooth boulders. The night air was crisp, cold, but I didn't let myself feel it. It reminded me of Hunter's embrace. A coyote yipped in the distance, and for a split second, the animal inside me wanted to chase it. It made me wonder if Hunter was hungry, if he'd gone in search of food. Or if revenge was the only thing on his mind right now, and he was stalking his father.

We scampered over dry, dusty hills, disturbing wildlife with our supernatural presence as we went. Owls hooted at us from their homes high in the branches, snakes slid into the safety of their dark crevices, and foxes skittered into the underbrush. Even nature knew we were at the top of the food chain.

Eventually, the trees thickened into a dense forest, and I struggled to keep the pace my parents were setting. I wasn't even sure where we were going, or why we were going there. My parents either. As we paused under a clump of trees so I could catch my breath, my mother asked, "Where are we going, Teren?"

Dad shook his head, "I don't know. I just thought if hunters were after him, he might be hiding."

I huffed out quick breaths as my heart sped in my chest. "This would be a safe place to rest. Humans would have a hard time following him here."

Dad's concerned eyes washed over my weary body. "Mostly human vampires too. Are you okay? Want a ride?" He turned and offered his back.

I started to tell him I was fine when I caught a very faint scent in the air. Blood. Mom and Dad smelled it, too, and shifted to face the wind. We all inhaled, cataloging the smell and registering it as not-animal, not-human. Vampire. I pushed myself away from the tree I was leaning against, no longer needing its support. "Hunter …" I took off after the scent.

I heard my father telling me to wait, but I ignored him. He would follow me, of that I had no doubt, and I couldn't lose this trail. As I tore through the crowded wilderness, it became clear that I couldn't continue without the light my parents provided. I tripped and stumbled with nearly every step. Even though it pained me, I waited two seconds for my parents to catch up to me. With Dad lighting the way, and Mom following close behind, we took off toward the source of the blood. A sudden sound pricked my ears. It was a suppressed whimper, a controlled grunt of pain. Was it Hunter? Was he hurt? Or was my imagination getting the best of me.

Around me, I began to see evidence that someone had been through this part of the woods recently. Branches were snapped off, rocks were kicked over, brush trampled. It was careless, destructive, not like Hunter at all. A lifetime of stalking vampires had made him stealthy, like a cat tracking its prey. His conversion had only enhanced his silence. If he was leaving a trail of destruction in his wake, it was because he couldn't help himself.

When we got to a small clearing, I spotted the blood we'd been smelling. A medium sized boulder near a tree was covered in it. It looked like a murder had happened there. Or a sacrifice. A chill went up my spine, and I started to shake as I approached the splatter that looked black in the darkness.

While my father leaned down to smell it, I searched the trees. Nothing. No trace of Hunter, no trail of blood leading away. No clear sign of a disturbance to guide us another way. It was like he'd vanished. My dad cast me a cautious glance as he told my mother, "It's vampire. Fresh."

I tried to keep the panic from swelling in my heart. I couldn't, though, and Julian's concern for me raised a notch. "That's a lot of blood, Dad. Why would he be bleeding? Whatever is wrong with him, he should have healed instantly."

Dad shook his head as he pulled out his phone. "I don't know, honey." He glanced at the screen, then cursed. "We're too far away from the tower, I don't have a signal. I can't let Great-Gran know we found something." He put the phone away and looked between Mom and me. "We'll just have to keep looking for him on our own."

The anxiety of the moment amplified the sense of loss in my body. Even with my family standing right beside me, I felt cut off from the world in these isolated woods where something horrible had clearly happened. My emotional bond with Julian was my only saving grace; I clung to his feelings like a lifeline.

Mom squeezed my shoulder sympathetically. "We'll find him."

We mentally flipped a coin as to whether we should head north or south. Dad figured Hunter might be heading back to the ranch if he were injured, so we headed north. Luck was on our side, and we caught another heady waft of blood on the breeze. This one was at the edge of the forest, where the trees were beginning to thin out again. The same careless destruction was around the gory mess, like Hunter had crashed through the trees in pursuit, or in pain. Then the trail vanished. It was frustrating, to say the least.

Since we'd successfully found the trail again, Dad kept us on a homeward bound path. It lightened the darkness in my heart a little that Hunter seemed to be heading toward the ranch. The realization that he was somehow inexplicably hurt squelched that brightness though.

We found a few more pools of blood as the green life started giving way to barren desert. Each time there was no visible trail of Hunter. But the pools were fresh, so he couldn't be too far ahead of us. I was sure that no human hunter could have followed the path we'd just traversed, at least, not at anywhere near our speed. Hunter had to know he was safe from pursuit, which made the fear in me grow exponentially. What was he running from?

As the landscape gave fewer and fewer places to hide, my desperation grew. We had to find him. We'd gone several miles without even a whiff of blood, though, and it was impossible to know for sure if we were on the right path. For all we knew, he wasn't heading home, and he'd gone east or west, or even south again. There was no way to know for sure, so we kept plugging along, hoping we'd find something to lead us to him.

Just when I was positive we'd lost his trail forever, a trace amount of blood wafted by. We locked onto the new smell, and adjusted our path to a more northwest direction. Then, suddenly, as we scrambled up a treeless hill, a pained cry drifted through the night air. All three of us were instantly alert. When the sounds of a scuffle followed the cry—rocks sliding, the hard hit of a body falling—we took off toward the noise. Hoping beyond hope that it was Hunter, I used every ounce of strength I had left to blur past my father.

The sight I stopped at was not what I'd expected. I was at the precipice of a deep canyon. I barely saw the drop-off in time to stop myself from rocketing over the edge. The steep walls of the cliff made seeing completely inside the hole impossible. I was sure it remained dark down there even in daylight. I thought I heard a lazy river flowing through the bottom of the canyon, but it seemed disastrously far away. The fingerlike stretches of land standing high above the canyon floor sent an instinctual warning through my brain: *Danger! Do not go any farther!* But the blood was leading me closer to the edge of the steep ravine, and I needed to see what was at the end of that heavenly scent.

As I stepped toward the side and peered over the ledge, my father joined me. He pulled me back a foot, so I was farther from the edge. I felt like a woman possessed as he held me back. It was how I imagined a worried mother must feel when her missing child was almost within sight. Hunter was down there, I just knew it. "Dad, he's here, I know he is!"

Dad handed me off to Mom's firm hands, then squatted to inspect the dusty ground. More blood covered the rocks, darkening the dirt. God, why was he bleeding? What was wrong with him? Kneeling, Dad peeked over the edge of the cliff. He inhaled, but I knew that wouldn't help him here. The wind was blowing across the canyon, so if Hunter was inside it, the smell wouldn't reach us. "Hunter?" he called, his voice echoing around the solid rock walls.

Nothing but the faint scampering of wildlife answered him. My heart thudded in my chest as I watched Dad's eyes scanning the darkness. His gaze returned to me. "I'm not seeing anything, Nika. I don't think he's down there."

I pulled against Mom's hand. "We have to go look. We have to be sure."

Dad looked pained. A trek down the canyon walls wasn't exactly a safe journey, especially at night, especially if we weren't positive that Hunter wasn't being chased. Dad stood, the wind around him buffeting his jacket. I held mine tighter around myself. "I'll find a way down and check it out. You two stay up here, okay?"

Even though he'd asked a question, I knew it wasn't really a question. He wanted me to stay put. Since Dad's senses were stronger than mine, he would have an easier time picking up Hunter's trail, so I nodded. Mom grabbed Dad's elbow as he twisted back to the ravine. "Be careful," she said. Her full lip twisted into a concerned scowl. "I don't want you falling and accidentally staking yourself."

Dad crooked a smile. "Your faith in my skills is inspiring." His face settled into seriousness and he gave her a quick kiss. "I'll be as careful as possible."

He jogged along the edge of canyon, looking for a trail that led down the sheer cliff. I watched him leave, then peered over the edge again. As I inhaled the blood near me, and searched the wilderness for some sign of my boyfriend, a prickling sensation tickled the back of my brain. It was the strangest feeling I'd ever had, and I scratched my head to try and make it go away. It wasn't, though. It was only getting stronger. That was when I realized what it was. The family bond was returning. The shot was wearing off.

The itching slowly turned to stinging, and I held my breath. I hoped the bond coming back wasn't as painful as the bond being shut off. Mom noticed my distress. "Are you okay, Nika?"

I nodded as I smiled. "The bond is coming back."

Mom's eyes narrowed as she examined me. I knew she was trying to sense my location in her head. "I can't feel you."

Looking over the cliff face, I smiled even wider. "Hunter gave us the shot a little bit after he'd taken it. If mine is starting to wear off, then his must nearly be gone. We'll be able to feel him soon. We're going to find him."

That was when I heard something far to the right of me. Like he was standing beside me, whispering in my ear, I heard Hunter's raspy voice drifting up from the canyon's depths. "Nika ... help me."

Without a second thought, I streaked away from my mother and slipped over the edge of the ravine.

Hunter

I'D NEVER FELT so sick in all my life. Every step I took was painful, every movement I made, agony. I'd tried to take this damn arrow out of my chest a half dozen times, and every time I worked up the nerve to touch it, the act of moving it made me throw up. All I'd managed to do was fall against it, impaling it even deeper into my body. The entire shaft was buried now.

After every failed attempt to remove it, I'd blurred away toward the ranch. I had to get back to the nest before the hunters stormed it. I couldn't stomach the thought of that beautiful, diamond-shaped home being burned to the ground. I couldn't even comprehend any of the vampires inside it being harmed. Or killed.

That fear drove me ever onward, until the agony eventually became too much, and I crashed to the ground, writhing in torture. Through my pain-filled fog, I recalled the landscape changing from woods to barren desert to rolling hills. I trudged forward through it all, only stopping when I could no longer continue. Not being able to run as fast or for as long as my body normally could, I hadn't made it nearly as far as I would have liked, and time was running out. My brain started prickling with a burning sensation that only added to my discomfort. How much more grief could I endure?

Near delirious with pain, I made one last attempt to pull the arrow out. My hand burned as if I'd put it in a fire; my chest was already engulfed in those flames. I minutely tugged on the stiff end of the bolt, and my head swam. Woozy, I fell to my hands and knees, and lost my stomach. Blood gushed from my mouth, chilly and sweet. I could feel the pricks of my fangs against my tongue, but I could do nothing to retract them. I was losing myself to the pain. I had no idea where I was anymore. I was quickly losing sense about *who* I was. The only thing in my mind was my mission: Save the nest.

I struggled to stand, to blur back home, but my weak hands gave out and I toppled to the side. To my surprise and terror, there was no dusty ground to catch my aching body. I felt myself falling through the oblivion of nothingness, like I'd been kneeling at the edge of the Earth and I'd just toppled over it. Then the land caught up to me.

Rocks and branches smashed against my face, twisting and jerking my body as I plummeted down what I could only assume was the side of a mountain. Each and every impact shoved the arrow farther into my body. I briefly cried out, but then I ran out of air. I couldn't inhale after that. I felt bones breaking as my useless limbs flailed about. It brought new meaning to the word agony. When I finally skidded to a stop, I just wanted it to end. *Someone stake me. Please. I can't take this anymore ...*

I felt like I was still in a precarious position when I finally stopped moving. Even though every fiber of my being screamed in pain, I laid perfectly still as I waited for the various aches to heal. I knew my chest wouldn't improve as long as the silver from the arrow was infecting me, but slowly the pain everywhere else started receding. I huffed short, fast breaths while waves and waves of agony seeped through me. This torture had to stop at some point, didn't it?

I wasn't sure how long I laid there in pain, fading in and out of consciousness. I could already feel the edge of blackness seeping into my vision as complete and total darkness offered to give me reprieve, if I only let it. I fought against the bleakness, though. I had somewhere to be, family in danger I needed to warn. I couldn't keep lying here, hoping to die. I couldn't move either. I thought I heard my name being yelled, but maybe that was wishful thinking. I was all alone out here. I was alone, cut off, and no one was going to find me. No one was going to save me. Now, when I'd finally accepted what I was, I was going to wither away and die. Or at least, it felt that way.

Not knowing what else to do, rusty words escaped my tight throat. "Nika ... help me." I knew it was a useless plea. Nika was nowhere near me, and had no way to find me.

As the darkness closed in around me, strange sounds pressed in on my ears. Sharp, commanding voices. A scuffle. The sound of rocks sliding. My imagination even went so far that I thought I could feel pebbles flicking my skin, dust billowing into my face, making me blink. But that couldn't be. I was alone out here. Completely and utterly alone. My eyes fluttered shut as I conceded to the nothingness that wanted me. I didn't have the strength to resist anymore.

Through the fog of pain enveloping me, I heard movement above me, felt a body slide to a stop beside me. I tried to open my eyes, but even that small motion was too hard. Something soft touched my cheek, brushed my hair back from my face.

A panicked voice breathed in my ear, "Hunter?"

Small hands rocked my shoulders, trying to flip me over, and I cried out in pain. My eyes flashed open, and I saw an impossible sight illuminated by the weak glow extending from my hazy vision. An angel of mercy, come to save me. "Halina?" I whispered, my throat rough and raw. "You came for me ... ?"

Her face contorted into an expression of sorrow and joy. "Of course I came for you. I love you."

She tossed her arms around me, burying her dark head into my shoulder. I wanted to hug her back, I wanted to weep with joy, but I hurt so much all I could do was whimper. The movement of her clasping her arms around me shifted the arrow in my chest, and my stomach clenched in a disturbingly familiar way. Quickly turning my head away from her, I heaved up a stream of blood. The silver was slowly poisoning me. I knew it, yet I couldn't do anything about it.

Halina instantly released me. "Jesus, Hunter, what's wrong with you?"

I could only vomit again in response. Despite my weak, pain-filled protests, she flipped me over. I gasped, then whimpered. I was tired of pain. I just wanted it to end. "Help me," I pleaded.

She hissed as the silver instrument of my torture became clear to her. Bracing herself, she grasped the end of the arrow and pulled it out of me. Since both of us were sensitive to the cursed metal, we screamed in pain together. Halina tossed it into the darkness while I panted, recovering. I heard my name being shouted from above. It sounded like Nika. Had she found me too?

Halina was letting out a steady stream of low, fast Russian. I was sure she was cursing everything under creation. I was doing the opposite. I was suddenly grateful for everything. Especially the fact that the pain in my chest was fading with every breath I took. It was a slow process, though. The silver from the arrow had leached into my body. The immediate pain was gone, but the ache lingered. Moving was difficult, but now that my head was clearing, I suddenly remembered that I couldn't lie here much longer. I had somewhere I needed to be. We all did.

As Halina made a move to scoop me up like a ragdoll, I put my hand up to stop her. "Leave me here. You need to go, and I'll only slow you down."

She narrowed her bright eyes at me. "I just found you again. I'm not leaving you behind."

Exhausted, I shook my head. "You have to. He's going after the ranch. He could already be there."

"Who ... ?" Instantly realizing who I meant, her voice darkened. "Your son-of-a-bitch father?"

I nodded as I peeled open my eyes. "He sent people to clean the nest. You have to stop him. Don't let him destroy our home."

She cupped my face, her expression overjoyed for half a second. Then my words sunk in. Cursing again, she threw her arms around me and lifted me into the air. A grunt left me as she effortlessly tossed me over her shoulder. A part of me wanted to make the journey back to safety on my own, but I knew I couldn't right now, so I let her carry me.

How far I'd fallen quickly became apparent as she zipped me back up to the top. In some spots, she had to shove her fingers deep into the rocky cliff wall as she scrambled upward. It was awkward with me holding on to her, but she was strong enough that she got us there in only a few minutes.

Once we were at the top of what I could now tell was a steep canyon, Halina gently set me on the ground. She examined my body for other injuries while I groaned and laid my head back on the dirt. Her hands ran over my freshly healed limbs. While I felt okay, I knew that a couple of my fingers had healed at strange angles. Murmuring, "This will hurt," she broke the misshapen digits again. The surprise of the move blocked out the pain.

At first. When it did hit me, I gasped, then cried out, slamming my uninjured fist into the dirt beside me.

Nika was instantly at my side, smoothing back my hair and stroking my cheek. "Hunter, are you okay?" Leaning down, she started peppering my face with tender kisses.

Exhaling a slow breath as I felt my hand healing in the proper way, I nodded. God, I hoped she didn't find any more out-of-place bones on me. Lifting my head, I looked down at Halina examining my legs. "You don't have time for this. You need to go."

Teren had been watching his daughter cover me with affection, but trained his eyes on my face once he heard the urgency in my voice. "Go where? What's going on?"

Shooing Halina from my aching body, I struggled to sit up. A wave of nausea struck me, and I couldn't speak for a second. When the feeling passed, I was panting. Nika put her arms around me, and I leaned into her body, grateful for the support. Focusing as hard as I could on not being sick, I lifted my eyes to Teren. "My father has sent hunters to the ranch. They could already be there. You need to go."

Teren's eyes widened, then his head snapped around to stare toward where I assumed he could feel the others; I still couldn't, but the burning sensation in my head told me I probably would be able to soon. Nika's arms around me tightened. "Dad ... Julian ..." Her voice wavered, and Teren returned his gaze to her. "He's worried. I thought he was worried for me, but ... maybe that's not it."

Teren glanced at his wife, then pulled out his phone. He looked at the screen, checking for service. We must have been close enough. He pressed a few buttons on his phone, calling someone, while Halina cursed and gave me soft eyes. She was torn. She didn't want to leave me. But she had to. I would only slow her down. Teren cursed as he ended the call that had switched over to voicemail. He called someone else, and I could again hear voicemail pick up. He cursed again, and I told him, "It's started. You need to go. Now."

Teren's eyes were wide when he shoved his phone back into his pocket. "He's right, Great-Gran. I can't get a hold of anyone."

Imogen stared toward the ranch, her face strained with worry. "Alanna ..." she whispered.

Suddenly, Nika shot to her feet. With her support gone, I slumped back to the earth with a groan. "Dad! Julian's scared."

Nika looked about ready to run to him, but like Halina, she was torn. She didn't want to leave me. Her father grabbed her elbow. "Great-Gran already had to save you from plummeting over a cliff wall today. And she just barely managed to catch you in time." Nika rubbed her shoulder while I wondered just what she'd done to try to get to me. Frowning, Teren added, "Let's think for a second before we react."

Nika nodded, but she was biting her lip, and I could tell she wanted to be doing something.

Halina immediately took a protective stance in front of me. "I can't leave him like this."

Teren shook his head. "You're the fastest and the strongest. None of us can get back there as quickly as you can." He swallowed a pain-filled lump in his throat. "Mom and Dad need you. Julian ... needs you. Please." He indicated my prostrate body. "I'll stay here with him. I'll protect your child, if you protect mine."

His voice was ripe with pain. I thought my earlier torture was nothing compared to his grief over not being able to run home. Halina hesitated just a fraction of a moment, then sank to her knees by my side. Kissing my forehead, she told me, "I'll come back for you as soon as I can. I won't be gone long."

I clutched her arm as she pulled away from me. I could barely believe the passion in my voice when my words left me. "Be careful. I can't lose you."

Halina gave me a sad smile as she nodded. Then she crooked a grin. "Have no fear, beloved. Hunters run from *me*, not the other way around."

She gave Teren a stiff nod, then looked to Imogen. "Let's go protect our family, daughter." Imogen nodded, eager to leave.

Just as they were about to streak off, Nika's mother stepped forward. "I'm coming with you."

Teren grabbed his wife's arm. "No."

Emma shook her head as she gave him a stern expression that clearly said her mind was made up. "Stay here with our daughter. I'm going to our son."

A look of torment crossed Teren's face. It was a look I knew well. Here was a man divided. I attempted to stand, to make it to the ranch with the others so no one had to stay behind with me, but I was still too weak; the residual silver coursing through my veins was taking its toll. I still felt nauseous, and had to clench my stomach to keep the blood inside my body.

"Em ..." he whispered, begging her to stay.

Smiling, she gave him a soft kiss and murmured, "I'll be fine." Then she gave Nika a swift hug, telling her, "Watch after the boys." She nodded a farewell to me, then the trio of women blurred away to go save their home. I wished them well.

An expression of sorrow and loneliness was etched on Teren's features as he closed his eyes and fisted his hands. Knowing he had sired Nika's mother, I wondered if he was feeling the same pulling sensation from the bond that I was feeling—and that was when I realized the shot had completely faded and I was connected to the family again. Closing my eyes, I welcomed the discomfort of feeling Halina leave me. Because even though it was an uncomfortable ache, feeling it was by far a better feeling than being cut off from her ... from all of them.

Teren twisted to me after a second of contemplation. "Let's get you on your feet, and we'll follow after them. Maybe we'll get there in time to help ..."

His voice trailed off as I nodded. We wouldn't get there in time, not when every movement was a struggle for me, and the attack was happening now, but we could at least pretend we wouldn't be too late.

Teren lifted me. Pulling against him, I struggled to my feet. My stomach heaved as my vision faded to black, and I immediately sank back down to my knees. "I'm sorry, I can't yet," I panted. Breathing slowly and surely, I waited with my head down for the effects of the silver to pass. I could feel time ticking away, and I wanted to stand and run, but I couldn't leave yet. I needed a few minutes to collect myself.

Nika rubbed a circle into my back. "Why are you still hurting? Grandma pulled the arrow out?"

I shook my head. "It was in for too long. The silver got into my bloodstream. It's going to take a while before I recover." I looked between the two of them. "You should leave me here and go with the others. You can feel me now ... you can come back for me."

Teren's lips pressed into a firm line, like he'd been thinking the same thing. What he said though, was, "I gave my word that I would stay and protect you. I won't go back on it."

I sighed, wishing this honorable man beside me could somehow be less honorable. Several minutes passed before I felt somewhat okay enough to stand. Halina and the others were speeding toward the ranch; they must be over halfway there by now. I cursed myself for not being strong enough to go with them. If anyone died tonight, I'd never forgive myself. God, I hoped no one died.

Teren again helped me to my feet, ducking his shoulder underneath mine. Nika immediately supported me under my other arm. With the pair of them acting as crutches, I managed to stay standing. I felt wobbly, like I'd had too much to drink. My vision swam, my fingers trembled. I even gagged as my stomach lurched. I'd never realized as a human just how awful silver was to vampires. We knew it hurt them, but the lingering weakness from the exposure was something that had never occurred to me before. The group of us took a hesitant step forward. I felt more in control than I had during my mad, panic-driven dash with an arrow in my chest, but without the adrenaline rush giving me strength, moving was wearisome. Getting home was going to take me a while in this condition.

Just as I was considering begging Teren to leave me behind, a loud crack sounded through the air. It echoed around the canyon walls behind me, silencing the minute sounds of nature nearby.

All three of us snapped our attention to the source of the unnatural noise. Another loud bang pierced the night, and the ground at my feet exploded in a small puff of dirt as a bullet punctured the Earth. I instinctively positioned myself in front of Teren and Nika, pushing them back a step, while still leaning on them in support. We didn't have far to retreat, though; we were still very close to the cliff wall.

I had no idea how it was possible that he'd found me after my mad dash from the cabin, but my father stepped into the circle of light that Teren's and my glowing eyes provided. Astonishment flashed through me. How had he found me? Again?

A music player in his pocket streamed hard, fast rock into his ears. It was at a frequency that our family had discovered completely blocked the trancing effect of vampires. The human mind couldn't be coerced if it couldn't hear the commands. Dad walked toward us with his weapon raised to chest level. I froze, not sure how to get all three of us away if he started firing. True, we were marginally faster than bullets, but he would still likely hit one of us. I wasn't at my best right now, and Nika wouldn't heal like Teren and I would.

Dad gave me a sad smile as he showed me a tracking device in his other hand. I could see my location blinking on the screen. He must have put another one on me during our scuffle earlier. Shaking his head, he murmured, "You didn't think I'd let you get away that easily, did you?" He sighed, and his face momentarily looked as conflicted as Teren's had earlier. "Not when we have unfinished business, Hunter. I'm very sorry about this."

And then, without wasting another second, the man I'd loved and idolized, the man who'd taught me everything I'd ever known, pulled the trigger.

CHAPTER TWENTY-THREE

Julian

GETTING SHOT SUCKED, and as I lay in my bed at the ranch, I decided I never wanted to experience it again. Arianna clasped my fingers, her expression worried. I threw on a smile for her so she wouldn't stress over me. I was fine. The bullet was gone, and my leg was stitched up. My small wounds were even still numb from the anesthetic my grandmother had used. An anesthetic I was pretty sure my family had obtained in less than conventional methods. A perk of having a compulsion-wielding pureblood in the nest.

"How do you feel, Julian?" Arianna whispered, brushing some hair off my forehead.

Her touch felt wonderful. My head buzzed, and my brain itched a bit, but I was pretty sure that was just the bond returning to me. Either that, or I was having a really strange reaction to the drugs I'd been given. Ignoring the prickling, I focused on my sister's stress pushing in around me. She was back in Flagstaff searching for Hunter, and by the feel of things, the scouting mission wasn't going well. I compressed my lips, which made Arianna's frown deepen. Shaking my head, I told her, "I feel fine. It's Nika who's losing it. She's worried about Hunter ..."

Arianna looked even more concerned over my pronouncement. I think it still wigged her out that Nika and I were empathically linked. "Oh ..."

Her gaze drifted to our interlaced fingers. A tension grew between us, filling the air with apprehension. I could almost hear the words *We need to talk* vibrating in the silence. I really didn't want to hear anything she might have to say, and I suddenly wished my grandparents were still in the room. But Alanna and Grandma Linda had left after I was all patched up. They were downstairs with Grandpa Jack, discussing the situation with Hunter. They weren't sure what to do about him either.

Arianna cleared her throat, and I tensed. Wanting to distract her from what I was afraid she was going to say—that being with me was too much for her—I sputtered, "It was nice falling asleep with you last night."

I stroked her thumb as I said it, reminding her that while that moment had been laced with fear and aggravation, it had also been full of comfort. Once Hunter had left us alone in a house we couldn't leave, Arianna had wanted out of the dungeon-like basement. Since Hunter hadn't forbidden us from leaving the room, I'd taken her upstairs. My stubborn sister had stayed behind to wait for Hunter to return. Looking back on it now, I probably should have dragged her ass with us, but I'd wanted to be alone with Arianna.

Waking up with my arms still draped over Arianna's body had been just as amazing. We hadn't done anything the night before, but somehow just sharing the intimacy of resting together had brought us closer. We'd had a quiet brunch with the old man, who'd seem completely unfazed that we were squatting in his house, then we'd tinkered throughout the home, looking for things to do until the sun went down. That was when we'd spotted the hunters outside with large gas cans. I'd never had a surge of adrenaline quite like that as I'd watched a trap being set. But still, I hadn't panicked, hadn't had an "episode." I'd known that Arianna, Nika, and I needed to leave, but before we could do that, Hunter had to release his hold on my girlfriend. So, I'd done what was necessary to make that happen. Even though the entire event had been scary as hell, I was proud of myself for not falling apart. Maybe I could be the hero my dad was after all.

Arianna's voice in my bedroom pushed away the fragments of my memories. "Is life with you always going to be this ... crazy?" she asked, her voice hitching.

I clenched her hand tighter, wishing I could just lie and tell her no. "I don't know, Arianna. Maybe. In spurts." Since Halina wasn't anywhere close enough to hear her answer, I asked, "Is it too much for you?"

My heart thudded as I waited for her response. It felt like it took forever in coming. Lifting her shimmering hazel eyes to mine, she shrugged. "This is a lot more dangerous than I'd anticipated, but maybe I shouldn't be surprised, considering how we got together. I just thought …" she bit her lip as she mulled over her answer, "when you first told me what you were, I didn't really think about what that might mean. I just liked you so much, and wanted to be with you … I think I allowed myself to overlook a few things." She shook her head as a shimmering teardrop fell onto her cheek. "I'm only sixteen, Julian, and I've already been shot at twice now because of your family. Then there's Raquel being attacked, this weird bond with your sister, your grandmother wanting me to get pregnant, Nika's boyfriend threatening to take every memory away from me. It's just … a lot to take."

She hung her head, like she was filled with guilt for admitting that to me. I didn't blame her for her feelings. It would be a lot for me, too, if I were in her shoes. Lifting her chin, I made her look at me again. Her eyes danced everywhere, looking at anything but me. "Hey, look at me, Arianna."

She closed her eyes as a deep sigh left her body. Opening them again, she stared at my face like she was seeing all the way into my soul. My mouth felt dry, and my leg ached. I didn't think it was because of my wounds, though. It was the question I was about to ask her. A part of me didn't want to ask, but I needed to know. "Do you still want to be with me?"

She opened her mouth to answer my question, but no words came out. The only answer I got was more tears spilling down her cheeks. I didn't take that as a good sign. Sitting up with a grunt, I cupped her cheek, wiping away her tears with my thumb. A desperate panic ran through me, and I did the only thing I could think to do. I pressed my mouth to hers, needing to physically show her how much I cared about her.

A sob escaped her, and I tasted salty tears on her lips. It sent of jolt of pain through my heart. My fear of losing her now matched Nika's fear of losing Hunter. Yet again, we were feeling the exact same thing. Even through my own pain, a spark of worry for Nika flashed through my brain.

"Don't do this, Arianna," I whispered through our anxious kisses. "Don't give up on us."

She whimpered under my administrations, her lips frantic against mine. Then, with pain clear in her voice, she croaked, "I'm not. I'm not, Julian."

Relief poured into my kiss as I slipped my tongue into her mouth. She groaned in a way that made me delirious with delight. She wasn't leaving me. Not yet. Just as I was about to lean her back on the bed and show her what I couldn't show her last night, my bedroom door swung wide open, banging against the far wall.

Arianna squeaked in surprise while I jumped about a foot in the air. My heart racing like I'd run a marathon, I snapped my head around in time to see Gabriel storming into the room. Face stern, he swiftly said, "The two of you need to come with me."

Concern pricked my stomach. Halina had asked him to leave, and I was pretty sure she hadn't meant for him to leave with my girlfriend and me. "What? Why?"

Gabriel shook his head and motioned with his hand for us to follow him. "There isn't time to explain. We need to get you both downstairs. To safety."

Electricity zinged up my spine. Safety? Arianna hopped off the bed while I got up a bit more gingerly. Alanna had stripped off my jeans, which was a little mortifying with Arianna in the room, then she'd made me put on some sweats once I was all bandaged up. I was only in my socks though, so I slipped on my shoes when I was sitting on the edge of the bed.

Gabriel glanced from me to the door and back again, clearly not liking how long this was taking. Frowning, he called over his shoulder, "Starla. Jacen. Get these two down to the lowest level. I'm going to check the perimeter."

He was gone in a flash. While I went from a sitting to a standing position, my pseudo-mother and her boyfriend appeared. Arianna's confused face matched mine. "What's going on, Julian?" she asked.

Since I had no idea, I redirected the question to the two adults in the room. "What is it, Starla?"

Her brow pinched together, creating deep lines that were surely going to give her wrinkles, something she usually avoided. She blurred to my side, scooping me into her arms. "The ranch is under attack," she whispered, with no trace of her usual snarky attitude.

My jaw dropped as I glanced at Jacen picking up Arianna. "What?" I had to have heard her wrong.

Starla's eyes were wide with fear. Seeing it on her spiked my feelings of trepidation. Jacen spoke in his matter-of-fact way, but even his voice was laced with tension. "Hunters are here. At least a dozen ... maybe more."

Arianna started breathing faster. I did too. No. This couldn't be happening. I had no idea what to do or say. But there wasn't time for words anyway. I clung to Starla as she blurred us away, to the relative safety of the lower floors. Were they safe enough though?

Right as we entered the living room, three of the spacious windows shattered, and we were flecked with debris. Out of shock and the desire to avoid being hit by stray shrapnel, Starla and Jacen dropped behind the couch for shelter. Arianna screamed and held onto Jacen so tight her fingers were bone white. Fear sliced through my body as I separated myself from Starla; I was sore, but I could make it the short distance on my own. I could hear other windows breaking throughout the house as our home was penetrated, and I couldn't stop the odd thought that this was going to be a bitch to clean up. Assuming any of us lived, of course.

From our vantage point, we could see the bookcase that covered the entrance to the hidden rooms below the earth. It was swinging open. Ben appeared from the recess, and frantically motioned at us to hurry.

We sped through the opening, and Ben closed the secret door. Aside from a tiny, barely-used lock, there was no real way to brace the door. The home just hadn't been built with defending a siege in mind. Ben used his body instead, telling Jacen, "Go! Get them downstairs with the others!"

Jacen was still holding Arianna and immediately blurred away with her. Starla and I followed. We didn't stop until we got to Halina's bedroom; aside from Gabriel and Ben, everyone else was already there, waiting—Alanna, Grandma Linda, Grandpa Jack, Olivia, and Tracey. Jacen set Arianna down while I rubbed my aching leg. Grandma Linda immediately tossed her arms around my neck. Olivia attached herself to my waist, burying her head in my stomach like she was hiding; I stumbled a bit.

While Olivia screeched my name, Grandma Linda cooed, "Oh, thank God, Julian, Arianna. I was so worried." Pulling back, she bobbed her head to Starla and Jacen. "Thank you, both."

Jacen gave her a curt nod, then turned to face Starla. His face businesslike, he told her, "Leave all of the doors open. I don't want you soundproofed and unable to hear what's going on. I'm going to wait for them in the hallway with Ben. That's where they'll most likely attempt to enter from."

Tracey groaned as she ran her hands through her hair in a nervous, repetitive fashion. Olivia tightened her grip on me so hard, I cringed. Starla grabbed Jacen's elbow as he started to leave. When he swung his head around to her, she grabbed his face and kissed him, hard. When she came up for air, she fervently intoned, "Do *not* die on me, understand?"

Breathless, Jacen nodded. "I wouldn't dream of it."

He gave her one last kiss, then streaked away. Starla swallowed about five times in a row as she looked around the room. Alanna put her hand on her shoulder, but didn't offer her any comforting words. Somehow, that filled me with more dread than anything else had.

After peeling Olivia off me and passing her over to her very pale mother, I balanced my weight on my uninjured leg and put a comforting arm around a trembling Arianna. Alanna straightened her shoulders and took a protective stance in front of all of us. The seemingly youthful woman probably looked like an unlikely bodyguard, but I knew how tough she really was. Her long black hair streamed down her back, as she rolled up the sleeves of her plaid, button-up shirt. She did the same thing when she was about to make dinner ... or when she bled the cows.

Glancing back at her husband, Alanna murmured, "I'm glad Teren and the others aren't here. I'm glad they're safe." Her pale eyes flicked to Grandma Linda, Tracey, Olivia, Arianna, and me, and I knew she wished we were away from the ranch with Dad.

While we waited for something to happen, Tracey repeatedly murmured, "I can't believe this is happening." Looking up at me, Arianna's hazel eyes seemed to be saying the same thing. While I rubbed Arianna's arm and tried to be comforting, I felt Nika's concern skyrocketing. Were her feelings because of me? Did she know what was going on, or was she feeding off my fear? It was so frustrating at times to not know the reason behind the feelings.

There was a crash from upstairs, and I just about jumped out of my skin. It was followed by men cursing, groaning, growling, someone crying out in pain. I had no idea if that was Jacen. Anxiety twisted my stomach. Starla rushed forward, but stopped when Alanna held out her arm. "Jacen and Benjamin can take care of themselves. We need to protect them," Alanna whispered, glancing back at the group of humans huddled in the center of the room.

Starla's eyes watered, but she nodded and stayed with us.

The sound of snarling and fighting drifted toward us from upstairs. I knew Ben had experience fighting vampires with Dad, and I knew Jacen had experience fighting as a part of Gabriel's guard duty in his old nest, but I didn't know if they could take on multiple hunters. All they had to do was keep them out of the hallway, though. I supposed that was easier than a full-fledged assault.

While Tracey, clearly scared as hell, clutched at her daughter, Olivia mainly just looked confused. "Mom, what's going on? Why are we hiding down here? Are men really attacking the house? Shouldn't we be calling the cops?"

She asked several more questions until Starla finally rounded on her. "Would you shut up! We need to be able to hear what's going on!" Olivia furrowed her brow, and I realized her human ears couldn't hear what my family's sensitive ears could. She really couldn't tell what was going on, and she was the only one who had no idea she was in a house full of vampires, and that a group of zealous hunters were trying to exterminate them. I wasn't sure if her ignorance was a blessing, or a curse.

Suddenly, there was growling and shouting from a different section of the house, much farther away than the living room hallway. Starla's face brightened as she turned her head toward the sound. "Father," she murmured.

I knew she meant Gabriel, and a bit of hope seeped into me. Gabriel was ancient, strong. It still wasn't nearly a fair fight, but he'd definitely help even the odds.

I wasn't sure how long our fighters fended them off; it felt like an eternity passed while I waited with the others. I was sweating bullets, which immediately cooled against my skin, leaving me chilled. I was sure each bang and crash I heard was the end of Gabriel, Ben, and Jacen. Starla was sure, too. She was rigid with tension. Tracey looked scared but indifferent. Maybe her ears being less acute was a good thing.

Everything was peaceful where we were for quite a while, but eventually, we heard a scuffle in the hallway directly above us, and heard Ben let out a loud curse. Footsteps pounded down the hall, then Jacen called out, "Starla! They're coming!"

He'd said it loud enough for all of us to hear, even the humans. Arianna started hyperventilating. I squeezed her hand tightly, told her it was okay, then pushed her behind me. If we were about to get in a fight, I wasn't going to let anything happen to her. Grandpa Jack pushed Grandma Linda, Tracey, and Olivia behind him while Alanna and Starla blocked us all. I wanted to blur up to the front of the line with Alanna and Starla, but I knew I wasn't cut out for fighting vampire hunters with my bum leg.

As the sound of running feet grew louder, Tracey looked around at all of us; her fear was so evident it wafted around the room like perfume. "What do we do?" she asked.

In answer, Alanna twisted to face Grandpa. Her expression was bleak and stoic at the same time. "Take them outside, Jack. Run as far as you can. Starla and I will hold them off."

Grandpa's mouth opened as he stared at Alanna in disbelief. "I'm not leaving you."

Turning to face him, Alanna gave him a hug filled with passion. "You have to, my love." Running a hand through his silver hair, she whispered, "We talked about this moment coming one day, and you know this is the way it has to be. We decided that together. Please, get our family to safety."

Grandpa's aged eyes watered as he stared at his wife. "Alanna…"

She gave him a swift kiss. "I love you. Please go."

I wanted to give Alanna and Starla a hug, beg them to change their minds and come with us, but the pounding feet were dangerously close now. There was no time for goodbyes. It broke my heart to leave them, but protecting the rest of the family was Grandpa's and my responsibility now, and I wasn't about to fail my job. Corralling Arianna and Olivia, I hobbled after Grandpa as he hurried Grandma Linda and Tracey to the back of Halina's massive walk-in closet.

Grandpa pressed against what looked like a solid piece of dark cherry wood behind a rack of Halina's dresses. It slid back to reveal a hidden pocket door with a smooth stone hallway leading into pitch-black darkness.

"It's like the entrance to Narnia," Olivia muttered as Grandpa moved her into the hallway.

Tightly holding Arianna's hand, I followed her. "It just leads back outside. If all the … burglars … are in the house, then no one will notice us leaving." I looked behind me. "Right, Grandpa?"

"That's the plan." Grandpa closed the closet door once we were all inside the tunnel. The door sealed tightly shut, blocking out the weak light coming from the house. Since these deep underground entrances were just for the vampire's convenience, there was no external light source, and we were blinded by blackness. I waited for a familiar panic attack to drop me to my knees as the emptiness compressed around me. It didn't come, though; I had too great a burden placed on my shoulders right now to cave into that childhood fear.

Sounds of a scuffle filtered through the door. The hunters who'd made it past Jacen and Ben had already found Alanna and Starla. Whispering, "Go, go, go!" I pushed on whoever was in front of me as I dragged Arianna behind me.

Olivia whimpered as we dashed up the hallway. "I don't like this, Mom. Why isn't Dad with us?"

Tracey, maybe realizing just how serious this was, told her daughter, "I know, honey, I don't like this either, but we'll be out soon, and Daddy will join us. I know he will."

I strained my ears, listening for any sounds of pursuit, but I didn't hear anything that led me to believe we were being followed. The floor of the escape tunnel had a steep incline to it as it reached for the surface. My heart was beating harder, my breath was faster, and my leg felt like it was on fire. The humans around me, especially the older humans, were struggling just as much as I was. Grandma Linda sounded pained, but she carried on without complaint.

Just when I thought we'd never get out of this hallway, I saw a crack in the darkness, a slim section of blackness that wasn't quite as black as everything else. A weary exhale of relief left me. Thank God. Now, hopefully nobody was around when we burst out of here.

When the bodies in front of me came to a stop, I paused with them, tenderly rubbing my leg. The ground had leveled now that we were at the surface. I knew from experience that this exit opened at the back of a large wood shed. My nose told me that, too, as the smell of dry cedar logs stung my senses. Grandpa's voice drifted back to me, along with the sound of a door jiggling. "It's locked on the other side. Julian? Can you break this?"

Olivia snorted in surprise. "Julian? He's barely bigger than I am ..."

I ignored her unintentional insult as I weaved through the crowd toward Grandpa's voice. "Yeah, hold on."

The light was a little better at this end of the tunnel, and I could just make out Grandpa's shape. When I got to where he was standing, I put my hands on the wooden sheets of plywood barring our escape. From the other side, they just looked like the building's walls. A high stack of wood in front of them blocked the iron bar with a padlock. The door was locked on the other side to keep curious possible intruders out of the house; the tunnel was used more as an entrance, than an exit. It wouldn't keep me in, though.

Holding up a hand behind me, I tossed over my shoulder, "Stand back."

I heard shuffling as my family did as I asked. Inhaling a deep breath, I drew strength from the vampiric heritage inside me. Just like I could handle being in this cold, dark place, I could do this. With every ounce of supernatural force I possessed, I thrust my shoulder into the door. The iron bent, then pulled away from its hinges, and the wooden doors broke apart under the pressure.

I stumbled through the remains of the doorframe, crashing into the stacked pile of wood that was a couple of feet in front of the concealed door. I accidentally pushed a section of the cut logs forward, knocking them onto the floor of the wood shed with a resounding crash. Cursing, I froze. I felt like my heart was going to break through my ribcage. I could almost hear my sister reprimanding me—*Way to be stealthy, Julie.*

As my family inched their way through the door, I heard someone to my right say, "What was that?"

Another voice answered, "I don't know. We'd better check it out."

I rolled my eyes as I righted myself. Seeking out my grandfather, I told him, "Someone heard that. They're coming."

Face grim, he nodded as he indicated the slight break in the logs that led through the rows and to the exit. As quickly as our motley crew could go, we left the confines of the wood shed.

When we got into the open air, Olivia turned to me, wide-eyed. "You're the strongest man I've ever met."

She gave me a lovesick smile, and I turned her around. "We have to go!"

From over my shoulder, I heard someone say, "There!" and then a gun went off.

Everyone flinched, then started running. My leg ached so much I thought I might topple over, but I ran with them as another shot echoed in the night. We were all silent as we ran, but I could hear how difficult it was for the weaker people in our group to keep up. They wouldn't stand a chance against those hunters once they caught up to us. And they would catch up; we were going far too slowly. It took me less than a second to know what I had to do.

Yelling up to my grandfather in the lead, I said, "Grandpa, get them to safety!"

He looked back at me, pain in his eyes, but he knew, just like I did, that I was the only one left who could fight back. I started to turn around, to go back the other way, but Arianna grabbed my forearm. "No! You're coming with us!"

Another shot rang in the air. I heard the bullet hit a tree just a few yards to my left. Grabbing Arianna's face, I gave her a quick kiss. "I'll meet you there. I love you." I didn't give her another chance to try and stop me. I didn't have time. Wrestling my arm back, I blurred away, toward the danger everyone else was running from.

I swung wide of the pair of men crashing through the brush after my girlfriend and my family. Turning around, I came up behind them. Hopefully, with the element of surprise, I could get the drop on them. Zipping back to the woodshed, I grabbed a heavy, durable log. Hoping I had the courage to inflict harm on another person, I charged the one closest to me. Moving blindingly fast, I smacked him across the back of the head with the log. He went down with a thud, and I twisted to his partner. The guy saw me, though, and swiveled his gun and fired before I could attack him. I instinctively ducked, and the man kicked me, hitting me just under the chin.

My vision hazed as I fell onto my back. I'd never been kicked like that before. I swore my jaw was broken and my teeth were cracked. My ears rang, and I saw everything in triplicate. I knew I didn't have time to dwell on the pain vibrating through my skull. I didn't have time to fixate on any of the myriad sensations percolating throughout my body. Nika, my family, the noises coming from the house, all of it was lost on me as I watched my attacker shove his gun into his pocket and pull out a thick, wooden stake. Wow, I was about to get staked, just like in some lame vampire flick.

The man was no bigger than me, but when he sank to his knees, straddling my body, I suddenly felt powerless. That wasn't true, though, so I forced my mind to fight through the fear paralyzing my body. It was a bit alarming when I realized my breathing was heavy, my body was shaking. It had been an eternity since I'd had a panic attack. Calming my body, I brought my hands up to block the stake barreling toward my chest. I stopped the weapon an inch before my rib cage.

My attacker didn't say anything; he just tried a different tactic. Leaning down, he head-butted me. I'd never experienced that before either. I saw stars as blackness choked my sight. My limp hands fell to my sides, leaving my chest exposed. I knew I needed to move, but I just couldn't get my body to cooperate.

Hoping I'd at least given my family enough time to escape, I made one last attempt to get my body to do what I wanted it to do. My arms felt like lead as I lifted them, and I felt like I was shoving them through tar as I reached out for the man's chest. Since he was moving forward to shove a sharp stick through my heart, his body met my hands more than the other way around. Wanting him away, I pushed against him with everything I had left.

Surprisingly, he flew off me. I cracked open my eyes, disbelieving my own strength. A growl filled the air as I watched my assailant soaring through the night sky. He struck a nearby tree with a sickening thump. He didn't get back up after he fell to the ground.

"Julian, are you okay?"

Cold hands felt my forehead as familiar glowing brown eyes examined my injured face. "Mom?"

I could feel her location pinging in my head as she knelt beside me. I could feel everyone's. The bond had crackled into life some time ago, but

I'd been too preoccupied to really pay attention to it. I could sense Nika, Hunter, and my father several hundred miles away, and Halina was rushing into the house to help with the rest of the intruders. I relaxed in my mom's arms as her cooling fingertips soothed my injuries. Even though we were still in the middle of the battle, I felt safe.

"Did Grandpa and the others get away?" I murmured, feeling sleepy.

"Yes, sweetheart," she cooed, kissing my forehead. "Mom is taking them to Peter's, getting them away from the property. You saved them," she added, pride in her voice.

She helped me to my feet. I felt wobbly, like I was going to fall again, and I clung to her for support. "I didn't do that much," I muttered, wishing my head would stop throbbing.

"You helped them get away, and now I'm going to help you get away." Her voice was fast and low, still laced with tension. This fight wasn't over.

Mom scooped me into her arms while I listened to snarls and growls echoing from inside the house. I hoped every member of my family was safe. I couldn't bear the thought of losing any of them. Just as Mom turned to dash away with me, an emptiness greater than anything I'd ever felt seared my soul. I gasped and clutched at my chest. It felt like a chunk of me had been ripped away. It hurt more than being staked. Mom paused, looking down on me with worried eyes. "Julian, what is it?"

I couldn't breathe for a second while I tried to understand just what I was feeling. There was a nothingness in my body where something warm and loving used to be. I felt shallow, scooped out, void. The hollowness brought tears to my eyes. I couldn't wrap my head around my growing despair. Why was I feeling this way? Was it Nika's emotions that were getting to me? They shouldn't be affecting me this strongly, considering our distance. I tuned in to her, paying more attention to the blip on my heart that was her. That was when I understood.

Eyes wide, I looked up at my mom. "I can't feel her. She's gone. She's just … gone."

Mom was confused for a second, then she gasped as she understood. "You can't feel Nika's emotions? Why? Why would they just disappear?"

She looked over her shoulder, to where we could both feel Nika's presence. That bond was still there, still pinging her location. Our emotional bond was different though. Gabriel's shot, and the shot I'd been given as a child, had proven that the two bonds were independent of each other. I didn't want to say it. I didn't want to think it. But only one answer rang through my head. If I wasn't picking up on her feelings anymore, it was because she wasn't having them. And if she wasn't having them … then she was dead. I just knew it.

CHAPTER TWENTY-FOUR

Nika

WITH MY SHOULDER propped under my boyfriend's arm, I watched in horror as his father fired a gun at his chest. At this close range, there was no way Connor would miss. I couldn't believe we'd come this far, just to have Hunter's father kill us now. I silently said goodbye to my brother. Whatever he was doing now, he was scared. As a wisp of smoke escaped the gun and a sharp boom cracked the stagnant air, I prayed that Julian and the others got through the night okay.

With the small amount of strength he had left, Hunter shoved me away from him. It wasn't enough of a move to spare him from being hit, but it got me out of danger. I cried out in fear and anger, since it was the only thing I had time to do. Then, quicker than even my eye could process, my father twisted in front of Hunter to block the shot. I held my breath as I watched the bullet lodge into his back.

One injured, one depleted, I watched two of the most important men in my life sink to the ground. Fury ran up my spine, temporarily silencing the fear. I would *not* let this man destroy my family. I blurred over to Connor. Could I take him on my own? Well, of course I could. I wasn't your average teenage girl. I was a vampire, born from a long line of proud, vampire women, and I could handle one lone hunter.

Ramming my shoulder into his chest, I knocked him over, making him miss his next shot. The discharge of the gun echoed in my ear as I crashed on top of him. Lightning quick, I yanked the gun out of his grasp and it skittered across the ground toward my dad and Hunter.

Connor strained against me, but with my enhanced strength, I kept his forearms pinned to the ground. I could hear my dad grunting as he stood, could hear Hunter working his way to his feet. Dropping my fangs, I snarled in Connor's face. It felt good to relieve the tension, but Connor didn't appear to be the slightest bit afraid of me as he continued to fight against me. Maybe he thought that I wouldn't cause him any actual harm. And he would be right. I wouldn't. I couldn't even contemplate hurting anyone.

Wondering what to do with him, now that I had him sort of trapped, I did the only thing I could think to do—I pulled the earphones out of his ears and opened his mind to the power of suggestion.

"Hunter! Tell him to stop!" I called out, twisting to look behind me. Hunter and Dad were on their feet, Dad wincing in pain, Hunter stumbling and looking nauseous. You would think the pair of them had been duking it out all night by their slow reactions. I breathed a sigh of relief that the bullet that had struck Dad hadn't hit his heart.

I'd released one of Connor's hands when I'd pulled out his earphones. When I twisted back around to him, I had just enough time to see that he'd grabbed a jagged knife from his belt. While he still could, he plunged it into my body. My eyes widened when I felt the sharp metal slicing through the tender flesh of my stomach. Then the pain hit me, and I cried out.

I heard Hunter yelling at him to stop moving, but he was a fraction of a second too late. The damage was done. Connor had already moved the knife up my gut, then yanked it out. At Hunter's order, he froze beneath me, bloody knife in hand. Rolling over to the hard-packed dirt beside him, I panted as waves of pain radiated throughout my body. It was all I could focus on—that one incessant source of agony. I clutched my stomach, instinctively wanting to hold the wound closed; my chilled fingers instantly warmed as hot blood oozed through my soaked T-shirt.

"Dad," I whimpered, almost more scared than pained.

He was beside me an instant later, his pale eyes scanning my face, then my body. His hand lifted my shirt, gently moving my fingers aside so he could see just how much damage Connor's knife had done. "Jesus," he muttered. I didn't take that as a good sign.

Hunter moved to the other side of me. Fear on his face, he watched as my father pressed his hands upon my stomach, trying to staunch the flow of blood. I struggled to hold in my pain-filled cries as the pressure amplified my torture. Hunter's fangs dropped as the smell of blood filled the air.

"She's losing blood too fast," my father told him, his words quick and clipped.

"Do we take her to a hospital?" Hunter asked him.

My father's pale eyes shimmered as he locked gazes with me. "We're too far away. She won't survive the trip."

His words hit me, and tears leaked from my eyes. Was I going to die here? Would Julian know? Forcing my fear aside, I tuned into his emotions. He was scared as well. Maybe he already knew? Or maybe he was about to die too? Not knowing was as torturous as the agony in my belly. Although, that ache was feeling better as time passed. I was more tired than anything now.

"It's not so bad, Daddy. I can barely feel it ..." My words felt slurred to me, my mind thick, my lids heavy.

I felt cold hands on my cheeks, moving my head from side to side. It made sleep evasive, and I frowned at the person trying to interrupt my slumber. "Nika, you need to stay awake, baby."

Hunter's concerned voice was in my ear. I tried to lift my hand to touch his face, but my body wasn't responding to my commands. "Five more minutes," I muttered. I wished I had a blanket. My hands and feet were freezing.

Hazy words met me. "Teren, what do we do?"

"I don't know. She's bleeding internally. I can't ... I can't fix this."

My dad sounded so scared. I wanted to tell him not to worry ... I felt fine. I felt great. Just cold. And sleepy. So sleepy. If I could just rest a minute ...

Hunter

NIKA WAS LOSING blood fast. Her heartbeat had already slowed to a point that was dangerous, and she wasn't responding anymore when I shook her. Not even a groan escaped her lips now. Teren was right; she wasn't going to make it to a hospital. She wasn't going to make it at all.

The wound up her abdomen was deep, massive. Teren's hands upon her stomach were holding her organs in place as much as slowing the flow of blood. I didn't want to think about how cut up she was on the inside. I didn't want to contemplate the fact that she'd never be the same after this moment. I just wanted to rewind the night. I wasn't sure what I'd do differently to change this, but I would try.

No, I knew exactly what I'd do differently. I never would have run away from my nest. I would have told Halina and the others that my father was sending assassins after me, and we would have dealt with the problem as a family, because that was what we were. A family. A family who was about to lose a member. Because of me, and I couldn't handle that fact.

Teren's grievous face looked up at mine. "We're losing her. She's slipping ... her heartbeat is so faint."

I'd never seen someone look so devastated. Was this how my father had looked when I'd died? Somehow, that made what he'd done to me easier to bear. What would I do to save someone I loved? What was I going to do now? There was only one thing I could think of.

Not knowing exactly what to do, I relied on the vampiric instinct coursing through my veins. My fangs had crashed down ages ago, when Nika's blood had first filled my senses. I brought the sharp points to my wrist. They ripped through my flesh as easily as a human's. It hurt, but I endured it. This pain was nothing compared to Nika's. Instead of nice clean holes, I tore open a section. Nika needed blood. I had blood.

Teren snapped his gaze to me when he realized what I was doing. When I brought my wrist to Nika's mouth, he grabbed my arm. A deep growl rose from his chest. "What are you doing?" he asked, venom in his voice.

That instinct inside of me told me we were running out of time. Eventually, even this option wouldn't save her. As gently as I could, I told him,

"She's going to die if we continue to sit here and do nothing. We can't move her. We can't fix her. But I can turn her."

Teren shook his head. "No. She wouldn't want this."

I exhaled in a quick huff. "I didn't want it either, but ... some things are preferable to death. I see that now." I glanced down at her pale face; her mouth was relaxed, pain-free, and her slim fangs were visible as she rested. As she died. "She's already a vampire, Teren. She'll be okay with this."

"She'll be a pureblood. Condemned to darkness. She's only sixteen. A child ..."

His voice hitched, and I returned my eyes to his. "I will be with her. She won't be alone. It's the only way to save her ... you know I'm right."

Teren's head dropped, then he nodded. He eased his hand upon her body, and the blood now free from its restraint, gushed from her, completely staining her shirt. I waited a few minutes, until some innate part of me knew she was ready to receive my blood in exchange of hers.

My wrist had healed already, so I ripped open my flesh again and placed it to Nika's sweet lips. The blood poured from me, into her. As her mouth filled, my father, immobile thanks to my command, barked out, "Creating a monster from a monster. You're truly one of them now, aren't you?"

As I stroked Nika's forehead with my other hand, I murmured, "Yes. I am one of them. And I'm grateful for it." When Nika's mouth was full, she automatically swallowed. I reopened my wrist to feed her again, while my father continued berating me for the life he'd given me.

"I really have lost you. I should have let you die that night. I should have killed you myself before you converted. You're an evil bloodsucking creature of the night now. If your sister only knew what you've become ..."

A snarl left my throat as I stared over at my father's prostrate body. "Stop talking! You don't ever get to mention her to me again! She loved me. Above anything else, she loved me, and she would have tried to accept what I'd become. She would have attempted to love me, even like this. She never would have sent our friends to kill me. As far as I'm concerned, Dad, out of the two of us, *you* are the one who has shown yourself to be the true monster."

My father opened and shut his mouth, obviously wanting to retaliate with harsh words of his own. I ignored him for a moment, and focused on feeding Nika instead. Even as her heartbeat faded, she drank from my wrist with more fervor than before. True to our species, she was dying and living at the same time. While I watched her swallowing, I glanced over at Teren. He had long tear tracks down his cheeks, but he was smiling as he watched his daughter recovering. When he noticed me watching him, he whispered, "Thank you."

I frowned. "I got her into this mess. You shouldn't thank me."

His smile turned sad. "The past is over. What you're doing now is what matters to me, and without you, she'd be dead, so thanking you is the very least of what I should be doing for you." He put his hand on my shoulder in a fatherly way. "You may have fought against it, but you've adapted to this life and remained a good man. You should be proud of that fact."

I was speechless as I stared at him, and could only nod in lame acknowledgement. Pride wasn't one of the things I felt, but maybe … acceptance was. Over Teren's shoulder, I saw my father silently fuming. Considering my options with him, I murmured, "The past is the past."

Knowing he was a problem I could deal with later, I refocused my attention on Nika. I wasn't sure how long I needed to feed her. I would give her every drop of me if necessary. It felt like an eternity, but eventually she stopped swallowing what I gave her. Panicked, I looked up at Teren. Blood filled Nika's mouth, overflowing from her lips, but she wasn't drinking it. Teren's eyes scanned her body as he tilted his head to listen to her heart. Worried, I listened too.

The low thump of life within her was faint, thready, and I could swear each beat was weaker than the rest. While my blood sat useless in her mouth, the ineffectual organ in her chest struggled to remain alive. I knew it would stop soon, and I wanted to cry with the loss of it. If it weren't for me, her heart would still be beating. She'd live to see seventeen. She'd grow into a woman. But the past was the past, and all I had was the here and now. Grabbing her hand, I squeezed it tight. "I'm right here with you, Nika. Go ahead and sleep. I'll be here when you wake." *God, please let her wake.*

After my words left me, she swallowed the last bit of blood in her mouth. Then a slight breath escaped her lips. There was no reciprocating inhale. Her heart gave one last weak thump, then it didn't beat again. Teren brought his hands to his face and began to weep for his dead daughter. Leaning over, I placed a light kiss on Nika's forehead. My jaw quivered, but I held in my tears. She wasn't gone. She was dead, yes, but she wasn't gone. My blood had to have saved her ... I couldn't go on without her.

While Teren worked on regaining his composure, I turned my attention to my father lying stiff and still beside us. His eyes tightened as I approached. He probably thought I was going to rip him to pieces for what he'd done to Nika. Maybe I should. But this cycle of violence had to stop somewhere. And it was going to stop with me.

Kneeling beside my dad, I inhaled a calming breath; it was a struggle. I felt like my entire body was vibrating. "You probably think I'm going to kill you. I'm sure you would kill me if our situations were reversed, and you had the upper hand." I shook my head. "I'm not, though. I'm not angry at you anymore. I'm not upset about what you did to me." I glanced over at Nika's unmoving body. "I'm not even upset over what you did to her. Not entirely. You felt you had no other choice. I get that. But I have several choices, and I'm not going to take the easiest one right now."

Feeling steadier, both physically and emotionally, I stared him down, trapping him in my hypnotic gaze. Voice calm, I said, "I want you to listen to me very carefully, and follow my instructions to the letter." The residual defiance left Dad's eyes as he stared at me. When his expression was tranquil, I told him, "I want you to call off the attack at the ranch. Tell them to retreat, that you have new information that can't be ignored. Have them all meet you at our old house in Salt Lake. Then I want you to call every single person who knows about me or the Adams. Have them all meet you at the same house. You will not remember me telling you to do this. You will believe that you are going to tell them something of the utmost importance, and you will be adamant that they meet you there in the next twenty-four hours."

Dad nodded. Reaching into his jacket pocket, I pulled out his cell phone and extended it to him. "Go ahead and call them."

Free to move, Dad took the phone and called a number. As he brought the cell to his ear, I glanced back at Teren and Nika. Nika was the same, Teren had composed himself some and was watching me with curious eyes. I smiled at him, sure my plan was going to work. I was going to end this once and for all.

When the line picked up, Dad's gruff voice broke the silence. "It's me. Change of plans. Stop whatever it is you're doing, gather up everyone, and meet me at the house I was renting in Salt Lake, the one I told you about." There was a pause as the other person spoke. I could hear they were upset; I could also hear fighting in the background. Dad's expression darkened. "I don't care if you have them cornered. I've got something much bigger than the Adams, something of utmost importance. Gather everyone and wait for me at the house. I'll be there as soon as I can. Now go!"

He hung up the phone with such assurance that I knew he felt positive the other man would obey. It worried me some that the hunters had "cornered" my family, but worrying about it wouldn't do me any good. When Dad finished with that conversation, he started in on the others. I breathed a sigh of relief as I looked back at Teren again. At least the ranch was safe now. That was one positive to come out of this mess.

Teren's phone rang as he lovingly tucked a strand of hair behind Nika's ear. He closed his eyes before pulling it out of his pocket, and answered it without even looking to see who it was. After he said hello, I recognized Emma's concerned voice. "What happened? Is Nika okay? Julian says he can't feel her emotions anymore. Why, Teren? What's going on?"

Curiosity swelled in me. Julian could feel Nika's emotions? That explained a few things, like Julian showing up just in the nick of time when I'd inadvertently scared Nika with the fang markings on my sister's urn. He'd known she was terrified.

Teren's voice cracked when he told Emma what had happened to their daughter. My chest squeezed with pain as I remembered it. Emma started crying, and I momentarily cursed my enhanced ears. Teren soothed her with comforting words about Nika being fine once she finished her conversion. He sounded surer of her completing the process than he looked. When Emma's sobs eased, he asked, "Have the hunters left the ranch? Are you safe?"

Emma hiccupped, then softly told him, "Yes. They all fled a couple of minutes ago. Halina chased after a couple of them, but several got away…"

Gritting my teeth, I spoke loud enough that Emma would hear me. "It's okay. They won't get away for long."

While Teren consoled his wife, I turned back to my father. He'd finished with his calls, and was looking at me with impatient eyes. Thanks to my instructions, he now wanted to be away from me. He wanted to meet up with those hunters, and pass on his "vital' information. In his mind, he had a highly important mission that didn't involve me. Only, it *did* involve me. The plan I'd just put into motion only involved me; my father wasn't needed anymore. Now that every person who could possibly want to harm the Adams or myself was on their way to one specific location, Dad was free to retire.

Locking gazes with him, I said, "I want to thank you for all the years you kept me alive. For doing your best raising Evangeline and me after Mom died. For teaching me everything I know." With a smirk, I amended that. "Almost everything. The Adams have added on to your lessons a bit. Compassion, understanding ... acceptance ... forgiveness." Dad didn't react to my statement. He couldn't. I hadn't given him permission to talk freely. Wanting to keep this simple, I left him mute. "I'm going to do something you wouldn't let me do. I'm going to let you live, and I'm going to give you a new life. I'm going to wipe your mind of everything and let you start fresh. But, before I do, I want you to know, I forgive you for all of it, Dad."

Dad's eyes widened, and his mouth opened in silent protest. He knew what I was about to do. I was obliterating him as surely as if I were driving a stake through his heart. But unlike an actual death, he would rise from the ashes of his destruction, and he'd be a better man for it.

As I started to speak, Teren grabbed my arm. He was still on the phone with his wife, but he was giving me a contemplative expression. I wasn't sure why he was stopping me—my father had to be wiped or killed. There were no other options.

He chewed on his lip for a moment, then told me, "You could keep him ... as your father. Erase the parts about him being a hunter, but keep the parts about him being your family. Let him know you're a vampire, or hide it, that part is completely up to you, but it doesn't have to be all or nothing."

I sat back on my heels as I stared over at him. "He hunted your family, shot your best friend, killed your daughter ... and you would be okay with him staying in my life? In Nika's life?"

Teren's jaw tightened, and I knew what he really wanted to say. He didn't say it, though. Instead, he told me, "Family is important. It's possibly the most important thing there is. And if there is a way for you to keep at least one member of yours ... then, yes, I think you should."

I smiled, pleased beyond belief that he would offer me that kind of comfort after everything I'd brought down upon his loved ones. Putting my hand on his shoulder, I whispered, "I'm not losing my family by wiping him clean, Teren. Halina, Nika ... you ... I have more family now than I ever could have hoped for. I'm okay with this. Keeping him around would just remind me of a past I'm not proud of, a past I'd sooner forget."

Teren gave me a small smile and a stiff nod. Turning back to my father, I gave him a final once-over. The scar on his jaw from a vampire in St. Louis, healed puncture marks on the side of his hand, worry lines around his eyes, weariness in the hollow of his cheeks. Had our life, our mission, given him any joy at all? I tried to remember the last time I'd seen him truly happy. It was well before Mom had died. Well before she'd gotten sick even. It was probably decades ago, back when Mom was alive and hunting by his side. Dad had darkened after her death. He'd buried her fang-marked urn in Missouri. He'd said she deserved her rest after a lifetime on the road. I think it had just been too hard for him to keep her close. I knew it had felt that way sometimes with my sister. Nika keeping watch over her ashes for me had actually been a blessing in disguise.

"Dad, when I'm done speaking, you won't remember a thing about me ..."

After I was finished reprogramming him, I helped him get back to his truck. It was parked quite a bit away, along the side of the highway. I ordered him to wait beside the truck while I cleaned out the inside. I removed everything that might have given him some clue about who he really was—all his weapons, all of his notes and journals, and a picture of my sister and I that I found tucked in the visor. I did the same with him, removing everything but his cash and his license from his wallet, and every concealed weapon. I also took back the device he'd used to track me. He wouldn't be needing it now. When I was done, I had one of his large duffel bags slung over my shoulder, filled to bursting with a hunter's arsenal.

"You can get in now," I warmly told him as I held open the door.

He nodded with a polite smile. "Thank you, young man."

I hid a smile as he climbed into the truck. I was already a stranger to him. Giving him one final command, I said, "I want you to keep driving north until you're almost out of gas. Whatever city you end up in, I want you to stay there, find a job, and begin your new life. And I want you to be happy, optimistic, at peace. Life is full of promise, if you take the time to look for it." I smirked at my own sentimental ramblings. With a shake of my head, I finished with, "You won't remember me helping you, the second you start to drive away."

He blinked at me with a blank expression, and I gently closed his door. He proceeded to start his truck and pull away from me as if nothing odd had just happened to him. Staring after his taillights, I whispered into the darkness, "Thank you for saving my life." Then I wished him the best, turned around, and let him go.

When I got back to Teren, he was still with his daughter. He looked up when I stepped into his ring of light. "Her stomach has healed. That's a good sign. The conversion is working." His voice was bittersweet, tired with emotion.

Indicating her stone-still body, I asked, "How long will it take before she ... wakes up?"

"Pureblood conversions take at least twenty-four hours," he whispered.

"Let's take her home," I replied.

Teren started to scoop her into his arms, but I leaned down to stop him. "If you don't mind, I'd like to carry her."

He raised an eyebrow in question. "Do you feel strong enough?"

I nodded. The silver was finally gone. The only exhaustion I felt now was emotional, but I wouldn't let that stop me from taking care of her. Teren stared at me for a second longer, then slowly rose to his feet. I knelt to take his place, sweeping Nika into my arms. She felt feather-light as I held her to my chest, and she offered no resistance as her arms dangled and her head fell back. She was dead, her heart silent, her breath stopped. But she would live again. This wasn't the end.

As Teren watched me holding his daughter, I remembered that he'd taken a bullet for me. Pursing my lip, I indicated his back. "You okay?"

He grimaced, like he wasn't looking forward to something. "Yeah, I'll be fine. But the bullet will have to be removed."

My face tightened in sympathy. I could easily imagine how much that would suck. Vampires might heal quickly, but we still felt pain. "You took a bullet for me. Thank you."

His eyes flicked down to Nika. "You're family," he whispered.

It took Teren and me a long time to get back to the ranch. He offered numerous times to take Nika from me, but I didn't want to let her go. I was attached to her already, like a pre-bond was anchoring itself into my heart. I couldn't stomach the thought of not being close to her. I knew without a doubt that things were going to be different from now on, and for more than one reason. Nika had been the love of my life before, but now she was a part of my soul. We were connected as deeply as two people could be connected.

When we got within a few miles of the ranch, another bond pulsed through me, warming me. Halina. She held the other corner of my soul. When Teren and I reached the circular drive of the ranch, one of the three sets of front doors burst open, and a multitude of streaking bodies rushed out to meet us. They were followed more slowly by the group of humans who I shared a home with.

Halina tossed her arms around me, murmuring tender Russian words that filled me with peace. Or maybe that was just her presence. I looked her over, anxious for any physical sign of trauma upon her, but aside from some bloody smears and tears in her clothing, she appeared fine. Any wounds had healed long ago. Her long, dark hair whipping around her in the breeze, she turned her attention to her granddaughter.

With a sigh, she ran her fingers across her forehead. "Nika," she murmured, sadness in her eyes.

The rest of the family crowded around Nika, anxious to see her. There wasn't much to see, besides her lifeless body, her T-shirt soaked with blood. Julian pushed his way through the family to get to his sister. His eyes bloodshot, he grabbed her face and twisted her to look at him. "Nick? Can you hear me? Are you okay? Please don't be dead ... please."

"She'll be fine, Julian. She's converting right now." Supporting Nika's weight with one hand, I tentatively reached out to him. He flinched away from my touch.

"What the hell did you do to her!" he yelled at me.

I opened my mouth to speak, but Teren beat me to it. "He saved her life, Julian. Without him, I'd be bringing home a corpse."

There was sniffling in the group, sounds of light crying. My eyes roved over every member of my nest, looking for anyone who might be missing. Aside from Gabriel and his group, everyone seemed to be there—Emma, Imogen, Alanna, Jack, Linda, and oddly enough, an older couple I didn't know; Teren introduced them as Ben and Tracey. Their daughter, Olivia, was resting upstairs. While the humans looked exhausted, and a little scratched up—Ben had one hell of a black eye—none of them seemed severely injured. It would appear they'd successfully held off their attackers. If it weren't for the body in my arms weighing down my joy, I would have been beaming with pride.

Wanting to get Nika inside, into a warm bed where she could rest in comfort, I stepped forward. The crowd parted like the sea, allowing me access to the house. Arianna was waiting inside the entryway; she looked on the verge of an emotional collapse. She took one look at Nika's body in my arms and immediately broke down into hysterics.

"Nika, no!" She rushed up to me, touching Nika's body, feeling her sodden shirt, fumbling for a pulse in her throat, trying to warm her chilly extremities. She kept repeating no, over and over, and no matter how many times I told her Nika would be fine, she didn't seem to believe me. She didn't even seem to hear me. Julian eventually had to pull her off Nika and forcibly lead her toward the entryway. I was sure the girl needed a Valium. Someone should take her home. She was in a severe state of shock, as was most of the teary-eyed family.

I headed for the underground levels of the home, since Nika would need protection from the sun now. I was astonished at the disaster that surrounded me. Tables were knocked over, vases full of flowers shattered, their pools of water staining the floor. Portraits on the wall were crooked, if not fallen. An ornate painting of a sunrise was ripped in half. Dozens of windows were shattered; shards of glass covered the ground like a crystalline carpet. The walls had huge craterlike cracks in them, like bodies had been thrown against the plaster. The furniture was torn, toppled, broken. Bloody smears and droplets were everywhere. It looked like a warzone, which of course, it had been.

The bookcase entrance to the secret bedrooms had been completely ripped from the wall. It was lying on its side, partially blocking the hall, its contents spilling everywhere. I sighed as I stepped over the piles. All this chaos, because of me. I could hear family members quietly following me as I took Nika to my room. When I paused to open my door, a voice behind me said, "We have other rooms. She doesn't need to be in yours."

I looked back at Teren, watching me with furrowed brows. "She will want to be with me." I glanced between him and his wife. "You understand?" Teren opened his mouth, but shut it instantly as he locked gazes with Emma. He understood how the bond worked. Nika would need to be with me now. We would both need it.

Everyone gathered around the doorway while I placed her on my bed. Even though she wouldn't need its warmth, I covered her with a blanket. I didn't want to look at the blood anymore. I also didn't want to disrespect Nika by changing her while she rested.

Emma entered the room and stood beside me. Looking down at her daughter, she whispered, "Thank you for bringing her home. Thank you for saving her life." When I met eyes with her, hers were wet. "If you wouldn't mind, Teren and I would like to be alone with our daughter for a while."

I nodded, and left the parents to their grief. I naturally gravitated toward Halina. She stared at me a moment, sighed, then wrapped her arms around me again. A feeling of completeness washed over me as she held me, and I knew with absolute certainty, I would never try to leave her again.

CHAPTER TWENTY-FIVE

Julian

I WAS AN emotional basketcase. A part of me wanted to go downstairs and be with my sister, and another part of me wanted to stay as far away from her as possible. Looking at her now would be too painful, would only emphasize the void in my soul. I couldn't feel her emotions anymore. Granted, her feelings would have been quiet anyway, since she was … resting … but this was different. They were gone. Stripped away. I felt raw inside, like I'd had a bandage removed and my skin stung. It went deeper than my skin, though. The ache went to the bone.

I wasn't the only one negatively affected by the sight of my sister. Arianna was borderline psychotic as she endlessly paced up and down the cobblestone driveway. The entire time she moved, she muttered, "She's dead. My best friend is dead. I can't believe this. I can't believe this …" I wanted to tell her Nika wasn't really dead, but I was too shell-shocked to speak. Like it or not, things would be different now.

Just as I was wondering if I should somehow get Arianna home—Dad's car was still abandoned along the highway, his keys still in my pocket—a trio of vampires walked out the front door. Looking over, I stared at Gabriel, Jacen, and Starla with impassive eyes. Arianna didn't even notice them. Gabriel tilted his head as he examined my girlfriend. "I could give her a sedative, if you like?"

Not really wanting anything from him, I shook my head. "She'll be fine. I just need to get her home."

Gabriel nodded at me, then turned to Starla and Jacen; both mixed vampires were worn and bloody, like they'd gone a round or two with an MMA fighter. Or a dozen of them. "Go get the cars, please. We'll head back to L.A. at once. We'll collect our things later."

They both nodded, then plodded off toward the garage. Gabriel watched them leave, sadness in his eyes, then his expression returned to neutrality as he looked at me again. "If you'd like, Julian, we could take her home before we leave."

A sharp voice behind him cracked the stillness in the night air. "No. I need to take her. Her family will need adjusting. It's a miracle her parents haven't come to collect her yet." Halina strode from the open front door to stand by Gabriel.

He quirked a smile. "Since you were preoccupied, and the girl wanted to stay, I had an acquaintance of mine in a neighboring city pay her parents a visit. I can assure you, they haven't been missing her."

I flashed a glance at Arianna, hoping she didn't understand what that meant. I didn't think she'd be okay with her parents receiving visitors from strange vampires. Hell, I wasn't entirely sure *I* was okay with it. I trusted Gabriel, though. In this, at least. He wouldn't send anyone dangerous to her house.

Halina agreed with my assessment. Her face remained cool, but her tone slightly warmed. "Oh, well, thank you. The last thing we needed tonight was frazzled parents at our door." After a moment, she raised an eyebrow at him and said, "You stayed and fought with my family, protected them, even after I ordered you to leave. Why?"

Gabriel looked over at me and smiled. It was a genuine smile, full of warmth. It was a little odd to see on him, since he was generally very guarded with his emotions. Turning back to Halina, he told her in a soft voice, "They are as much a family to me as my own. I would give my last breath to keep them from harm, my love."

Halina looked touched, then she frowned. "Not all of them."

Gabriel's smile evaporated. Furrowing his brows, his lips mimicked Halina's scowl. "With regards to Hunter, I am truly sorry I let jealousy cloud my judgment. That was most unlike me. I can't even remember the last time I felt that way." He looked over her shoulder, lost in thought for a second. When he refocused on her, his gaze was resolute. "It was wrong of me to attempt to break your connection with Hunter. You have my sincerest apologies. I am highly disappointed in my actions, and even though I do not deserve such a kindness, I pray that when I am gone, you will remember our good times together, and not how we ended. I would wish for your thoughts of me to not all be unkind, although, I would certainly understand if they were." He flashed a glance at the tattered home behind him. "I'll leave your family in peace now. Goodbye, my love."

He turned to leave, but Halina snatched his elbow. "Wait." When he looked over at her, she rolled her eyes. "You may stay. We need help cleaning up anyway." She shrugged.

As Starla's shiny BMW and Gabriel's sleek sedan stopped right beside my pacing girlfriend, Gabriel gave my grandmother a cautious glance. "You have forgiven me?"

Halina narrowed her eyes. "Not yet." She sniffed. "But I will ... in time." With a sigh, she ran a hand down his arm and grabbed his fingers. "You have nothing to be jealous of with Hunter. He is my child, you are my lover."

"Are?" he asked, climbing a step to be equal with her again. "As in, I am *still* your lover?"

Halina nodded as she grabbed his other hand. "For the time being." She gave him a crooked smile. "Just make sure you don't piss me off again."

His eyes lowered to her lips, and, sensing an intimate moment that I didn't want to see, I turned away. After a few soft lip smacks, I heard Gabriel mutter, "Duly noted, my love. Duly noted."

Starla was waiting in her car for Gabriel. She looked hopeful and happy as she stared at Gabriel and my grandmother making out through the window. For all her complaining, she liked being a part of our nest. Cracking open her door, she stood up. "Father? Are we really staying? Can we go home?"

Halina groaned, and Gabriel chuckled. Looking back at Starla, he nodded. "Yes, you and Jacen are free to go home now. We'll be staying in Utah after all, it seems. Please leave the sedan, Jacen. Halina and I will be returning the girl momentarily."

Jacen nodded and stepped out of the car, leaving it running. With a wide smile, he politely told Halina, "Thank you," then rushed over to Starla's car. Pulling her into his arms, he spun her in a circle; both were laughing, relieved by Halina's decision.

When they drove off a few seconds later, spinning the sports car's tires in their exuberance, Arianna broke out of her pacing-induced trance and looked up at me. "I want to go home, Julian."

My brief humor at seeing Starla and Jacen's joy vanished as I was reminded of my own situation. I sighed as I walked down the steps to join Arianna, and fervently hoped that she could handle everything that had just been thrown at her recently. I swished my hand toward the running car. "Come on, we'll take you home."

Halina and Gabriel took the front seats while I walked Arianna to the back. Pausing in the open car door, I told the house, "I'm taking Arianna home." One of the vampires inside would hear me and inform my grief-stricken parents that I was leaving. Not that they wouldn't know by the bond. They'd know the second Halina and I left the property, and as long as I was with her, they wouldn't worry. Too much.

Alanna appeared at the door and waved goodbye. She wiped a tear from her cheek; her hand was shaking. This night had put everyone through the wringer. Reaching into my pocket, I tossed her Dad's car keys, so he could fetch it later, then I slid into the seat beside Arianna. She was silent on the ride home. Silent and contemplative. It worried me. I tried holding her hand, kissing her fingers, but she ignored my affections. My heartbeat was fast with dread by the time we reached the city.

I endlessly searched my girlfriend's face while Gabriel drove us to her house. Her brows were knotted as she stared straight in front of her, and her green-flecked eyes shimmered with moisture. She had bags under her eyes and her cheeks seemed hollow, like stress, lack of food, and lack of sleep had sucked in her features. She'd had to deal with so much in such a short span of time. Was she okay? Or still on the verge of a collapse?

An ache ran through my injured leg, and I idly rubbed it. Arianna's eyes flashed to the movement. Her expression changed, and she suddenly looked very afraid. I could almost see her replaying the terrifying ordeal in her mind. Her heart raced, and her breath picked up. Abandoning my leg, I reached out for her face. "Hey, it's okay. We're okay. It's over."

"It will never be over," she muttered, panic rising in her voice.

I rubbed my hand over her cheek. "Yes, it will," I soothed, hoping that was true.

Her honey-brown locks flicked around my hand as she violently shook her head. "No. There will always be something, someone trying to kill you. I'll always be in danger with you. I don't want to die. I don't want to die. Nika died. Oh God, Nika died ..."

Sensing she was about to seriously lose it, I pulled her in for a hug. In the rearview mirror, I caught eyes with my grandmother. She had an eyebrow raised as she appraised my girlfriend. I had to be very careful here. One wrong step and I could lose everything. "The man chasing us is dead. We're safe. We won't be hunted anymore." I had no idea if those words were true, but it was all I could think to say.

Arianna was stiff in my arms, resisting my comfort. "I thought it was over when Nika's boyfriend was killed, when my mom's car was shot at. I thought that would be as bad as it got ..." She pulled back, and her face was ghostly white. "They tried to burn us alive. They shot at us. They destroyed the ranch trying to get to us. They killed Nika ... they killed my best friend."

Terror rose in her voice, and I ran my hand through her hair to try to sooth her. "They won't hurt us anymore. You're safe."

She pushed my hand away. I could sense the fear oozing from her, and I knew her reaction was based from exhaustion and terror, and not from her true feelings, but in her turmoil, she said the absolute worst thing she could have possibly said. "I can't be with you. You're dangerous. And I don't want to die. I don't want to die ..."

My vision swam as her words sunk in. I clutched for her hands, but she pushed me away. "You don't mean that. You're just tired, scared."

"Yes, scared of being chased, scared of being hunted. They wanted to kill me just because I was with you." She pointed at the bullet wound in my leg. "They shot you!"

"Arianna," I pleaded, "I love you. Please don't do this."

I tried to hug her, and she immediately started slapping me away; she'd completely gone over whatever slim edge of sanity she'd been keeping. "I don't want this! I don't want to die! I want to go home! Take me home!"

We were just about to her home anyway. I stopped trying to soothe her, and she huddled into a ball, murmuring, "I'm sixteen, I don't want to die."

Sighing, I glanced in the rearview mirror again. Halina's face was impassive as she watched Arianna, then her gaze shifted to me. I saw steel in her eyes, and I knew what it meant. She was firming her resolve to do something difficult. The car stopped in Arianna's driveway a few seconds later, and Arianna bolted. I wanted to run after her, but Halina cracked open her door. I grabbed her shoulder over the seat. "Please, don't. She'll be fine; just give her time to adjust."

Halina looked back at me, firmness on her face. "She's not strong enough, Julian. She's not the one for you."

I glanced Arianna's way. She was pounding on the front door, yelling for her parents. If they weren't worried before, they would be now. "Then make her strong enough. Make her calm down, make her be okay with what happened." I looked back at Halina; I could feel the tears dripping down my cheeks, but I was too worried to brush them away. "Please, I love her."

Halina's face softened for a second, but then her mask returned. "I'm sorry, Julian, but I won't alter her to suit you. If she can't handle our life, then she must be cut free. It's our way."

She began to move, and I panicked and followed her out the car door. Standing in front of her, I grabbed her shoulders. "Don't take it all. Take the girlfriend part away, but let her remember me. Please, at least do that for me."

Halina sighed as she looked down at me. From behind me, I could hear Arianna's parents opening the door, asking her what was wrong. Arianna started sobbing, and telling them ... everything. Halina clenched her jaw as she listened to all our secrets being exposed. "I'm sorry, Julian. If I let her remember you, she'll remember her feelings for you. We'll be right back where we are now." She brought her chilly hand to my cheek. "And I have no desire to hurt you like this twice. It is best to completely sever the tie. Then you'll begin to heal."

She looked behind her at Gabriel. He blurred to my side a second later. Arianna's disbelieving parents saw the supernatural movement and started panicking along with their daughter. I heard the front door slam as they all darted inside. Even though I knew she needed to fix this, I fought against my grandmother when she tried to move around me. But then Gabriel's steel fingers locked around my arms, freeing Halina, and I knew I was powerless to stop this.

"I'm sorry! I'm sorry!" I wasn't sure who I was shouting to—my soon-to-be ex-girlfriend, or my grandmother.

I watched in horror as Halina casually strode to the door, pushed it inward as if it were made of cardboard, and disappeared into the depths of the home. There was shouting, pleading, then absolute silence. I knew it was over, and I sank to my knees. Gabriel let me fall. There was nothing to be done now. He patted my shoulder in sympathy. "It is for the best, Julian. You'll find another."

Dejected, I stared at the ground. "I don't want another," I muttered. "I want her. She was in shock … her best friend was just killed. She should have been given time to mourn, to grieve … to adjust. This wasn't fair."

He removed his hand. "Many things in life are not fair."

I knew that, but knowing it didn't make anything any easier.

I stayed on the ground until Halina returned; I was still on my knees when she stood before me. I remained there, looking at the clumps of grass around my legs. I couldn't look at her yet. Not without anger. She lowered herself into a squat and waited. When I still didn't move, her hand forcibly raised my chin. Reluctantly, I looked up at her. As gently as she could, she told me, "I know you don't understand, but I did this for you, for all of us. We cannot afford to let those who cannot handle our lives keep their knowledge. And she will be safer this way, for she was right, our lives *are* dangerous. There is no denying that."

Lifting my chin, I spat back, "She was in shock. She would have been fine if you'd given her time. But you didn't, and now you'll never get the grandchildren you want. Nika can't create them, and I'll never love another woman. You just destroyed the line."

She gave me a patient smile. "Never say never, child."

I sprang to my feet. "I'm going home. I have school tomorrow, and I want to be alone."

Halina seamlessly stood up. "Yes, school. There are other adjustments I will need to make before morning. It does us no good if Arianna no longer remembers you being together, but everyone around her does." I stared at Halina in defiance, and she gave me a soft smile. "I already have the information, I got it from Arianna before I wiped her, so your stubbornness won't stop anything."

I stormed back to the car and slammed my door shut. Gabriel joined me, but Halina stayed outside. To Gabriel, she said, "I'll do this faster on my own. Take him back to the ranch."

I glared at her through the window. "I said I want to go home."

She gave me a smile that was clearly forced. "I am not leaving you in an empty house all night."

Narrowing my eyes, I muttered, "I'm sixteen, not six." When she didn't appear swayed by my argument, I exhaled in a huff. "Fine, then take me to Starla and Jacen's." In a softer voice, I whispered, "I can't be around Nika right now. I just … can't." It hurt too much.

Halina titled her head as she examined me, then she slowly nodded. "I'll let your parents know where you …"

Her voice trailed off as she turned to stare in the direction of our house. "What is it?" I tentatively asked her. I really couldn't handle any more tonight. I just needed a bed. And maybe a wall to punch.

Brows furrowed, she replied, "Hunter. He left the ranch, and is heading toward your neighborhood."

As I tuned in to the mental blip that belonged to Hunter—a blip I generally ignored—I discovered she was right. That surprised me, and then I was surprised that *anything* could still surprise me. "He left Nika? Why?" And even more odd, now that I was paying attention, I could sense that my father was moving too. What was going on now?

Still staring off in Hunter's direction, Halina murmured, "I don't know." She looked up at the dark, twilight sky, then her eyes returned to Gabriel. "I have time. I'm going to find out what Hunter is doing. Take the boy to Starla's."

She said Starla's name with a slight sneer, and Gabriel smiled at hearing it. "With pleasure." Lifting his eyebrows, he added, "Be careful, love."

She nodded at him. "You, as well."

Halina blurred away, and Gabriel started driving. I stared at Arianna's house until I couldn't see it anymore. She was gone. I could knock on her door right now and she wouldn't recognize me. It would be like the first day of school all over again. She'd had a class with both Nika and me back then. Arianna and Nika had hit it off instantly, and Arianna had just always been around after that. She'd always been flirty with me, and a part of me had known she'd liked me, but it had taken me far too long to realize just how much I liked her too.

I laid my head against the window in despair. I'd wasted so much time obsessing over Raquel. And now, oddly, Raquel was all I had. But she wasn't what I wanted, she wasn't who I loved. I wanted Arianna. But maybe all wasn't lost. Halina might have wiped Arianna's mind clean, but she wouldn't have touched her natural instincts—that wasn't Halina's style. She wouldn't change Arianna, make it so she was never attracted to me, and if Arianna had been interested in me from day one, then I was sure she could be interested in me again.

Sitting up in my seat, I mulled over my options. I could admit defeat, let Arianna go, and move on with my life. Or ... I could get her back. I could start over and win her back. Halina wouldn't like it, she might even attempt to wipe her again, but then, I'd just start over again. A slow smile spread over my face as I stared out the window. I'd start over as many times as I needed. I wouldn't stop, and I wouldn't give up. I couldn't. I loved her.

Hunter

I WANTED TO stay with Nika. I wanted it more than anything I'd ever wanted before. The bond was strengthening in me, molding itself around my very being. I could almost feel the ethereal tendrils of it wrapping around me, like steel links of chainmail encasing me in armor. It made the thought of leaving her difficult to bear, but I had something to do, and I needed to attend to it before the sun came up. My guests wouldn't wait forever.

Knocking on my bedroom door, I intruded on Teren and Emma's sanctuary with their daughter. "Teren," I whispered. "I need to meet my father's men. Would you ... want to come with me?"

Teren and Emma both lifted their gazes from Nika to stare at me. Emma, eyes bloodshot from tears, look startled. Teren looked grim, but determined. Emma looked at Teren, fear in her eyes. "The hunters who attacked the ranch? You're going to meet with them? How do you know where they are?"

Teren nodded my way. "He compelled his father to make them retreat. They're regrouping at Hunter's old home, near our house." He looked back at me, a small smile on his lips. "We can get rid of them all, in one fell swoop."

Emma grabbed his hand. "No, it's too dangerous."

Stepping into the dimly lit room, I shook my head at her. "They'll be expecting my father, not me. They won't be prepared for what I have to tell them." I stressed that last part, to remind her that my words were law. When it came to humans, at least.

She still seemed skeptical. Running a hand down Teren's back, she muttered, "Do you have to go? You've already been shot once today ... and your mother still needs to remove the bullet."

Teren grimaced. Alanna had already been down here a couple of times to operate on him once she'd found out about his heroics, but he'd sent her away each time. He'd claimed he wasn't ready to leave Nika, but I think he was just avoiding the unpleasantness. I didn't blame him.

"I need to see that this is taken care of, Emma," he told her. "For our children's sake."

Emma's eyes returned to Nika, still as a statue on my bed. Imogen had brought down fresh clothes from Nika's room here, and had helped Emma clean her up and change her. Aside from not breathing or having a heartbeat, Nika looked like she was sleeping.

Emma nodded. Teren kissed her forehead, then stretched across to kiss Nika's. He rose, and Emma squeezed his hand. "Be careful, and come back to me," she said.

"Always," he smiled.

Teren and I left the room together. Ben met us in the hallway. "You two look like you're on a mission." His pale eyes locked onto Teren's. "I want in."

Teren crooked a grin. "We're leaving on foot, so I'll have to carry you ... and I know how much you love that."

Ben made a face, then shook his head. "I still want to go." His eyes drifted to the closed door that Nika was resting behind. "I need to do something," he added. The concern in his voice for this family made me like him already.

Teren and I exchanged glances. Knowing Ben was human, I frowned. "If I compel them as a group, he'll be compelled with them."

Teren was about to speak, but Ben beat him to it. "Actually, I'm part-vampire. You can't compel me." He seemed very proud of that fact. Jerking his thumb at Teren, he added, "Asswipe here already tried."

Teren rolled his eyes. "Let it go already."

Not knowing what they were talking about, I simply shrugged and started heading back upstairs. We ran into Ben's wife in the hallway. She looked even more distraught than Emma. Wearily hugging her husband, she murmured, "I finally got Olivia to sleep. She doesn't understand anything that happened. She's asking a lot of questions, and I don't know what to tell her."

Ben hugged her, running a hand up and down her back. "I know. We'll think of something together."

His wife pulled back, giving him a small smile. Then she seemed to notice that Teren and I were impatient to leave. Looking at the three of us, she pursed her lips. "What's going on? Are you going somewhere?"

Ben sighed, clearly not wanting to have this conversation right now. I didn't either. The longer we waited, the fewer hunters there might be. I wasn't sure how long they would wait around for Dad to show up. "Trace, this is my job. My true job. If there is a problem with vampires, humans, or hunters, I'm the one who helps take care of it. To keep everyone safe."

Her crystalline eyes grew wide. "Is this what you do back home? Is this why you're always scraped and bruised?"

Ben nodded. "This is what I've been doing. This is what I've been keeping from you. I didn't want you to worry. And ... it wasn't my secret to tell."

She shook her head, and a small leaf fell from its resting place in her pale hair. "It's so dangerous ... do you have to do this?"

He looked around the house with a pained expression. "It generally isn't this dangerous." He locked eyes with her. "And yes, I have to do this. If I'm honest with you about what's going on, will you be okay with this?"

She hesitated, and I thought for sure she wasn't going to answer. I reached forward to grab Ben's elbow and tell him we had to go now, but

Teren halted my movement. He gave me a *Just give them a minute* expression, and I bit back my impatience.

Finally, Ben's wife nodded. "If you can be honest with me, then I can try and accept this."

Ben smiled, then kissed her nose. "Good, because I really love you." Squatting down, he looked her in the eye. "This won't take long, and I've got two vampire bodyguards. They'll keep me perfectly safe, so you have nothing to worry about, okay?"

I scoffed at the term bodyguard, and Teren elbowed me in the ribs. Ben's wife didn't notice the exchange; her eyes were all on her husband. She slowly nodded again, and I took the opportunity to drag Ben away by the elbow. "We'll keep him safe, but we do need to leave now."

Her brows furrowed, but she let us leave without complaint. When we got outside, Teren scooped Ben into his arms. Ben groaned, and Teren's lips broke into a wide smile. "Sorry, Ben. You may have a bit of vampire in you, but you can't do this." Ben laughed as he rolled his eyes.

It lightened my heart to see a bit of humor in my nestmates, especially considering Nika's tragedy. I grabbed hold of that feeling, soaking it in, then glanced back at the house. "I'll be right back, Nika," I whispered, then I took off.

Being at my old home was surreal. So much had changed for me in such a short amount of time. I'd lost my sister, been run out of L.A., tried to rebuild my life here. Even tried focusing on something other than hunting. I'd tried to build a relationship with an amazing girl who I really cared about. Then it had all fallen down around me. But I'd risen from the ashes stronger, and Nika would, too.

Lights were on in the rental, but by the *For Rent* sign in the yard, it was clear the house was still vacant. The owner had boxed up Dad's and my stuff when he'd figured out we weren't returning. He'd had to wait a certain amount of time before putting it back on the market, though, and luckily, no one new had rented it yet. That could change at a moment's notice, so I'd have to find the landlord and "convince" him to re-rent the house to me, so I could put the rest of my plan into place.

There was movement near the curtains, eyes watching the front door. We stopped well away from the house, and Teren put Ben down. Ben arranged his clothes and muttered, "Thanks for the ride."

Teren smirked at him, then turned to me. "How do you want to do this?"

I was about to answer him when I felt something. Holding my tongue, I looked behind me. Halina blurred to a stop and I inhaled a deep, cleansing breath at her presence. With an inquisitive brow, she regarded our odd trio. "And what are you boys up to?"

I gave her a sly smile. "We're going to wipe a dozen or so hunters. Care to join us?"

Her fangs crashed down as she grinned. "You don't have to ask me twice."

I put a hand on her arm. "I'm not killing them." She immediately frowned. Hastily, I added, "I have a plan, and I need you to trust me and follow my lead. I'm about to change everything for us, for our species." I gave her an encouraging smile as I let go of her arm.

Her expression betrayed her mixed feelings. She wanted to believe me, but I hadn't always been the most reliable person. Things were different now, though. I was committed to our nest, our family. Seeing the conviction in my eyes, she nodded. "As you wish."

Looking at the group, I laid out my plan. "They all need to be in one area, with no protection from compulsion. They'll be expecting my father, not me, so I think we'll be fine ... at first."

A few minutes later, the plan was in place. Halina headed to the back of the house, while I took the front. Ben was going in a rear bedroom window, while Teren was watching the outside, making sure no one tried to make a run for it. Between the four of us, we should be able to get everyone corralled and subdued.

I started the ball rolling by blurring through the front door. It was locked, but I burst through it with no problems. My extravagant entrance caught everyone's attention in the living room, and a half-dozen weapons were instantly raised in my direction. I squatted, lest someone shoot before I could speak. "No one move! No one make a sound!"

Since the group hadn't been expecting a vampire to show up in their midst, none of them had been protected from me. Like statues, they all halted their movements. Men and women, young and old, stared at me with guns, crossbows, and stakes at the ready. But for my command, I'd be dead already. There were noises at the other end of the house, where those who were far enough away from my voice had been able to escape its effects.

They were quickly shepherded down the hall by Ben and quieted by Halina as she came in through the kitchen. Teren walked through the front door a moment later, dragging a couple of groggy hunters with him. Once they came to enough, I ordered them to silence, then made them wait with the others. To make sure we had everyone together, I strolled through the home with Halina. We found a stowaway hiding in my old closet. He was plugging his ears, but that wasn't enough protection against me. I ordered him to join the others. Once I was satisfied that we had all of them, I went back into the living room.

Halina had them all unarmed and sitting on the ground in lines. There were ten of them. I wasn't sure how many men my dad had convinced to attack the ranch, but if these were the survivors, it must have been a hefty amount. We were exceedingly lucky to have come out of that battle unscathed. A pang went through me as Nika's comatose body went through my mind. Well, mostly unscathed.

"Answer my questions," I intoned, staring down the group. "Is this all of you?"

As one, they replied, "Yes."

I nodded. Good. Tracking down stragglers wasn't something I had time for tonight. "You probably think I'm going to kill you. Probably think I'm going to order your hearts to stop and watch you all instantly die." Muscles tensed and eyes widened as my words stirred innate fears within them. I recognized several people in the group, men and women I'd fought beside. Some of them had saved my life on occasion. Some of them I had saved. Shaking my head, I told them, "You can relax. I'm not going to do that. I'm not even going to erase your memories."

The fear shifted to confusion. Halina looked over at me, concern clear in her eyes. I hadn't told her this part of my plan, just asked her to trust me. I gave her a reassuring smile as I turned back to the group. "I'm going to open your eyes, like mine were opened. I'm going to enlist your help ... in protecting innocent vampires from persecution. Vampires like my girlfriend, and her family."

Halina smiled at me. The captive audience went from confusion to anger. I could feel it radiating in the air, filling it with tension. They'd kill me for that comment alone if they could. None of them believed vampires were innocent creatures who needed protecting. They all believed what I'd believed, that the demon blood obliterated the human host—destroyed the soul. But that wasn't the case. It amplified the senses, heightened the awareness, and created a craving for blood, but the person was still the person they were before. I was still me. I wasn't evil. And neither were my nestmates.

Peace came over me as I thought of who I was before, and who I was now. They weren't as different as I'd once believed. "What I have come to understand through my conversion is that vampires aren't inherently evil. We're people, as good or as bad as any other people." I pointed at each person in turn. "There are certain challenges we have to overcome, but they aren't insurmountable."

Tilting my head, I contemplated the hunger within myself. I hadn't eaten tonight, and I was still not drinking as often as a newborn vampire should, but nothing within me wanted to attack these people. I would wait until I got home to feed. And maybe tonight, because the last few days had been exhausting and I felt like trying something new, I would drink straight from the cow. But that didn't make me any more or less barbaric than a man who killed an animal for its meat.

With a rueful shake of my head, I told the group, "We should be helping those we can, and punishing those who deserve it, both human and vampire." Firming my resolve, I began changing the belief system of the vampire hunters in front of me. "I want you to listen to my words, and believe with all of your heart what I tell you. From now on, all vampires will be treated as humans are treated—innocent until proven guilty. If there is a heinous crime that a vampire has committed, then that vampire will be punished accordingly, but no more innocent blood will be shed. No more killing a vampire simply *because* he's a vampire. No more using unknowing humans as bait. No more torching a harmless man's home. A hunter's methods should never be crueler than the creature they are hunting."

I went on to explain more specifics of how vampires were to be treated. Halina interjected with her own ideas about what was and what was not acceptable. The two of us had a lively debate about the justified murder of killers and rapists. Halina, on occasion, liked to dole out her own form of justice. But what we needed for our two species to coexist peacefully was laws. So, in the end, we decided it was too much of a gray area to be allowed to remain unchecked. Permitting vampires to kill some humans and not others was opening a door that could lead to greater problems; same could be said of hunters too. Vengeance seeking would be discouraged on both sides. It was decided that any vengeance deaths—vampire or hunter—would be discussed by a panel of vampires and hunters alike, and they would determine whether the attack was justified. Both sides would be held accountable for their actions.

By the end of the night, the newly compelled humans were released from their constraints. They began actively engaging in the conversation, and I didn't have to compel them to get their compliance anymore. They fervently believed in what we were trying to do, in the justice we were trying to achieve. The final compulsion I gave them was for all of them to contact everyone they knew, and have them meet me here, so I could compel them too. If every new recruit brought in someone else, I could trance nearly every hunter on the planet given enough time. It was a daunting job, but it was one I felt I had to do.

Teren had actually given me the idea. When he'd suggested that I save my father, I'd begun to wonder how I could have kept one such as him in my life. The loss of his skillset in the world bothered me—there was still a place for hunters, after all, but not for hunters who blindly killed any vampire they encountered. The circle of violence had to stop somewhere.

I wasn't naïve enough to think that fixing the problem would be as easy as compelling the opposing side, but it was a place to start. The vampire side would have to be persuaded in a subtler manner to get them to cooperate with the new rules. And since purebloods could compel, they could undo everything I was trying to put in place with a few words. But I had to believe that most of them would want to live in peace with hunters. Not all, though. Like humans, some vampires enjoyed killing. And those ones wouldn't want to be brought to justice for their crimes. Other vampires might try and protect those brethren, even if they didn't hold the same beliefs as the murdering vampires. But the differences would be settled over time, and I firmly believed that having the hunters work *with* us was far better than having them continue to work against us.

An hour or so before dawn, the group of us finally left my old home. I was anxious to return to Nika. So were Ben and Teren. Halina had some errands to run first, something about fixing Julian's classmates. I left her to it, to rush home to my girl. Hopefully, when I woke tomorrow night, she'd be nearly done with her conversion. And hopefully she'd be okay with what had happened to her.

CHAPTER TWENTY-SIX

Julian

GOING TO SCHOOL the next morning was hard for me, and not just because Arianna no longer remembered me. I was going to school without Nika, and unlike other times when she was too sick or injured to go to school, she wouldn't be joining me again. Ever. She couldn't, now that sunlight was toxic to her.

But it wasn't really that fact that was making me glum as I drove toward the high school in the station wagon I shared with my sister. It was the separation from her emotions that filled me with loneliness. I'd never felt so vacant inside. Was this how everyone else felt? With only their own emotions to keep them company? I supposed I was better off this way in the long run, but I'd be lying if I said I didn't miss Nika's moods. The flash of delight when she had her morning cup of blood. Her annoyance when I wouldn't let her drive. Her resigned amusement when I gushed over my girlfriend ... my ex-girlfriend. Her joy for life. All of that was hidden from me now. I hoped that after her conversion, she still felt the same way about things. Especially about her life. I didn't want her to be sad, now that she was dead.

I pulled into a spot in the parking lot and shut off the car. Automatically, I looked over to Nika's side of the car, but only my backpack was keeping the seat warm. I really didn't want to be here. Guilt had kept me up all night. I should have gone back to the ranch to be with my family, but I'd chickened out and stayed away. Starla had told me she didn't blame me when she'd made up a guest room for me. Jacen had told me that Nika wouldn't know the difference. But *I* knew the difference. I'd run away from her. I wouldn't run tonight, though. I would be there to see her through her conversion, even if my parents forbade me.

They'd called late in the night, when it was clear I wasn't coming back. Dad had told me that was smart of me, that I should stay away from the ranch until Nika had eaten her first meal as a pureblood vampire. In fact, he was sending all the humans to our house today, just to be on the safe side. Nika would be starving when she woke up—so starving she might lash out and attack a loved one. Our family didn't take chances with conversions, and everybody with a pulse would be kept away. They couldn't keep me away, though. I wasn't leaving my sister again.

Snatching my bag, I hopped out of the car and slammed the door. Spring was in full bloom now, and while a chill still clung to the air, it would burn off around midday. This was typically my favorite time of year—not too hot, not too cold. Just right. But the buzzing sounds of nature reawakening were doing nothing for me today. Maybe it was exhaustion, but I just didn't give a shit about the renewal of life right now.

Trey met up with me when I made it to the football field next to the gym. His bleary eyes took a second to focus on me, then he looked back at my car. "Where's Little A?" he asked, his voice oddly nervous.

I shrugged. "She's sick." Halina and Hunter were going to have to wipe the school, erase her from everyone's memories. Or at least blur the details. Halina had already begun doing that with Arianna. I wondered how many of my schoolmates remembered us as a couple, and how many had absolutely no clue we even knew each other.

"Oh," Trey muttered. Looking back at me, he fidgeted as we walked. "She didn't, uh, mention me or anything, did she?"

Puzzled, I tried to think of any reason why Nika would have mentioned Trey recently. "No. Why?"

He exhaled in relief. "Oh good. I just thought she might have mentioned … we had a … weird moment at the dance."

Stunned, I stopped in my tracks. "You hit on my sister?"

Trey sheepishly met my gaze. "On accident. We were dancing, and she looked really good, and I felt bad about that jackass hurting her, so I kind of, sort of, leaned in for a kiss."

Shaking my head at him, I let out a snort and started walking. He quickly caught up to me. "We didn't, though. She took off before ..." His brows condensed as he tried to put together the odd events of that awful dance. "Hey, why does everyone think a janitor found Raquel when I saw you carrying her to the parking lot?"

I sighed ... Halina was going to have to fix that too. "Don't worry about it," I muttered.

Trey shrugged and let it go. "Anyway, I kind of feel weird about the whole thing now. I mean, Little A is practically my sister too. Is she going to be back soon?"

Knowing Trey was about to lose her as surely as I'd lost Arianna, I told him, "Yeah, I'm sure she'll be right as rain tomorrow."

Trey grinned and tucked a stray strand of hair under his cap. "Awesome."

From behind us, I heard a voice call out, "Julian, wait up!" For a split second, I thought it was Arianna calling me. I snapped my head around to look, but it was Raquel jogging down the field, not my girlfriend. Well, of course. Arianna couldn't pick me out of a lineup now.

I paused and waited for Raquel to catch up to us. How she was now in my circle of friends and Arianna wasn't was beyond me. Her tanned cheeks were flushed with color, her long dark hair windblown. Letting out a long breath, she clutched her backpack strap and smiled up at me. "How was your weekend?"

Since I couldn't tell her anything that had happened to me, I simply smiled and said, "It was great." I'd have to work hard to not limp today, which would be quite a feat, since my leg ached like a son of a bitch. Tylenol was going to be my best friend today.

Raquel's dark eyes clearly showed that she didn't believe me. Narrowing them, she examined my face. It made me a bit uncomfortable, and I looked away. "You're lying. You look like you haven't slept in weeks."

I scoffed at her. "You're basically saying I look like crap. Thanks."

She smacked my shoulder, then rubbed it. "I'm saying you look like something's bothering you, and I understand how stuff can eat away at you ... make you do stupid things." She looked down at the scars on her arms hidden under her jacket, scars she believed were self-inflicted. Friendship in her eyes, she told me, "Just know I'm here, and you can talk to me about anything."

Feeling a bit lighter, I nodded and accepted the friendship she was offering me. "Thank you."

The three of us started walking toward our respective classes, and I instinctively scanned the crowds for Arianna. Trey was preoccupied with a group of cheerleaders keeping pace beside us, but Raquel noticed. "Looking for somebody?"

Deciding to test what my grandmother had done last night, I shrugged and said, "Arianna Bennett. You know her?"

Raquel's forehead scrunched as she thought. "Yeah, I think I have a class with her. Why are you looking for her?" She nudged my elbow with hers. "Got a crush on her?" she asked, not a hint of jealousy in her voice. Our relationship had certainly shifted since Raquel's "accident."

Trey picked up on the teasing lilt in Raquel's tone. He glanced our way and joined in the mockery. "Julian's crushing on a girl? Besides you?" I shoved him away from me. Raquel laughed. "When did that happen?" he asked, unfazed.

Even as I smiled, sadness overwhelmed me. Halina had gotten to them last night, and they didn't remember that Arianna and I had been together. How close we'd been, how much we'd cared about each other, how great of friends we were. Like a puff of smoke, our entire relationship was gone, and all I had were my hazy memories of my time with her. I would hold them close, though. They would get me through the dark nights until she was mine again.

I eventually had a class with Arianna. Seeing her was like being hit by a semi-truck. It left me breathless, dazed, seeing stars. It fractured my heart, and scoured my insides. And not having Nika's comforting empathy to help ease the pain only made it worse. I was on my own.

When I walked into class, she was already there, obliviously laughing with her friends. None of them looked my way. Arianna looked amazing—vibrant, happy, full of life and hope. It was a far cry from the last time I'd seen her. Even though that had only been a handful of hours ago, it seemed like a lifetime.

I'd been procrastinating coming to class, so there were no open seats by Arianna, and I was forced to sit on the other side of the room. Most people didn't seem to think that was odd, but a couple of heads swiveled my way—Halina hadn't been able to get to everyone yet—just the key players. The few who still knew quickly brushed off the oddity, and went about their own business. High school couples broke up all the time. And Arianna and I were a low-key couple anyway, barely noticeable on the social scale. The two of us no longer talking wasn't exactly front page news.

I thought about what to say to Arianna all throughout class, but I was suddenly really nervous to be around her. I felt like a bumbling idiot in her presence. In fact, all I managed to say to her was, "Hi."

It was in the doorway, when I was stupidly standing beside it, waiting for her to leave. All her friends were clumped around her, and she wasn't even looking my way. I was positive she hadn't heard me, but then her caramel-colored head shifted to look back at me. Her hazel eyes scanned my face while her full lips momentarily pursed, like she was trying to place me.

"Hi," she muttered back, before her friends pulled her through the hole. Just that brief exchange made my heart pound. She turned to leave, then she looked back at me. A soft, interested smile briefly touched her lips, and butterflies instantly took off in my belly. She was still attracted to me. Halina hadn't taken that away. And if she was still attracted to me, then I still had a shot.

The moment she was gone, I did a little happy dance right there in the classroom. The teacher gave me a funny look, then shook her head in amusement. I didn't care. I was on cloud nine. My girl had smiled at me.

By the end of the day, I'd gotten her to smile at me three times. Each time felt like a huge victory, and filled me with hope. I got back into my car feeling so much brighter, and I wished Nika could feel what I was feeling. Wanting to see my comatose sister, I headed out to the ranch. I knew my parents wouldn't be happy about that, but too bad. My mind was made up. I was going to experience her conversion with her—physically, if not emotionally.

When I pulled into the circular driveway, my dad was standing there with his arms crossed over his chest. His face spoke volumes about his disapproval, and I halfway expected him to point back at the massive iron gate marking the entrance, silently ordering me to leave. He didn't, though. He just watched me stop the car in front of the house. When I opened my door, he sighed. "You shouldn't be here, Julian. I thought we talked about this."

I closed my door with authority. "We did. And there's nowhere else I want to be right now than with my sister." I smirked. "Besides, I can take her if she comes after me."

Dad slowly smiled as he shook his head, then he swished his hand toward the house. "It could be a long wait. We're not sure what time she'll wake up."

When I stepped to his side, I gave him a stoic nod. "I'll wait for her as long as I have to. I'm not leaving her side until this is over, until I know she's safe."

Dad put his arm around my shoulder. "I know, son." Together, we walked inside, to wait for the sun to set, and Nika to rise.

EVEN THOUGH THE sun was still lighting the Earth, everyone in the house was awake. The lower levels were bustling with activity, while we all prepared for my sister's conversion to be complete. Halina, Imogen, and Alanna were discussing which cattle would be best for Nika. Mom and Dad were quietly holding hands, each deep in their private thoughts.

Hunter was a wreck. He was sitting on a chair beside the bed, bobbing his knees and wringing his hands. He'd been doing that for the last three hours. Watching him stress about Nika was exhausting, so I tried to tune him out as best I could. I sat on the other side of the bed, holding her ice-cold hand. Knowing it would feel good to her, I cupped both of my hands around hers.

Gabriel watched me closely. As I wished for time to speed up, he asked me, "Are you sure the bond is gone? Maybe you simply cannot feel it while she undergoes the transformation?"

I looked over at him standing at the foot of the bed. "I'm sure. It's not just the fact that I can't feel her ... I feel the absence of her, like she's been ripped away from me." I looked back at Nika and sighed. "Like she's gone somewhere I can't follow."

Gabriel made an interested noise like what I'd said was fascinating. I ignored it and him. He found almost everything fascinating, and had been curious about our connection since the beginning. No doubt he'd test us once Nika was out of danger.

I didn't want to think about that part of her conversion. The scary, painful, possibly lethal part. My family would never let her starve to death, but they couldn't do much about her immediate discomfort. It would be quick, though. Nika wouldn't have to suffer too much.

After some time passed, both Halina and Hunter stopped moving, closed their eyes, and let out a slow exhale. Their identical reactions caught my attention. Anticipating what they'd sensed, I stood up. "The sun set. Are we moving her outside now?" The closer we could get her to food, the less pain she would have to endure.

Halina looked over at me and nodded. "It's time."

Moving before Hunter could, I reached down and scooped Nika into my arms. He frowned at me. "I can take her," he said.

"Yeah, you can, but I'm going to. Besides, you've done enough," I snipped. Hunter still wasn't my favorite person.

He ground his teeth and looked like he wanted to argue with me, but Halina said, "Drop it. We have more important things to do right now than bicker."

Hunter agreed, so he relaxed his posture and flung his hands at the door. "After you." His tone was only moderately mocking, but I couldn't resist smiling at him as I carried Nika out of his bedroom.

Imogen led us to a far pasture, away from the ranch hand's house. Nika's awakening could get noisy. There were six cows staked to the ground. They didn't look the least bit afraid of what was about to happen. They might not even realize their fellow cattle were dying until it happened to them. Cows weren't the smartest creatures. That fact made it a little easier to stomach them being lined up for the slaughter such as they were. Even still, I purposely ignored the one happily swishing her tail. *Sorry gals, my sister needs your help.*

Mom laid a blanket and a pillow on the ground, and I set Nika on top of it. The blanket was a deep red color that looked black in the glowing light of my family's eyes. That vampiric trait had skipped Nika and me, but since she was a pureblood now, her eyes would probably glow just like everyone else's when she woke up. That would be weird to see on her.

Much like in the bedroom, I sat on one side of Nika, while Hunter sat on the other. He cast me quick glances occasionally, and annoyed, I eventually lifted my eyes to his. "What?" I asked.

Hunter looked over at Mom and Dad. "Should he be out here with her? Should he be sitting right next to her? His heartbeat will be the first one she hears."

Dad's brow furrowed, like he was wondering the same thing. Frowning, I curled my fingers around Nika's hand. I wasn't going anywhere unless I absolutely had to. I narrowed my eyes as I stared Hunter down. "Just try and move me."

Halina smacked the back of my head, but when I twisted around to look up at her, she was smiling. She liked seeing this more aggressive side of me. "Play nice." Her eyes shifted to Hunter. "He may stay."

Hunter shrugged and returned his attention to Nika. I wasn't sure how long we waited, but I eventually began to shiver from the cold. Mom squatted beside me, wrapping a blanket around my shoulders. I'd barely registered her zipping away to get one—all my focus was on Nika. "Thanks," I muttered, looking up at her.

She smiled at me, then moved a strand of Nika's hair behind her ear. Watching Mom watch her daughter, I thought of all the stories that I'd heard about my family's conversions. None of them were pleasant. "This is going to hurt her, isn't it?"

Mom's smile faded some as she turned to face me. "Yes ... it will." I noticed the other vampires looking away, even Hunter; their expressions told me more than Mom's honest answer. Mom put her arm around me, squeezing me tight. "It won't last. She'll be okay."

Swallowing a knot in my throat, I nodded. Just for the time being, I was grateful my emotional bond with Nika was gone, and I wouldn't have to experience the pain with her. Then I felt guilty for feeling that way. I pushed both emotions aside. This wasn't a time to be selfish. I was here for Nika, and Nika alone.

I was lost in the details of my sister's face—the ridge of her nose, the outline of her lips, the wavy mahogany hair—when her eyes suddenly sprang open. She'd been still for so long, I instinctively jumped at the unexpected movement. Her eyes instantly locked on me. The dark brown depths that I'd looked into on countless occasions seemed completely different highlighted in the phosphorescent glow of our species. She was otherworldly as she stared at me. The effect of her eyes seeped into my bones. It was like soaking in a hot tub, or sipping a glass of warm blood ... completely relaxing. My heartbeat slowed as her gaze trapped me.

A low, menacing growl rumbled through the night. It sent a shiver up my spine, and it took me a minute to register that the sound had originated from Nika's ribcage. She'd never been able to make such a threatening noise before. Her mouth opened, and I could see her fangs were fully extended, as long and sharp as I'd ever seen them. Almost like she was pulling me into her with her eyes, I leaned forward. She leaned up, like she was going to whisper something in my ear. Her hand weakly clasped my neck; it was so cold, it felt like my skin was burning.

"Julian! Don't!" A hand on my shoulder stopped my descent and yanked me backward. I fell back on my elbows, and the jolt of the landing snapped me out of my reverie. Nika's expectant face instantly transformed into pain and grief as the agony of hunger struck her full force. Clearly biting back the urge to scream in pain, she clutched her stomach and curled into a ball.

I scrambled onto my hands and knees, but Halina's strong arms kept me at a distance. "Nika! You need to drink!" I shouted.

She didn't seem to understand my words as she growled and groaned. When Hunter laid a soothing hand on her, she snarled at him, tried to nip him. He didn't react to her attack, just soothingly told her, "It's okay. I know how hungry you are. Smell the food ... it will take the pain away."

Her eyes swung back to me. There was so much longing in her gaze, I took a step back. Hunter was right—I shouldn't be here. In jerking, pained movements, Nika rose to her feet. One hand still clutching her stomach, like the healed wound Dad had told me about was still there, she clamored to me. Mom and Dad stepped in front of me protectively, and Hunter grabbed Nika from behind. Shocking all of us, Nika growled at him, then jerked him over her shoulder. He landed a few feet away. Dad glanced at Mom.

We all looked back at Nika with trepidation. Ignoring the cows set up for her, she stormed my way. Dad held up his hands. "Not him, Nika. Look behind you. They're for you." Nika reached out with one hand and batted Dad aside like he weighed nothing. Mom's eyes widened, and Halina shoved me behind her, forcing me back several steps.

"I don't want to hurt you, Nika," Mom pleaded. "Please, turn around."

Imogen tried forcefully turning Nika around, but Nika shoved her back. Then Nika stumbled and cried out in unmistakable pain. It broke my heart. I wanted to comfort her, like I'd done all my life, but I knew if I took a step near her, she'd drain me dry without a conscious thought. Falling to one knee, Nika let out a choking sob. Hunter returned and kneeled in front of her. Cupping her cheek, he tilted her head to the cattle. "Drink," he urged. Ignoring his food suggestion, she swung her head back to me.

Dad returned and cast a worried glance at me. "You're distracting her from the cows."

Heart beating wildly now, I whispered, "Do I run back to the house?"

Dad shook his head. "That will only make her chase you. Just stay still."

I froze. I didn't even blink. Hunter tried coercing her again, but Nika wasn't listening to him; she was listening to my heart. Rising to her feet, she started walking toward me again. Her steps were erratic, like she was drunk. She seemed weaker than before, like staying upright was a struggle. Blood-red tears coursed down her cheeks as her face contorted in pain. I could only imagine how much she was hurting right now. And I was making it worse for her, and dangerous for the both of us. "I'm sorry," I whispered.

She halted at my words, tilting her head like she was trying to understand me. Dad blurred from my side, but I was too focused on my sister to really care what he was doing. Hunter put a hand on Nika's shoulder, trying to redirect her, but she resisted, taking a step toward me instead.

A pained cry filled the air, followed by the thud of a heavy body landing. The aroma of fresh blood blossomed around us—strong, sweet, intoxicating. It smelled good to me, but to Nika, it was an undeniable attraction. Turning from me, she groaned in pain, clutching her stomach. Hunter caught her, sweeping her into his arms. He blurred her to the cow Dad had just ripped open, and dropped her beside the beast. Mouth open wide, like a man dying of thirst, Nika dove for the cow's neck. Her grunts of pain shifted to light purrs of satisfaction. I exhaled in relief. She was eating, and she wasn't eating me. We would both be fine now.

Dad wiped the blood off his mouth with his sleeve. Beaming with pride, he watched his daughter. Hunter closed his eyes, then looked over at Dad. "Thank you," he told him, his voice earnest.

Dad smiled and clapped his back. "I wasn't about to lose my daughter, or my son."

Seeing Nika gorge herself was a distressing sight—before today, she wouldn't even watch Dad drain the small chickens he bought for dinner. I made myself step closer, though. I wanted to be there for her, now that she was more herself. When she finally lifted her head from the beast, her breath was heavy and her jaw was stained dark red; the slash Dad had made hadn't been subtle.

"Nika," I gently said. "Are you okay?"

Her face distorted in discomfort as she sleepily looked my way. "Julie? I feel ... funny. What happened?" Sympathy coursed through me. She didn't know. She didn't know she died, and Hunter converted her. I had no idea how she'd react once we told her. I was about to start in on the explanation when she blinked, then did a double-take. "Did I almost ... eat you?"

Her face looked so disgusted by the prospect that I laughed. "Yeah, you did. Bitch," I teased.

She laughed once, then her face contorted. "I'm so hungry. Why am I so hungry?" Her weary eyes searched out her maker. Hunter took her hand. "We'll explain everything soon, but you need to eat first." He indicated the string of cattle waiting. "These are for you. Drink."

Nika pursed her lips, an odd move around fangs, but she was too hungry to resist the shackled meals. Hunter helped her to the next one, and she almost timidly bit into it. Her movements became much more aggressive when the hot blood poured into her, though, and she easily subdued the whining animal. I turned away, not wanting to watch.

Sitting on the damp grass nearby, I listened to my sister fell two more cows. It was disorienting, to hear her, to see her movements from the corner of my eye, sense her location in my head, but not feel her emotions. I could only guess how she was doing, and I'd never had to do that before. It made me sad, made me feel alone, even though I wasn't.

I was contemplating if I would always feel this alone without her when she sat down on the grass beside me. Smiling, I looked up at her. She had blood all down the front of her shirt. Shaking my head, I pointed at it. "You, uh, got a little on you."

She glanced down at her top, then grimaced. "God, what a mess. I don't know what came over me. That was ... weird." I sighed, and Nika sighed with me. "I died, didn't I? I died, and Hunter turned me."

My eyes misted as I nodded. "Something like that. Hunter's father got you with a knife to the stomach." I looked down at my hands. "I'm so sorry I wasn't there, Nick."

She rested her head on my shoulder, and I rested my head against hers. I made myself ignore the fact that no heartbeat thudded in my ears, but the absence of it was too great to block out. As our family gave us a moment of privacy, Nika murmured, "I can't feel you anymore. It's like there's a hole in me where you used to be."

A stubborn tear ran down my cheek. "I know. It's like that for me too."

I sniffed, holding in my pain. Lifting her head, Nika grabbed my cheek, drying my tears with her ice-cold fingers. "Don't be sad. I'm okay. I'm still here. I'm still alive ... in a way. And maybe this is a good thing. Maybe this was the only way to shut off the bond. And it was time to shut it off. You deserve your privacy with Arianna. And I ..." She twisted around to look at Hunter watching her with hungry eyes. She inhaled a quick breath and held it. If the bond she shared with him was even remotely as strong as the bond between my parents, then their relationship was about to get very intense.

I forced a smile, even though my heart was cracking. She didn't know about Arianna yet either. That one was going to hurt her, too, although, not nearly as much as it hurt me. "Yeah ... maybe you're right."

Pulling her fingers from my face, I held her hand. It was clearly hard for her to do so, but she finally managed to stop ogling Hunter and turned her attention back to me. "Are you happy?" I asked. It might be too early for her to really know that answer yet, the news was still sinking in, but I needed to hear her say she was, even if it was just to appease me.

Her smile breezy, she nodded. "I'm completely content."

I smirked and bumped her shoulder. "That's probably because you just ate half the herd." She stuck her tongue out at me; it was still bright red. I laughed, the pain squeezing my heart easing. Glancing back at the two cows left standing, I more seriously asked her, "Did you get enough to eat?"

Nika patted her tummy with her free hand. "I will burst if I eat anymore. I don't know why they thought I needed that many."

Extending my aching leg, I gently massaged as close to the wound as I could get. It already itched. "Better safe than sorry, I guess."

Nika put her hand on my injury. The chill from her touch soothed my pain, even through my jeans. "I'm sorry I stalked you," she whispered.

I wrapped my arm around her shoulder, and she nuzzled into my warmth. "No harm done, Nick."

I thought to tell her about Arianna then, but Hunter starting walking toward us. Nika stiffened in my arms like he'd pressed a block of ice against her back. She snapped her head around to look at him, and a low growl burrowed out of her chest. His eyes danced with interest as a similar growl escaped him. It was obvious from the stiff way he moved that he was trying to control his actions as much as he possibly could. Nika didn't have his level of control yet. She zipped to her feet and blurred into his arms. They were all over each other after that. Hands and tongues, groaning and moaning, and, ugh, grinding. I started to look away, but Dad busted up the party before I could. He grabbed Nika by the elbows, and yanked her off Hunter. Hunter lunged for her, but Mom and Imogen grabbed him before he could take Nika back. Being held a few feet apart, the pair of newly bonded vampires were breathless, squirming, and fighting against their restraints to attack each other again. I was positive they'd have sex right here in this bloody field—regardless of who was watching—if either one of them was released.

I shot to my feet, eager to get away from them before I saw something that I wouldn't be able to un-see. Halina started belly laughing. Wiping tears from her eyes, she laughed out, "This is going to be so much fun!" By the annoyed look on Dad's face, I could tell he didn't agree.

CHAPTER TWENTY-SEVEN

Nika

MY LIFE WAS completely different, and yet, it was completely the same. I was still the hopeful, romantic girl who loved her family more than anything. I was just also undead and completely reliant upon blood to survive. But I was happy. I'd saved Hunter, and he'd saved me. And we now shared something so deep and meaningful, it nearly brought me to tears just thinking about it. I loved him, with every section of my unbeating heart, and I knew he loved me, too, just as much. That kind of unshakable devotion was comforting. It brightened all the potential dark spots. Like the downside to becoming a full vampire. And there were quite a few of those.

I wasn't thrilled that the sun was now off-limits to me. I'd enjoyed sunbathing, watching the rays sparkle off the water wall at the library, going to school with my friends. But all those things were impossible for me now. I was confined to darkness, just like Halina, just like Hunter. At least I wasn't alone.

The loss of the sun, along with the loss of food, being able to touch silver, ever physically aging past sixteen, and the chance of having children one day weren't what I missed the most, though. Not yet. No, what bothered me more than anything was no longer being able to feel what Julian felt. I hadn't been prepared for how much I'd miss that connection. There was a part of me that was empty inside, like it had been plucked out. I knew Julian felt the same hollowness inside him, but only because he'd told me. He hadn't told me everything he was going through, though. For the first time ever, Julian could keep things from me, and I didn't like it.

I saw his sullenness, the physical effect of some inner turmoil, but I didn't know the cause, didn't know the level of his pain. It was unnerving not to know. It put me on edge. All I could do was surmise what was wrong with him, and I hated having to rely on guessing. But he wouldn't talk to me about it, so what else could I do?

Sitting beside me, as he often was, Hunter rubbed my thigh. His hand was pleasantly comfortable, now that we were the same temperature. "You okay?"

He asked me that constantly, like he was sure that any minute now I was going to go into hysterics over what he'd done to me. But what he'd done was save my life, and I wasn't about to complain about being alive. "I'm fine. Just worried about Julian."

Hunter nodded, his nearly black eyes pensive but unsurprised. Me being concerned over my brother was nothing new. I'd only been a full vampire for a few days, but in those days, Julian had been my main focal point of distress. He was asleep at the moment, only separated from me by our mutual bathroom. It might as well have been an entire country, though, with how distant I felt from him.

"He's fine," Hunter told me. This also wasn't new. He often told me I had nothing to worry about concerning Julian, that we had much more pressing problems. And I supposed we did. Where we were going to live for one thing.

Ever since my conversion, Hunter had become my world. I was drawn to him as surely as a flower turned its petals toward the sun. If we were separated, even by just a few hundred feet, it felt like someone was pulling on a piece of me. It made my entire body ache. When he started to approach me, it had the opposite effect. I felt warmth in every cell, every muscle. Desire rushed through me like a tidal wave, nearly knocking me senseless. Hunter felt the same energy pulsing through him, and our unions were usually very explosive. It was more than a little embarrassing.

My father was being put through the wringer. He watched me close when Hunter was away, waiting for signs that the erotic bond was kicking in. He also watched me close when Hunter was nearby. It was a lose-lose for him. Hunter and I were going to be together, and there wasn't much Dad could do about it. He still tried, though. Every time the bond rushed Hunter and I together, Dad was there to pull our writhing bodies apart. We hadn't had a chance to consummate our vampiric bond yet, but we'd come very close.

Dad wouldn't let Hunter stay here in the city with us during the day, which meant Hunter had to run back to the ranch before every sunrise. He didn't like to part with me—our goodbyes usually took hours—and I was a little afraid that one day Hunter wouldn't make it back to the ranch before the sun rose. I wanted him to stay here at the house because of that. And to keep the fiery part of our bond under control. We were naturally attracted to each other, but the intenseness leapt a hundred notches higher when we were forced to separate and reunite. Dad groaned after every sunset, when he watched me nearly panting with desire because Hunter was running to me. Like I said, embarrassing.

Dad refused to let him stay here, though. He just kept saying that I was sixteen, and too young to live with a boy. He wouldn't let me stay at the ranch either. He seemed to think Halina and the others wouldn't mind Hunter and I together as a couple as much as he did, and he was right about that. None of them had Dad's level of aversion to the two of us having sex. They knew we were both head over heels in love, and that was enough for them. Dad just wasn't ready to give up his little girl yet. Even if her heart had stopped beating.

It was easiest on our bond if Hunter and I remained together. It kept our desires in check, although, every part of me still burned to kiss him. He was very attractive, after all. And sweet, strong, sensitive, and recently, determined. He was going to make the world a safer place for vampires, and in a way, for humans, too. By changing the way vampire hunters felt about our species, he was slowly turning the tides. He was bringing order to the chaos, laws to the lawless, peace to the violence. I was sure there were a ton of people who wouldn't like that fact, but I believed in him, and in what he was doing.

That was why I went with him every night when he went to convert a new group of hunters. It was dangerous, and Dad didn't like me going, but I was stronger now. I was also blessed with the power to compel humans, too, so I could help Hunter in his mission. It gave me purpose, and helped take my mind off Julian, and all the things I had lost.

Standing, Hunter extended his hand to me. "We should go. There will probably be a few hunters waiting for us, if we're lucky." Each group of tranced hunters was asked to contact other hunters and have them wait at Hunter and Connor's old home for "special instructions."

Rising from the bed I didn't sleep in anymore, I took his offered palm. "Okay, let's go change some minds."

From down the hall, I heard a sleepy voice mutter, "Nika ... I want you to stay in tonight."

I rolled my eyes and walked out to the hallway, pulling Hunter with me. Dad was at the end of the hall, leaning against his bedroom door. He looked exhausted, like any second he would topple over. He usually tagged along when Hunter and I went to meet with the hunters, then he stayed up afterward with his door open, listening for any sound of inappropriate behavior. Dad was burning himself at both ends, trying to watch over me all night long. Guilt washed through me as his haggard appearance cracked my heart.

Releasing Hunter, I walked toward Dad. He straightened, doing his best to look authoritative, even though he was dressed in his pajamas. Ignoring the stubborn stance he was giving me, I wrapped my arms around his neck. For the first time in my life, my father was no longer ice-cold to the touch; we were the same. "I love you, Daddy," I whispered in his ear. "But you need to let me go."

He buckled under my words. Arms tight around my waist, he murmured, "How am I supposed to do that? You're my baby ..."

Pulling back, I locked gazes with the pale blue eyes I had loved all my life. "And I always will be. Letting me go doesn't mean you have to give me up."

A corner of Dad's mouth twitched into the smile that made Mom giggle like a schoolgirl. Widening it, he tucked a strand of hair behind my ear. "You're so much like your mother. I think that's another reason why this is so hard for me." He looked behind me at Hunter. I itched to look with him. The bond buzzed in me, goading me to return to Hunter, but I shoved the feeling aside so I could focus on my father. He needed me more at the moment. Eyes intently focused on my sire, Dad said, "You're in possession of one of the most important things in my life. Treat her accordingly."

Hunter's smooth voice as he answered was like an electric current down my spine. "She *is* the most important thing in my life, and I won't let anything happen to her."

Dad returned his eyes to me, sighed, then kissed me on the forehead. "Be careful. You're a pureblood vampire now, but you're not invincible."

I kissed his cheek. "We'll be safe. Get some sleep." Dad gave me a face that clearly told me he wouldn't be sleeping so long as I was gone. I gave him one of my mother's famous do-not-argue-with-me expressions. "You need rest, you're about to keel over. I'll be fine with Hunter, and besides, Halina's in the city. You know she'll show up at the meeting spot. The tranced hunters will be there, too. We've done this all week, Dad. There's nothing for you to worry about."

Dad relaxed a little but then his eyes shifted back to Hunter. I could see the distrust there, and I knew it was more over my body than my safety this time. I moved into Dad's line of sight so he would look at me again. "We'll be good. I promise."

Even though he nodded at me, by the tight way Dad pressed his lips together, I knew he probably wouldn't sleep well tonight, if at all. Poor guy. We separated, and I returned to Hunter. The buzz from my body amplified as we approached each other. Even only being a few feet apart caused a reaction, albeit a much smaller one. Hunter had a euphoric smile when he wrapped me in his arms. I felt it, too, as I leaned up to kiss him. Dad cleared his throat, and I forced my lips to detach from Hunter's. It was difficult.

Looking back at him, I cringed. Wanting to change the focus, and maybe suffering from a little wishful thinking, I brightened my expression and asked, "So, since you're more comfortable with all of this, can Hunter stay with us now?"

Dad switched the scowl on his face to a smirk. "I never said I was comfortable, and no. No, he can't." He grinned at me as he added, "Nice try."

Hunter and I stepped outside, and I paused to take in the vibrant air. There was an energy to the darkness that I'd never noticed before. It pulsed around me, beckoning me into shadowy corners and moonlit pathways. Being nocturnal appealed to the vampiric blood pumping through my veins, and while I missed the sun, there was an abundant amount of beauty to be found at night, away from the could-be garish light of day.

It was the middle of the night for humans, which was the middle of the day for us. It astounded me some that I'd already acclimated to the time difference. I would have thought I'd be tired and sluggish for days after my conversion, but I'd felt fine from that very first night. It even felt natural being up all night long.

Hunter smiled as he watched me enjoying the twilight. "I can't say I'm happy about everything that has transpired recently, but ... you certainly are a sight to behold in the moonlight."

I laughed as I grabbed his hand. "So are you."

We walked at a human pace toward Hunter's old home, the place where I'd first laid eyes on him. Just before the house, we ran into Rory and Cleo. The pair of ex-vampire hunters were among the first batch that Hunter had compelled. Rory was a wide man, a six-foot-five wall of solid muscle. Even still, I could probably bench-press him if I wanted. Cleo was the opposite. Long, lean, and dark as the night, she was lithe and swift. She vanished so quickly at times, I nearly thought her a ghost. They were sort of Hunter's lieutenants now, helping him with everything and anything. They even saluted him when he came into view.

"Only three this time." Rory bowed his head. His dark hair was cut close to the scalp; a thin white line ran parallel to his right eye. He'd had a close call once. Probably more than once, considering his line of work.

"Three is better than none," Hunter said as Rory and Cleo fell into step behind us. Their heartbeats were low and smooth, untroubled. Whatever anxiety they might have once felt about our kind, they certainly didn't feel it now. Glancing over his shoulder, Hunter asked, "Any trouble with these three?"

Cleo shook her head. "No, they believe they're here for important intel. They're just waiting for the lead hunter to arrive ... Hunter." Her mouth curved into a one-sided smirk. She had the kind of lips men fantasized about—so plump you'd almost think she'd had them cosmetically altered. Cleo wasn't the type, though. Everything about her was natural. She wasn't out to impress anybody. Her mission was her life, and now her mission was Hunter's mission.

Hunter twisted back to the front and continued leading us to his old home. Some things had changed drastically since he'd last lived there. Some things were charmingly the same, like the effeminate salmon color of the walls. It appeared slightly darker at night, but it was still definitely pink. The familiarity brought a smile to my face, and I hoped the landlord never changed the color.

Halina arrived just as we reached the door. Gabriel was with her. She beamed at Hunter, but restrained herself from hugging him in front of the "troops." Instead, she merely nodded at him, then opened the door for us all. Rory and Cleo rushed inside first, to calm and gather the new trio of hunters who were about to be brought into the fold. Hunter paused for a moment, listening to the greetings, then strode in. Not expecting a vampire in their midst, the hunters in the living room were slow to react. Their brief hesitation was all we needed. Calm as a summer day, Hunter told them. "Don't move, don't speak. I have something to tell you, and I want you to listen very carefully."

Forty-five minutes later, we had three more eager volunteers ready to champion the cause for vampire rights. Hunter was very careful to stress that every precaution should still be taken when dealing with vampires, but now, vampires would be given a chance to prove their innocence and not just murdered unduly. It was a way to give vampires, like my family, a chance to live in peace. We wouldn't be hunted simply because of what we were. We could relax ... somewhat.

Once Hunter gave the new recruits the order to send any "uninformed" friends our way, we were free to leave. Halina gave Hunter a sad look as he told her goodbye. Even though she tried to hide it as she repeated his sentiment, I could see the longing in her eyes. Hunter had been spending all his time with me. That had to be hard on her, since they were bonded, too.

Since it was still early in the day for us, we took a long, slow walk around the city. I'd never remembered Salt Lake being so beautiful, or Hunter being more at peace. He was finally okay with what he was, and with what I was.

Whether planned or by force of habit, we ended up at the library before long. We walked up the sloping ramp to the rooftop garden. Being amid the plush green grasses and slumbering flowers was soothing. Sitting on a railing, we looked out over the twinkling lights of the city spread out around us. While I'd been taught to not get too attached to a place, since my life would be a constant juggling act of lies and movement, I thought Salt Lake would always have a place in my heart. *Different by Nature*, just like me.

Hunter grabbed my hand and stroked my fingers. Our bond was calm and quiet since we were together. Everything was calm and quiet. Remembering something that I'd grabbed for Hunter a few nights ago, before everything in my life had changed, I reached into my pocket and pulled out a small wooden puzzle box.

When I handed it to Hunter, his eyes widened. "How did you ... ?" He couldn't finish his question in his confusion.

My grin was enormous as I watched him finger the contraption. "It was in your jacket, in that old man's house. By the look on your face when you'd told me your dad had bugged it, I figured it was important to you." Pointing at the side of it, I added, "I took the tracker out, by the way."

Hunter stared at me, dumbfounded. "You figured out how to open it?"

Laughing a little, I grabbed it back. Simultaneously pressing on two smooth wooden sections, I popped it open. "Wasn't so hard." Truth was, it *had* been a little tricky, and I'd nearly smashed the stupid box against the wall, but the stunned look on Hunter's face was priceless, so I didn't mention that.

Hunter gingerly took the box back. The inside was lined with velvet, and the only thing that I had found inside—besides the tracker—was a picture and a ring. The picture was obviously of Hunter and his family, back when he and his sister were younger and his mother was still alive. They'd all looked so happy and normal, but even back then they'd been hunters, born and bred. Hunter removed the photo, smiling at the family members he'd lost. "My sister was twelve in this picture. She was given her first stake a few weeks later ..." He sighed and shook his head. "Odd how much things change. Dad asked me what she'd think of me now. Sometimes I wonder the same thing."

I ran my hand up and down his arm. "She'd see that you were doing the right thing, and she'd be very proud of you." I kissed his shoulder. "I'm very proud of you." He smiled down at me, and I pointed to the ring in the box. "Is that your mother's?"

Nodding, Hunter replaced the photo and pulled out the golden circle with a small, modest diamond solitaire attached to it. "Her wedding ring. Her first one anyway. Mom and Dad didn't have much in the beginning, doing what they did for a living. Dad eventually gave her a nicer one, but this simple one was always her favorite. Evangeline took it once Mom died. Now that she's dead, too ... I guess it's mine."

I folded his fingers around the ring. "It's beautiful."

Hunter grinned at me. "Maybe I'll give it to you one day? When you're older, of course." He laughed, and I playfully pushed him away from me.

"Maybe someday I'll agree to wear it ... when I'm older, and ready to settle down with one man."

I gave him a teasing smile, and he pursed his lips in feigned displeasure. "Mmmm hmmm."

Laughing, I leaned into his side. Hunter fingered his mother's jewelry, then lovingly put it back into the box, and back into his pocket. "Thank you for saving these for me. It means a lot."

I exhaled in contentment. "I know. You're welcome."

After a peaceful, quiet moment, Hunter whispered, "Are you hungry? We could get you some more to eat."

Even though I'd downed a huge glass of blood almost the instant I'd woken up, I was hungry again, almost on the edge of starving. That was a side effect of being a newborn. It didn't control me, though. *I* controlled me.

Resting my head on his firm shoulder, I murmured, "Yes, I need to eat again, but I don't want to leave just yet. It's too perfect here. With you."

I could feel Hunter chuckle, then felt him kiss my head. "Whatever you want, Nika. Whatever you want."

We stayed there longer than I'd anticipated, just enjoying the still night, the hard-earned freedom we'd won, and each other's comforting company. When only a few hours remained in our day, Hunter stood. With hardly any effort at all, he swept me into his arms. I laughed as I curled my arms around his neck. "If we stay here 'til sunrise, you'll starve to death."

I laughed a little harder. "And we'll both fry to a crisp."

His smile faltered, and I hurriedly gave him a soft peck. "I'm fine with my life."

His smile returned, although, not as bright as before. Keeping me cradled in his curved arms, he jetted off for my house. If I was going to eat, I preferred to do it from a steaming thermos like the rest of my family. Attacking cattle and wayward animals wasn't my style. And humans ... no ... I didn't ever want to bite a human. My teeth were reserved for Hunter, and Hunter alone.

Like we hadn't made love again yet, we also hadn't shared blood again either. I wanted to, but Hunter insisted we should wait until I was stronger. Personally, I thought I was plenty strong enough to handle him drinking from me, and now that the mild concern of Hunter possibly killing me was off the table, I couldn't wait to try it again. But I knew feeding like that made him slightly uncomfortable still, so I didn't push him on the matter.

Like a perfect gentleman, Hunter escorted me into my home, made sure I got something to eat, then twisted to leave me once I was finished with my meal. I grabbed his arm before the bond even had a chance to kick in. "And where do you think you're going? It's a couple of hours before daylight."

Hunter grinned as he wrapped his arms around me, then he sighed. "You saw Halina. She misses me, and, truth be told, I miss her too. Our bond isn't as strong as *this* ..." he squeezed me for emphasis, "... but it's still there." When he pulled back, guilt was clear on his face. "I'm sorry, but I'd like to spend some time with my sire."

Smiling, I shook my head. "You don't have to be sorry for that, remember. I'm used to this world, and I understand how it works. What you and my grandmother have is special, and I won't get in the way of it. If you need to go see her, then go. I'll be fine here with my family."

Peace smoothed his features. "Okay ... I'll miss you, though. So much, I think it will physically hurt me."

I patted his chest, where the ache between us when we were apart was the greatest. "It *will* physically hurt you. Me too." I sighed contently, loving him with every fiber of my being.

He kissed me. "Okay." He kissed me again. "Okay, I'm leaving now." He didn't move, just kissed me again. "Okay, for real now, I'm leaving." Again, he didn't move, and once he realized he hadn't, he laughed. "Hmm ... you may need to help me, or this could go on for the rest of the night."

I forcefully turned him around, pushed him to the entryway, then shoved him away from me. A shiver of discomfort rippled through my soul. I ignored it, and waved goodbye to him. Hunter nodded, inhaled a deep breath, then walked out the door with halting, jerky movements. As he streaked away from me, the ripples grew into waves that cruelly bashed against my heart with merciless abandon. I stomached the sensation, and closed the door on my love and the last few shadows of the night.

Twisting around, I debated going upstairs to my bedroom to read for a bit, or going straight to my hidey-hole beneath the earth. My new bedroom was originally put in for Halina, so she'd have a place to sleep if she was in town and wanted to stay the night. I'd taken it over since my conversion. It wasn't nearly as nice as the below-ground halls at the ranch, but it blocked out the sun, and that was really all that mattered.

The entrance to it was buried in the hall closet under the stairs. I had to weasel my way past winter jackets every night to go to bed. But secrecy was ingrained in us, and even if things were drifting toward peace, we relied on our clandestine ways to keep our existence a secret.

I was just cursing my family for having way too many clothes when I heard my brother's voice drifting down the stairs. "Can I talk to you a second, Nick?"

Wondering what Julian was doing awake, I shifted to head up to his room. When I got there, he was sitting up in his bed, rubbing his eyes. He was dressed in his typical pajamas—a black T-shirt and gray lounge pants. His hair was adorably tousled. Arianna would be all over him if she could see him right now. I wondered if she knew about me, and if so, why she hadn't called me yet. I'd been too preoccupied adjusting to my new life, and this crazy, intense attraction to Hunter to call her. That made me feel pretty crappy. I was being a bad friend. I made a mental note to call her tomorrow night.

Sitting beside Julian, I smiled and asked, "Why are you up so early?"

I expected him to smile in return, but he stared down at his lap, a slight frown on his face. "I ... uh ... wanted to talk to you in private. I've been wanting to all week."

Now I frowned. "Oh? What about?"

For some reason, dread filled my belly. It amplified along with Julian's dour expression. "School ..."

I blinked in surprise. By his face, I'd expected something much more sinister. Julian peeked up at me. "You know, what the kids and teachers think happened to you."

Wondering what he was getting at, I said, "Dad already told me. For now, most of the student body thinks I decided to go back to homeschooling to finish out high school." And then, after Julian graduated, the memory of both of us would be blurred from the students and staff. It was what my family had done for my father, although, it was going to be much trickier with us, since the school population was so much bigger than when Dad was in school. It wouldn't matter too much, though. The natural aging process would erase us from the minds of the people Halina couldn't get to.

Julian bit his lip and started working it between his teeth. I nearly expected him to gnaw through the tender flesh. "What?" I asked, a little irritated that I couldn't sense what he was feeling right now.

Sighing, he released his mouth. "It's not really about school. It's about ... Arianna."

My spine tingled. Why hadn't she called or come over yet? "I've been worried about her. Is she okay? She must still be in shock over what happened." A thought occurred to me, and I let out a weary exhale. "Is she scared of me now that I'm a pureblood? I know Halina and Hunter kind of freak her out. Is that why she's staying away? Why she hasn't called?"

Julian snapped his head away from me, but not before I saw his eyes start to water. The emptiness in my soul where his emotions should have been assaulted me with painful silence. "Julian ... where's Arianna?"

He looked back at me with a hard swallow. "She's gone, Nick. Grandma erased her ... she took everything."

I shot off the bed like he'd just lit it on fire; his tired eyes only watched me. "What? No, she wouldn't do that! Arianna is your girlfriend. My best friend. She wouldn't do that to us!"

His sad eyes lost focus as he stared behind me. "She did. I watched her. Arianna had a breakdown after what happened to you. She freaked out, broke up with me, told her parents everything." His eyes refocused on mine. "Grandma ... was on edge, I think. She wiped her clean, just like she promised me she would."

I collapsed on the bed, no longer able to stand. "I can't ... no ... she has to remember ..."

Julian put his hand over mine. "She doesn't. I see her every day at school, and she has no clue who I am. None of our friends remember us being together either. It's like the last few months never existed. Like I'd just been dreaming them ..."

He choked on his words, and I put aside my pain to focus on Julian's. He loved her, and she didn't know him. I couldn't even imagine how much he hurt, and it felt a little selfish, but for the first time, I was remotely happy that I couldn't feel it. Sympathy for him weighed down my spirit. "Julie ... I'm so sorry. Why didn't anyone tell me?"

He sniffed and looked at his lap again. "I told them not to. I wanted to be the one to tell you. I wanted to tell you right away, but ... I couldn't talk about it, and you had so much on your plate already."

"You should have told me. No matter what is happening to me, I want to know what you're going through." I sighed. "Especially now that we can't feel each other. Talking is all we have now." Julian nodded, but didn't comment.

I rubbed his back while we sat in silence. My vision hazed with red tears as I remembered all the times that I'd had with my quirky human friend, times that she didn't remember now. "I can't believe she's gone. I never got a chance to say goodbye."

Julian straightened and looked over at me. Wearing our grandmother's confidence, he told me, "I'm going to win her back, Nick. She might not remember me, or what we were, or what we had, but I know she's still attracted to me." He gave me a sly yet determined smile. "I don't care how long it takes, but I'm going to make her fall in love with me again. She'll love both of us again."

He seemed so sure of that, and I believed him. But still, love didn't guarantee that we wouldn't lose her. "Won't she just freak out again ... and won't Grandma just wipe her again?"

Julian shook his head. "With what Hunter has been doing, we shouldn't be chased and shot at anymore ... I hope. That was what freaked her out, not what we are. I mean, you had just *died* ... she was overwhelmed. Grandma shouldn't have wiped her so fast. She should have given her time to adjust."

He nodded with even more conviction. "That's what I'll do differently. I'll give her time to adjust. I'll go so slowly with her, we'll make snails look fast." He grabbed one of my hands with both of his. "I'm not giving up, so don't worry, okay. I'm going to fix this. I promise."

I smiled at his optimistic determination. "I believe you."

I knew it was probably going to take some doing on his part, and a great deal of effort, but I had no doubts that my brother would eventually win over Arianna again. And maybe this time, he'd get to keep her.

S.C. STEPHENS

THE END

ABOUT THE AUTHOR

S.C. Stephens is a #1 *New York Times* bestselling author who spends her every free moment creating stories that are packed with emotion and heavy on romance. In addition to writing, she enjoys spending lazy afternoons in the sun reading, listening to music, watching movies, and spending time with her friends and family. She and her two children reside in the Pacific Northwest.

You can learn more at:

AuthorSCStephens.com
Twitter: https://twitter.com/SC_Stephens_
Facebook.com/SCStephensAuthor

Also by S.C. Stephens

Dangerous Rush
Furious Rush
Untamed
Thoughtful
Reckless
Effortless
Thoughtless
It's All Relative
Collision Course
The Next Generation
'Til Death
Bloodlines
Conversion

Printed in Great Britain
by Amazon